New York Times bestselling author **Jill Shalvis** lives in a small town in the Sierras full of quirky characters. Any resemblance to the quirky characters in her books is, um, mostly coincidental. Look for Jill's bestselling and award-winning books wherever romances are sold.

Vi bsite **leisure** & complete book list a y blog detai e-mountains ad s. For other news, find her o llShalvis, r follow her on Instagram **@jillsha**

Jill Shalvis. Delightfully addictive:

'A wonderfully touching story about family, love, and second chances that will tug on the heartstrings and take readers on an emotional journey'
Harlequin Junkie on *The Forever Girl*

'Hot, sweet, fun, and romantic! Pure pleasure!'
Robyn Carr, *New York Times* bestselling author

'Shalvis capably weaves the complex, intertwining relationships into an appealing story of second chances. This is sure to satisfy'
Publishers Weekly on *The Forever Girl*

'Fans of the TV drama series *This Is Us* as well as love stories ripe with secrets waiting to be spilled will devour Shalvis's latest'
Library Journal on *Almost Just Friends*

'Jill Shalvis balances her trademark sunny optimism and humor with unforgettable real-life drama. A book to savor – and share'
Susan Wiggs, *New York Times* bestselling author, on
The Lemon Sisters

'Jill Shalvis's books are funny, warm, charming, and unforgettable'
RaeAnne Thayne, *New York Times* bestselling author,
on *The Lemon Sisters*

By Jill Shalvis

The Family You Make

Jill Shalvis

HEADLINE ETERNAL

Published by arrangement with William Morrow,
an imprint of HarperCollins Publishers

First published in Great Britain in 2022
by HEADLINE ETERNAL
An imprint of HEADLINE PUBLISHING GROUP

1

Cataloguing in Publication Data is available from the British Library

ISBN 978 1 4722 8442 6

Offset in 10.78/15.67pt Minion Pro by Jouve (UK), Milton Keynes

Printed and bound in Great Britain by Clays Ltd, Elcograf S.p.A.

MIX
Paper from
responsible sources
FSC® C104740

Headline's policy is to use papers that are natural, renewable and recyclable
products and made from wood grown in well-managed forests and other
controlled sources. The logging and manufacturing processes are expected
to conform to the environmental regulations of the country of origin.

HEADLINE PUBLISHING GROUP
An Hachette UK Company
Carmelite House
50 Victoria Embankment
London EC4Y 0DZ

www.headlineeternal.com
www.headline.co.uk
www.hachette.co.uk

The Family You Make

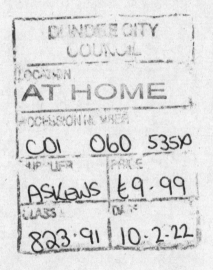

CHAPTER 1

It wasn't often that Levi Cutler came within a hair's width of dying. But if he'd known biting the dust was on today's agenda, he might've done things differently, like called the waitress who'd tucked her number into his pocket the other night or learned to brew his own beer.

Forgive himself for his past mistakes . . .

Sitting back on the gondola bench, he looked out the window at the afternoon winter wonderland of North Diamond Ski Resort. The sky had been clear when he'd arrived, but in the past twenty minutes, that had changed. Snow came down like white fire and brimstone, leaving visibility at zero. He knew what he'd see if it'd been clear—three hundred and sixty degrees of jagged snow-covered mountain peaks stretched as far as the eye could see, and a glimpse of Lake Tahoe due east, its waters so blue, so deep and pure, you could see a dinner plate three hundred feet beneath its surface. One of his favorite science facts, and he had many, was that if by some cataclysmic event the entire lake tipped, the spillage would cover California under fourteen inches of water. As a kid, he'd really wanted to see that happen. As an adult, he preferred the water right where it was.

A gust of wind jostled the gondola. The storm that no one had seen coming was kicking into gear. He'd hoped to get a few runs in before having to face the reason he was back in Tahoe in the first place, but that wasn't seeming likely. Nearing the top of the mountain now, the gondola rose past towering pine trees coated in thick, powdery snow, swaying in the wind, resembling two-hundred-foot-tall ghosts.

The gondola, built for sturdiness, swayed with the trees, giving him a quick, stomach-dropping vertigo. But being in the business of knowing risks and algorithms, he knew the chances of dying in a gondola were nearly nil.

On the other hand, the risk of dying while skiing—especially in this weather—was a different game altogether. The smart decision would be to turn around at the top and go back down the mountain. Especially since the snow kept coming, harder and faster now, thick and heavy, slanting sideways thanks to the strong headwind. The gondola did the same. He might spend most of his time on a computer these days, creating tech solutions to fix supposedly unfixable problems, but he'd grown up here. He'd spent his teen years working on this very mountain. As he knew all too well, anything could happen in a blink of an eye.

Even as he thought it, the gondola swung again, hard enough to rattle his teeth. Yeah, he was definitely going back down. No reason to be that guy who didn't pay attention to his surroundings and ended up *splat*, face-first into a tree.

The gondola peaked the top ridge and slowed as it slid toward the end of the ride. A lift operator opened the door. He was maybe seventeen, and he gave Levi a "stay seated" gesture. "Sorry, sir, but we just got word, right after you boarded."

"No problem." Levi had been there, with his job on the line as he told belligerent tourists that no, as a matter of fact, they couldn't risk their lives on the mountain. "Need any help clearing people out?"

The kid shook his head. "We've been sending guests back down and got almost everyone off the mountain. The gondolas in front of you are empty. We're just waiting on one more employee. After she loads, I'll be right behind you on a snowmobile."

A woman appeared in the doorway. She nodded at the kid, then stared down at the one-inch gap between the platform she stood on and the tram floor. With an audible gulp, she clasped her necklace in a fist and hopped over the gap the same way that Levi's six-year-old niece, Peyton, did when getting onto an airplane.

The woman darted past him to the opposite bench, as close to the window as she could get, and even though they were the only two people on the whole thing, she didn't acknowledge his existence. Instead, she closed her eyes and began to mumble to herself, something about how ironic it was to have "survived a whole bunch of bullshit only to die in the storm of the century while inside a tin can hanging by a hook on a mountainside."

The gondola bounced and she gasped, flinging her hands out in front of her like a cat trying to gain traction on linoleum. She was covered from head to toe in heavy winter gear, the only thing visible being the long strands of her wavy dark red hair sticking out from under her ski cap.

As the gondola made the turn and began heading down the mountain now, she brought her legs up on the bench and dropped her head to her knees.

"You okay?" Levi asked.

"Absolutely," she said to her knees. "Just very busy having a freak-out here."

"About?"

"About leaving my lunch—a triple-decker peanut butter and jelly sandwich—in my locker back there. I don't want to die on an empty stomach."

"We're not going to die. At least not today."

Not lifting her head, she made a snort of disbelief.

Okay, so the unannounced storm had muted nearly all daylight, and the snow looked like white lines slashing through the air like spears. It was stunning, but he could admit it might also be construed as terrifying to some. "It's actually far less scary if you watch."

"I'll take your word on that. We're a million feet up."

"Five hundred and fifty."

"What?"

"We're five hundred and fifty feet above ground. Approximately the same as five and a half stories, or the height of a roller-coaster ride, at least a good one—"

"Oh my God." Her head jerked up, hitting him with some seriously green eyes. *Why would you tell me that?*

"Sometimes, if you're afraid of something like heights, knowing all the facts helps."

She stared at him as if he'd grown a second head, but her spine snapped ramrod straight. "Do I look like I'm afraid of heights?"

she asked, just as the gondola jerked so hard that she gasped and grabbed for the oh-holy-shit bars on the side closest to her.

"You're right," Levi said. "You're clearly not afraid of heights at all."

She tightened her grip on the bar and glared at him. "Hey. For your information, it's not heights that get me. It's tight, enclosed spaces. Especially tight, enclosed spaces that are swinging five and a half stories above ground."

"Shift to the middle of the bench," he said. "Away from the windows. You'll feel better."

This got him a vehement shake of her head that had her hair flying about her face. "I've got to be at the window so I don't miss the crash." She grimaced. "Don't even try to make sense of that, or me for that matter—you'll just hurt yourself."

The next gust hit hard. Everything in the gondola flew to one side, including his companion. He caught her and pulled her down onto the bench at his side, keeping ahold of her for a minute. "You okay?"

"No! Not even close! We're an inch from falling and dying, and I don't know about you, but I had things to do today. Like *live*."

"A gondola fall is extremely unlikely," he said. "Maybe one in a million."

They rocked again and she drew a deep, shaky breath. "You know what I need? Silence. So if you could just stop talking, that'd be great."

He laughed, because having come from a family of talkers, he was often mocked for being the silent one.

"I don't see how this is funny—" She broke off with a startled scream as the next gust hit violently, knocking them both off the bench and into each other on the floor. On their knees, swinging wildly, they turned in unison to look out the window just in time to see . . .

The gondola in front of them appear to drop a few feet and then fall, vanishing from view.

She gasped in horror. "Oh my God! Did that gondola just . . . ?"

"Yeah. Hold on," he said grimly. As he said this, their gondola came to a sudden stuttering halt, leaving them swinging wildly back and forth, flinging both of them *and* all their stuff far and wide. Levi went with the momentum and ended up face-planted against the window, kissing the cold glass.

Something hit him in the back.

His pack.

And then a softer something. His companion. She hurriedly scrambled clear of him to stare out the window at the gaping chasm where the previous gondola used to be. "Ohmigod," she whispered, her nose to the window, as if that could help her see past the thick, swirling, all-encompassing snow. "Was anyone in it?"

"The lift operator told me that the three cars in front of us were empty."

She leveled him with those amazing eyes, narrowed now. "So much for a gondola fall being one in a million!" She yanked out her phone and stared down at it. "Dammit. I forgot it's dead."

"Don't worry. They'll know what happened at base. They'll come for us."

She let out a slow exhale, looking pale and shaky.

"We're still on the cable," he said, looking out the window in front of them. "It didn't break. That gondola in front of us snagged on something on the track, or there was a malfunction in the grip—"

She let out a distressed sound and squeezed her eyes shut. "You know what really gets me? I put on mascara today. A waste of five minutes that I could've used to stop for a breakfast burrito. I mean, that's what a girl needs on the day she's going to die, a solid breakfast burrito to hold her over to the ever after."

"I like breakfast burritos," he said. He didn't offer any empty platitudes because the truth was her fears were valid. Their gondola wasn't moving now, no forward or reverse motion at all, nothing except the relentless swinging in the wind. He didn't know what had caused the gondola in front of them to fall, but if theirs did the same, the odds of them walking away were slim to none. First up was getting them to stop swinging so freely, and he began to calculate the balance and weight needed to stabilize the car. "Hey, do you think you can get all the way into that back corner there?"

She blinked, but didn't question him, just did as he asked, crawling to where he pointed while he moved into the opposite corner.

"You do realize this only works if we weigh the same," she said.

"We'll use our gear to even things out." His backpack was at his feet. "What have you got with you?"

She lifted her hands out to her sides. "Just what you see."

"You came up on the mountain with nothing on you—no snacks, no water, no emergency gear or equipment?"

"Didn't say that. And judgy much?" She emptied out her many pockets. Steel water bottle, a single-serving bag of beef jerky, a pack of gum, and . . . a small first aid kit, which she held up for

Levi to see. "Safety first, right?" she murmured, irony heavy in her tone.

He'd noticed the medical patch across the back of her jacket. "Ski patrol?"

"RN," she said. "I'm a traveling nurse, working a rotation at each of the five urgent care medical clinics in the North Shore area." She once again waved her first aid kit. "I'm qualified to save people's lives—even if I can't manage to get my own together."

He started to smile, but another hard gust of wind hit and they spun like a toy, so fast they just about went topsy-turvy. There was a sound of metal giving way—the shelf above his head for passenger belongings—and Levi lunged to shield her body with his.

Everything flew in the air like they were in orbit, and for a single long heartbeat, gravity seemed to vanish. Levi wrapped himself tight around his companion, her head tucked into his chest when something hit his head.

And then it was lights out.

CHAPTER 2

When the gondola finally stopped moving, Jane couldn't breathe or see. Oh, God. She was dead.

Wait.

Her eyes were closed.

She blinked them open. Okay, whew, but either she was paralyzed or something was on top of her, something heavy.

No, not a something, a some*one*. The guy who'd been unfailingly steadfast in the face of her rising panic, and he was a dead weight. Carefully, she crawled out from beneath him, because while they hadn't yet fallen to their deaths, it could still happen at any second. At the thought, she broke out into a cold sweat, despite the frigid temps. "Hey." She leaned over the man with her and checked his pulse, nearly whimpering in relief when she felt it. Thready, but he was alive. "Can you hear me?"

Not so much as a twinge.

Mr. Talkative was out cold, leaking blood like a sieve from a dangerous-looking two-inch cut that sliced at an angle through his right eyebrow and along his temple. Normally she saved swearing for bad traffic, but as she looked around them, she let out a string of pretty impressive oaths, if she said so herself. Because now what?

It was still snowing like a mother, but the wind had calmed enough that the gondola was now swinging almost gently compared to the violence they'd just endured. The floor looked like a garage sale gone wrong, their stuff scattered everywhere. On top of everything lay the steel shelving rod that had broken loose, probably what had hit Mr. Talkative in the head.

This was bad. Very, very bad. "Come on, Sleeping Beauty, time to rise and shine." The guy had lunged across the gondola to tuck her into him, saving her from getting hit. *What was that?* She was a perfect stranger. She checked his pulse again. Still faint, but steady.

She looked around for her phone before remembering it was dead. And anyway, who was she going to call? Not the clinic she'd just left; she'd been the last staff member out and had locked up herself. Logically, she knew that security at the base would figure out what had happened to the gondola in front of them—after all, *someone* had shut them down, right? Surely they'd be working their way toward them for extraction.

The man still hadn't moved. Not good. She ran a hand along his body, checking for other injuries. Nothing obviously broken, but when she turned him onto his side, beneath his jacket she found his shirt sticky with blood. Shoving his layers up, she found two slashes across his back and shoulders, also bleeding freely.

Well, hell. "You had to play the hero." She shrugged off her jacket to stuff it beneath his head as a makeshift pillow. "Isn't that just like a man." She stripped off her scrubs top and the thermal she had on beneath, using the former against the scratches on his back. The thermal she pressed carefully against his head wound to slow the bleeding. "Okay, seriously, if anyone's going to nap, it should be me. I've just worked a long shift. So rise and shine, okay? No fair letting me be the only one awake when we die."

Nothing.

Stripping further, she pulled off her outer gear ski pants, which she rolled and used to prop him up on his side so he didn't lie on those wounds. Then she checked herself over. She looked like a horror flick victim. She was pretty sure the blood was all his, but dear God. She'd been through a lot of shit in her life, almost all of it she'd dealt with on her own. And most days she was okay with that, but today? Today wasn't one of those days where she wanted to be alone.

She twisted around to look for her first aid kit, which was not in immediate sight. It had to be twenty degrees in the gondola and the blizzard didn't seem to be interested in slowing down any. And here she sat, stuck a million feet in the air. No, make that five hundred and fifty feet in the air, in a glass prison wearing only her sports bra and thermal leggings because her patient was currently bleeding through everything she had. "Come on," she cajoled, leaning over him. "If I have to be the one in a million to die in a gondola, you have to wake up to die with me."

Not even a flicker. So . . . she pinched him, right on the ass. As it was a very fine, very taut ass, there wasn't a lot to work with, but she managed.

He let out a grunt and she nearly collapsed over him in relief. "That's it," she murmured. "Now open those pretty gray eyes of yours and tell me once again how we're going to be just fine."

He groaned, sounding rough. "You actually talk more than I do, did you know that? How long was I out?"

"A few minutes."

Still not opening his eyes, he gave a small smile. "You think my eyes are pretty. *And* you touched my ass. Admit it, you want me bad."

Had she really told him his eyes were pretty? Maybe she'd hit her head too. "Why did you use yourself as a shield for me? That was so stupid."

"*Always* save the person with the first aid kit."

Leaning over him while trying to balance in the still-swaying gondola, she pulled back the shirt to check his head. Blood welled up. She quickly put it back.

"I didn't want you to get hurt," he said quietly, sucking in a breath when she applied pressure.

She didn't want to react to his statement, but she honestly couldn't remember when anyone had done such a thing for her, stranger or otherwise. Then she realized his color had gone from tan to white to green, and she knew what that meant. "Breathe in through your nose. Hold for four seconds, then slowly let it out to fight the nausea." She breathed with him to keep him on track. "For the record," she said quietly, "I'd have been fine on my own."

"Most people might say thank you."

"Yeah, well, I'm not most people. And I stand by my statement— it was a stupid move." Once again, she lifted her blood-soaked shirt and inspected his gash. It was deep and he *still* hadn't opened his eyes, pretty or not. "Are you dizzy?"

"I'm fine."

Guy speak for yeah, he was dizzy as hell. At least this she knew how to deal with. Her hands had stopped shaking, her heart no longer pounded in her ears, but the truth was, they were still hanging, possibly by a thread, and in need of extraction.

Don't think about it.

"It's my mom's fault," he murmured.

Great, he was delirious. "Your mom?"

"She taught me to protect others, always."

The blood was soaking through her shirt, so she deepened the pressure, making him wince. "Yeah? And how is that working out for you?"

"Great. And *Jesus* . . ." He tried to sit up, but she held him still. Or at least he gave her the illusion of letting her hold him still, because he was a big guy. As he lay on his side on the floor of the shuddering gondola—*Nope, don't think about that!*—his long legs took up much of the room, and what little was left, his broad shoulders covered.

When she'd first noticed him sprawled out on the bench opposite of her as she'd boarded, she'd done her best to ignore him. That had been easy because she'd been distracted by her hatred of small, enclosed spaces. But it was impossible to ignore him now, on her knees and snugged into the curve of his long body, her face close to his as she checked his pulse again, his blood on her hands.

Closest you've been to a man in a long time, came the entirely inappropriate thought, which vanished at the shocking grinding sound of metal. She gasped and involuntarily clutched at his arm. "What was that?"

She expected him to come up with some smartass answer, but he didn't speak at all. "No. Hell, no, don't you dare. *Stay with me.*"

He groaned, and she almost burst into grateful tears. "What's your name?" she demanded. "Mine's Jane."

His voice was gravelly and barely audible. "You Jane, me Tarzan."

With a startled laugh, she sat back on her heels. "I don't know whether to worry that you're hallucinating or that you're an imbecile."

"Imbecile," he said. "At least according to my older sister."

Keep him talking . . . "Well, for future knowledge, it's Jane Parks, not Tarzan's Jane. You're close with your family?"

"Unfortunately. I'm also the black sheep."

"Is that because you tell stupid jokes?"

His lips quirked, but other than that, he didn't move, and worry crept into her voice. "Open your eyes, Tarzan. Right now. I mean it."

"Bossy." But he cracked open one slate, bloodshot eye.

"*Both* eyes."

It took him a moment, and it made him grimace and go green again, but he managed.

"Are you dizzy? Nauseous? Is there a ringing in your ears?"

"Yeah."

She assumed that was yes to all the questions. Damn. She took one of his hands and directed it to hold the compress on his head, freeing up both of hers. "Now track my finger. *Tarzan!* Pay attention."

"*Levi.* My name is Levi."

"Well, Levi, are you watching my finger?"

"Yep. All twenty of them."

Oh crap, his pupils weren't tracking either.

Again, he tried to sit up, but she held him down. "Your only job is to stay still, you hear me?"

"That bad?"

She pasted her sweet nurse smile on her face. Yes, she had a whole repertoire of smiles. She had a professional smile. She had a fake smile. And her personal favorite, her don't-make-me-kick-your-ass smile. "No. Not bad at all."

A very faint laugh escaped him as he closed his eyes again. "Don't ever play poker, Red."

"Jane." And she *did* play poker. The skill had come in handy in college. Especially since she had a fondness for having food in her belly and a roof over her head. Or a tent. She wasn't picky. After growing up tether-less, a tumbleweed in the wind, she'd never needed more than the bare minimum to get by.

Levi had closed his eyes again.

"Hey. Hey, Levi, stay with me. Where did you grow up?"

"Here." He swallowed hard, like he was trying not to throw up. "Tahoe. Not the gondola."

She smiled. "Funny guy."

"I try. Where did you grow up?"

"I didn't. Not yet." It was her automatic, by rote, don't-give-too-much-of-herself-away answer, and she usually got away with it.

But Levi opened his eyes, then managed to narrow them slightly as he reached out and touched her cheek. His fingers came away with blood on them. "You're hurt," he said, sounding more alert now, carefully scanning his gaze over her. She watched as he took in the fact that she was crouching over him in just her bra, but his gaze was brisk and methodical. "Just a scratch," she assured him.

He made a quick assessment anyway. Patting her down, checking the bloodstains on her.

"It's *your* blood." She caught his hand. "Levi, I'm fine." Okay, so maybe she was a *little* dinged up, but she'd had worse. "Really. I'm good."

He gave a nod so slight she almost missed it. "You are," he agreed. "And brave as hell." Then he closed his eyes and lay very still.

She checked his pulse again.

"My ribs are bruised, but not broken, I don't think," he murmured. "And you know head wounds always look worse than they are. I'm fine."

"Yeah? You're fine?" There might've been the slightest touch of hysteria in her voice. "Then maybe you could put all those well-honed muscles to use and pry us out of this tin can."

That got a very small smirk out of him.

"Oh please, like you don't know that you look like a walking/talking *Outside* magazine cover. Let me guess. You're a wildland firefighter. A hotshot."

His small smile widened a bit. "Data . . . scientist. Consultant."

"Sounds very . . . cerebral."

His smirk remained in place. "You think scientists can't have . . . what did you call them . . . well-honed muscles . . . ?" His voice trailed off.

He was fading, and panic surged anew. "What does a data scientist consultant do?" she asked desperately.

He shrugged, which caused him to grimace in pain. "I . . . extract and design data modeling . . . processes . . ."

"*Levi.*"

"Hmmm?"

He was clearly having trouble finding words and keeping track of the conversation. He needed X-rays. An MRI. "What else does a data scientist consultant do?"

"Create algorithms and predictive models . . . for business needs, stuff like that."

She looked around once again for the first aid kit that had to be here somewhere. Yes, there it was in the corner. She hooked it with her foot and opened it up. "Could you create an algorithm to tell me which fast-food joint is most likely to give me a stomach-ache when I'm inhaling food after a twelve-hour shift?"

"The answer is *all* of them. And that's a long workday."

"Betting you work long hours too."

"I do. How about I feed you real food after this?"

She snorted. "Are you flirting with me right now, Levi the Data Scientist Consultant?"

The man managed a small smile, sexy as hell even with him sprawled out on the floor, bleeding. "I'm stuck in a gondola with a beautiful woman who took off her clothes. The least I can do is make her laugh."

She did just that as she found the antiseptic and gauze and doctored up his head the best she could for the moment. "This isn't exactly a laughable situation."

"I know. I didn't even get mouth-to-mouth—"

He broke off as another huge gust of wind hit them like a battering ram, rocking them violently.

Jane crouched over him to keep anything else from hitting

him. "Wonder how many gondolas have fallen at this resort," she asked with what she wanted to be a calm voice, but which sounded thin to her own ears.

Levi reached up and covered her hands with his. "Until tonight? Zero."

"You better not be lying to make me feel better."

"I'm not. I mean, I'd *totally* lie to make you feel better, but it's also the truth. A gondola has never fallen in the Tahoe region. Scout's honor."

"Until now."

His steely eyes held hers. "Until now."

She realized their faces were inches apart. Pulling back, she began going through the stuff littered around them, finding a bottle of water. "Are you allergic to acetaminophen?" she asked.

"No."

She handed over two pills from the small sample packet in her first aid kit. He propped himself up and popped them into his mouth, swallowing them before she got the bottle of water open. He lay back down and closed his eyes again. A muscle ticking in his jaw was the only sign he was in pain.

"What else do you need?" she asked.

"Can you reach into my front pocket?"

"Not even in your dreams."

That got her another almost smile. "To get my phone."

"Oh." Right. The fact he was no longer flirting with her and his face was pinched with pain made her even more worried. Worried enough to indeed reach into his pocket and pull out his phone. She handed it over and watched as he sent out a quick text, getting an even quicker response. "I've got a friend on the search-and-rescue team here. He says the resort security alerted them. There's already a team in place, but they're being held up at base because there's zero visibility." He gave a very tense smile. "He said to hang tight."

Jane risked another look out the window and was startled to realize she couldn't see an inch past the glass, nothing beyond a swirling, vast void that seemed all encompassing. She swallowed hard. She'd done a lot of things in her lifetime that would be considered dangerous. The locales of some of the places she'd been sent to deliver health care, for instance. Or when she'd been mugged on a train in Europe. And then there'd been the time she and a group of other medical workers had been flown to a remote village in the Philippines that had caught on fire while they were there.

But this. Hanging by a thread, facing a fall that she knew neither of them could possibly survive . . .

Levi reached for her hand, his big and warm. "We're going to be okay."

She stared down at his long fingers gripping hers. "That would be more believable if you weren't gripping me hard enough to make the muscles in my fingers cramp. Tell me the truth: you think we're going to die, don't you."

"We don't actually have any muscles in our fingers," he said. "Their function is controlled by the muscles in our palms and arms."

That was actually true. She knew it from nursing school. He was trying to distract her the way she always distracted her patients when she had a needle coming for them. "You can't distract me. I'm indistractable."

He managed a small smile. "I'd like to prove you wrong, but right now I'm all talk. How about we don't put it out there into the universe that we're going to die, okay? Let's put it out there that we're going to make it, that there's no alternative."

Looking into his eyes, she almost believed him. Then he flashed a small smile. "Besides, you haven't thanked me for saving your life yet. Can't die before that." He held out his phone.

She stared at it. "What do you want me to do with that?"

"Call your family," he said quietly.

To say goodbye, he meant, and suddenly her heart was in her throat again.

CHAPTER 3

Jane stared down at the cell phone, then glanced to the windows again. Snow blowing sideways, still zero visibility, still absolute chaos, but in here it was oddly quiet, insulated, almost . . . intimate. It felt odd to look out into the wilderness, so close that without the glass, she could've reached out and touched one of the towering heavily snow-draped Norway spruces. She felt like she was inside a snow globe in an enchanted winter wonderland scene.

Still lying down, Levi was patiently waiting for her to make a call, even though he was the one in pain and injured, and yeah, okay, they were *both* in an impossible situation, but his was most definitely worse than hers.

And he'd offered her his phone first. "My cat can't answer a phone," she said. "It's an opposable thumbs thing."

His lips quirked. She hadn't been trying to be funny, but rather distract from the truth—she had no family to call.

"Your parents?" he asked.

Her mom and dad had been troubled teens when she'd come along and disrupted their lives. By the time she'd been born, her dad had peaced out and had never been a part of her life. Her mom hadn't stuck around much longer, leaving Jane with her grandparents. Eventually her mom had grown up, settled down, and gotten herself a new family. Deeply embarrassed by her wild youth, her mom hadn't spoken to her in years, and Jane had no intention of wasting her last few moments on earth trying to get her on the phone. "They're not in my life."

His eyes softened, but since she couldn't handle sympathy, she cut him off before he could speak, handing him back the phone. "You should hurry, your battery's nearly dead."

Not moving anything but his finger, he activated a call on speaker, presumably so he didn't have to exert the energy to lift the thing to his ear. A female voice answered with a soft, joyous-sounding "Levi!"

He drew a deep breath and closed his eyes. "Hey, Mom. Listen—"

"Oh, honey, I'm so glad you called! You left so quickly I didn't get a chance to ask what you'd like for dinner. I mean, it's so rare you get up here from San Francisco— Hold on a second. *Jasper!*" she yelled. "*Stop that!* Oh, for God's sakes, he's digging in the yard. We've got gophers in the grass again. They're making holes all over the place, and Jasper fell into one and nearly broke his leg."

Jane looked at Levi in concern.

Levi put a thumb over the microphone. "Jasper's her dog. Also known as 'Stop that!' and 'Drop it!' He's a huge goofus golden-doodle she rescued. Trust me, he's indestructible." He pulled his thumb from the microphone.

His mom was still talking.

"I mean, those holes . . . one of these days they're going to be the death of someone," she was saying. "Yesterday at my yoga class there was a woman whose son created a system with a camera that lets her know if there's a gopher in her yard. He's going to sell it and get rich."

Levi looked pained. "Mom, anyone can buy a security camera—"

"Sure, but you could make something like the gopher camera and get rich."

"I'll get right on that," he said on a barely-there sigh that made Jane smile. "But about why I'm calling—"

"I mean as long as it didn't take any time from your personal life," his mom interrupted. "You need a personal life, Levi, you work too much. You haven't even made time to date since—"

"*Mom.*" Levi ran a hand over his face.

A blizzard and possible death hadn't rattled him, but this clearly did. And now Jane wanted to know what the *since* meant.

"Mom, I'm trying to tell you something."

"Oh, I'm sorry, honey. What?"

"I'm . . ."—he locked eyes with Jane—"going to be late picking up Peyton from her after-school dance program."

Jane would bet her last ten bucks that hadn't been what he'd planned on saying.

"Oh no," his mom said. "Levi, you promised. Peyton told everyone in her class you were going to show them that magic trick you do, you know, the one where you make a volcano out of a soda? Oh! And did I tell you our plumbing problems are back . . ."

Levi ran a hand over his head, which undoubtedly hurt like hell. "Mom—"

"The toilet in the upstairs master keeps running, and sometimes it even overflows, and I know you say it's because your dad doesn't give a courtesy flush, whatever that means, but there's *got* to be a fix."

Levi looked pained far beyond his injuries, and Jane couldn't help it: a laugh escaped. They might die at the next gust of wind, but his mom had gophers and plumbing problems.

"Who was that?" his mom asked, apparently possessing bat-like ultrasonic hearing. "I heard a laugh. A feminine laugh. You're with a woman? *That's* why you can't pick up your darling niece? *Levi!*"

Jane winced for him, thinking he was about to get yelled at.

"Ohmigod, you finally have a girlfriend! How wonderful! How exciting! Why didn't you just say so? What's her name? I want to meet her, put her on the phone."

Jane went from laughing to walking backwards with her butt cheeks while miming *no-no-no* with her hands. She had zero experience with parents to begin with, which meant she was especially bad with dealing with *other* people's parents.

Levi took in her panic and smiled, and, oh great, he was going to hand her the phone and she'd have to kill him. That is, if their fall down the rocky mountainside didn't.

"Mom, I'm not putting Jane on the phone."

"Jane! What a lovely name! Is she nice? Does she look after you? Not that you need it, you're a grown man who's been taking care of himself for a long time, but the thing is, you're thirty years old and all you do is . . ." She paused. "I'm sorry. I always forget what exactly you do. It's something with data."

Before Levi could answer, they were slammed by another gust of wind. Over the unbelievable noise of that came the unmistakable sound of metal straining, and Jane covered her mouth with her hand to keep her startled scream to herself.

"Levi? Levi, can you hear me?" his mom asked, sounding tinny. "What was that?"

Before he could speak, his phone beeped and Jane knew what that meant. The battery was on its last breath. It was now a race as to who would die first, the battery . . . or them.

Levi's gaze met Jane's, and in that single heartbeat something changed for both of them. Acceptance. He reached for her hand as he spoke into the phone. "Forget my job, Mom," he said with surprising gentleness, eyes still locked on Jane's. "I just wanted to tell you that you're right. Jane's my girlfriend."

"Oh!" his mom whispered, clearly touched to near tears. "Oh, Levi, that's wonderful. A dream come true for me, to know my baby is happy. You are happy, yes? Is she sweet?"

"Very," he said.

Jane bit her lower lip and shook her head, needing him to know she was the furthest thing from sweet.

He just held her gaze and kept talking over the raging storm and the blood whooshing in Jane's ears. "She's sweet, she's caring . . . she's everything you've ever wanted for me."

"Oh, honey, really?"

He looked right into Jane's eyes and lied through his teeth. "Really, Mom."

Jane was boggled. Both at the obvious love he had for his mom, and also how she should've been embarrassed to be intruding in such a private moment, but instead only felt . . . fascination.

"I can't wait to meet her," his mom said, sounding happy, so damned excited that even Jane's cold dead heart warmed and rolled over in her chest. "Does she live in Sunrise Cove? When can I meet her?"

"We'll do details another time," Levi said. "I've gotta go now, Mom. Kiss Peyton for me. Love you—"

Beep.

His phone died.

Swearing beneath his breath, Levi looked down at his cell, expression tight with pain but also worry, and yet Jane knew that not one single ounce of it was for himself. It was for his family, whom he clearly loved beyond anything.

That selflessness got her. She'd felt it once, with her grandparents. But like most good things in her life, it hadn't lasted.

Levi's hand slipped into hers, and she started.

"It's going to be okay," he said, comforting her even though he was the one who was hurt. "We're going to be okay."

That's when she realized she was shaking.

Swearing again, Levi sat up with some difficulty, but determined, he leaned against the bench, where he tucked her into his side so that they were sharing body heat, snuggling her in close. "Hug me," he said. "I'm scared."

She looked into his eyes. He wasn't scared—or at least he wasn't letting it show—but she took the out and pretended it was for him anyway, gratefully moving in against his body.

"We really are going to be okay," he said softly near her ear.

And even though she knew he was just trying to make her feel better, the same way he'd done with his mom, she found herself nodding. "I know." The guy had an optimistic outlook, like he truly believed deep in his soul that someone would come for them.

Since she couldn't remember anyone *ever* coming to her rescue, this blind faith was utterly foreign to her. That's when she realized the weight of his arm had just gotten heavier. "Levi? Stay awake."

"Tired."

An adrenaline crash and also a likely concussion were causing that, but he needed to stay awake. "Hey, so how often do you come home to visit your family?" she asked urgently.

"Mostly only when it's a command performance . . . by the one person on the planet who can guilt me into it."

She tilted her head to look up at him. "Your mom?"

"She likes to remind me that thirty years ago she labored for well over twenty-four hours to birth me, ruining her figure in the process. Translation: I owe her."

Jane started to say something like how horrible of her, but Levi's voice had been warm with affection. They were quiet for a moment, in their bubble from the real world, Levi's arm around her, her body curled into his side, sharing body heat. Daylight was fading as the snow swirled all around them, blocking out everything else.

"Any regrets?" he asked.

"You mean because we might die?"

"Let's not."

She let out a rough laugh. "Agree, let's not."

"So . . . ?"

She shrugged. "I hate regrets. I try really hard not to have them."

"Which didn't answer my question," he said.

"Okay, fine, maybe there are a *few* regrets . . ." She drew a deep breath as she thought about how she'd lost touch with her grandpa. She supposed no matter how hard she'd tried, she did indeed have regrets. "I lost touch with someone important to me," she admitted. "And the more time that goes by, the harder it is to figure out how to find my way back."

Levi's eyes held hers as he gave a barely-there nod of understanding. "I get that. I . . . hurt someone important to me once." His gaze went faraway, like he was lost in the memories. "She wanted more than I was capable of giving her back then."

She had to admit to being curious, but she was grateful he hadn't pressed her for more details, so she had to afford him the same courtesy. "And now?" she asked.

"And now it's too late."

Something else she could understand all too well. "So we both suck," she said.

He snorted, and they were quiet a moment.

"If you could have one thing," he finally asked quietly, "whatever you want, right now, what would it be?"

That seemed like an unanswerable question. "I think you should go first on that one."

His eyes were closed again, his voice slower than before, worrying her. "I'd want to see my niece, Peyton . . . Her dad just bailed on her and my sister, and she's lost so much. I'd want one more day with her, taking her skiing or playing tea party, whatever she wanted to do."

The words rumbled through his chest to hers, and warmed her every bit as much as his delicious body heat.

"Now you," he reminded her. "Whatever you want, what would it be?"

She wasn't actually sure. Maybe to have a family unit, like he did. Impossible with the life she led, of course. She came to work the ski season in Tahoe every year. The rest of the time, she was all over the world, wherever she was needed, working for organizations like Doctors Without Borders. Her next contract was already lined up in Haiti. The job was a labor of love. Hence the annual Tahoe gig, which paid her more over these two months than she would earn for the entire rest of the year. Plus, it was easier, fewer hours, and she loved the snowy terrain.

But none of that was why she really did it. Her reason was her own and deeply personal.

And not something she intended to share. "Well, I was going to say a cookies 'n' cream cupcake from Cake Walk," she quipped, needing to lighten the mood. "But now that just sounds shallow."

Eyes still closed, he smiled. "There's *nothing* shallow about a cookies 'n' cream cupcake from Cake Walk. What else, Jane?"

"I guess if I could have one thing right now . . ." she repeated, stalling. "Um . . ." Maybe it would be to have enough battery to call Charlotte. When Jane was here in Tahoe, she stayed in a big old house owned by Dr. Charlotte Dixon. Charlotte was a trauma surgeon who collected people around her like some women collected shoes, and was the warmest, kindest, and most incredibly stubborn, bossy person Jane had ever met. Once Charlotte decided on having someone in her life, that was that. So yeah, Jane supposed if she could do one thing, it'd be to thank Charlotte for collecting her.

"You've got a cat?"

"It's more like an alley cat I feed when he lets me."

"What's his name?"

"Alley Cat."

He gave a small laugh. "Do you let him inside?"

"No, he's an alley cat." Jane might have had a real home for only a brief window at her grandparents', but she knew what a home should be, all warm and cozy and welcoming, with people in it who loved one another. She couldn't offer that to Cat, not when she'd be gone in five or six weeks.

"Do you let him in at night?" he asked.

"That would just confuse him when I'm gone, and then his alley would seem cold and hard, and that's hardly fair."

He squeezed her gently, his eyes serious now. "See? *Sweet*."

"If you knew me better, you'd know how funny that is." But her smile faded quickly when she realized he'd tipped his head back against the wood bench behind him. He was pale, too pale, and his mouth was a hard grim line.

Definitely still in pain and possibly fighting to stay conscious. Given what he'd done for her tonight, she knew she'd do just about anything for him in return, so she opened her mouth to give him a truth, to confess what she'd *really* do with her last moment on earth. But in that very moment, the gondola came to life with a little jerk and . . . started moving again.

"Oh my God!" She looked around with shock and relief, having really thought her number might be up. "We're going to make it!"

When Levi didn't answer, she tightened her grip on him. "*Levi*."

But he was out cold.

CHAPTER 4

Sunrise in Tahoe was magical. Jane knew of no other way to describe it. One minute the sky was like black velvet dotted with diamonds, and the next, a kaleidoscope of colors. No matter the season, when the sun peeked over the Sierra Nevada and showed off her beauty in all its glory, the view was so stunning it could almost make her forget she'd already had a shitty day.

Almost.

Because she was currently inside the ER, unable to see anything other than the curtain surrounding her cot.

Five minutes after Levi had passed out on her, their gondola had returned to base, where they'd immediately been taken to the hospital.

The ER had been overloaded. She'd sat with Levi in the cubicle until his wounds had been cleaned and stitched up and he'd been wheeled off to Imaging, which had been hours ago. She'd since been checked over, and at the moment sat in a cubicle on her own, worrying about Levi.

Dr. Mateo Moreno slipped in past the curtain. He was one

of her very favorite ER doctors, and not just because he treated nurses with respect and kindness instead of the usual assholery they got from most doctors, but also because he lived next door to Charlotte's house, where Jane rented a room, and he was a friend.

Or at least as much of a friend as Jane allowed herself.

"If you needed a nap after your shift at North Diamond, you could've just said so," he wisecracked as he pulled up a stool. "You okay?"

She snorted in amusement. "Isn't that your job to know?"

His own amusement faded as he met her gaze. "I'm betting your experience was terrifying."

One hundred percent, but it was a personal rule not to do vulnerable. "Nothing I can't handle."

"How did I know you'd say that?" He began to peck on the computer at her bedside. "You call the boss yet?"

This was a joke reference to Charlotte. Thirty-nine-year-old Dr. Charlotte Dixon was five feet of pure heart and soul encased in hard steel with a southern accent. Nothing and no one got by her, and God help you if you ended up in a skirmish with her, whether that be at work or at the local bar's pool table or at her weekly poker night, because the woman was fiercely competitive. And yet she loved with everything she had. If you were lucky enough to be in her close circle, she couldn't help herself, she'd be this gentle but demanding presence in your life as she coaxed/bossed the best out of you, whether you wanted to be your best or not. "I'm waiting until I'm cleared," Jane said. "So I can show her in person that I'm fine. Otherwise she'll freak."

He laughed softly in agreement. "She just got off her shift. I don't know if she's still in the building, but if you don't leave her

a message before you go, you know she'll find out and freak anyway."

"Not if you hurry up and get me out of here. With a little luck,
she's still in the staff room gabbing with everyone like she does, and
I can go pick up her favorite breakfast and coffee for a distraction
and beat her home."

"Just when we all think you don't care at all . . ." he teased.

"Ha-ha, you're a laugh a minute. You missed your calling—
being a comedian would've saved you all that college debt."

"I like this paycheck better."

She knew it was about far more than his paycheck. The guy
cared about people almost as much as Charlotte did. "You about
done yet?"

"Almost." He went back to his pecking, making her sigh in
frustration. "Almost" in doctor-speak could be anything from five
minutes to never.

"So . . ." she said with as much nonchalance as she could mus-
ter, "how's the guy they brought in with me?"

"Hmm?"

"The guy who was on the gondola with me. Head injury. Is he
okay?"

He hesitated, which was odd for Mateo, who was a straight
shooter. Then he slid her a look. "Professional interest?"

"Of course," she said, because personal interest would yield her
nothing thanks to privacy laws.

Mateo looked at her for a long beat, then shook his head.
"Damn, woman. You and that poker face. But you know the drill.
If you want info on a patient, you're going to have to see if he'll
allow visitors and talk to him yourself."

She sighed. "Or you could just give me a hint."

"I'll say this. You and Levi both got damn lucky."

"You know his name."

"Yeah. I know his name."

"You worked on him in the ER?"

"I did. And also . . . we go way back." And then he went back to typing, shoulders a little atypically tight.

Seemed everyone had their secrets.

As for her and Levi getting lucky, she wasn't sure luck had anything to do with it. Levi had thrown himself across the gondola to protect her body with his. If he hadn't, he'd be fine. And she'd be . . . not fine. "I'll take lucky any day of the week," she said softly.

Mateo's eyes softened. "Same. And since you're not going to ask on the details about yourself, I'll just tell you. Your wrist is sprained and the contusions on your jaw and cheek, while probably painful, are nothing to worry about."

"So you're releasing me to go home and take a nap for real."

"Yes." Mateo pushed the keyboard away and turned back to her. "How you going to get there?"

"I don't know yet." The old Subaru she drove, which was Charlotte's spare car that she always lent to Jane when she was in town, was still in North Diamond's parking lot. Problem was, she'd lost her keys at some point between the gondola and the hospital.

"I'll take you home," Mateo said. "I was off thirty minutes ago. I stuck around to spring you free."

She smiled at him. "You're the best, Dr. Hottie Patottie."

He face-palmed. "You promised you'd make all the nurses stop calling me that."

One of the five urgent care clinics she rotated through, Sierra North, was attached to the hospital. There was some staff crossover, and she knew a lot of the same nurses he did. "Oh, I got them to stop." She hopped off the cot. "That was just for me. I enjoy watching you squirm."

"You're a sick woman."

"Tell me about it. Let's go."

Mateo went to get his stuff and Jane took a stroll down the ER hallway, gait purposeful so people would assume she was on official business.

She needed to see Levi for herself and know he was okay on top of lucky. Because actually, thinking about it, it would just be just plain rude to not check in . . .

He wasn't in any of the ER bays. Wasn't in Imaging either. She found him in a patient room, hooked up to an IV, asleep. "Thanks for saving my life," she said softly. "I owe you one."

He didn't give so much as an eye flicker, so she turned to go and . . . bounced off Mateo's chest.

He gave her a long look as he shrugged out of his jacket and wrapped it around her shoulders. He didn't say anything, not on the walk out of the hospital and not when they walked across the snowy, slippery parking lot to his car. On the heavily foot–trafficked path, the thick layer of newly fallen wet snow crunched beneath her feet, giving away slightly with each step like a sponge. A few snowflakes drifted down from the sky utterly silently, looking innocuous, landing on her head. She tilted up her face, feeling them settle on her eyelashes, gentle as a kitten's kiss, making her marvel at the difference between this morning's weather and yesterday's.

He turned on the engine and cranked the heat to high, aiming the vents at her before finally pulling out of the lot.

They stopped at the Cake Walk, which was Sunrise Cove's local bakery. Jane was convinced the place was actually heaven on earth. She quickly grabbed Charlotte's favorite muffin and coffee, and then they got on the road again.

Slowly. God, so painfully slowly. She looked over at Mateo. "You know, for a guy who works in the ER, moving at the speed of light all day long, you drive like a grandma."

"You're just panicked because you want to beat Charlotte home so you can shower and get to bed before she indeed freaks over what happened to you and then mothers you to death."

"Yes! Join my panic, won't you?"

He laughed and turned onto their street. Then he stopped laughing. "Uh-oh."

"Uh-oh? What uh-oh?" She leaned forward, trying to peer out at the bright morning, but she didn't have her sunglasses. Sun on snow glare was the absolute worst. "You know I don't like uh-oh."

Mateo pointed to the car in front of them.

Charlotte's.

Shit. Jane sank down low into her seat. "Just park and get out of the car and leave me in here. I'll sneak out once she's inside."

Mateo made chicken sounds.

"Oh, like you're in the clear. You're still totally in the doghouse with her for clearing our driveway of snow in that last storm."

"Yeah, and maybe you can explain that to me. She actually put the snow *back*."

Jane laughed at his confused expression. Men were slow sometimes. "She doesn't like to accept help. She's . . . stubborn."

"Takes one to know one."

Okay, true. Jane was incredibly stubborn. She knew this about herself. She wasn't sorry. "Just don't let her see me."

Mateo's and Charlotte's houses shared a driveway that split off at the top to two different parking areas. There was enough room for two lanes of cars at the top, but Mateo stopped right next to Charlotte's car.

"Wow," Jane said, still scrunched down low, out of sight. "*Seriously?*"

"Hey, if I'm going down, I'm taking you with me." He opened his door, got out, and . . . *didn't* shut his door.

"Payback sucks," she warned him, then braced to get fussed over. But somehow she got lucky, because when Charlotte got out of her car, she didn't so much as glance over at Mateo's. Instead, she stood there, hands on hips, in her midnight-blue scrubs, her white doctor coat, and a thick pink down jacket, unzipped, which billowed behind her in the chilly breeze. Same with her blond hair, loose from its usual bun, flying around her face like a halo, giving her the look of an animated action hero. She gave Mateo a single nod and said "Doctor" in a tone so chilly Jane almost got frostbite.

"Doctor," Mateo repeated back to her, sounding amused.

Charlotte stared at him, but Mateo didn't turn to stone. "It's going to snow again later." She said this in that classy southern drawl of hers, the one that always sounded like maybe she was on the way to an opera or something equally sophisticated and elegant. "When it does, don't even think about plowing my driveway."

"Just trying to help," Mateo said lightly.

"Who said I needed help?" She shivered and then zipped up her pink down jacket.

Mateo's lips twitched, and Jane knew his amusement resulted from the fact that the badass Charlotte had one weakness—for anything pink. Then he slid a knowing look at the strings of twinkling Christmas lights lining Charlotte's house's eaves.

Charlotte was back to hands on hips. "They're hard to get down."

"I offered to help you."

"Maybe I just want to be ready for the holidays ahead of time."

"It's only February."

She dismissed this with a wave of her hand. "You know what I mean."

"I do," Mateo said. "You don't need any help on anything, *ever.*"

"Now you're getting it. And anyway, I don't see you plowing Stan's driveway. Or Peter's."

Stan and Peter, both elderly men, were neighbors. And Jane knew that Mateo had indeed plowed their driveways as well, many times. But Mateo didn't tell Charlotte that or try to defend himself. He just stood there with a small smile on his face. Like Charlotte being all hoity-toity and contrary somehow amused him.

Jane had never understood why Charlotte didn't like Mateo. The woman liked almost everyone, but if you were one of the few unlucky ones—well then, she could cut you dead with a single slice of her icy blue eyes. And those eyes were frigid right now. She might be a sweet steel magnolia who never swore in public or wore white after Labor Day, but she never, *ever* backed down from a confrontation.

The cold air coming in the open car door was sucking the

breath from Jane's lungs. Plus, she was hungry, tired, and needed to pee. With a sigh, she got out.

Charlotte glanced over and paled.

Jane hoisted the coffee and pastry bag. "Look, breakfast!"

Charlotte drew in a deep breath before sending Mateo a hard look that had something else in it as well, something Jane couldn't place for certain but thought was maybe . . . hurt?

"It's not what you think," Mateo told her calmly.

That was when Jane realized she was wrapped in Mateo's jacket—which covered her from chin to her thighs—hood up, arriving home with the guy at just past dawn, like two teenagers trying to sneak back into their house without getting caught. "*Definitely* not what you're thinking," Jane said, with a face that made Mateo give out a rough laugh.

"Thanks," he said dryly and then turned to Charlotte. "She landed in the ER while you were in surgery."

"*In the ER?* Oh my God." Charlotte moved quickly toward Jane. "What happened? Are you okay?"

"Yes." With a sigh, Jane let the hood fall back to reveal her small facial injuries and pushed up a sleeve to show the wrist wrap. "It's nothing."

Charlotte aimed a dark look at Mateo.

He put up his hands. "Hey, you should've seen her when she first arrived at the ER. This is her actually cleaned up."

"You should have told me." Charlotte turned her attention back to Jane, unzipping the jacket to see that Jane wore a set of the scrubs in the colors reserved for the ER.

Where Jane never worked. Her rotations were in the urgent care clinics, not the hospital. Even more pale now, Charlotte cupped

Jane's face, looking it over carefully. "What happened? And where are your clothes?"

They'd been caked with Levi's blood, but that's not what Charlotte was asking. Jane stepped closer, making sure to keep eye contact. "I'm not hurt," she said. "Not in that way. I promise." She handed the coffee and pastry bag to Mateo to hold so she could put her hands over Charlotte's. She knew the woman's mind would take her to the worst possible place, assuming someone had hurt Jane on purpose. Badly. As Charlotte had once been hurt on purpose. Badly. "You heard about the gondola that went down last night?"

"Yes," Charlotte said. "No one was on it. It was downplayed for the press, presumably so as not to dissuade the ski season traffic in any way."

"It's true that no one was on the gondola that went down. But I was on the one just behind it, with another passenger. We got tossed around some, but I'm fine."

"Oh my God." Charlotte tugged her in and hugged her hard. "Do you know what could have happened?"

"But it didn't," Jane said.

"Why on God's green earth didn't you call me? I was right there at the hospital." She turned on Mateo like this was his doing.

"Yep, and there's my cue to go," he said, handing Jane back the bag and coffee.

Charlotte's eyes narrowed. "Isn't that just like a man, turning tail and running from a discussion."

Mateo stopped dead in his tracks, his dark eyes flashing something more than good humor for once. "You're not looking for a discussion, Charlotte. You're looking for a fight. And I'm not backing down from either. Name the time and place, babe. And I'm there."

The air seemed to crackle.

Jane, who'd been enjoying *not* being the center of their attention, suddenly straightened and stared at them both because . . . *what*? What was this? If she didn't know better, she'd call it sexual tension. But Charlotte didn't do sexual tension, ever. She'd cut that part of her life off entirely. Not exactly healthy, something that even Jane could recognize, but it was the truth. Fascinated, she watched as Charlotte, under Mateo's sharp gaze, seemed to . . . squirm?

Jane had never seen the woman squirm, not once.

Instantly curious, Jane eyed Mateo, who looked to be both amused and annoyed at the same time, which made things even more interesting because Mateo rarely showed annoyance. "Oh my God," she said, pointing at them. "You two are doing it?"

Charlotte gasped and put a hand to her chest.

The southern belle does denial.

Mateo's expression didn't change.

"You are!" Jane said in surprise.

Charlotte crossed her arms. "No, we are in fact *not* doing it."

Mateo shrugged. "I've asked her out. She's turned me down. Multiple times." He spoke to Jane but never took his eyes off Charlotte. "She knows the ball's in her court."

Charlotte stared at him right back. "I don't play ball."

"Then pick something else. You know where to find me." And with that, he started across the driveway toward his house.

"Hey," Jane called after him, "you're just going to leave me with her?"

"I've already been yelled at this week, both for the snow removal and when my car was an inch over the center divider of the driveway. Your turn."

"Excuse me, I don't yell," Charlotte said to his back. "I speak strongly, as is my right as a woman, thank you very much. And it wasn't *your* car blocking my driveway, it was a blue Toyota, so unless you occasionally wear a blond wig . . ."

Mateo stopped and turned back. "Whatever you do, *never* tell my cousin you thought she was wearing a wig."

Charlotte blinked. "Your cousin?"

"Yes. You know my family lives nearby. You've just never met them because, again, you've turned down all my attempts to get to know each other better."

"I can't believe I missed all this," Jane muttered to herself. "I thought you two didn't like each other. But it's actually the opposite, you two—"

"Finish that sentence and you're doing dishes for the rest of my life," Charlotte said. "And while this has been a whole bunch of fun, I'm going inside to eat and then sleep." With that, she strode, nose in the air, toward her house, blond hair quivering with indignation.

"Now who's turning tail?" Mateo asked, almost lazily.

Charlotte, her back to Mateo, froze.

Oh boy, Jane thought, torn between making a run for it or staying to watch the show. Because what Jane knew, and what Mateo had no way of knowing, was that Charlotte had been turning tail when it came to men since the night of her eighteenth birthday, when a string of bad decisions had nearly derailed her entire life.

Jane stood there, caught between two people she cared deeply about, not sure how to help. Thankfully, Mateo's phone went off. He looked at the screen and ran a hand down his face.

"I'm being called back into the hospital," he said. "Trev can't make his shift."

"No," Charlotte said, bad 'tude gone, replaced with something that looked suspiciously like worry. "You're too tired. Let them call someone else."

"I'm fine." He gave her an unreadable look, then got back into his car and drove off.

Jane felt for Mateo, she really did, but at the end of the day, her first alliance was with Charlotte, *always*, and her heart pinched hard at the look on her friend's face. Slipping her hand in Charlotte's, Jane knew exactly what to say to the good doctor, whose greatest joy was taking care of others, to redirect her. "Let's go inside. My head and wrist are aching."

Charlotte gasped. "And you let me stand out here dithering on?"

"Well, I know how you love to dither."

Charlotte snorted indignantly but slipped an arm around Jane and drew her inside.

Charlotte had bought the old Victorian to celebrate getting her residency. But burdened with heavy debt from medical school, she typically rented out three of the five bedrooms to hospital staff. Anyone of the female persuasion who needed a room qualified, from nurses to cleaning crews. She kept the master for herself and the one extra room as a den.

And a bedroom for Jane when she was in town.

For Charlotte, it was kind of the-family-you-make situation. Her parents were sweet and wonderful but lived in Atlanta. And since Charlotte couldn't often make herself go back there without experiencing crippling anxiety and panic attacks, she'd created a home and family here in Tahoe as well.

To Jane's shock and surprise and eternal gratitude, she was a part of that homemade family.

The house was an extension of Charlotte herself, warm and cozy, right down to the comfy furniture and thriving plants—more thanks to the high-altitude sun that came in from her floor-to-ceiling windows than any green thumb. Just walking inside, Jane could actually feel her blood pressure lowering. "That was fascinating, brand-new information, bee tee dubs. You and Mateo . . ."

"Hush." Charlotte took the pastry and coffee. "Are you really okay?"

"Yes," Jane said. "Promise."

"If you're sure, I'll make us a big breakfast. Then we'll split the pastry for dessert and both go get some sleep."

"Sounds perfect. I'll help."

"You mean you'll watch me cook, then do the cleanup."

Jane smiled. "Unless you want my help cooking?"

Well aware of Jane's lack of talent in the kitchen, Charlotte shuddered. "Please, no."

Two women were in the living room, both on yoga mats, stretching into some sort of twisted-pretzel poses. Charlotte greeted them warmly and announced she was making breakfast if they were interested.

They were.

Jane waved at them but didn't engage, just followed Charlotte into the kitchen. "What?" she said when Charlotte gave her an amused glance while stripping off her pink down jacket. "You said the magic word—*breakfast.*"

"They're our roommates." Charlotte was pulling out ingredients. "They've been here two weeks and you still don't know their names."

"Sure I do."

Charlotte put a pan on the stove top and gave her an *I'm waiting* look.

Shit. "Um . . ."

Charlotte snorted. "Michelle and Stacey."

"Yes! You took their names right out of my mouth."

"Uh-huh." Charlotte was cracking eggs into a bowl. "Or is it Chloe and Emma . . ."

Jane narrowed her eyes. "You're messing with me."

"You're an easy mark. And FYI, it's Zoe and Mariella."

"I knew that."

Charlotte poured the eggs into the hot pan, making them sizzle. "Honey, you're taking lone wolf to a whole new level this time."

"I know. I'm a jerk."

"No. You're an introvert. There's nothing wrong with that. But even a lone wolf has to come inside and get warm once in a while." She added peppers and onions to the eggs, which made the kitchen smell like heaven. Then she pointed the spatula at Jane. "You're so great with your patients—I've seen it. Sweet and personal and caring. They rave over you. But when it comes to making any real connections, you turn all thumbs. Why is that?"

Jane pulled some leftover bacon and chicken from the fridge and crumbled it into a small bowl. "I don't see the point of making connections. Not when I'm going to be gone soon."

"Ah. Right. Your favorite motto."

Jane ignored this and headed to the back door, where she found herself caught in the cross hairs of the biggest cat she'd ever had the pleasure of knowing.

Cat, as she called him—short for Alley Cat—sat on the back stoop, looking quite at home. Big but not overfed, a sleek, dark gray predator with slightly crossed light gray eyes. He eyed Jane for a long moment, letting her know she was in some sort of disfavor for being late with his breakfast.

"Sorry," she said, setting down the bowl. "I nearly almost died, but don't you worry, I've got your food."

"Let him in," Charlotte called out.

"He doesn't want to come in. He likes being free, living how he wants." Jane watched as Cat began to inhale the meat from the bowl, making some *yummy yummy* noises deep in his throat.

As far as she knew, he belonged to no one but himself. He made the rounds through the neighborhood daily, but seemed to spend the most time with Jane. She sat on the step at his side and stroked his fur in thanks for his blessing her with his presence. It was ridiculous how much she cared about him after only a few weeks, but as she kept telling everyone, she was leaving at the end of the season. It really would be cruel to introduce him to the fine life of indoor living, only to have to put him back out on the streets when she was gone.

She stayed with him until he'd finished his food and sat back on his haunches, washing his face. Done with that, he gave her another look, one she liked to think meant *thank you*, turned, and with a flick of his tail, was gone.

Other than Charlotte, it was the best relationship she'd ever had.

Back in the kitchen, Charlotte was still working on the food, and since Jane was starving, she revisited the fridge and this time came out cradling a glass container labeled JANE's. "You're my very own personal angel," she told Charlotte, grabbing a fork for the vegetable lasagna.

"That was for last night, which of course you missed, and you really should heat it up first—" Charlotte broke off with a grimace of distaste, but didn't further waste her breath as Jane dug into it cold.

"Yum."

Charlotte sighed. "Your cat was just making the same appreciative noises."

Jane snorted. "Are you comparing me to our alley cat?"

"*Your* alley cat, and yes." Charlotte paused and met Jane's eyes. "Where's your car, still up at North Diamond?"

"Yeah."

"I'll drive you to get it after breakfast."

"Thanks," Jane said gratefully.

"Of course." Charlotte paused, studied her for a moment. "You want to talk about it?"

"About what?"

"Almost dying."

"I was being dramatic."

"Jane, you're never dramatic. Tell me. I get it, you know."

Jane did know, and to her surprise, found herself fighting emotions. "I was coming home from work when the storm hit, it all went bad, and— Oh, no." She broke off, set the food down, and clutched at her throat where her necklace normally lay.

It was gone.

"I lost it," she whispered. "*That's* what happened. *Dammit.*"

"Your grandma's necklace?"

"Yes." And the only thing Jane had of hers. She pulled out her phone and called North Diamond's urgent care. No one picked up, so she left a message, detailing the necklace she'd lost, also asking them to check with ski patrol.

Knowing exactly what that necklace meant to her, Charlotte came around the island. "Honey." She slid an arm around her. "Someone will find it and contact the resort."

Jane nodded, but the dread in her gut told her it would be like trying to find a needle in a haystack.

"How about pancakes with your veggie lasagna and eggs?"

Jane wasn't the only one who could distract with the best of them. "With chocolate chips?" she asked.

"Is there any other kind?"

CHAPTER 5

The waves washed over the pebbled sand rhythmically, waking
Levi. He took a deep breath. Fresh pine trees and cool, fresh air.
Nice. The stunning sky matched the color of the lake in front of him,
a sea of blue, surrounded by the jagged Sierra peaks. Next to him
on the beach sat an urn.

Amy's ashes.

Lake Tahoe had been her favorite place on earth. Levi had been
her favorite person on earth, going as far back as middle school,
when they'd crashed into each other on the monkey bars and
cracked heads.

She liked to say he'd knocked himself right into her soul, that
there would never be another for her. She'd known that from age
twelve. He'd never fully understood it.

Or appreciated it.

Guilt washed over him in tune to the water hitting the sand.
Except . . . hold up. The sound was shifting from gentle waves to an
obnoxious beep, beep, beep . . .

"Levi? How we doing?"

He didn't recognize the voice, and he sure as hell wasn't going to open his eyes, because suddenly something was hammering away at the base of his skull. A sledgehammer. He actually lifted his hands to his head to hold it on his shoulders and felt the tug of an IV.

Damn. That, along with the scent of antiseptic, was a dead give-away.

He cracked his eyes open and immediately regretted it because the pain behind his eyeballs exploded. "*Jesus*," he gasped.

"Take your time. Slow breaths or you'll get sick."

No kidding. The urge to throw up was suddenly his number one problem. He drew in a very slow, shallow breath. And then another, not moving a single inch until the nausea retreated slightly.

"Good."

He fought his eyes open again. Given the slant of light coming in the window on his left, it was midmorning. On his right stood a nurse, checking his vitals.

"I'm fine," he said.

"Of course you are." She smiled at him. "If not just a little roughed up. And welcome back."

"Wait." His brain felt scrambled. "Jane." He had to clear his rough throat, the sound causing more stabbing pain behind his eyeballs. "Where's Jane?"

His nurse moved closer, adjusting his IV line before patting his hand. Her name tag said *Daisy*. Her warm, caring eyes said her regret was genuine. "I'm sorry. I wasn't here when you were brought in. Is she a relative? Your wife?"

He struggled to think, to remember, but his entire head felt constricted, like his skull was too tight. "I just need to know if she's okay."

At the look on his face, Daisy took sympathy on him. "All right, hon, I'll ask around. What's her last name?"

He opened his mouth and then had to close it again because he didn't know her last name.

"Okay, so not a relative, and definitely not your wife," Daisy said dryly. "Hang tight. I'll get your doctor."

Levi lay back and stared up at the ceiling. The night was a blur, a jumble of snapshots he couldn't seem to put in the right order. Frustrated, he started to push up from the bed, and immediately his world started spinning.

Beep, beep, beep . . .

"Whoa," Daisy said, back at his side, gently pushing him to lay down. "You're not quite ready for prime time yet." She took his vitals, made notes, and smiled at him. "Hang tight, your doctor will be here any second."

The next sound he heard was the curtain rings sliding on the metal rod, reminding him of another metal sound. From last night, when the gondola had tipped and the steel rod had slid out of its holder and . . .

Hit him in the head.

Suddenly the images in his head shifted and fell into order. Leaving San Francisco for the drive up the mountain to Lake Tahoe, his childhood home. And then after an hour with his parents, a familiar sense of restlessness had come over him, and needing to clear his head, he'd gone to North Diamond. Getting on the gondola, he'd felt his first sense of excitement in a long time, looking forward to the rush he always got from skiing.

Then Jane. Flirting with her. Irritating her . . . All while the storm increased with shocking speed, battering the gondola and rocking them like a ship at stormy sea.

Then the gondola ahead of them had gone down. Jane's soft gasp of horror, and his own oh-shit feeling as their dangerous predicament hit him. They'd both known that at any minute they could fall to their certain death, and still Jane had remained calm. Not fearless. Nope, she'd definitely been afraid. Hell, they'd both been terrified. But she was good in an emergency, and damn, that had been attractive.

Lying on the floor of the swaying gondola, the storm beating them up from every angle. Jane sitting with his head in her lap, holding pressure to the cut on his head. Being with her had been quiet and peaceful . . . that is, if nearly dying could be quiet and peaceful.

He remembered the ambulance ride. Jane had been at his side, talking in medical jargon to the EMS team, and he also remembered thinking how hot that was. She'd been here in his room too, sitting in the chair in his cubicle. Someone had given her fresh scrubs and she'd stayed with him while his head was cleaned and stitched until he'd been taken away for X-rays and a scan of his head.

When he'd been brought back, she'd been gone. Which meant she had to be okay, right?

The doctor who appeared from behind the curtain wasn't a stranger. Dr. Mateo Moreno wore scrubs and an opened white lab coat, his face dialed to eight hours past exhaustion. He'd been Amy's brother, and once upon a time, also Levi's best friend. It'd been a few years since they'd seen each other.

Levi's fault.

Mateo stepped up to the side of the hospital bed. His eyes, once always filled with laughter, mischief, and the genuine affection that came from a lifetime of hanging out together, were hooded now. "How you feeling?" he asked in a doctor-to-patient voice.

"Good enough to go home."

"Nice try." Mateo paused, then sank into the chair with both weariness and wariness. "About time I run into you, even if it's because you landed in my ER looking like death warmed over."

"That bad, huh?"

Mateo shrugged. "You've looked worse. Like when we drove my dad's truck up to the summit and did donuts on the ice and you fell out."

Levi laughed, then groaned at the pain. "You mean when we *stole* your dad's truck, and *you* did donuts on the ice until the passenger door opened and I was flung over the embankment?"

"Semantics." But Mateo smiled, his real one this time. "It was fun until you had to make it about you."

"Ha-ha." But it had been fun, just one in a long string of fun times they'd shared. "We're lucky we survived all the shit we got into."

"True story. And speaking of surviving, you're being held for observation because of the concussion and stitches, but you should be good as new in a couple of weeks with a lot of rest. Good thing your head's so hard."

Levi snorted, which caused a new stab of pain, but he sucked it up. "Good thing."

Mateo nodded, eyes serious. "It's been a minute."

"Too many." Levi had thought being in Sunrise Cove again, seeing Mateo, would hurt. Instead he just ached. Some from his injuries, but mostly from the loss of one of the best relationships he'd ever had. "I'm sorry."

Ignoring this, Mateo stood and hit some keys on the computer. "I called your mom, told her you were going to be okay. I also told her visiting hours didn't start until nine A.M., so you're welcome and you owe me." And then he started to go.

Levi did owe him, big-time. And he'd missed him. "I was a dick."

Mateo stopped, glanced back. "They say recognizing the problem is half the solution."

Levi let out a low laugh, and then a groan because damn, his head.

"You need to take it easy. You scrambled your brain good."

"Could be worse."

Mateo, eyes still serious, nodded. "Yeah. You could've been on the gondola in front of you."

True story. And then he'd be dead, without ever having this conversation. "I meant it. I'm sor—"

Mateo gave him the hand. "You're injured. We're not doing this now."

"I need to," Levi said. "I shouldn't have vanished."

"No, you shouldn't have. It wasn't your fault, what happened to Amy."

"I hurt her."

"Because you didn't let her drag you down the aisle?" Mateo shook his head. "You weren't ready."

"We'd been together all our lives, I should've been ready. A wedding was all she ever wanted, and I didn't give it to her before . . . before it was too late."

Mateo looked down at his bootee-covered shoes for a long

beat. Then he sighed and came back to Levi's bedside. "Is that what kept you away? Guilt? You think any of my family blamed you for not marrying her when she wanted you to? We didn't, Levi. What we blamed you for was leaving and not looking back. Like none of us ever meant a damn thing to you."

Levi felt his throat tighten, and the ache was now in his heart, not his head. "You did mean something to me. You all did. You deserved better from me."

"Damn straight," Mateo said, voice not quite as cool as it'd been.

Levi took a deep breath and was grateful he didn't throw up. "I need one more favor," he said quietly.

"You're racking them up."

"Actually, two favors."

Mateo just raised a brow.

"I want a do-over."

They'd started the do-over thing in middle school. When one of them did something incredibly stupid—which happened a lot— the other could choose to give a do-over. Or not.

But they'd never *not* given each other a second chance.

Mateo took his sweet-ass time answering. "Okay," he finally said. "You get a do-over. I'll take it in the form of pizza and beer when you're cleared to drink."

Levi let out a breath he hadn't known he was holding. That was more than he deserved. "Deal."

"And the other favor?"

"I was brought in with a woman named Jane. Do you know if she's okay?"

Again, Mateo looked at Levi for a long moment, eyes solemn, arms crossed over his chest. "I do."

"And?"

"And she's in far better shape than you." With that, Mateo walked out, sliding the curtain shut behind him.

Levi blew out a breath, and to stave off all the memories piling onto memories inside his aching head, he opened his palm and looked down at the dainty gold locket in his hands. An old friend on the local search-and-rescue had shown up in his ER cubicle after they'd found it on the gondola. Levi had promised to get it back to the owner. He flicked it open now and found a smile. The tiny pic on the right was a little girl of around eight with wild dark red curls exploding around her head like a halo. Jane, dressed like a sugar plum fairy. The older woman in the opposite picture could be anyone, but he'd guess a grandmother. As for how he was going to get the locket back to her when he didn't even know her last name . . . well, he'd figure that out when he was released.

A commotion sounded on the other side of the curtains, and then came a shrill, nervous woman's voice. "Where is he, where's my son?"

"They said the third room on the left, Shirl," a man said. Levi's dad. "One more room down."

"I can count, Hank. Why are you walking so slow?"

Levi stared up at the ceiling, not ready for this. Not that it mattered, as ready or not, his mom, dad, sister, and niece all crowded into his room.

"Honey!" his mom cried, rushing to his side. She was dressed up, hair and makeup in place, no sight of her always present bright blue glasses, which meant she was wearing her contacts. Which she hated. This was all unusual enough to have him taking a second look at her.

Worry lines were etched into her face. "Mom, I'm okay."

Not satisfied, she looked him over carefully. Levi was, and always had been, the odd man out in his family. His parents ran a sporting goods store, and if there wasn't a ball or a kayak or a tent involved, they weren't interested. Levi had grown up outdoors and loved it, but what he loved more was books, science: taking things apart and putting them back together in a better way; gathering data and then creating ways to manage that data.

Bottom line—his brain worked differently from the rest of the Cutlers, and while he had no doubt they loved him, they'd never really understood him.

And yet here they were, ready to smother him with love in the only way they knew how. "Really, I'm fine."

"You sure?" his mom asked.

"Very."

"Okay then. Tell us everything."

"You already know everything," he said. "Mateo told me he called you."

"He said you were okay and that visiting hours started at nine A.M. The end. Honestly, both you boys need phone manners."

Levi glanced at the clock on the wall. It was five minutes before nine.

"Your nurse let us in early," she said.

Translation: she'd badgered the front desk until they'd caved. No one, and he meant *no one*, had ever been able to tell Shirley Cutler what to do.

"She said you have a concussion," she said. "No one would tell us anything about Jane."

He felt a twitch begin behind his eye. Could one feel a vessel bleed? And if it was bad enough, could he pass out and miss the rest of this visit? "Who's manning the store?" he asked.

"We're opening an hour late," his mom said.

This was a shock. The store his family owned and operated was called Cutler Sporting Goods, located in the Tahoe area. It was closed for Easter and Christmas, and nothing else *ever*. The store had its ebbs and flows like anything else, but it was largely successful. Mostly because Hank Cutler was so tight with money he squeaked when he walked.

"So," his mom said. "Where's Jane?" She looked around like maybe Levi was hiding her somewhere in the tiny room.

"I'm probably going to be discharged soon," he said, hoping to distract from the fact that the girlfriend he'd made up last night had never really existed. "You guys didn't have to all come check on me."

"Oh, we didn't," his sister, Tess, said. "We came to meet your girlfriend."

"Where's Mateo?" his mom asked. "He'll give me a straight answer."

"Shirl, listen to the boy," his dad said. "Everyone's fine, and he would know otherwise."

"Uncle Levi!" Peyton yelled, jumping up and down. "Grandma said you might be getting married soon. Can I be the flower girl?"

Levi looked at his mom, who had the good grace to wince. He shook his head at her, then smiled at Peyton. "Hey, sweetness. And there's no wedding on the horizon."

"That's okay!" The six-year-old beamed at him, her two front teeth missing. "Hospitals smell bad. Like medicine and burnt toast and Grandpa when he forgets to spray after going potty."

"Peyton," Tess said, sounding like she was holding back a laugh. "You can't possibly smell all those scents at once."

"Actually, you can," Levi said. "The human nose can distinguish at least a trillion different odors."

His mom, dad, and sister stared at him, but Peyton laughed in delight. "Is a trillion a lot?"

"*A lot*, a lot," he said.

"More than the stars in the sky?"

"In our galaxy, yes," he said. "But not in the universe."

His dad tossed up his hands. "He gets his head bashed in, but can still cite weird random science facts."

"That's why he beats you at Trivial Pursuit," his mom said. "It's also why he can fix anything and everything. It's how he's wired, Hank, you know that."

Levi had taken a lot of teasing over the years for being the family fix-it guy, but he hadn't been able to stop Amy from dying, or keep his sister from getting dumped by her asshole husband, Cal. And no matter how hard he'd tried, he hadn't been able to fix the emptiness inside of him that he was beginning to be afraid was just a part of him now.

Peyton patted his IV-free hand and smiled at him so sweetly and adoringly it almost hurt. "Mommy told me I can pick a candy from the 'chine!"

Tess looked pained. "Every time I say no, she hears *ask again*. Giving in was the path of least resistance."

Peyton tried to climb up onto his bed. Tess attempted to stop her, but Levi leaned over and gave Peyton an assist. It hurt his head, but hell, so did life.

Peyton sat on his bed at his hip, her smile slowly fading as she got a closer look at him. "You haz an owie!" she said, pointing at his head.

"It'll heal."

She nodded, then leaned over and gave him a very wet kiss on his cheek. "I bring you candy from the 'chine. Grandma! We haz to get him some candy!"

"I've got something better." Levi's mom sat in the corner chair and started going through her bag. "Power bars. I made them myself . . . where did they go . . ."

Tess sighed and shifted closer to Levi. "Thanks for the car ride over here with her, by the way," she whispered.

"Oh, I'm sorry, was my near-death experience inconvenient for you?"

His mom raised her head with her ultrasonic maternal ears that could probably also hear his heart rate. "Your *near death*?" she repeated, eyes wide.

"He's just kidding," Tess said.

Levi risked his head falling off by nodding.

"Let's talk about Jane," his mom said. "Where is she?"

"She's been released."

"Released . . . Well, for goodness sakes." She sat down, removed her contact lenses while muttering about how annoying they were, and then slid on her bright blue glasses. "Why isn't she at your bedside? And how come you've never mentioned her before? How did you meet? Is she from here or San Francisco? What does she do?" She was looking around as if waiting for another bed to miraculously appear, and suddenly the hairdo and makeup made sense.

She'd dressed for Jane.

Making up a girlfriend had definitely not been a good son moment. It'd seemed so logical when he had been staring death in the
face, but now . . . "Listen, about—"

"Oh, no." His mom put her hand to her mouth. "You were
dumped."

"No—" He blinked. "And why would you think I'd be dumped?"

She had the good grace to wince. "I mean . . . it happens to everyone at least once, right?"

"I wasn't dumped. I made her up."

His mom dropped her hand from her mouth to her heart. "Are
you telling me you'd rather lie to my face about not having a girlfriend just so that you don't have to introduce her to me? You're
that ashamed of us?"

There wasn't enough pain medication for this.

"All I've ever wanted is for you to be happy," his mom said softly
with the threat of tears in her voice. "And you having someone
in your life was the best news I've had in a long time. It means
everything to me."

He exhaled slowly and felt himself cave like a cheap suitcase.
"Jane's not been in Sunrise Cove for long. And as for what she
does, she's a nurse."

"A nurse," she repeated, sounding impressed. "I'd so love to
meet her, and before you say no, I promise to not embarrass you."

"Mom." He reached for her hand. "You don't embarrass me."

"Good. Then you can invite her to our big fortieth anniversary
dinner."

The regular Cutler family dinners were a mixture of bickering,
disagreeing, and once in a while, a good food fight to boot. Holidays were regular family dinner times two. His parents' fortieth

anniversary dinner, four weeks from now, would be *exponentially* worse. He wouldn't wish it on his worst enemy. "Mom, that's really not necessary—"

"Oh no, you don't." She sucked in a deep breath, her eyes sparkling with sudden tears. "You think I don't know that you're underplaying what happened last night? How we could've lost you? With Jane, you've *finally* moved on from Amy's passing and are ready to live your life, and in one fell swoop it could've been over."

There was a single beat of uncomfortable silence. The Cutlers didn't do emotions well. No one, not his dad and certainly not his sister, wanted to discuss feelings. Ever.

Levi wasn't much better. Yes, Amy had been the first person in his life to understand him, to get who he was, and he'd adored her for that. With her, he'd never had to explain himself or his differences. She'd actually been a lot like him, and while he'd never been as convinced as she that their genuine affection and love for each other meant that they were *in* love or that they'd make good life partners, he *was* afraid he'd never find that easy acceptance again. Thinking about her gave him a definite ache, but after two years, he'd finally gotten good at dealing with his shit. "You didn't lose me, Mom. I'm right here."

"I know, and I'm grateful for that. And I love that you're *finally* seeing someone," she said in that fierce mama bear tone she'd been using with a hundred percent success rate on him since birth. "All I'm asking for is a chance to meet the woman who brought your big, beautiful heart back to life."

His so-called big, beautiful heart pinched. Calling home last night had been beyond stupid. But more, it'd been selfish.

"I thought we'd lost you," she said quietly, desperately.

"I'm really okay—"

"I meant when you left Tahoe. We hardly ever see you anymore."

Okay, true. But that hadn't been just about losing Amy. It'd also been because he'd felt . . . smothered here. San Francisco had been good for him, really good.

His mom came close and cupped his face. "When you called last night, there was something in your voice."

Yes, because he'd been pretty sure he'd been about to die a terrible, horrible death.

"You had love in it," she whispered. "I could tell you were deeply moved. Clearly, Jane did that for you. I want to meet her, Levi. I want to hug her and thank her. And feed her. At my anniversary dinner."

Yeah, he was a selfish idiot. "Mom, that's weeks from now. By then I'll be back in the city. You and Dad usually go out, just the two of you."

"Not this year. This year I'm having a dinner party with my family, and that means you. And you can't leave and come back. Mateo said you'll have to rest for several weeks at least. So see, you *will* be here for the dinner."

"That is not anything close to what he said."

"That's what I heard." His mom looked at Levi's dad. "Tell him, Hank."

Levi's dad turned to him. "You should do what you want, son. You always did."

There was a lot to unpack with that statement, but Levi's head was throbbing and his vision was blurry and all he wanted was to close his eyes. "I can take care of myself while I heal."

"Levi Anthony Cutler, we're perfectly qualified to help you and care for you even if you're smarter than the rest of us put together!"

"Hey," Tess complained, then shrugged. "Okay, *maybe*. But probably the concussion killed *some* of his brain cells, right? It might've knocked his high IQ down a few points and evened the playing field."

"You'll stay," his mom said to him.

Resistance was futile. "For as long as medically advised," he said—as much as he was willing to concede.

His mom beamed from ear to ear. "I'll cook, you'll eat. And . . . we're going to get to meet Jane!"

Welp, he'd walked right into that one. Which actually put his so-called high IQ in question. "I'll still need to work," he reminded her.

"You're your own CEO. You can work from anywhere."

That might be true, but *unlike* everyone else who shared his last name, he needed his own space to function. A quiet space, and order.

And possibly a lobotomy.

Daisy came in, took one look at Levi, and shook her head. "Everyone out," she said. "My patient needs quiet."

Levi nearly asked her to marry him on the spot. When the room was blessedly empty, he gave her a look of gratitude. "Thank you."

"Don't thank me. They won't go far."

Didn't he know it. He ran his thumb over Jane's locket. She'd want it back, he knew that much. Pretend girlfriend or not, he was going to have to find her. And why that gave him his first real smile of the day, he wasn't sure he wanted to know.

CHAPTER 6

Charlotte walked through the hospital, realizing that even after ten straight hours of being on her feet, she was feeling
good. Even cheerful. Weird as it might be to anyone not in the
field, she loved her life here. Loved everything about what she did.
Helping people. Healing people.

It distracted her from her own life.

As for why she needed that distraction in the first place—well,
she wasn't one to dwell, so she didn't go there.

Realizing her stomach was grumbling and that she hadn't eaten
in far too long, she headed toward the staff room. Surely it was
someone's birthday and there would be goodies.

She loved goodies.

As she entered, the large room went silent. Interesting. They
weren't a silent bunch. They were highly educated know-it-alls
with a social immaturity that came from being in college for half
of their lives. She narrowed her eyes. "What?"

It was dinnertime, so the room was fuller than normal. There
were staff on the two couches, at the two tables, standing in the
small kitchenette area.

All looking at her.

"Did I miss a call?" she asked.

"You won the pool." This from Mateo. His voice was its usual husky tone, the one that tended to give her goose bumps. Goose bumps she pretended meant he grated on her nerves.

A big fat lie. "Which pool?"

Valid question. Important too. There were at any given time ten to twenty different pools going on at the hospital. Yes, the staff members were swamped and run ragged almost every minute of the day. But in those rare seconds they could socialize, it was almost always about their ongoing wagers.

Could Lonny make it through his shift without one of his four-year-old twins calling 911 to talk to their "daddy."

Could Rae keep herself from pranking anyone.

Could Mateo manage to not get hit on by a patient or patient's family member.

Could Charlotte keep herself from going in on a new bet for a whole shift.

Note that the last one had been the only bet she'd failed so far.

"You won for the most compliments in a twenty-four-hour period from non-hospital staff," Mateo said. "Which I had to double- and triple-check because I still don't get how your patients and patients' families never fail to make sure everyone in the hospital knows how amazing you are."

"You doubt the compliments are genuine?"

His eyes darkened. "No. Because I know exactly how amazing you are."

The parts of herself she'd closed off squirmed. She ignored those parts. "Then what's the problem?"

"You've won every pool this week."

"And?" she asked.

"And you're getting rich off us."

She laughed and held out her hand for the envelope of cash, not a single regret in her mind because everyone in this room made enough money. "So I'm a little competitive, so what?"

Mateo snorted. "A little? You still haven't forgiven Montana for beating you out on the number of surgeries you performed in a twenty-four-hour period last week."

"That's because she cheated."

"I did not!" Montana pointed at her with a soda can. "It's not my fault I got called onto the floor for one last surgery before the end of shift."

"It was fifteen seconds until the end of your shift. It shouldn't have counted. In fact, let's just have a redo."

Montana suddenly beamed. "Yes, let's."

Charlotte nodded her head.

"Ha!" Montana practically bounced up and down as she clapped. "You just lost today's bet, the one where you promised not to go in a pool today."

Well, damn.

"Your hot streak is over," Montana said.

"Temporarily only," she said.

The crowd went back to talking and eating. Well, everyone except Mateo, who was just watching her, slowly shaking his head.

"What?" she asked.

"Nothing."

"It's something," she insisted. "Let's hear it."

He looked at her for a long moment. Then he smiled with his eyes. "Maybe another time."

"Why?"

"You're not ready."

And then he walked off. She found herself watching him go. "When will I be ready?"

He turned and caught her staring at his ass, and the smile hit his mouth. "Maybe sooner than I thought."

AN INCREDIBLY LONG week—which felt like five years—of "rest and relaxation" later, Levi finally escaped the family house for a doctor's appointment. After an exam and the removal of his stitches, he walked out of the doctor's office to where Tess was waiting for him in the parking lot. He slid into the passenger seat of her car, relieved as hell.

"Well?" she asked. "Is your head still scrambled?"

"Only slightly. Headaches might be a thing for me for a while yet." He could live with that. "The good news is my freedom's been obtained. I've been cleared to drive again." And the relief was nearly overwhelming. He'd forgotten what it'd been like to live at home.

"Prepare for the inquisition, then," Tess warned. "You know Mom's been holding back for this very moment, trying her very best not to hound you about Jane, and why she hasn't checked in on you."

"Maybe we've been texting and calling."

"Maybe." Tess looked out at the parking lot. Her voice was flat when she asked, "You're going to hightail it out of here now, aren't you."

"Eventually," he said. "But not yet."

She looked over at him, her eyes too shiny. "Not yet?" She sniffed. "Really?"

"Yeah, really." He was surprised by her show of emotion, and also concerned. It wasn't like a Cutler to be anything other than "perfectly fine." "It'll be another few weeks before I'm fully recovered, and you know Mom wants me to stay until their anniversary party." She still hadn't told him what she'd called him up to Tahoe for in the first place, insisting it was nothing for him to worry about while he was recovering. "What's going on, Tess?"

"Nothing."

"Try again."

She sighed. "I didn't tell Mom and Dad, but Cal and I didn't have a prenup." She drew a deep breath. "He took all the money out of our accounts before he ran off to Bali with the babysitter."

"What the—" He scrubbed a hand down his face. His anger wasn't going to help her. "What did the police say?"

"Turns out that neither screwing the babysitter nor taking money out of joint accounts is illegal."

Maybe not, but Levi would like to have a minute alone with Cal to teach him a little respect. With his fist to the guy's face. Since that was not the reaction Tess needed, he kept it to himself. But the money thing, that he could do something about. "I could help—"

"No. I don't want your money. I want my own life back." Angrily she swiped a few tears from her cheeks. Then she gripped the steering wheel tight and leaned in closer to the windshield to eyeball the car cutting in front of her in the roundabout. "Hey! Asshole!" she yelled, punctuating each syllable with her horn. "I have the right of way!" Then she took the roundabout on two wheels.

"Maybe I should drive."

"I'm fine!"

"Yeah, I can see that—" He winced. "There's another car coming—"

"*I have the right of way!*" She sped up, and when the second car honked at her, Tess told him he was number one. With her middle finger.

Five minutes later, she whipped into the parking lot of Cutler Sporting Goods. Levi let out a relieved breath and uncurled his fingers from the dashboard. Look at him. He'd survived a blizzard *and* his sister's driving.

"I've got to get to work," she said. "I'll get a ride home with Mom or Dad. Take my car and go rest."

"You're picking up a lot of hours."

She shrugged. "I'm taking on extra shifts when I can fit them in between Peyton's dance classes or when she's at a friend's house."

"Saving up to move out?"

"To fund my depression drugs."

"*Tess,*" he said quietly.

"It was a joke. Well, sort of. I am eating a lot of barbecue-flavored potato chips. Supposedly not habit forming, though, so no worries."

When Tess got out of the car, Levi moved into the driver's seat. Funny how adrift he'd felt while being unable to drive, how out of control. Felt good to be in charge of his destiny again.

He ran two quick errands, stopping for a pizza and then at the

Cake Walk for a specialty cupcake. He took the pizza to the hospital and asked for Mateo.

His oldest friend appeared at the front desk five minutes later, looking surprised to see Levi. "You okay?"

"Getting there, thanks to you." He pushed the pizza across the greeting desk. "I didn't bring the beer to go with it since you're working."

Mateo picked up the box. "I don't need the thanks. But I definitely need the pizza." He looked at Levi. "Is this a do-over pizza?"

"Yes. Is it working?"

"Possibly." Mateo started to walk away, but stopped to say, "Keep them coming."

Levi left the hospital and drove up to the North Diamond Resort. He parked and stared out his windshield at the imposing snow-covered mountain in front of him.

The sun was out, making the snow sparkle like diamonds—hence the resort's name. At 7,500 feet, the air was crisp but somehow also warm at the same time, and the sky was so clear and sharp blue it looked photoshopped. Feeling an odd and uncomfortable sense of déjà vu, he got out and breathed in the harsh, cold, crisp air of winter, welcoming the freezing freshness of it. He turned his face up to the sun, but the air was too cold, too all-encompassing, to warm him. He didn't mind. Winter worked for him. Winter invigorated him.

Even if it'd almost killed him.

The parking lot was full, the lifts were running, and given all the skiers and snowboarders on the ski runs, business was booming in spite of what had happened with the gondola only a week ago.

The investigation had yielded a decision that it'd all been a freak accident. Earlier on the day of the storm, there'd been some construction work done and somehow a piece of debris had been left behind. A small chunk of wood. The vicious wind had knocked it onto the track.

The odds against such a thing were astronomical.

But Levi still didn't get onto the gondola.

Instead, he found a friend who happened to be on ski patrol and hitched a ride on his snowmobile up to the urgent care clinic at mid-mountain. He entered the clinic and asked if Jane was working. He'd called earlier. He'd called all the clinics. He couldn't get anyone to tell him who was on duty. So here he was . . .

"She's not on our schedule today," the nurse at the front desk told him.

He drove to High Alpine Resort next. No luck there either.

Two hours later, Levi walked into the last urgent care clinic in the area. This one was in Sunrise Cove, right next to the hospital.

There was no one behind the front desk, but he didn't need help because Jane was standing in the middle of the room wearing scrubs and a familiar attitude, staring up at the only other person in the room—a huge guy, at least six-five, and clearly a fan of daily lifting at the gym.

His expression was dialed to royally pissed off, his entire body taut with tension. "Hell, no," he growled at Jane. "Not happening."

Jane, *maybe* five-four, and that was including the pile of wild dark red hair knotted on top of her head, was hands on hips, head tilted back to see the guy's face, clearly not at all impressed by the macho display. "We've been through this before, Nick," she said calmly. "And we both know who won. So you can either walk to the back of your own free will"—she gestured toward the door behind her, which presumably led to the patient rooms—"or I can call your wife again."

The guy seemed to shrink. "Ah, man, why do you gotta be so mean? I'll come back tomorrow."

"No. You need a Tdap shot *today*."

"I don't need whatever that is."

"It's a tetanus shot, and yes you do. You stabbed your thumb on a rusty nail. But I promise, it's just a little prick."

"*You're* a little prick," he muttered, then swiped his hand down his face. "Shit, I'm sorry. That was automatic."

"Understood. Now can we . . . ?" Jane pointed at the back again.

Nick and his mountain-wide shoulders sagged. "I just don't see why it has to be today. I said I'd come back another time."

"Please refer to my earlier answer of no."

Nick huffed out a huge sigh and started shuffling into the lab. Halfway there, he turned back.

Jane was still pointing.

With a huge sigh, he vanished through the doorway.

Jane turned to Levi, registering nothing but a quiet surprise. "Tarzan."

He grimaced. "Tell me you remember my real name."

"Of course I do. But then again, I'm not the one with a head injury."

"I'm fine." He knocked on the top of his head. "Hard as a rock. And you?" He gestured to her wrist, which wasn't splinted.

"I'm good." Her dark green eyes gave nothing away, including how she felt at seeing him again.

As for what he felt, it seemed a whole lot like relief. "I wanted to thank you for saving my ass."

"You'd have been fine if I hadn't been there. You only got hurt because you were trying to protect me."

"I liked the company," he said, and while she looked to be absorbing that comment, he made another. "You ducked out on me at the hospital."

"Hey, I made sure you were going to live first."

This made him laugh. "Thanks."

"No problem. Are you in need of medical attention?"

"No."

She looked him over anyway. He'd like to think that there was some attraction as well as assessment in her pretty eyes, but she was damn good at holding her own counsel. "Okay then," she said. "Welp, I gotta get back to work. Make sure the door shuts behind you. The latch doesn't always catch."

He smiled at being so thoroughly dismissed. "Nice bedside manner. Sexy. Only you're not the boss of me, Jane. I mean . . . unless you ask real nice first."

"Now you're just *trying* to fluster me."

"Didn't know I could."

She rolled her eyes and pushed a few loose strands of hair out of her face. "Like you don't know you have that effect on most women."

"But not you."

"I'm not most women. How did you find me anyway?"

"First, I braved North Diamond's mountain looking for you, only to find out that you weren't scheduled at that urgent care today. Or at Sierra North, Homeward, or Starwood Peak . . ."

That won him a low laugh, but her smile slowly faded. "I'm off rotation at North Diamond for now."

He hated the idea that she was afraid to go back up there, but he certainly understood it. "I nearly had a panic attack at the idea of getting on the gondola," he admitted. "I had to get a buddy from ski patrol give me a ride on his snowmobile."

That had her looking at him again, her gaze softer now. "It's not often people try to find me," she said. "Usually it's been the opposite."

That effectively swiped the smile from his face, remembering what she'd told him, that she didn't have family. His family was a huge pain in his ass, but he couldn't imagine not having them. "Can we talk?"

Those sharp eyes assessed him, taking in the scar the stitches had left through his eyebrow. "I'm glad you're okay. But I don't know what there is to talk about."

"Maybe I needed to know you're okay too."

"I'm fine."

He smiled at his own usual mantra and his gaze settled on the bruise along her jawline. Very gently, he ran a finger along it. "I'm sorry about what happened that night, Jane."

She swallowed hard, then shook her head. "None of it was your fault. And I'm sorry, but I've really got to get back to work. So unless you've got another of your fascinating facts for me, I'll see you around—"

"If you burned all the new data from just one day onto DVDs, you could stack them on top of each other and reach the moon—twice."

She blinked, then looked impressed. "Okay, that's a good one."

"Also, I brought you something." He reached into his pocket.

"At least you didn't ask me to get it out for you this time."

He grinned, and that felt good. Too good. He held his hand out to her, palm still closed, and her eyes narrowed. "What is it?"

"Suspicious much?" Reaching for her hand, he dropped her necklace into her palm. "One of the search-and-rescue guys found this that night, but they missed you at the hospital. I promised to get it back to you."

She stilled and stared down at the necklace, her eyes going shiny before she closed her fingers around the locket and brought it up to her chest. "Thank you," she whispered, voice thick. "You have no idea how much this means to me."

Looking at her stare at the necklace again, he thought maybe he did. "I'm just glad you have it back. Jane . . ."

She lifted her face.

"Do you want to talk about it? About what we went through?"

"No. We're both okay, there's no need." She took a step back. "But I owe you one."

"Actually, you saving my life trumps me getting the necklace back to you. Can I buy you lunch on your break?"

"I'm not hungry." Then her stomach growled and she grimaced, looking embarrassed. "Okay, fine. I'm starving. After I finish with my patient, I get a break. Meet me at the hospital cafeteria. It's in the next building over, ground floor."

He smiled. "It's a date."

"It's not a date. I don't date."

"Never?" he asked.

"Well, maybe once in a blue moon."

His eyes twinkled with mischief. "Then here's hoping for a blue moon. See you in the cafeteria, Jane."

She nodded, then watched him walk out of the urgent care—which he knew because he looked back and caught her at it.

With another grimace, she vanished into the back, and he smiled all the way to the hospital cafeteria.

CHAPTER 7

Fifteen minutes later, Jane walked into the hospital cafeteria. This was a bad idea. Like, a *really* bad idea, mostly because while she could say she wasn't interested in starting anything with Levi, she seemed to conveniently forget that when looking in his eyes.

Stupid, sexy eyes.

Sandra, a fellow traveling nurse, caught her at the entrance. "Jane! Hi, what's new?"

"Not much," she said neutrally.

"You sure? 'Cause there's a really hot guy waiting for you." Sandra tilted her head in the direction of a table off to the right and waggled her eyebrows.

"And?" Jane asked.

"And . . . there's a really hot guy waiting for you." The unspoken question was clearly *Where did you find him?*

The medical network here in Tahoe was impressive, but behind the scenes, it was like high school. High school with really smart kids who practically lived the job, so they were all far too tangled up in one another's lives.

And Jane didn't plan to be the latest watercooler story. A quick peek over her shoulder revealed Levi leaning back in his chair, scrolling through his phone. And damn, Sandra was right. He was sexy as hell, maybe even more so now with that new scar line through his right eyebrow.

"Are you really going to give me nothing?" Sandra asked. "Come on, my day's sucked so far."

Jane laughed but shook her head. "Did you really come all the way down from Labor and Delivery to get gossip?"

"No, actually I came looking for you. I was wondering how long you're staying at Charlotte's this year. The hospital offered to extend my contract by another couple of months, but there's no available housing. And you're always saying you're going to be gone soon, so I guess I'm wondering if that's true?"

Jane had spent the first part of her life being asked to move along. It was always done in a roundabout way, starting from when her grandpa hadn't been able to take care of her on his own. She'd been handed off from one distant relative to the next. *Jane, wouldn't you like to go stay with cousin so-and-so for a while . . . ?*

But this wasn't that, she reminded herself. "Have you spoken to Charlotte?" she asked Sandra.

"Not yet. Thought I'd check in with you first."

The thing was, Charlotte was such a bleeding heart, Jane knew the woman would sleep on her own couch to make sure Sandra had a place to stay.

And then there was the fact that Charlotte would make more money off Sandra, a lot more, because she never took enough money from Jane to begin with.

But the real truth was that Jane wasn't sure she could handle

Charlotte asking. She'd rather leave on her own than face that ever again. "I'm contracted for work until the season is over, but maybe we could work out a shared-room situation. See what Charlotte wants to do and let me know."

Sandra squeezed her hand. "Thanks, hon."

When Sandra walked away, Jane drew a deep breath and headed toward Levi's table. He looked up, smiled in a way that pushed the lingering bad memories away, and stood. "Hey."

"Hey."

He pushed a tray loaded with food to the center of the table. "I know you're short on time, so I got one of everything."

It was ridiculous how much this charmed her, and she laughed as she grabbed a grilled cheese and a cup of soup, and then on second thought, also the French fries.

Looking pleased, Levi took the burger and small salad. "I really enjoyed watching you handle the big guy today."

"Nick?" She smiled. "He's okay. He's really just a gentle giant."

Levi laughed. "Whatever you say."

They were eating their food when Levi leaned in. "We've got an audience. Your three o'clock."

She turned and looked and found Sandra, along with a few other nurses, watching them with avid interest. She gave them the shoo gesture and they scattered. "Sorry," she said. "It's like they've never seen me with someone before." She paused. Grimaced. "Okay, so they've never seen me with someone before. They have no idea this is just a lunch between two people who nearly bought the farm together." She laughed.

Levi didn't.

She paused with a French fry halfway to her mouth. "It *is* just a lunch between two people who nearly bought the farm together, right?" she asked.

"It's whatever we want it to be."

For some reason, this kicked her heart into gear.

He pushed a white box across the table. It had a pretty red bow on it, and she stared at it like it was a coiled snake. "What is it?"

"It's a Thanks-for-Not-Letting-Me-Die present."

"No. I don't do presents."

"Would it change your mind to know it's a cookies 'n' cream cupcake from Cake Walk?"

She gasped. "Don't you tease me."

"Wouldn't dream of it."

She practically tore off the bow, making him laugh, but she didn't care. Calk Walk's cupcakes were the gold bar of cupcakes. They were better than a day off. They were better than sex—at least she was pretty sure. It'd been a while. "You actually remembered," she said as she sat staring down at the huge perfect cupcake, lunch forgotten, mouth watering.

"Yeah. You moaned a little when you were talking about it."

Well, that was embarrassing. And true. "So you wanted to hear me moan again?"

"You already did." He smiled a bit wickedly, and . . . damn. It was a good smile. The kind that could give a girl some seriously dirty thoughts, which she also hadn't had in a while. Uncharacteristically ruffled, she grabbed a knife, carefully cut the cupcake in two, and handed him half.

"You absolutely positive they're even?" he asked.

She eyeballed them again. "Yes," she finally said and caught his grin. "You're still teasing me. But you should know, I take these cupcakes very seriously."

"Then I'm *seriously* touched that you'd share." He held up his portion in a cheers. "To not dying."

"To not dying." She took a big bite and moaned again. "I can't help it!" she said when he grinned at her.

"Not complaining." He took a bite as well and . . . let out a very male moan himself.

Laughing, she pointed at him. "See? Better than sex, right?"

His smoky eyes heated. "I'll admit, the cupcake is amazing, but nothing's better than sex. Not if it's done right."

Well, you walked right into that one. Determined to get out of the danger zone, she concentrated on her next bite, not even realizing that her free hand had gone to her necklace, back around her neck where it belonged.

Levi's gaze went there too. "Looks good on you."

Earlier when he'd dropped her grandma's necklace into her palm, she'd had to fight tears. He'd noticed, she knew he had, but he hadn't pushed her to talk. Instead he'd remained quiet, letting her recover. "Thank you again," she said softly.

"The way you touched it when you got on the gondola, I figured it was important to you."

It took her a minute to be able to speak. "Very. It was my grandma's." She opened the locket and looked at the picture of herself, the happiest she'd ever been in her life up to that point because they'd just gone to see *The Nutcracker.* "It's the only thing I have of her." She paused. "Actually, it's the only thing I have of my childhood."

"I'm glad you've got it back." Reaching out, he gently touched the fading bruise on her jaw. "You're really okay?"

"Yes." She looked at the healing cut slicing through his eyebrow. "I should have asked you before how you are feeling."

"Same as you, I imagine."

She drew in a deep breath. She hadn't wanted to discuss what had happened up there on the gondola with Charlotte when she'd asked, saying she couldn't go there yet. She hadn't wanted to have to admit she'd pulled herself off the North Diamond's clinic rotation schedule, how she'd had more than one nightmare about that night, how ever since then she'd felt . . . she wasn't even sure. Lost? Until now, anyway. With her necklace back, she could face anything. "I'm a master at shoving my hot-mess-ness deep."

A rough laugh rumbled up from Levi's chest. "Same."

Their eyes met and locked. Maybe she hadn't been able to talk to anyone else about what happened, not wanting to relive it. But Levi had been right there with her, so he already knew. She didn't have to tell him any of it. There was an odd comfort in that, and she went back to her cupcake, trying not to inhale hers, trying to savor it. "I'm sort of regretting giving you half," she said around the next mouthful.

He hadn't devoured his. He was taking his damn time, and while he was doing so, he casually sucked a dollop of frosting from his thumb.

Jane looked at her thumb, hoping for her own dollop to lick, but no go. She took her last bite and eyed the baking paper, wondering if she could lick that without embarrassing herself.

"You ever going to tell me why you disappeared on me that night?" Levi asked.

"I didn't disappear."

He gave her a look.

"All right, fine. I took off because I knew you were in good hands and that you'd be okay. There was nothing left for me to do." Plus, the longer she sat at his bedside, the longer she'd wanted to stay. She played with the cupcake paper until she felt his hand on hers.

"Hey," he said quietly, waiting until she looked at him. "Just so you know, it's normal after a situation like that to bond with the person you survived it with. I never knew how true that was until a week ago. We're the only two who know what we went through. After you left, in the days after, I was just . . . worried, I guess, thinking about you out there, maybe going through a bad time because of it and not having anyone who'd understand."

She didn't want to be touched, but she was. She was also unwilling to admit she'd been indeed having a hard time. "I face life-or-death situations all the time for a living. If I formed an attachment to every patient, I wouldn't last long."

He looked at her for a long moment. "You and I both know that what happened up there that night was far more than a patient/practitioner relationship."

She looked into the cupcake box, but a second cupcake did not appear.

"And you face life-and-death situations every day at work?" he asked.

Clearly, the sugar high had loosened her tongue, and he was too damn smart because he'd caught the one little tidbit she hadn't meant to let loose. "I told you I'm only in Tahoe for the ski season. The rest of the year I'm out working for Doctors Without Borders and other organizations like them." She genuinely loved helping others, loved helping to make people feel safe—ironic since she'd never felt particularly safe growing up, or . . . ever. But mostly she loved the temporary nature of the contracts she took. Loved knowing she got to leave on her own terms. That the end date was decided going in. No one had to ask her to leave because she'd become inconvenient. She couldn't be returned.

And yeah, that was her deep, dark, sad, secret truth . . . she was terrified of staying past her usefulness.

Levi was looking at her like she'd surprised him, but he didn't comment, for which she was grateful. She never knew what to say when people responded with *wow*, or *that's amazing*, or *thank you for giving back* . . .

She realized he still had his hand on hers, and he was rubbing his thumb back and forth over her palm, a look of fascination on his face. "You keep surprising me, Jane."

"Yeah." She pulled her hand free. "I get that a lot."

"I meant in a good way."

She took in the seriousness behind the playful light in his eyes, behind the several-days-old stubble on his jaw, at his slow smile because she was still just staring at him. "Oh," she said brilliantly.

"*Oh*," he repeated with a small smile, and slid the rest of his cupcake back toward her. He'd taken only two small bites.

"You're giving it back?"

"I like watching you eat."

"You're a strange guy."

"No doubt," he said agreeably.

Not willing to look a gift horse in the mouth, she took the half cupcake. Bit. Chewed. Swallowed. And then stilled at the realization. "You want something."

"It's a small thing."

Damn. She knew it. She stopped eating. "What?"

"You disappeared before my parents could meet my . . . *girl-friend*."

Her tummy quivered, and not necessarily in a bad way, which made her need the clarification. "You mean your pretend girl-friend."

"My mom wants to meet the woman willing to put up with me. She wants her to come to their fortieth anniversary dinner."

"Again, not seeing how this is my problem." Just thinking about it had licks of panic racing through her, even while being fasci-nated by this family of his.

"It'd be just one family dinner."

"Oh no," she said, snorting to hide her rising horror. "No, no, no."

"Okay, great. So you'll think about it."

She had to laugh. "So your Male Selective Hearing is intact."

"Well, I am a male, so . . ." With a smile, he stood. "Take your time, the dinner's not for three weeks." And then he took his sexy ass—yes, it was indeed very sexy—and walked off. He passed the table of gawking nurses and winked at them. "She's thinking about it," he said conspiratorially.

In unison the whole table swiveled their heads and stared at Jane.

"No," she said. "I'm not."

"Can *we* then?" Sandra asked.

Jane thunked her head on the table.

THE NEXT MORNING when Jane's alarm went off at four forty-five, she was still doing nothing but thinking about it. She didn't have to be at work until eight, but she still got up, showered, and hit the Stovetop Diner by five.

The early bird always gets the worm.

That's what her grandpa used to say. Which was why she was really here. Not just the diner, but Lake Tahoe in general.

Last year she'd been here for the ski season as usual, and she'd caught sight of her grandpa in this very diner. At the time, she'd been too shocked to talk to him. She wasn't proud of it, but she'd ducked out before he could see her.

She hadn't been ready to make contact. Hurt and resentment and her ever-present fear of rejection had ensured that. Complicating things was that her grandpa also inspired some of the best memories of her childhood.

This year, she still felt the same roller coaster of emotions, so she was no closer to making a decision about talking to him.

But none of that stopped her from wanting a peek at him. So she parked at the diner, because if she knew one thing about her grandpa, it was that he was a creature of habit.

The building had been constructed just after the Prohibition era, standing tall as a distillery for decades. In the 1950s, it'd been bought and turned into the first diner on all of the North Shore, complete with black-and-white-checkered floor tiles, red vinyl booths, and jukeboxes. The look had since lost some of its luster, but the food was amazing, ensuring that the place remained a mainstay for the area.

The alcohol license didn't hurt.

She eyed the table across the room, where indeed her grandpa sat with his cronies drinking their morning espresso and telling stories about growing up here in Tahoe before it'd become a popular tourist destination. "Back in the day . . ." one of them was saying, "you could jump off the cliff at Hidden Falls and not get in trouble."

Her grandpa chuckled. "Back in the day, Secret Cove was still a nudie beach that no one had ever heard of except for us locals. Watch out for the geese, though—they like to nibble at the frank and beans."

Jane watched him, heart torn between love and hurt as she sipped her coffee in disguise; her ski hat pulled low, scarf wrapped around her neck, and coat still on to hide her scrubs. She was in an out-of-the-way booth, not easily seen, sitting with a spare to-go coffee to take to Charlotte at work—unless she ended up drinking both out of sheer nerves.

Her grandpa tipped back his head and laughed heartily at something one of the men said, and it both hurt and felt good to hear it. She'd spent a lot of years suppressing her emotions, so the waves of nostalgia, heartbreak, and guilt hit hard.

When someone unexpectedly sat at her table, Jane nearly jumped right out of her skin.

"Some PI you are," Charlotte said, stealing Jane's coffee. She was in her usual scrubs and her ridiculous pink down jacket. "You didn't even see me coming."

"You need a bell around your neck. And hey, the one in the to-go cup is yours."

Charlotte took both, looking pleased with herself. "I'm stealth, baby. Ask me how stealth."

Jane eyed her warily. "How stealth?"

"Stealth enough to know that a hot guy brought you a cupcake to work yesterday, and that you had lunch with him."

Jane gaped.

"And that he asked you something and you're thinking about it."

"*How in the world . . . ?*"

Charlotte grinned. "Heard it from an intern, who heard it from a lab tech, who heard it from Radiology, who heard it from a nurse who was at the table with Sandra."

"Wow." Jane shook her head. "And you're missing a whole bunch of details. Your sources are slipping."

"Actually, their exact words were that you were caught sharing a postcoital lunch with Sexy Gondola Guy." She leaned in, hands on the table. "Let's discuss."

"Sure," Jane said. "We'll discuss as soon as *you* discuss our very handsome next-door neighbor—also your coworker—and why you pretended to not like him this whole time when you secretly *do*."

CHARLOTTE CHOKED ON her sip of coffee and nearly snorted it out of her nose. But that wasn't what had her heart pounding. Pretending she hadn't just burned her windpipe, she leaned casually back as she studied her best friend. "I don't know what you're talking about."

"Then neither do I," Jane said with a smirk. She saw right through Charlotte.

She was Charlotte's own personal miracle. No one saw past her walls. Not at work, where she was practically a dictator. Not with her circle of friends, who were amused but not bothered by her almost OCD need to control . . . well, everything. No one. She was that good at hiding in plain sight.

But Jane. Jane had seen right through her from the start, to the real Charlotte. Terrifying at first, but now comforting. Even more so was the fact that she gave the same sense of security to Jane.

They were two peas in a pod, which allowed Charlotte to relax with Jane like she could with no one else.

But right now, staring at each other, with Jane clearly hiding burgeoning feelings for a man for the first time since Charlotte had known her, and with Charlotte doing almost the exact same thing . . . Well, it would have been funny if it hadn't been so scary.

They stared at each other. Charlotte broke first. She always did. She'd never met a silence she could endure, and she knew that about herself. It was irritating as hell so she did what she did best, she went on the defensive. "I also know you sat at Sexy Gondola Guy's hospital bedside for several hours before coming home."

Jane went from smirk to . . . unsure? And Charlotte's heart kicked for another reason altogether. She was a worrier, always had been, but with Jane, she was also somehow a warrior. She leaned in. "What does he need from you? Do I have to kick his ass?"

"No!" Jane let out a small laugh. "Ohmigod, we're both out of our minds. But no ass-kicking necessary! Stand down, Dr. Dixon."

"You sure? Because you know I'd do it." She flexed. "I'm tiny but mighty."

This won her another rough laugh, which coming from Jane was the equivalent of a belly laugh. "I never doubt you," Jane said. "But what Levi wants, it's, um . . ." She squirmed.

Fascinating. Jane *never* squirmed. Jane never gave herself away like that. At least not to anyone except Charlotte, which was a huge source of pride for her. Jane had been a tough nut to crack, but Charlotte didn't know how to take no for an answer. It'd taken her six years, but she was fairly confident Jane finally considered her family. "It's what?" she pressed.

"Personal."

Charlotte's eyes widened.

"I know what you're thinking," Jane said on another low laugh. "But it's not *that*. When Levi and I were on that gondola and we thought we were going to die, he called his mother to say goodbye."

Charlotte gasped, a hand to her chest. "Oh my God," she whispered, trying to imagine calling her mom to say goodbye. She couldn't imagine it, not without her throat tightening and her eyes burning with unshed emotion.

"Yeah." Jane let out a breath.

"I really can't fathom making that call," she said softly, reaching for Jane's hand. "Oh, honey."

"The thing was, he couldn't actually do it. He told her he was happy and in a relationship."

"Sweet. But I can't help but notice I didn't get a call."

Jane shook her head. "I couldn't do it, not to you."

Charlotte took a moment to just breathe past the image of losing her. "Next time I want a call." She squeezed their fingers together. "But let's not have a next time, okay?"

"Agreed." Jane took a breath. "Anyway, now Levi needs a pretend girlfriend for some big family dinner in three weeks."

Charlotte took this in. Jane was . . . blushing a little. And not making eye contact. Fascinating. "You going to do it?"

"He brought me my locket back."

Charlotte felt a smile crease her face. "You're going to do it."

"I don't know. Wait— How do you know I sat by his bedside? You were in surgery."

"Someone told me."

Jane stared at her. "Dammit. Now I'm going to have to kill Mateo."

Mateo. The only man who could make her feel like she didn't know what she was doing. At any given moment of any day, she wasn't sure if she wanted to wrap her fingers around his neck and squeeze or climb him like a tree. Not that she would admit either under threat of death. Nope. Her ridiculous little crush on the man who was sexier than the legal limit was going to stay her own personal secret. For a whole bunch of reasons, not that she could name one at the moment.

"I knew it!" Jane pointed at her. "See, you *don't* want him dead."

"Well, I never said I wanted him dead, did I? I said I wanted him to stop flirting with me." A total lie.

"Admit it," Jane said. "You have no idea how to deal with a good man trying to get your attention. I mean, you're not quite as screwed up as I am, but you're close enough."

True story. Charlotte'd had a good childhood, but she'd also had her share of trauma, which had left her just as awkward and uneasy at romantic entanglements as Jane.

"He wants to go out with you."

Charlotte ignored the butterflies in her belly at that thought and shook her head. "He's a flirt. That's what he does. He flirts with *everyone*."

"Wrong," Jane said. "Mateo's one of the rare good ones. Yeah, he's nice to everyone on the floor, from surgeons to nurses to the cleaning crews. But there's only one person he flirts with, stares at, moons over, brings coffee to. And that's you. And— *Ohmigod*."

"*What?*"

Jane squeaked and ducked low, beneath the table.

Charlotte stuck her head under the table. "You drop something?"

"Yes, my marbles! I think my grandpa saw me— Oh my God, don't look!"

But Charlotte was already looking, feeling her heart harden on the spot. "I want to see the man who deserted you when you were eight."

"He didn't desert me."

"Bullshit," Charlotte said.

"He wasn't well."

"And you were eight."

"Yeah," Jane muttered. "Hence me being under the table like I'm still eight."

Charlotte stuck her head under the table, softening when she saw Jane's genuine panic. "Honey, what have I always told you?"

"Um . . . Men suck?"

"Okay, and what else?"

"Always make the time for lip gloss because we're not animals."

"Aw! You *were* listening." Charlotte felt so proud. "And . . . ?"

"And . . . family is earned, not inherited."

Charlotte nodded. "So you have to decide. Are you ready to go there? Open up some old wounds?"

The look on Jane's face said she was undecided.

Fair, given what she'd been through. "Whatever you decide," Charlotte said softly, "you know you have people who love and support you."

Jane hesitated, then nodded. "I'm still getting used to that. I let you barge in past all my walls."

Accurate.

"And Mateo too," Jane said. "And now maybe Levi? It feels like too much. It's like . . . the quintessential nightmare of going to school naked. I'm out there hanging out in the breeze, vulnerable, just waiting for someone to say it's time for me to move on."

"I'll never say that," Charlotte said fiercely. "And you know that no matter what happens with your grandpa—or doesn't happen— you're going to be okay because . . . why?"

Jane gave a reluctant smile. "Because I've got you at my back."

"Aw. You've grown up so fast—" Charlotte caught a glimpse of the tall man in scrubs who strode into the diner. She gave an unladylike squeak and slid all the way out of her chair and under the table too.

Jane stared at her. "What the—"

"Mateo's here," Charlotte hissed.

Jane blinked. "And?"

"And this is not a drill! Congratulations, you've taught me how to be ridiculous. Hope you're proud. Now scoot the hell over and make some room!"

Jane snorted, but scooted, just as Mateo spoke from above them. "Morning, ladies. Did you drop something?"

Jane smirked at Charlotte.

"Don't you dare leave—" But she was talking to air because Jane was gone as if she had the hounds of hell on her heels.

Not Charlotte. It wasn't the hounds of hell chasing her. It was her past.

Which felt just as scary.

CHAPTER 8

Levi woke up to the unmistakable sound of paws scrambling in his direction, but he didn't move or open his eyes, hoping he was invisible. Not likely though, as he was on the pullout couch in the Cutler family den slash office.

Which was how a very hot, wet tongue was able to lick him from chin to forehead.

"Thanks, Jasper," he murmured.

Apparently encouraged by the greeting, his mom's goldendoodle slash Wookiee leapt on top of him, wiggling all ninety pounds with the grace of a bull in a china shop, breathing his doggy breath all over him.

Levi managed to hug the silly, lovable dog while protecting his favorite body parts, not an easy task with Jasper's four massive paws. "Good boy, but time to get down."

Jasper lay down—on top of Levi.

He had to laugh. Who'd have thought he'd actually miss his childhood bedroom? But after Tess and Peyton had moved back in for the duration of her ugly divorce, his room had been turned into a proud princess palace. They'd offered to move out for his stay, but he'd refused, saying the couch was fine.

Not that it mattered where he slept in this house, because he'd always felt just a little misplaced in it. The square peg shoved in a round hole. For one thing, he'd been an oops baby to his parents, who'd thought they were done after having Tess nearly ten years earlier.

The three of them had been a tight unit by the time he'd come around. Levi had done his best to fit in. He'd been a good skier and probably could've gone somewhere with it, but even though he'd gone to the University of Colorado, where he could have skied competitively, he'd concentrated on getting his data science degree instead. Which of course had baffled his parents beyond belief. As far as they were concerned, he'd taken his athletic talent and walked.

Looking back, Levi understood their point of view, but he also knew they'd never understood his. He'd worked at the family store growing up, putting in his time, even if he'd always had his nose in a book or been on the computer creating software and apps, and then later working in tech before, during, and after college to support himself.

More than Levi being good, he'd been lucky, making the right connections, and now his start-up, Cutler Analytics, was thriving. Yes, he missed the mountain. Actually he missed the mountain a whole bunch, but hadn't missed feeling like that square peg again.

He'd done well on his own and had learned how to be okay exactly as he was. Sometimes he was even more than okay. Sometimes there was actual joy and excitement—like five minutes ago when he'd still been sleeping, his dream starring one sexy, smartass nurse named Jane. Unfortunately, his reality was as far from that erotic dream as humanly possible.

That was when his niece, Peyton, bounced into the room like the Energizer Bunny in a tutu and tiara, waving a sparkling staff.

Jasper jumped down—finally—and ran to his favorite person.

"Down," the six-year-old commanded, the one who weighed less than the dog.

Jasper lay down like a perfectly behaved dog. Probably because Peyton was also carrying a bowl of cereal, and Jasper knew only good boys got bites of cereal.

Peyton leaned over Levi, her warm little girl breath scented like the Froot Loops she'd carried in. When she saw his eyes were open, she grinned her toothless grin. "Uncle Levi! Uncle Levi! Uncle Levi!"

"Yes, baby."

"Is your girlfriend here?"

He narrowed his eyes. "Did your mom tell you to ask me that?"

"No. Grandma."

Levi sighed.

She giggled. "Where is she hiding?"

He had no problem bending the truth for his nosy mom and sister, but he wouldn't lie to Peyton. "Can we talk about something else?"

"Okay, let's talk about my tea party. It's soon. You're coming." She had a purse around her neck, one of Tess's, and from it she pulled a small notebook and pencil. She opened it and made some scribbles and quickly closed it back up.

"What's that?" he asked.

"It's my secret diarrhea."

He bit his lower lip so as not to laugh. Maybe one day he'd correct her, but today wouldn't be that day. "What do you write in there?"

"Important notes. Mommy writes important notes in her diarrhea to save and show Daddy so she can kick his *ask* if he comes to visit." She lowered her voice. "Don't tell her I said *ask*, okay? *Ask* is a bad word."

Levi mimed zipping his lips closed.

"Do you think my daddy's coming soon?"

"I don't know, baby." But he'd gladly help Tess kick the guy's "ask" for leaving two of his favorite females hurting. He sat up and realized that his dad sat only a few feet away, behind his desk, head bent to an awkward level so he could peer over the top of his glasses instead of actually using said glasses. He was muttering about "bullshit, crap internet reception" as he pecked with his index fingers on his computer's keyboard.

Paying none of them any mind at all—not the dog, the man, or the little girl. Just as well. Peyton was back to jumping up and down, and shit, she was making him dizzy as hell.

"Can we have a tea party?" She put her face back close to his. "Can we? Can we? *Can we?*"

"I might need a nap first."

"But! But! But!" Peyton liked to repeat herself. At high decibels. "I'm ready now!"

"Peyton!" Tess yelled from somewhere down the hallway, also at high decibels. The apple never fell far from the tree . . . "*Don't wake up Uncle Levi!*"

"He's already awake! Jasper did it!" Peyton squatted down and carefully picked up her bowl of . . . yep, Froot Loops. Sans milk because everyone was tired of slipping or sitting in spills that never got reported. "I brought you breakfast," she said, the bowl balanced precariously in her little hands.

Levi leaned in to take a Froot Loop, but she held up her wand. "Any color but red," she said very seriously. "The red ones are my favorite."

"How about the yellow?"

"Those are my next favorite."

"Green?"

"You can haz green," she decided.

"Thanks." He popped one in his mouth and she grinned at him, a sweet guileless toothless grin that tugged at his heart. He playfully pulled on a strand of her hair. "You know they all taste the same, right? They're not individually flavored."

She blinked, this new intel sinking in. "The reds are the prettiest."

"Understood."

She did the Energizer Bunny imitation again. "Get up, get up, get up!"

"Okay, okay." He started to sit up before remembering he'd stripped down to just boxers last night. "Uh, why don't you get the tea party all set up and I'll come meet you after I shower."

"Yay! Yay! YAY! DON'T BE LATE!" And she skipped out of the office.

Silence filled the room except for his dad's two pointer fingers continuing to pound away on his keyboard.

Levi stood up and groaned. The bed sucked. Or maybe it was his life.

His dad slid him an unimpressed glance. "'Bout time you got up. I don't know what you do in the city, but here in the mountains, our mornings start before ten."

Levi had always operated on the assumption his dad enjoyed pushing his only son's buttons. And he was good at it. It hadn't been easy growing up knowing he'd been expected to stay in town, take over the family business, and live happily ever after—without following any of his own hopes and dreams.

He'd gotten past all that. Okay, so maybe he still harbored a *little* resentment. But since his stint in the hospital and now his stay here at the house, Levi was starting to realize that maybe it wasn't that his dad didn't respect or understand his son's choices. Maybe . . . maybe the guy was just doing the best he could to get through his own day, and being a cynical ass helped him do that. "What's going on, Dad? What's with all the mumbling?"

"Don't ask when you don't really want to know."

The family store was the only sporting goods store on North Shore, which meant it was highly trafficked and did great business. But there wasn't a huge profit margin in it, and Levi's family had struggled plenty—something he hadn't appreciated growing up because his parents had never let on about any financial strain.

Knowing that they'd protected him and Tess from that stress usually gave him more patience when his dad pulled the holier-than-thou crap. But he felt pretty rough this morning, and was definitely short on patience. "Dad, just tell me what's going on."

His dad pushed his chair back from the desk, looking disgusted. "The store's books are a mess."

For the past decade, Cal—Tess's soon-to-be-ex-husband—had been doing the accounting for the store. He'd started right after college, the first nonfamily member to ever handle the books.

But when Cal took off with the babysitter a month ago, he'd walked away from the job. If he was being honest, Levi hadn't even given it a single thought, knowing someone else would now be handling the bookkeeping.

Apparently that someone had been his dad. This wasn't good because, though the man knew his stuff, he was impatient as hell when it came to the business side of the store.

His dad tore off his reading glasses and tossed them onto the desk. "Cal's a piece of shit."

"Agreed." Levi took a closer look at his dad and saw the tight grimness to his mouth and the stress lines around the eyes. "What's wrong?"

His dad rubbed his eyes. "It's not good."

Levi's heart sank. "I'm going to need you to be clearer. Did Cal mess up the books, or did he help himself to the kitty?"

His dad opened his eyes and looked at Levi. "I'm not sure. But I think the second thing."

"Jesus, Dad."

The guy shook his head. "It's just a gut feeling. I haven't been able to find anything."

"The software I sent you last quarter should've alerted you to anything out of the norm going on."

"Yeah, I couldn't make heads or tails out of that program. And why change something if it's not broke."

"Are you kidding me—" Levi broke off and drew a deep breath because nope, not getting baited into a fight. "Mom told me it was working out great."

"Because that's what I told her." His dad looked away. "It was complicated to load and I never got around to it. Obviously, not my smartest move."

A surprising admittance. But the thing was, Levi's program

wasn't complicated. It was simple. And no one would have had to do anything but let the program run in the background. Levi drew a deep breath. "Dad." He couldn't believe he was about to say this. "Why don't you let me take a look and see what I can figure out?"

"What, so you can get it all working, only to go back to the city?" His dad waved his glasses around. "I don't want to be left trying to undo something someone did."

Levi swallowed the automatic defense bubbling in his throat. "I'm not Cal, Dad. I've never left a mess behind."

His dad sighed, scrubbed his hand down his face. "Yeah, I know. Sorry. I don't mean to take this out on you. But shit, that asshole left us in a bad place."

"Then why do you always say everything is fine when I call?"

"Your mother didn't want me to bother or worry you. And anyway, you've never wanted the store, you've never been happy here, so what does it matter to you?"

"Jesus, Dad." He started to scrub a hand down his face and realized he'd inherited the tell from his dad and stopped. "I love it here," he said. And it was true. He loved it on the mountain, loved knowing that he could have any outdoor adventure he wanted. "I want to help."

"You do?"

"Yes." That he'd not given the store a single thought after knowing Cal had gone, leaving them in a lurch, had guilt swamping him. "Let me go through the books with a fine-tooth comb and see what I can find."

"I can't ask you to do that."

"You didn't ask. When I'm done, I'll install the software for you, which will do the job of finding these problems when I'm not around."

His dad looked uncertain, and wasn't that a kick to the gut. Levi made a living, a really good living, and a lot of that came from solving people's problems. Problems just like this. But because he was the baby of the family, and let's face it, *different*, his dad had a hard time seeing his value to the family.

"Dad, let me help." He gestured for him to move out from behind the desk so Levi could get to the computer.

"You going to put on some pants first?"

"Yeah." He grabbed his jeans from the floor and stepped into them. A T-shirt too. He didn't live like a slob at home, but here all he had was the couch, so things naturally ended up on the floor around it. When he sat behind the desk, he caught the look in his dad's eyes. Maybe relief. Maybe hope. Hard to say, as the man wasn't in the habit of giving much away.

Guess it could be said that Levi himself, the apple, hadn't fallen far from the tree either.

His dad put a hand to Levi's shoulder. The Cutler equivalent to a warm, hard hug. "Thanks."

Levi slid him a look. "You must be *extra* desperate."

His dad smiled ruefully. "I was two seconds from chucking the laptop out the window before you woke up."

Levi supposed he should be thankful for the small things. For instance, it was better to have been woken up by a dancing fairy demanding a tea party than by the sound of a laptop crashing through the window and falling to its death two stories below.

CHAPTER 9

Jane woke up late, a rare treat. It wasn't often she had a day off. Typically when she was in Tahoe, she worked every shift she could get. Because she'd had some lean years with no one but herself to rely on, working her ass off and saving for a rainy day had become second nature.

But lying in bed, contemplating the ceiling, she knew what she'd told Charlotte was true. She wasn't on her own anymore.

She touched the locket. Normally it invoked memories of her grandma, but there were new memories attached to the locket now. The way Levi had looked at her when he'd brought it back. She'd known he had a killer smile, that he was also funny as hell, and could more than hold his own in an emergency—all super attractive things.

But she hadn't imagined he could do sweet, and her eyes drifted shut as she smiled—

And then flew open when the bed shifted.

And began to purr.

"What the—" She leapt out of the bed, yanked back the covers, and came face-to-face with a pair of slightly crossed gray eyes, tail twitching in annoyance at losing the covers. Alley Cat.

"Oh my God, how did you get in here?"

He stood, stretched, turned in a circle, then lay down, his back to her.

She had to laugh. "You can't be in here. This house is a pet-free zone, and plus, I only pay rent for one." Scooping him up, she strode down the hall to the kitchen, unable to resist nuzzling her face against his, making him purr louder. Damn. If she'd been one to stick somewhere and put down roots, she'd keep him in a heartbeat. But she wasn't, so she couldn't. "Please understand," she whispered against his fur.

Charlotte was at the table, glaring at her laptop. "You'd think that paying bills online would be so much more calming. It's not."

Jane passed by her to the back door and set Cat outside.

His tail switched back and forth for a few beats. Then he stalked off.

"He'd have kept your feet warm," Charlotte said.

"Is that why you let him in?"

They looked at each other, Jane waiting for the confession, Charlotte not looking sorry at all.

"You know I can't keep him," Jane said softly. "And you know why. Don't make this harder on me."

Charlotte sighed as Jane poured herself a coffee and then re-filled Charlotte's cup as well, nudging a chin toward the laptop. "You know you could double what you're charging people to live here, since we all know you don't charge enough, and then the bills wouldn't be as stressful."

"Not doing that."

Jane tossed up her hands, and Charlotte smiled. "You love me."

Jane rolled her eyes.

"You do," Charlotte said.

"Maybe," Jane admitted. "But I don't love you sneaking the alley cat into the house and opening the door to the den so he could get onto my bed."

"First of all," Charlotte said, "he wanted to come in. Secondly, he's not an alley cat, he's *your* Cat, and he went looking for you, crying outside your door—which isn't the den, it's your bedroom."

Jane's chest tightened at the thought of Cat crying for her. "I can't keep him. You know I'm leaving. It wouldn't be fair to him to live with me for the next month, and then be out on the street again." She picked up a piece of paper with a list on it. "What's this?"

Charlotte shrugged. "My family and some others keep asking for my birthday wish list."

Jane slid her a look. Charlotte hated accepting gifts, but it was the "some others" that interested Jane. "Is one of them named Mateo?"

Charlotte pretended not to hear her. "I made the list, but it seems greedy, so I'm not sending it to anyone."

Jane stealthily pulled out her phone and snapped a pic of the list. If Charlotte wouldn't take her damn money, then she'd give the woman a hell of a birthday gift, and make sure others did as well. The southern belle would never, ever, turn down a gift—it would be rude.

"So . . ." Charlotte said.

"So . . . what?"

"You going to do it? Be the hot guy's girlfriend?"

"I knew I was going to be sorry I told you about that. I'm going to shower and then run errands." Jane turned to go.

"Don't forget to buy a bed for Cat to sleep on in your room," Charlotte yelled after her.

"Sure, soon as you stop taking care of everyone but yourself," Jane yelled back.

Back in her room after she'd showered and dressed, Jane pulled out her phone and sent the photo of the list to Mateo with a text:

> **JANE:** She's made herself a list and she's checking it twice. I'm attaching a copy. Calling dibs on the ski jacket.
>
> **MATEO:** Look at you showing your sweet.
>
> **JANE:** Take that back.
>
> **MATEO:** You're a good friend, Jane.

Not sure that was actually true, she shoved her phone into her pocket and headed out for the jacket. Charlotte didn't put a lot of stock into material things, unless it involved skiing. The woman loved to ski.

Jane wasn't as big on clamping two skinny boards to her feet and flinging herself down a steep mountainside. But she could appreciate the need for good equipment, so she was going to Cutler Sporting Goods.

Had she picked the jacket to give herself an excuse to go there? No. Definitely not. Or at least *probably* not . . .

Okay, yes.

Yes, she had.

The store was downtown, which consisted of a four-block-long area called the Lake Walk, lining the lake the length of Sunrise Cove. It was filled with bars, cafés, touristy stores, galleries, anything and everything that might lure more tourists in. The buildings were mostly from the early 1900s, and though they'd all been renovated many times over, they still held a certain Old West style that was hugely appealing. At night, every storefront and tree on the sidewalk would be bright with thousands of twinkle lights that reflected off the lake and made the place look like a postcard.

But even by daylight, the charm was still there. Cutler's was done up like an old warehouse with turn-of-the-century sporting equipment decorating the walls and hanging from the open rafters. Old-time skis and sleds, wood surfboards, and the like.

Jane walked in telling herself her mission was to get in, find the jacket, and get out—all without catching a glimpse of Levi. She had no idea if he was even here, but she strode directly toward the ski section, not looking left or right, just straight ahead, stopping at women's jackets.

Girlfriend.

Levi had wanted her to pretend to be his girlfriend.

If he'd known her better, he'd have laughed at the idea of her doing any such thing. After all, she'd never been successful at making a real relationship work, much less a pretend one.

But there had to be someone out there for her, right?

Damn. She needed to stop secretly watching the Hallmark and Lifetime holiday movies. She found a jacket that seemed to match Charlotte's description and pulled it out. When she caught site of the price tag she almost passed out.

Damn.

You can't put a price on friendship, she told herself. At least not when it came to Charlotte's friendship and all she'd done for Jane. Calculating how to cut her food bill down for . . . oh, the next year, she headed to the checkout counter and stood in line. The woman ahead of her was saying, "Don't forget the fifty percent off employee discount, which is of course why I'm getting too much. I couldn't resist. Thank God Robby loves working in your bike department, right?"

Employee discount . . .

Did pretend girlfriends qualify?

"Good morning," the checkout clerk said when Jane was up. "You find everything you need?"

"Actually, I just realized I need to check on something. Do you know where I can find Levi Cutler?"

The girl pointed up.

Jane looked up. And up. And up . . . The entire back wall was a climber's paradise. The wall itself was divided into three different climbing heights, the tallest being the entire three stories of the building, and there was Levi near the top and, close as she could tell, the only thing holding him up there was a very thin-looking rope.

The man was clearly insane.

She walked up to the wall and stood next to a tall, lanky guy in cargo shorts and a store employee shirt. His pale blond hair was a wild mane around his face. His name tag said *Dusty*.

"Can he hear me if I yell up to him?" she asked.

"Dude hears *everything*. We think he might have bat hearing."

"It's true," Levi said calmly, like he wasn't hanging high above them.

"Hey, Tarzan," she called up. "Have you lost your marbles?"

He smiled. "Nope. They're all in play."

"Really? Because you've had a concussion, which comes with blurry vision and dizziness. So being a hundred feet up is a bad idea."

"It's thirty feet and I've been cleared by my doc."

She crossed her arms, and his smile went to a full-out grin. "You're worried about me. Cute."

Cute? She was a lot of things. Sarcastic. Irritated. Stubborn . . . not cute. "We need to talk," she said.

He grinned down at her. "Sure. Come on up."

"Funny."

His laugh floated down to her. "Thought you weren't afraid of anything."

Turned out, she was afraid of plenty, including how just looking at him could change the rhythm of her heart.

Kicking off from a rock, Levi suddenly arced into the air, making her gasp as she looked over at Dusty, who stood there hands on hips, just watching. "Wait, aren't you belaying him?"

"He's on an auto belay system."

Levi dropped to the ground, landing lightly on his feet like a cat. A sleek, powerful wildcat. Eyes bright with the thrill of adventure, Levi flashed Jane a smile and killed a bunch more of her brain cells.

"You do that on purpose," she murmured.

"Do what?" he asked innocently.

Dusty snorted and moved off.

Jane went hands on hips. "There's no way you're cleared for rock climbing. Who's your doctor?"

"Mateo Moreno."

She blinked. "Dr. Mateo Moreno?"

"Yep, and he's an old friend. Best friend, actually, from middle school. So trust me, he knows me well and realizes climbing in here is tame in comparison to half the shit the two of us did growing up."

"Huh." How had she not known this?

Levi cocked his head. "You know him?"

"He lives next door to the house I'm staying in. He's a good guy."

"The best," Levi agreed. "And he cleared me for whatever I felt up to doing." He grinned and she was momentarily stunned by all the sexy testosterone and pheromones.

"You are a menace," she decided.

"And you're here at the store. Either you missed me or you need something."

As far as guesses went, it was fairly accurate. Not that she would admit it. He studied her. "Interesting." His eyes were lit with good humor. "You're here to agree to go to a family dinner as my girlfriend."

"*Fake* girlfriend," she said. "And . . ." She bit her lower lip. "Maybe."

"I like the maybe." He gestured to the wall. "Want to try?"

She opened her mouth to say he was delusional, but he raised a brow, his eyes filled with the unspoken dare. And damn if her competitive nature didn't have her lifting her chin. "I'm not trained."

"We've got an expert on staff."

"Where?"

He smiled.

"You?"

He shrugged. "Seen a guy do it once or twice."

She narrowed her eyes and he laughed. "Grew up climbing this wall. And every mountain peak around here. And did I mention there are Calk Walk cookies 'n' cream cupcakes for people who climb?" he asked.

She narrowed her eyes. "You're teasing me."

"When I'm teasing you, you'll know it."

Okay, so there went the funny quiver low in her belly again. She pointed to the shortest of the three walls, the single-story one. "What are my chances of dying on that?"

"On average, there's two point five accidents per ten thousand hours of mountaineering."

"Two point five?" she asked in disbelief. "How do you get a point five fall? Do you half fall or what?"

He grinned at her. "It's just a statistic."

"But it doesn't make any sense."

"Neither does the bravest woman I've ever met turning down a simple challenge."

The bravest woman he ever met was stunned. She'd never thought of herself as particularly courageous. In fact, she often felt the opposite. Running scared from connections, ties, roots . . .

Maybe it was time to stop running. She blew out a breath. "Any tips?"

"Don't look down."

She laughed and then tipped her head back to take a closer look at the wall. The highest one, where Levi had been, was actually inverted for the last ten feet, making her shudder in horror. The middle peak looked only slightly less intimidating, but the lowest one . . . there were two kids on it. How hard could it be? "Okay. But that one."

He got her harnessed so quick that she knew that he knew she was a flight risk. "Safety first," he quipped, using her words from the night of the blizzard.

She snorted. "'Safety first' is a bunch of crap you say only when you're worried or a complete idiot."

He smiled. "Do I look like either of those things?"

She had to admit he did not.

After a surprisingly professional rundown on what exactly she'd be doing and when, he added, "I'll be climbing too and will be right beside you the whole time. Dusty will be belaying you. I promise you're perfectly safe."

She looked over at Dusty, who'd come back when Levi had gestured for him. "Look," she said, "I'm sure you're nice and all, but I'm not big on blind trust."

"You already signed on for the blind trust program when you filled out the release form," Dusty said.

"Um . . ."

Dusty flashed a grin.

"Not funny. If I fall—"

"You won't," Levi said. "Dusty will be right below you on the rope. He's on the local search-and-rescue team and is the best of the best."

Jane stared at Dusty. "I *knew* you looked familiar. You were there that night of the blizzard."

Dusty's smile faded and he nodded. "Yeah, and that was the closest you're going to come to dying on my watch. You got your necklace back?"

She pulled it out from beneath the neckline of her sweater. "Yes. Thank you so much."

"Don't thank me, thank him," Dusty said, nodding at Levi.

Levi's gaze locked with and held on to hers.

"He said he'd do whatever he had to in order to get it back to you," Dusty said. "You okay with heights?"

Jane jerked her gaze from Levi with some difficulty. She felt a little dizzy with the rapid subject change. Or maybe it was from realizing what a good guy Levi really was. "I'm better with heights than enclosed spaces."

Dusty laughed softly in commiseration. "Say stop at any time, and we'll get you down."

She smiled her thanks and turned to Levi. "So I need a real live belayer, but you don't?"

"Yes," Levi said firmly.

Dusty nodded.

All righty then. She began to climb, with both men quietly, calmly offering helpful tips. As he'd promised, Levi was right at her side. Whenever she struggled to find the right hand- or foothold, he'd make a suggestion with a quick explanation, and though she wanted to say, "I do it!" like a toddler, she listened to what he was saying and began to understand—and get into—the rhythm.

Until she looked down to check her progress. Stupid, stupid move. The ground felt a mile away, and instantly her head spun and she thought she was going to throw up.

"Jane."

She dropped her forehead to the rock, closed her eyes, and

gulped in air. "Sorry, can't talk right now, *very* busy having a panic attack."

Levi curled an arm around her. "Breathe," he said softly into her ear. "Just breathe for a minute."

She opened her mouth to tell him she was already breathing, only to realize she actually wasn't. Dammit. Her heart pounded in her ears and the muscles in her legs trembled. Logically, she knew she couldn't fall, but mentally it was a whole other ball game.

"You're doing great. And you're safe, I promise." He had an arm around her. "You can't slip or fall. The rope has you. Dusty has you. And I've got you."

I've got you . . .

And suddenly she was even more scared. Not at the idea of falling. Not of suddenly knowing that she was definitely going to agree to be his pretend girlfriend. Not even at the idea of spending an evening having dinner with his family—well, okay, so she was a little scared of that.

But what scared her most was the idea of him having her back.

When was the last time she could say that about a man? She couldn't remember. Unable to help herself, she took another peek down and let out a wimpy whimper. "It's like the blizzard all over again."

"Except there's no wind, no snow, and we're not dangling seven hundred and fifty feet in the air."

"Wait— Seven hundred and fifty? That night you told me we were at five hundred and fifty!"

"Is there really a difference?"

Good point, but she opened her eyes to glare at him anyway.

His gray eyes weren't stormy today, they were a shiny silver. And damn, he had long dark lashes that wouldn't require mascara. "Unfair," she whispered.

"That I lied?"

"That you have ridiculously long eyelashes."

His lips quirked and her gaze went rogue, dropping to his mouth, which slowly curved as she watched.

"Jane?"

"Hmmm?"

"We going to finish this climb?"

"Yes. And I'm going to beat you to the top." She had no idea why she said that. Oh, wait, yes she did. She couldn't handle losing.

Apparently amused by her competitive spirit, he laughed, but she went back to climbing. And a few sweaty minutes later, she had to admit, it actually was a huge rush, even when she faltered or took a moment to find the right hold. And when she scrambled to the top and rang the bell, she found herself sweating and smiling from what felt like Mount Everest. A twelve-foot-high Mount Everest. "I did it."

Levi grinned at her. "You did."

She nodded and then sat right there at the top because her knees were knocking. He handed her a bottle of water and sat with her. "I'm impressed," he said. "Turns out, you're a badass in an emergency, *and* a badass in a competition." He smiled. "I like it. I like *you*, Jane."

She snorted the water up her nose and then choked.

He rubbed her back until she could breathe. "So you aren't comfortable with compliments. Noted."

Actually, it was the "I like you," which she hadn't expected. Or her own reaction. She played with the condensation on the water bottle. "So . . . about that pretend girlfriend thing. I've got questions. And stipulations."

"Hit me."

"You've got a close-knit family."

"If by close-knit you mean half the time we want to kill each other, then yes."

She met his gaze then. "Look, I assume from how important it was to you that you call them when you thought we were going to die, that they love you very much. I just don't want to be the one to screw that up for you."

He looked baffled. "How could you possibly screw it up?"

"Trust me. Families don't like me." *Starting with her own . . .*

"Jane, there's no way they aren't going to immediately fall in love with you."

She felt her face heat up and got annoyed at herself. "I'm . . ." She searched for a way to make him understand. "I've got a weird sense of humor. I laugh at things no one else thinks is funny. I'm sarcastic. I say what I think, and it's not always . . . nice."

"There you go," he said. "You'll fit right in."

She stared at him. Why wasn't he scared off?

"What else?" he asked.

She took a deep breath. "What would this thing entail exactly? I mean, nothing . . . physical, right? Pretend or otherwise?"

When he spoke, his voice was serious now. "I wouldn't want *pretend* physical anything from anyone. Especially you, Jane."

She frowned. "Because . . ."

That got her a small smile. "I think I'll let you wrestle with that one."

She drew a deep breath. Oh boy . . .

"You mentioned stipulations," he said, sounding amused.

She nodded and tried to remember what they were. "You have to promise me that this thing stays pretend no matter what, that you won't fall for me."

He smiled.

She pointed at him. "Hey! It could happen!"

His smile faded. "I have no doubt."

Her heart did a somersault. "Promise me," she whispered.

He was quiet a moment. "I get it," he finally said. "Us falling for each other wouldn't be smart. We're both leaving Sunrise Cove sooner rather than later, and we lead very different lives that would make it nearly impossible to maintain a relationship."

Well, if he was going to be all grown up about it . . . And yet, she appreciated that. His honesty. She appreciated it a lot, and it made her feel a whole lot better about things.

"My turn for a question," he said. "You mentioned not really having a family. What happened to yours?"

Moment of truth. She looked away, eyed the high warehouse ceiling and the lighting, the people milling in the store—

"Jane?"

"I'm not in contact with them."

Gently he turned her face back to his. "None of them?"

"Not in a long time, no."

"Jane," he said softly.

"Believe me, it was for the best."

"What happened?"

She shrugged. "I got bounced around a lot as a child between anyone even halfway related to me. Kind of soured me on the idea of family." She shrugged again and even smiled, though she hated to talk about her childhood.

Hated.

And then there was the way Levi was looking at her, like he felt sorry for her. The thought of anyone pitying her made her feel anxious again, and though she knew how much worse it could have been—that she'd had her basic needs taken care of, had never gone hungry or without clothes—thinking back on her life never failed to make her feel like a spare button, the ones that came attached to new sweaters but were easily removed and tossed aside. "My turn now," she said. "Do fake girlfriends get the friends and family discount?"

He laughed, breaking the emotional tension, but his eyes remained serious. "Fake girlfriends get whatever they want. Why?"

"I was hoping to buy my roommate the jacket sitting at the checkout counter."

He smiled. "Smart. Funny. Sexy. *And* a shrewd businesswoman. You got it. So . . . we're doing my parents' dinner party?"

"Yes."

He nodded. "We should probably spend a little time getting to know each other before the dinner."

She blinked. "Like a date?"

"*Great* idea," he said. "Yes, a date."

She stared at him.

He smiled.

She narrowed her eyes. "Did you just trick me into going out with you?"

"Or . . . did you just trick me into getting the discount?" he countered.

She had to laugh. "Smooth. We're talking a *pretend* date, though, right?"

"Whatever you want, whenever you want. Just name the time and place."

She hesitated, shockingly tempted. "I don't know . . ."

"If it helps, you could consider it a fact-finding mission on your pretend boyfriend. We can get to know each other."

"When I'm ready."

"When you're ready," he agreed.

At just the thought of what she was agreeing to, meeting his family while playing a role that she'd never been any good at—doting girlfriend—she quivered with more nerves than she'd battled while climbing up this wall.

Levi's mouth curved, like maybe he was reading her thoughts. "You trust me, Jane?"

"No."

"Damn." But he was grinning again, clearly, unabashedly *not* worried. "Then this isn't going to be nearly as much fun."

"What isn't?"

He stood and took her hand, pulling her back to the edge of the wall.

"What are you doing?" she asked.

"My first act as your boyfriend is to get you safely to the ground."

"*Pretend* boyfriend," she corrected, and then screamed all the way down.

CHAPTER 10

Charlotte cranked up the radio and mainlined a huge mug of black coffee to keep herself awake as she drove home from her shift. She was coming off twenty-four straight hours in the OR, and thanks to the season and all its icy snow, she'd been on her feet the entire time.

Car accident victims had arrived on top of car accident victims. Heaven forbid people slow down or take the road conditions into account as they leave their cities and hit the mountains. Nope, they were on vacation, so caution went out the window.

She used the drive home to decompress. She breathed deeply and calmly, sang along with the radio even though she couldn't carry a tune, and did her best to stick with happy thoughts. All to shed off the horrors of the day, the shocking and devastating results of those accidents that rivaled any episode of *Grey's Anatomy* she'd ever seen.

By the time she parked at the top of her driveway, she felt almost human again, and out of habit, glanced over at Mateo's house. No vehicle in the driveway. He hadn't been on shift, but he wasn't home either. At the crack of dawn.

Doing her best not to think about whose bed he was in if he wasn't in his own, she let herself inside her house. It was quiet. Empty. She knew Zoe and Mariella were at work. She had no idea where Jane was. There was a stick-it note on the fridge in Jane's scrawl that read *Don't worry*.

Jane's idea of letting Charlotte know she was alive and okay.

In truth, it was a huge step from the beginning years. In those days, Jane hadn't understood that Charlotte actually cared about where she was and if she was okay. So Jane's leaving a note now was the equivalent to shouting out from the rooftops that she considered Charlotte family. Her feral wolf cub was growing up enough to realize that other people might actually worry about her whereabouts.

Progress.

She was a decade older than Jane, but if you compared Jane's life experiences to hers, Charlotte was the youngster. Still, she loved to smother Jane in affection, because one, near as she could tell, Jane didn't let anyone else do it, and two, because it was fun to watch Jane squirm trying to figure out how to accept said affection.

She'd planned on showering, pulling down her blackout shades, and going to bed, but, restless after her shower, she pulled on jeans and a sweatshirt and went out into her backyard. Hands on hips, she stared up at the roofline of her house, where her Christmas lights twinkled at her mockingly.

"I know, I know," she said. "It's February and you're embarrassed to still be up there."

At work, there was always an ongoing bet of some kind or another for comic relief. Charlotte was rarely the instigator, but she almost always was the winner.

She couldn't help herself, she hated to lose. Last month the bet had been who could go the longest without a bathroom break. This had stemmed from the fact that the staff bathroom between the ER and OR had been closed due to renovations, leaving all of them having to run up a floor and use the Labor and Delivery staff bathroom as needed. They'd installed a small camera at the entrance of said bathroom to make sure to catch everyone entering so they could see who didn't enter—and that would be their winner. They'd even installed a camera on the third-floor staff bathroom to make sure no one bent the rules.

But they hadn't installed a camera on the fourth floor, figuring no one would have that kind of time. Charlotte had won a nice pot of two hundred bucks, thanks to the hospital president being a personal friend and having her own office and attached bathroom.

She'd won the last five bets and had no intention of losing any time soon.

The other day in the staff room at the hospital, there'd been a poll on who still had their holiday decorations up, and you couldn't bet on yourself.

She could still remember the light in Mateo's eyes as he'd laughingly collected the bounty because he'd been the only one to know that she had hers up.

"They light up my bedroom at night," he told her later when they'd been alone. "Makes me think of you."

What would he say if she told him the truth—that she thought of him too. Way too much. But she still hated that she'd lost the bet on a technicality. She pointed up at her lights. "I'm coming for you."

They twinkled at her mockingly, and she wondered if Mateo would notice that they were gone.

He'd asked her out, multiple times. But she'd always declined. Not because she was going for celibacy. And not for a lack of interest either. She'd have to be dead and buried to not be attracted to the man whose easygoing mannerisms conflicted with his heart-stopping magic in the ER in the most fascinating of ways.

Not going there . . .

She drew a deep breath of determination and dragged her ladder from the garage to the backyard, wrestling it up against the roof. Not easy on any day, but she still had a foot of snow in her yard, even more up against the house. She snugged the ladder against the packed snow and hoped that it would make her feel more secure.

If Jane had been here, she'd have done this for Charlotte. Jane was good with ladders. Jane was good with just about everything. Charlotte was first-rate in an operating room. She was also excellent at holding on to the past, not that she was proud of it.

It was why she lived all the way out here on the West Coast. Because she couldn't fathom living in the city where *it* had happened. Where everyone knew and pitied her for it. Yes, she was lonely for her parents, but she was also furious that one bad decision on one terrible night had stolen not only her trust in others but in essence her family as well.

Quite over herself, she climbed to the top of the ladder and began to lift the string of lights from the hooks in her eaves. Two minutes in, she faced a quandary. Roll them up like a lasso and hang them from her shoulder, or let them drop to the ground and possibly break.

She was still deciding on a plan of action when she heard the doorbell ring. Grumbling, she backed down the ladder.

Please let it be a food delivery.

Since she hadn't ordered anything, the odds were against her. Stalking around the side of the house, she stopped in surprise at seeing Jane standing on the porch. She was in jeans and a thin sweater that accented her slender, deceptively lightweight figure. No jacket, no doubt because she'd forgotten it. Long wavy hair blowing around her pretty face. She had a big bakery bag in one hand and kickass boots on her feet that were a statement and told people not to underestimate her.

Charlotte certainly never did. She'd met Jane years ago at a medical clinic in Colombia, where they'd both been on a Doctors Without Borders stint. It'd been one of Charlotte's first overseas forays, and she'd been told to expect it to be rough.

But it'd been even more of a nightmare than she could have dreamed of. One night, rebels, guns blazing, had come into the clinic to confiscate all the meds and meager amounts of cash. Charlotte had been by the door, just locking up. The rebel guarding their exit had sidled up to her.

She hadn't been able to understand everything he'd said, but his intent had been clear in the way he looked at her while fingering her hair, bringing a strand of it up to his face to sniff at exaggeratedly.

She'd frozen, completely frozen, mentally yanked into an old nightmare of another situation she hadn't been able to control. And when she hadn't responded to the guy, his grip on her tightened. Before she could draw a breath to scream, one of the American nurses shoved her way in front of Charlotte, hands out at her sides to keep Charlotte behind her as she stared up at the rebel. "Take the drugs and money and get the hell out of here."

He'd laughed in her face, but Jane, all five feet four inches of her, hadn't backed down.

And the rebels had finished their looting and gone.

Charlotte had fainted. *Fainted.* Even now, six years later, just thinking about it made her face heat with embarrassment and humiliation.

She'd taken a lot of self-defense classes since then, and had also had counseling. She'd like to think if anything like that happened now, she'd hold her own and be brave.

Brave as Jane had been that day.

But she'd not taken on any more of those clinics, instead staying in Tahoe and working at the local hospital. She loved it, loved the people, and yes, okay, it was safe.

But she liked safe.

Lived for it.

And the fact that she was living at all was thanks to Jane, and she'd never forget it.

Jane had her hand up, just about to ring the bell again, when she caught sight of Charlotte coming around from the side of the house. "Hey," she called out, her smile fading at whatever she saw on Charlotte's face. "Everything okay?"

"Yes, except for the fact that you're ringing the doorbell. You have a key, and I know damn well you use it when I'm not home. You live here, Jane. You pay rent."

Jane thrust out the bakery bag to Charlotte. "Heard about your rough shift. And you don't ever take my money."

Charlotte took the bakery bag, because there was stubborn and then there was stupid. And she refused to be stupid. "I could marry you for whatever is in this bag. And I do so take your rent money."

"Charlotte, I checked my bank balance yesterday. You haven't accepted my Venmo payment."

Charlotte opened her mouth, but Jane pointed at her. "Did you accept Zoe's and Mariella's?"

Charlotte sighed.

"Thought so." Jane shook her head. "You know I love what you're doing here. Renting to women, making sure they're safe. I know why you do it, and I admire it so much. But I want to be a part of it too. I want to help."

"You already have." Charlotte could feel herself getting emotional when she didn't want to. "And what does this have to do with you refusing to let yourself in with your key?"

"Since you won't take my rent, I'm technically not a renter. I'm a guest. And guests ring the bell." She paused and softened her tone. "It's not my room, Charlotte. It's your den. I know you like to keep it open for me, but you could be renting it out and making money. We both know Sandra's looking to stay longer."

Charlotte opened the pastry bag. Her mouth watered at the huge blueberry lemon muffin, her favorite. Even knowing it was her entire day's calories wasn't going to stop her. "Okay, first, you don't have to bring me food, but thank you for doing it anyway. And second, that room is for me to choose what to do with. And I choose to keep it a den slash bedroom. For *you*. You aren't a damn guest, Jane. You're family."

"You just swore," Jane said, looking shocked. "You never swear."

"Then I must mean it." Charlotte opened the front door and walked inside.

Jane laughed and followed her in. "I bring you food because you do so much for me and I feel like it's the only thing I can do for you in return."

"Oh my God," Charlotte said, tossing up her hands. "It's like you want me to yell at you." She turned and put her hands on Jane's shoulders. "Listen to me. You're my dearest friend, you're always there for me, hardly ever try to boss me around, and after long, tragic, horrific days in the OR, you make me laugh. You make me feel human. So trust me when I say, *I'm* the one that gets the most out of this relationship."

Jane blinked, looking thrown off balance. "I . . . didn't know any of that."

"Well, now you do."

Jane took a deep breath and headed through the living room. She opened the sliding glass door, stepped outside, and sat on the stoop so that the huge gray cat waiting for her could hop into her lap.

Charlotte stepped outside too, shutting the door behind them before reaching out to stroke the cat, who allowed it once, twice, and on the third attempt, batted Charlotte's hand away, making her laugh. "Oh to be a cat and simply slap the shit out of anything I don't like."

"I'm sorry," Jane said as the behemoth cat jumped lithely down to wrap himself around Jane's ankles.

"Why are you sorry if he's not your cat?"

Jane rolled her eyes. "No one owns this cat. Sometimes he chooses to come visit me, that's all."

With a heavy thud, the cat jumped onto the patio table. Jane nudged him down. "No furniture."

The cat sat on his haunches looking offended.

Charlotte snorted. "Feed your stray, then let me feed mine."

"Are you comparing me to the cat?"

"You have to admit, there are some similarities." Grinning at Jane's grimace, she went into her favorite room in the house. The kitchen. Five minutes later it was already scented with the bacon and eggs she had going. She set out plates and grabbed the pitcher of iced tea from the fridge.

Yes, it was winter in Tahoe, and the outside temperature was maybe thirty-five degrees with a wind chill that made it seem half that, but Jane loved iced tea.

And Charlotte loved Jane, so iced tea it was.

Jane came into the kitchen, prepared a bowl of food for Cat, and set it down at the back door where he was waiting. She was quiet. Not a seething quiet, but a thoughtful, reflective sort of silent that meant she was thinking and thinking hard about something.

"What is it?" Charlotte asked.

Jane looked up suspiciously. "What's what?"

"Something's bothering you."

Jane smiled warmly. "Have you met me? Everything bothers me."

"Has something happened?"

Jane hesitated.

"Spill."

"I might've done something potentially stupid."

"You don't do stupid."

Jane laughed a little mirthlessly. "I agreed to go out on a date—a *pretend* date—with Levi."

Charlotte gaped. "Hot guy from the gondola."

"I really wish you'd stop calling him that."

"Just calling it like it is," Charlotte said. "And the date's pretend . . . why?"

"I told you what he did when we thought we were going to die."

"Yes. He told his mom he had someone in his life so she wouldn't worry." Charlotte smiled. "So incredibly sweet. But still not hearing the potentially stupid part."

"Because the *pretend* date is to get good enough at being his *pretend* girlfriend for his parents' fortieth anniversary dinner."

Charlotte stared at her and then laughed.

Jane pointed at her. "Stop that."

"No promises." Charlotte loaded up two plates and handed Jane one. "You know what I love? How you go kicking and screaming into anything good in your life, like you're afraid it's going to turn out to be a bad thing. So hey, if you have to tell yourself this is pretend, whatever, I'm all for it."

"I'm not *telling* myself it's pretend, it *IS* pretend. It's just so that it seems believable and all that."

"Uh-huh."

Jane rolled her eyes as she dug in. "Oh my God, this is delicious. Oh, and I bought your birthday present, so don't go snooping."

Charlotte was turning forty next week and would really rather not. "I told you not to get me anything."

"I didn't listen."

She sighed like she was put out, but in fact, presents were both rare and a secret thrill. "Okay, so let's see this present."

"No way." Jane was looking smug, which meant she was comfortable enough to be looking smug, and *that* was actually the gift, whether Jane knew it or not. "You don't get it until your birthday next week."

"Spoilsport." Charlotte watched Jane push around the food with her fork. "What else?"

"How do you know there's anything else?"

Charlotte just looked at her.

Jane sighed. "I went and visited my grandpa again yesterday."

"A visit implies you had a conversation. Did you two have a conversation?"

"Okay, correction," Jane said. "I spied on his weekly lunch with some of his old work buddies."

Charlotte studied Jane's face. "So far this season, you've stalked his weekly breakfasts with friends and now his weekly lunch with his old work buddies."

"Yep."

Charlotte looked at her.

Jane sighed. "Yeah, yeah, I'm ridiculous."

Charlotte's heart clenched tight at the unsure look on Jane's face. "Only if you hide under a table again."

Jane smiled. "You want to talk about hiding under tables?"

Okay, so that hadn't exactly been one of her finer moments. "Extenuating circumstances."

"Uh-huh. And no, I didn't hide under the table." Jane paused. "I stayed outside and watched through the window."

Charlotte laughed. "We've made progress."

"We? The only way *we* made progress is if you ran into Mateo today, didn't hide under a table, *and* agreed to go out with him."

Ignoring this and the flutter low in her belly, Charlotte went chin up. "How does he look?"

"Sexy as hell," Jane said. "Dr. Hottie Patottie's got that whole laid-back, easygoing charm down, and matched with that leanly muscled runner's build and the fact that he's brilliant—"

"I meant your *grandpa*!" Charlotte said. She didn't need to know how Mateo looked, he was imprinted on her brain. And Jane was right, he *was* sexy as hell.

Jane grinned, then thought about it as she took a few bites of food. And her smile slowly faded. "He's a little pale, a little tired. Clearly still recovering from his heart attack. His last EKG showed minor damage, but sufficient blood and oxygen supply to the heart."

Charlotte's heart skipped. "Tell me you didn't break any HIPAA laws, putting your job, not to mention your license, in jeopardy to get that information."

"I didn't break any HIPAA laws to get that information." Jane paused. "I eavesdropped on his conversation with one of his friends in the parking lot after his lunch." She looked at Charlotte. "You're not going to suggest I go talk to him?"

Hell, no. "I'm still not sure he deserves you."

Jane leaned in and gave Charlotte a very rare hug that got her right in the feels. "Better than rent money," she quipped, making Jane snort.

Jane gathered the dishes. Charlotte got up to help as well, and Jane shook her head. "You cooked. I clean. That's the rule."

"We don't have any rules between us."

"Yes we do, and you made them." Jane held up a finger. "Rule number one: I must come to Tahoe for this job every year and I must stay with you."

"Well, that one's just good sense," Charlotte said.

"Rule number two: we tell each other when we're standing on the edge looking down, ready to jump."

Charlotte nodded. It'd happened. To both of them.

"Rule number three," Jane said. "And this is more of an unspoken rule: you cook because *I* don't, and I clean because *you* don't. Now go. Go be free." She made a shooing motion at Charlotte with her hands.

She laughed and then went outside to finish with the lights. She was back up on the ladder, her headphones on full blast, dancing in place on the rung, singing to herself as she worked.

When someone unexpectedly put a hand on her foot from below, she nearly jerked right out of her skin. Reacting purely instinctively, she kicked.

And caught Mateo right on the chin.

He staggered back a step. "Nice one, tiger."

Yanking out an earbud, she stared down at him in horror. "Are you all right?"

"No blood no foul," he said, seeming more amused than irritated. "And a hundred percent my fault."

Okay, now that she could breathe again and he probably wasn't hurt, she climbed down. A proper southern woman always looked a person in the eyes while she yelled at him. "*Why in the world did you sneak up on me like that?*"

He shrugged. "When I made myself known the other day at the hospital cafeteria, you ran off. So I figured I'd try a new tactic."

"You figured wrong."

He cocked his head, smile fading as he studied her. She knew what he saw. Her eyes were misty, her hands were shaking. And while she'd meant to sound angry, the words had caught in her throat, giving herself away.

His expression serious now, he said, "I didn't mean to startle you. I won't do it again."

She swallowed hard at the sincerity in his voice and the regret in his eyes. "Thank you." She turned to climb back up the ladder.

"Charlotte."

A sigh escaped her, but she hesitated.

"You're shaking. Give yourself a minute."

"I'm fine."

"I know," he said quietly. "But do it for me."

She hesitated, but eventually nodded because she really was still shaking. Annoying as hell. And clearly also far too revealing, because he slowly—so slowly it made her ache—drew her in . . . pausing to look into her eyes before he hugged her.

Yeah, she'd *definitely* given herself away, maybe even more than she thought, because they'd never touched before.

Not once.

And dear sweet baby Jesus, *why hadn't they ever touched before*? His arms . . . they were almost as good as his chest, which she had her cheek pressed to.

He drew a deep breath as if he was just as unexpectedly shaken as she by the physical contact, then pressed his face into her hair. "Charlotte?"

"Yeah?"

"I like this."

"Yeah, well, don't get used to it." Not that she made any effort at moving away.

And maybe the best part of all was that he didn't either. Closing her eyes, she let herself absorb the feel of a man's arms around her. This man. He was big and warm. And he smelled good. Too good. Up against him like this, she found it suddenly far too easy to let her walls down and be vulnerable. Only she never did those two things.

Just then Jane opened the back door. "Hey, Charlotte—" She stopped short at the sight of them hugging. "Ohmigod, so sorry." She started to go back in, then stopped and grinned. "Carry on!"

And then she was gone.

Charlotte buried her face in Mateo's neck. Not out of embarrassment. She just wanted one last big sniff of him before forcing herself to pull back.

He was smiling. "Did you just smell me?"

"I believe it's called breathing."

Onto her, he smirked, but didn't press further. Instead, he looked up at the holiday lights, half still on her eaves, the other half dangling from the roof to the ground. "Need help?"

"No. I—" But then she was talking to herself because he was climbing the ladder. "What are you doing?"

"It's called lending a helping hand."

"I've got it," she called after him, doing her best not to stare at his butt, but honestly, it was a pretty great one, so she might not have tried as hard as she should. He was wearing work boots, dark jeans, and a black T-shirt with an unbuttoned flannel shirt over it, which flared away from him at the breeze. "Why doesn't anyone wear a jacket around here? You're going to turn into a Popsicle."

"The way I see it, you've got two choices," he said. "You could ask me to come down so you can do this all on your own, or . . ." He was rolling the lights up as he unhooked them from the roof, the strings fully cooperating and coiling in a nice lasso around his shoulder.

"Or?" she asked, curious in spite of herself.

"Or you could accept some neighborly help in the spirit it was intended, which is not to make you feel helpless, but to free up your rare free time for something else."

Hadn't she just lectured Jane about accepting help? Yes. Yes, she had. So maybe it was time she took some of her own advice. "Fine." Her eyes were back on his very fine ass. "But you have to let me do something for you in return."

He glanced down at her, smiling when she jerked her gaze off his butt. "You have my full attention," he said.

She rolled her eyes. "I'll feed you after."

He grinned. "Sold."

CHAPTER 11

Jane was on hour sixteen of what should have been a twelve-hour shift. Her stomach was now eating itself. When she finally got a break between patients, she dashed into the cafeteria, grateful to be at Sierra North's urgent care today, as she could run to the adjacent hospital and to the cafeteria there. She piled up a tray with food and sat with a grateful sigh. She picked up the can of soda that was her treat for surviving the day so far—briefly wishing that it was something with alcohol—and cracked it open.

It sprayed her in the face. With a gasp, she stilled in disbelief as it dripped off her nose. "That's what I get for wishing you were alcohol."

"Here." A woman handed her a stack of napkins. "And yeah, a martini would be great about now."

"Thanks." With a wry grimace, Jane began to mop herself up. "And I've actually never had a martini."

"That's a crime against alcohol. Is this seat taken?"

Jane gave up dabbing at her face and soaked scrubs to look up at the woman who'd handed her the stack of napkins. Maybe late thirties, she was in yoga gear and had her brown hair up in a ponytail, her gray eyes behind boxy glasses. She wore a welcoming, warm smile that said she liked to talk.

And here was the thing. Jane liked to be lonely on her breaks. She looked forward to it, but she couldn't be outright rude, so she nodded. Plus, she wasn't going to lie: the fact that the woman's tray was filled with desserts said they were probably soulmates.

The woman sat and reached for her own can of soda.

"I'd be care—" Jane started but gave up when that can blew up too.

The woman laughed as Jane got up and brought back more napkins. "Should've seen that coming," she said ruefully.

Jane eyeballed the woman's tray—all desserts—and had a hard time keeping her gaze off the stack of miniature lemon squares.

"Take them," she said. "I've got my eyes on the big soft brownie anyway."

Jane shook her head. "Oh, I couldn't—"

Her new companion took the plate of mini lemon squares from her tray and set it on Jane's. "For sharing your table."

Jane was a lot of things, but she was not a person who turned down dessert. So she dug in. "Thanks."

"Been a long shift?" the woman asked in sympathy.

"It turned into a double."

"Damn. They always overwork the unsung heroes."

Jane pretended not to hear this as she shoved in another lemon bite. She was always uncomfortable when someone thanked her for her work or referred to the job as being heroic. It was a job, and okay, yes, she loved it, but it was a paycheck.

Her table mate smiled. "My name's Tess. I come here for lunch sometimes before picking up my daughter from the after-school program because it's right across the street. Saves me some time, and also I like the food here. How about you?"

"Jane." She took another lemon bite, then pictured Charlotte rolling her eyes at Jane being so miserly with words. So she sighed. Swallowed. "I'm a nurse at the urgent care clinic next door, and I come here during my breaks for the same reason. Plus I forgot to pack anything."

"You must meet a lot of interesting people in your line of work."

Jane thought about how she'd met Levi while hanging apparently seven hundred and fifty feet in the air and had to laugh a little. "Yeah."

Tess smiled. "You look like you've got a good story to tell."

Pleading the fifth, Jane stuffed in another bite.

"Sorry." Tess sat back, looking embarrassed. "I'm a mom. It means I don't have boundaries anymore. Plus I find myself asking everyone I run into about their relationships because mine just blew up in my face."

"Oh, I'm so sorry."

"Don't be. I was stupid." Tess shook her head. "I let my soon-to-be ex-husband handle all our financial affairs, which means I don't get to be surprised he ran away with the babysitter and all our money."

"That's awful," Jane said in genuine sympathy. "Men suck." She had a quick flashback to Levi moving to protect her with his entire body as their gondola thrashed about in the wind like a toy. How he'd coaxed her into the new experience of rock climbing. And then given her the discount for the jacket for Charlotte's birthday, saying it was the least he could do for his pretend girlfriend saving his life. "Well, maybe they don't all suck," she corrected.

Tess lit up with painful hope. "Yeah? You've got someone special in your life, then? A good guy? They exist?"

"Um, not exactly. I'm only here for the ski season. After that, I'll be contracted somewhere probably far away from here. Not exactly relationship material."

Tess was quiet a moment. Reflective. "That sounds . . . lonely," she finally said. "Is it hard to always be on the go, no connections?"

There was that word again. Connections. "I'm not that great at connections."

Tess nodded. "You've been hurt, too."

"Haven't we all?"

Tess laughed a little mirthlessly. "Touché. Tell me you're in a relationship with someone good. Give me some hope."

"In a relationship?" It felt silly to say *I feel a deep connection to a man I met only a couple of weeks ago when we nearly died together* . . . "No, but . . ."

"Oh don't stop there," Tess said with a smile. "That 'no, but' sounds exciting."

Jane let out a small laugh. "To be determined, I guess."

Tess knocked her soda can to Jane's. "To the 'to be determined,' then."

LEVI COULDN'T REMEMBER the last time he'd felt nerves bubble in his chest, but he felt it now. It was date night—*pretend* date night, as Jane would say. A few days ago, Jane had agreed via text they could practice getting to know each other over dinner somewhere.

Louie's on the Lake was just as its name proclaimed—right on the water, and a popular local dining spot that would be extremely public. As for neutral, he was going to try and remain just that *and* stay awake. He was exhausted, having spent the past few days catching up with his own company, while also doing a deep dive into Cutler Sporting Goods accounting.

The store's situation wasn't good. In fact, it was bad, really bad, but at the moment, the knowledge of that was all on his shoulders. He needed to talk to his family but wanted another day to finish going through everything first.

Either way, it was going to suck. At the heart, his mom and dad were good people who didn't have filters or personal space boundaries because they expected the best of everyone.

And Cal had clearly counted on—and taken advantage of—that and them. And Tess. When she found out, it'd kill her. It was keeping him awake at night.

As was something else.

He'd been here two weeks. Longer than any other time since living here. He should be feeling claustrophobic and desperate to get out of town; he should be feeling San Francisco pulling at him to go back.

But he wasn't. Oddly, Sunrise Cove was the thing pulling at him, calling to him. Being back here, even under duress, reminded him how damn alive he'd felt living in the mountains again.

He'd left because he'd needed some space.

But at some point, that need had gone away.

When his phone buzzed with an incoming call from his dad, who never called him, he answered with a quick "Everything okay?"

"Yeah, why wouldn't it be?" his dad asked, sounding puzzled, and Levi had to let out a rough laugh.

"Because you never call me?"

"I do so," his dad said.

"Name one time."

"When your sister had Peyton."

"Dad, that was six years ago."

"Still happened."

Levi put a finger to his twitching eye. "What's up?"

"I'm in the store's office. There's a stick-it note on my computer that says to revamp the book section, that the books shelved aren't selling."

"That's right. They're the same four titles you've been selling for a hundred years."

"Hey," his dad said, "those books are on wilderness, exploration, and the history of the region. They're fascinating."

"Dad, they were written in the 1970s and are out of date."

"I like them."

"Then take them home, stick them in your bathroom, and read them during the three hours you spend in there every morning."

"I'm not going to take them home."

"Because . . . they're not riveting?" Levi asked dryly.

His dad sighed and hung up.

Perfect timing. He could see Jane walking toward him in dark jeans, a sweater the same gorgeous green as her eyes, and some seriously sexy boots, and suddenly he knew staying awake wasn't going to be a problem. Just one look at her and he felt more present than he had since . . . well, since the last time he'd seen her a few days ago, screaming with laughter in his ear all the way down the rock wall.

Best climb ever.

The weight of his stress and exhaustion faded, making him feel light for the first time since she'd agreed to this farce. And not just because she was saving his ass once again. He felt light whenever he was with her, pretend or not, although certain parts of his body told him there was nothing pretend about this attraction between them. And for once, those body parts and his brain seemed to be on the same wavelength.

Jane sat down across from him and without preamble, swiped her iPad awake and pushed it across the table to him. She'd loaded a site called How to Get to Know Someone in 100 Questions. He looked at her. "Seriously?"

"Okay, so we can skip the obvious ones, like how do you react in a life-or-death situation?"

He snorted, making her smile. "Just pick a random one," she said. "Here." She let her finger land on the screen. "Number fifty-two. What's your most unusual talent?"

He smiled. "In or out of the bedroom? Oh, and hi, by the way."

She softened with a low laugh. "Hi." She pointed at him. "Now answer the question. And OUT of the bedroom is all I'm concerned about."

He smiled.

"It is!"

Her defensiveness had him laughing. "Okay, okay, my unusual talent . . . Gadgets. Robotic gadgets."

"I said *out* of the bedroom!"

God, he adored her. "I was actually being serious. I like to build robotic gadgets."

"Oh." She blushed. "Sorry."

Their waitress turned out to be an old classmate of his. Kendra smiled warmly at him. "Hey, hot stuff," she said. "Heard you went off and made good on that fancy brain of yours. You get paid to tell all those big CEOs in the Bay Area what to do with their data now, right?"

"More like I offer suggestions," he said. "In a consulting capacity."

Kendra grinned. "Still, gotta be fun."

"Sometimes," he admitted, and gestured to Jane. "Kendra, this is Jane. Jane, Kendra."

"We went to high school together," Kendra told Jane. "We sweated out AP Chemistry. And then blew off steam in the back of my daddy's truck a couple of times."

To Levi's relief, Jane laughed. "Nice way to get through the worst class in the history of worst classes," she said.

Kendra grinned. "Right? So what can I get you kiddies tonight?"

Levi gestured for Jane to go first.

"I'm trying to decide between the sweet potato fries and the shrimp kebab," she said.

"I'd take both," Kendra said. "They're amazing. All the appetizers here are. And your main?"

"Oh . . ." Jane paused. "Um, just the apps, thanks."

Levi didn't know if she wasn't that hungry or if she was worried about the prices. "Hey, why don't we order a bunch of appetizers and share?" he asked her.

She smiled. "Okay."

"Is there anything you don't like?" he asked, wanting to give her the damn moon.

When she shook her head, he looked at Kendra. "How about one of each of the five appetizers." And then he added a flight of beer to share, getting Jane to pick the flavors.

"Also, we've got s'mores on the menu now," Kendra said. "You get all the makings for them, which you take out on the patio to the fire pits and create yourself."

Levi looked at Jane, who had lit up at the word *s'mores*. "I think that's a yes."

Kendra gave him another wink and took off.

"An ex, huh?" Jane asked.

"An ex implies we were in a relationship," he said.

"Ah. So you were one of *those* guys, the hot ones who had girls throwing themselves at you. Let me guess, it was hard to resist them all."

He laughed. He couldn't help it. "Not that either," he finally managed, trying to lose the smile when she glared at him. "No, seriously, if you'd known me then, you'd get why it was so funny."

"Enlighten me, Tarzan."

"I was the science geek."

"Doesn't seem like it hurt your game any."

"I had *zero* game. Luckily for me, just after I graduated from high school, my best friend told me we were in a relationship."

"Mateo?" she asked in surprise.

"Mateo's sister, Amy. They lived on my street growing up, and we were all close. Amy and I got closer that summer after graduation, and she changed colleges to go with me to Colorado."

"How long were you with her?"

"Until the year after college. I've dated on and off since then, but nothing serious." He really wasn't ready to explain what had happened to Amy because there was no way to do that without taking the mood to a somber place. He'd spent a lot of time in that state and didn't want to go there tonight.

Luckily, Kendra was heading toward them with their beer and

food. She set everything down and smiled at Levi. "You sure did grow up real nice, Cutler." She turned to Jane. "So is it true what they say about the geeks? That they only get better with age?"

Jane looked at Levi, and he found himself holding his breath on her answer.

"One hundred percent."

Kendra laughed, and when she left, they continued to stare at each other for another beat.

"In for a penny, right?" Jane finally said and picked up a sweet potato fry. "Also, there's no way we can eat all of this. It was sweet of you, but impractical."

That made him laugh because he was the most practical person he knew. In fact, normally by now on a date, he'd be mentally cataloguing the reasons she'd drive him crazy. It'd been his way of keeping himself emotionally unavailable. It was both funny and horrifying that she was doing it to him. "Impractical?" he asked. "My brain doesn't even know how to compute that."

She shrugged. Not her problem, apparently. She took the last sweet potato fry. "Yum. Wonder how they get them so sweet."

"The longer they sit, the sweeter they get."

She laughed. "I should have known you'd know. So . . . why did you stop seeing whoever you were seeing last?"

He thought of Tamara, the woman he'd met at a conference a few months back. They'd gone out to dinner and she'd eaten off his plate. Without asking. She'd taken the last of his fries, actually, and the irony of that made him laugh. "We weren't compatible. And you never told me your most unusual talent."

"To piss people off, which is self-explanatory," she said. "Robotic gadgets are not."

"It calms my brain."

She cocked her head and studied him. "Yeah, I can see that. You know what calms my brain? Cupcakes." She picked up a shrimp kebab, dragged it through a mountain of sauce, and pointed it at him. "Now stop trying to distract me with all your sexy nerd hotness. We've got a mission, or at least I do. I need to get to know you fast if I'm going to pull this dinner off, and let me tell you something about me—I don't like to fail." She went back to her iPad. "Next question—"

"Oh no." He put a hand over her iPad. "You're not getting away with telling me your talent is pissing people off. Play fair."

"But it's true."

He cocked his head and studied her. She actually believed this. "You haven't pissed me off."

"Give me time."

He leaned forward, waiting until she met his gaze. "Not going to happen."

"Maybe . . . but only because I'm going to be gone soon."

"That seems to be your life motto."

She shrugged.

"Still not going to happen, Jane."

"You don't know. You might disagree with me on stuff. Or not like my opinions, of which I have many."

"There's nothing wrong with disagreeing or having varying opinions. I actually like that."

She looked at him for a long beat. "You're different."

"Now you're getting it."

CHAPTER 12

Levi smiled when Jane just stared at him. The air seemed charged with something he hadn't felt in a long time. And given the suddenly wary look on her face, she felt the same.

All around them were the sounds of people talking and laughing, silverware against dishes, music . . . The table between them was small.

Intimate.

"Pretend," Jane said, pointing at him. "This is pretend."

"Are you reminding me or yourself?"

"*Both.*" She shoved his hand off her iPad and read the next question. "Is a hot dog a sandwich—and why."

He grinned. "Once again, in the bedroom or out?"

She shook her head. "I walked right into that one."

He flipped the case closed on her iPad.

"But—"

He crooked his finger.

She narrowed her eyes, but leaned in. "What?"

Their faces were close. Not as close as they'd been the night of the blizzard, when she'd shown him the depths of her courage. Or when she'd shown up at the store and climbed the wall, revealing she also had determination, a sense of adventure, and a willingness to laugh at herself.

"Hello," she said. "Earth to Tarzan."

"You've got pretty eyes. They've got a ring of gold around the irises. When you're irritated, it turns to fire. I like it."

She snorted, and he grinned, but let it fade. "You do know that for this to work, we need to know more about each other than how we categorize a hot dog. So ask me a *real* question, Jane."

"Okay . . ." She studied him thoughtfully. "You're clearly smart as hell, successful, and some women *might* find you attractive . . ."

It was his turn to snort. "I don't hear a question."

"Why do you need a pretend girlfriend?"

He was the one to break eye contact this time, turning to look out the windows at the lake. "I spend my whole day at work selling people on the idea that I'm the solution to all their problems. When I get home, I don't want to have to be that guy. I just want to be me. And I guess I haven't met a woman who's okay with me as is. I'm a simple guy with simple needs."

"I get that," she said, and nodded. "And same."

Easy acceptance. A surprise because no one had ever understood this about him. He shook his head.

"What?"

"I'm just sitting here thinking you're one of the most fascinating, amazing women I've ever met. I guess I'm just stunned that you're . . . available."

Her lips quirked. "Are you asking me why I'm single?"

"If you're willing to answer, then yes," he said. "Why are you single?"

"You mean other than most men suck?"

He smiled. "It's true, but I suspect you've always known that. So . . . ?"

"So . . ." She lifted a shoulder. "I spend nine months of the year in other parts of the world dealing with real people with real problems, and at the end of the day, it makes dating seem . . ." She searched for a word. "Frivolous, I guess."

This made sense, but it gave him a pang deep in his chest for her. She reached for the iPad, but he gently pushed it away. "I want to get to know the *real* you, Jane, not how you would answer an impersonal website survey."

She leaned back, picked up one of the shots of beer, took a sip, put it down. Straightened her silverware.

"You're nervous," he realized.

"Am not."

He put his hand over hers. "I was nervous tonight too. Until I saw you."

She gave a small smile. "It's actually the opposite for me. I wasn't nervous *until* I saw you. Good thing this is only pretend, right?"

He gave her fingers a squeeze. "We'll start easy, okay? Tell me something about your day."

"About my day? I don't know . . . it was pretty ordinary." She thought about it. "I did meet someone new at lunch. I usually try to eat alone because it's nice to get a minute of downtime between the rush of patients. But today this woman asked if she could sit with me. At first I was irritated."

"Not you . . ."

She snorted. "But she was really nice. We actually exchanged numbers. She loves martinis, which I've never had, so we're going to go for martinis soon. She's a single mom, getting a divorce, loves skiing . . . Tess something or another."

Levi froze. No. No, it couldn't possibly be . . . "*Tess*," he repeated, trying to hide his sheer disbelief.

"Yeah. Her daughter's school and after-school program is across the street from the hospital. She was *very* chatty. Her daughter thinks she's a fairy princess. Oh, and she has a totally annoying brother."

"Really," he said dryly. "That must suck for her." He really should've seen this coming, but his sister, and undoubtedly his mom as well, had clearly been cyberstalking Jane. He shouldn't be so stunned at the level of duplicity and lengths they'd gone to in order to butt their noses into his business, but he was.

And they wondered why he'd chosen to live in San Francisco.

"Yeah, I guess he's home for a bit," Jane said, "and he acts like he's still a teenager, leaving his clothes everywhere and dirty dishes in the sink. I never had any siblings, so it must be really hard to have to deal with that."

Oh, goody. They were still talking about *him*. "Must be," he managed.

Her smile faded a bit. "How big is your family again?"

"There's five of us," he said. "Though sometimes it seems like triple that."

She didn't smile, his first clue something was wrong.

"And they're . . . nice?" she asked.

She was anxious about meeting them. "They're going to be *really* nice to you, and very busy trying to figure out why you're with me."

She did give him a small smile at that, and he paused before bringing up her family again. "You've not said much about growing up, other than you were passed around a lot. You're not close to your family, I take it."

"No." She pushed around the empty glass. "My mom was a teenager when she got pregnant and my dad didn't stick around, so it's an understatement to say she wasn't ready to take care of a baby. It was tough for her to keep up with school and have a life, so we bounced around for a while, stayed with friends or family friends."

"Not family?"

"Not then," she said. "She'd burned some bridges."

"And you? What happened to you?"

"I don't remember much of this, but apparently when I was two, my mom got an opportunity to go away to college. I was sent to my mom's older sister, Aunt Viv. But she had five kids of her own and worked all the time, so I ended up at my grandma's sister's daughter's. I stayed there a bit, until she got married and wanted to start a family of her own."

"What was wrong with keeping you too?"

"I was a needy thing." She shrugged. "Got sick a lot."

Levi shook his head. "I can't imagine what that must have been like for you."

"I was fine, I don't really even remember much of it," she said quickly, as if she didn't want him to feel angry on her behalf, or worse, sorry for her. "And anyway, that's when my grandparents took me in. And that was . . ." She smiled a little, as some of the fond memories appeared to beat back her bad ones. "The best. They lived here in Sunrise Cove in a tiny cabin. I loved everything about that time."

"Here?" he asked, surprised. "They're here in Tahoe?"

"Just my grandpa now. My grandma . . ." She paused, her liquid jade eyes revealing pain. "She died when I was eight."

"Aw, Jane. I'm so sorry. Did you get to stay with your grandpa?"

"Her death was . . . hard on him. They'd been together since they were kids. They had an amazing relationship. He'd hide things for her to find. Food, cheap little knickknacks, seriously expensive jewelry, it didn't matter. It was a game between them. He'd give her hints and she'd run around looking. She was just as happy to get a box of cookies as a diamond bracelet. He'd just sit there and laugh the entire time she was hunting for whatever it was."

"They sound amazing."

She nodded. "My time with them holds my favorite childhood memories."

"What happened after your grandma died?" he asked softly.

"My grandpa had problems. Grief, and some health issues. My aunt Viv took me back in so I wouldn't bother him or put any burden on him."

"Damn. You couldn't catch a break."

"Maybe if I'd been an easier kid—"

"Jane, you were just a kid. Someone should have given you the choice and made you feel wanted. Someone should have *asked* you to stay."

She shook her head. "Real life's not like that. Memories stay. People go."

He hated that *this* was the lesson she'd gotten out of her childhood, and put his hand over hers. "What happened next?"

"I bounced around, and when I turned sixteen, I emancipated myself."

Yeah, brave as hell, and he had a whole new appreciation for what she'd done with her life. But damn, he hated that she'd never really had a home to call her own. "Do you see your grandpa when you're here?"

"No. Thinking about it, though. Maybe." She met his gaze, caught the look on his face, and shook her head. "Don't feel sorry for me. It wasn't all bad."

She'd been through hell and *she* was comforting *him*. His heart tightened at that. "Your family failed you."

"They did the best they could. And I never had to go into the system." She shuddered. "I know people who are still scarred from that life."

He squeezed her hand. "Still, it couldn't have been easy."

"Yeah, but when is life ever easy?"

She was amazing and resilient, and he wanted to hold her. He wanted to do other things too. She was beautiful, and he was extremely attracted to her, but more than anything, he wanted to make her smile. Make her feel as special as she made him feel.

Kendra came by and gathered up their plates. "Your s'mores platter is ready when you are."

Levi stood and took Jane's hand, pulling her up. "Come on. They'll serve it by the fire pit."

There were six fire pits spread out on a snow-covered patio. The sitting arrangements were low benches. They claimed a spot by themselves and Kendra brought a platter that held three bowls filled with marshmallows, chocolate bars, and graham crackers.

"I've never done this before," Jane said.

Levi smiled and handed her a spear. "You just load a marshmallow—" He broke off as she loaded not one, not two, but *three* marshmallows on her spear and held it over the fire, looking so excited that he laughed as he loaded his own spear. He held his marshmallow over the fire too and gently tapped it to hers.

She looked up at him from where she'd been deep in concentration on her marshmallow.

"Thanks for tonight," he said.

"I haven't been out in a long time," she admitted.

"How long is long?"

She thought about it. "Maybe over a year. My last relationship was a long-distance one, and it didn't work out."

"What happened?"

"Long distance." She lifted a shoulder. "I got a new assignment, and we weren't serious enough to make it work." She pulled her marshmallows back from the fire and beamed with pride. Perfectly golden. She carefully sandwiched them with chocolate and then graham crackers.

"Thought you'd never done this before."

"Haven't," she said. "But that doesn't mean I didn't always want to try." She took a big bite, and he became enthralled with the dollop of melted marshmallow at the corner of her mouth.

"What happened between you and Amy?" she asked.

The question surprised him, but he supposed it shouldn't have. He'd hesitated to tell her before, but he didn't like the idea of hiding Amy. She deserved more than being a secret.

Jane narrowed her eyes at his long pause. "Did you cheat on her?"

"No."

"Just checking. You don't seem to have a lot of obvious faults, so I had to ask. Did you know your marshmallow's on fire?"

"Shit." He yanked his spear from over the pit and blew out the fire, eyeing the black lump that used to be a marshmallow.

Jane laughed.

He looked at her clearly enjoying his discomfort and had to shake his head. "See? *Plenty* of faults."

"Uh-huh, and one of them is being good at coming up with distractions when you're asked uncomfortable questions. You make crap s'mores. And you don't have a poker face."

She was still smiling, and damn if it didn't bring out one of his own. "I have faults," he said. "Lots of them."

"Yeah? I'm all ears."

"Okay . . ." He thought about it, not wanting to give away the farm, but wanting to be honest. "I hyperfocus on work and lose track of everything else. And when I'm in that headspace, I can apparently be . . ." He thought about the biggest complaint Amy and his few other shorter relationships had always had. "Distant."

"Me too," she said and bit into her s'more. Her moan cut through him. As did her next question. "So. Amy. What happened? You've known her since you were a kid, she told you that you were in a relationship, you went to college together, and then . . . ?"

"We got engaged." The year after college, they'd played house and they'd been happy. Or so he thought. But then she started pressing for that wedding she'd been dreaming of since seventh grade. He made some agreeable noises and she'd been so happy, but he'd stalled on setting a date.

And then she'd died—without the wedding, which had been all she'd ever wanted.

These days he never made promises. Ever. He looked at Jane

and felt a pang, because if he was the promising type, she'd be the woman he'd want to make promises to.

"Levi?"

Shit. Why had he pushed for deep tonight? He was allergic to deep. Maybe when he'd hit his head, he'd been more injured than he'd originally thought. Although it wasn't his head aching now, it was his chest.

Something to think about.

But for now, there was no getting around this. "She passed away unexpectedly a year after we were engaged," he said. "An aneurysm."

"Oh my God." She set down her s'more. "I'm so sorry, I shouldn't have pushed—"

"No, it's okay. And what was it you said? It sucks. Life sucks. But then you learn to live with it. You don't necessarily forget, but you move on."

Her eyes were warm. Regretful, but also understanding. She didn't offer empty platitudes, for which he was grateful. She simply nodded and then went about toasting another perfect marshmallow. Then she created a s'more with it and handed it to him.

That was when he realized that the more he got to know her, the more real he wanted this to be.

"This was a very unusual date," she said, eyes dark by the fire's glow, mouth utterly kissable.

He smiled. "You said *date*."

"*Pretend* date," she corrected. "You promised me, remember?"

Right. He'd also promised not to fall for her. Guess he did make promises after all. Really bad ones. "I remember."

She nodded. Stared at his mouth. "A *very* unusual pretend date."

"Do you go on a lot of pretend dates, then?"

She shook her head. Nibbled on her lip, which was what he wanted to do too. He should be pulling away rather than wanting to extend the evening for as long as possible, but he didn't want to go anywhere. What he wanted was to see her again. And again.

"I'm going to be gone soon," she reminded him as if she could read his mind. "So are you too, right?"

"I thought so." He nodded at her surprise. Then he voiced the thought that had been in his head for days now. "Yeah, it caught me off guard too, but I'm actually thinking of moving back. I've missed connections, and I have a lot of them here. More than I wanted to remember."

She looked across the outdoor patio to the lake just beyond, dark and beautiful. "I can see why you'd want to stay here."

"And you?" he asked.

She slowly shook her head. "I'm not really a one place sort of girl."

Then right now would have to do. Assuming, of course, she was feeling the same. And though he could tell by her body language that at least a part of her was, he knew she hadn't even come close to deciding on him as something she couldn't be without.

Real or otherwise.

It began to snow, lightly at first, but by the time they laughingly gobbled up the last of their s'mores and walked out front, it was coming down pretty good.

Jane stepped out from the protective cover of the awning and tipped her face up to the falling flakes. "I never get tired of snow. It's got such potential to do serious damage, and yet it's so beautiful."

He thought maybe that could describe Jane too. "Where's your car?"

"Oh, I walked."

"Let me drive you home," he said, reaching for her hand.

"I'm okay. I like to walk."

But she held on to his hand and he smiled. "Then let me walk you home."

She met his gaze, her head dusted with powdery snowflakes, a few more on her lashes and her cheeks, making them rosy. "Then you'd just have to walk back here to get your car."

"I don't mind."

"There you go hiding your faults again, seeming too good to be true."

"Jane," he said on a rough laugh, "I can promise you I'm not too good to be true."

She studied him for a long beat, while he did his damnedest to look like something she couldn't live without. "A ride home would be nice, thank you," she finally said softly.

He followed her directions to an older neighborhood about four blocks up on the hill from the lake. Homes here had been built decades ago, were close together, and were mostly not renovated. He stopped before two old Victorians that shared a driveway.

"We're on the left," Jane said.

Levi had never been to Mateo's. Mateo had bought this house after Levi had moved to San Francisco, but it suited him. The front yard was good sized, with two huge pine trees, all of it covered with snow. Levi turned off the engine and started to get out of the car.

Hand on the door handle, Jane looked over at him, startled. "What are you doing?"

"Walking you to your door."

"That's hardly necessary."

He got out of the car anyway and met her at the front of the car. "Cute place."

"It's a full house this season." She was silent on the way to the door, then turned to him on the porch. She looked at his mouth. "You should know, pretend first dates don't come with a kiss."

This had him smiling. "But you're thinking about it."

She laughed. It was a good laugh. "I'm not inviting you in, Levi."

"I know."

"Do you? Because we're pretending for *your* family. The people in my life don't need to know about you."

"Ouch. And I thought you told me you didn't have anyone in your life."

"Fine. I have my landlord and aforementioned roommate."

The front door swung open. A pretty blond smiled out at him. "Charlotte," she said. "Landlord and aforementioned friend, though I'm amending what she said to add I'm also her *best* friend. And her family."

Levi recognized the protectiveness and appreciated it. "Nice to meet you." He slid Jane a smile. "Seems we have plenty of reasons for a second date." Then he started to walk back to his car.

"Hey," she called.

He turned back to find her standing there on the porch, lit by the glow of a single-bulb light. "What's the first reason?" she asked.

He smiled. "That kiss you want."

And when she didn't deny this, he smiled all the way home.

CHAPTER 13

It wasn't a real workday until someone yelled at Jane. It could be a doctor, a patient, whoever. It always happened at some point, and it was the least favorite part of her job. Today it was a belligerent patient named Jason Wells. "Your wounds are deep," she told him. "They need to be cleaned out or you risk infection."

"Get the hell out of my face and get me my phone!"

Jane took a deep breath for patience—which didn't come—but stepped back from the thirty-year-old, who'd purposely gone snowboarding off trail—not permitted here at High Alpine—and had hit a tree.

With his face.

Working on the front lines of patient care meant interacting with the general public, and one thing she could count on was that pain brought out the worst in people.

She'd been attempting to irrigate the worst of the guy's cuts so he could get stitched up, but he wasn't having it. Bleeding profusely from several places, and all he wanted was his phone. "Phones aren't allowed in the treatment rooms, sir."

"The hell with that." He struggled to sit up. Probably because his wrist was broken, but he didn't want anyone touching that either. "Help me up, I'm outta here."

His buddy, who'd dragged Jason into the clinic twenty minutes ago, appeared through the privacy curtain. "Dude, I can hear you yelling at her from the waiting room. Calm down, she's just trying to help you."

Oh boy. Never in the history of ever has telling someone to calm down worked.

"I don't need medical attention." Finally managing to sit up, Jason swung out with his uninjured arm, nailing the tray, scattering the medical supplies across the room.

Mateo, who was the doctor on staff for the day, having been sent over on loan from the hospital when the scheduled doctor hadn't been able to get to work, also appeared in the doorway. "Jane." He gave her a chin nudge indicating he wanted her to move farther back, out of Jason's reach.

Before she could, Jason's friend pushed past her and . . . punched Jason in the face.

Jason fell back, unconscious, and his friend looked at Mateo and Jane. "Sorry about the mess he made, but you should be able to treat him now."

And so went Jane's day. There were many things she loved about being a nurse. Helping people, sure. But it wasn't completely altruistic. She somehow felt better about herself when she was taking care of others. It wasn't easy to explain, so she rarely tried.

But another big draw was that she never had the same day twice. Take today. After Jason had gotten punched out by his buddy, they'd had to call the police, but it turned out that Jason had only recently come home from Afghanistan, and after three tours of duty for the good old US of A, was suffering from debilitating PTSD. His friend had truly just been trying to help.

Nope, never a dull day . . .

She took a late lunch break on the deck of High Alpine's lunch lodge and watched the skiers hurl themselves down the mountain. Her thoughts quickly drifted to her date with Levi the night before. Correction: *pretend* date, and though she was a whole lot curious about the kiss he'd mentioned, she knew it was a dangerous proposition to go there.

Didn't mean she couldn't fantasize about it.

Mateo came out and sat next to her holding a glass container she recognized. "Charlotte made you lunch?"

He grinned. "Jealous?"

"Hell, yes. Is that her famous three-cheese lasagna?"

"The one and only." He pulled out two forks and handed her one.

"You are a God among men," she said fervently.

"While I'm not opposed to that title, it was Charlotte's doing. She gave me this container on the demand that I share with you, because, as she said, you probably packed a protein bar and a soda."

They both looked down at Jane's protein bar and can of soda.

Mateo laughed and began eating. She did too, and they raced each other to the middle, because if there was one certainty on this job, it was that no break lasted long.

After a few minutes of blessed silence stuffing themselves, Jane pointed her fork at Mateo. "So what's up with you and Charlotte?"

"Other than that she finally allowed me to help her take down the holiday lights? Nothing."

"She fed you. She only feeds the people she cares about."

Mateo smiled hopefully. "Yeah?"

"Yeah." She jabbed her fork in his direction again. "Hurt her and answer to me."

"Hurting her is the very last thing I want to do."

It was Jane's turn to smile hopefully. "Yeah?"

"Yeah."

"Then good luck to you," she said seriously. "The odds are against you."

"No kidding. Got any tips?"

"I wish I did. But the fact is, she's dead set against opening her heart."

"Why?"

Jane shook her head. "Not for me to say, but trust me, she has her reasons."

He looked troubled as he nodded. "Yeah. I'm getting that loud and clear."

She put her hand over his. "Just don't give up too soon, okay?"

"I won't."

"Good. Oh, and while we're doing this, *your best friend is Levi*? How did I not know that?"

Mateo shrugged. "Until the gondola incident, I hadn't seen him in a few years."

She set her fork down. "Because of Amy?"

He lifted a shoulder.

"I'm sorry about your sister, Mateo."

He sighed. "Yeah. Me too."

"Why didn't you tell me you knew Levi?"

"You mean that night in the hospital? He was a patient. HIPAA and all that . . ."

She nodded. "And after?"

He looked at her. "Until right this very minute, I didn't realize there was anything to talk about."

Crap. "There isn't."

He laughed. "Uh-huh. You do realize you're about as forthcoming with your emotions as Charlotte, right?"

"Pretty sure I'm worse," she admitted.

"Yeah, well, knowing it is half the battle." He paused. "Levi seem okay?"

She met his eyes and saw genuine concern. "He says his headaches and dizziness are mostly gone."

"I didn't mean that. I mean . . . shit." He scrubbed a hand down his face. "I'm not as bad at this as you and Charlotte are, but I'm not good at it either."

"You're worried about him."

"He cut himself off from friends and family, like maybe he thought he didn't deserve that kind of connection. Which is bullshit, of course. I'm glad he's back, but he's still here only because of the gondola accident."

"You think he's going to vanish again?"

"Well, not until you go anyway."

"So you do know something." She shook her head. "It's not like that."

"I hope you're wrong."

"It's a long story," she said. "But I'm just pretending to be his girlfriend for some family dinner."

Mateo stared at her and then grinned. "Oh, man. You're so in over your head."

"Why? Is his family awful?"

"No. They're amazing."

Her phone pinged an incoming voice mail. It was from the local humane society, offering free shots for rescue animals. The email went on to stress the importance of keeping the immunizations of rescue pets current so they remained healthy, and offered a phone number to call for a free appointment. She looked over at Mateo. "Should I get Cat his shots even though he's not mine?"

"Yes, and yes he is."

She hit the number and was surprised to get an opening for five o'clock. "I don't have a cat carrier," she realized when she'd disconnected.

"Charlotte has one in her garage. I don't know why. I think a previous renter had a cat."

So that's how Jane found herself after work wrestling Cat into the carrier she did indeed find in Charlotte's garage. He went into it willingly enough, but narrowed his eyes at her when she shut the crate's door.

Then proceeded to howl his displeasure all the way to the animal shelter.

"*Free*," Jane told him via the rearview window. "And it's important to your health that you get your shots."

He had a lot to say about this, but she carried him into the shelter anyway, still yowling his displeasure.

The woman at the front desk looked up and smiled. "Oh my," she said. "He's got quite a voice."

"Sorry, and yes, he does. My name's Jane, and I have an appointment."

The woman's smile widened, her eyes friendly behind a pair of bright blue glasses. "Hello, Jane, how lovely to meet you. I'm Shirl. We didn't actually get the name of your lovely cat."

"It's Cat. Short for Alley Cat."

If Shirl thought this was odd, she didn't show it as she had Jane fill out a form and then took her and Cat to a patient room.

"Oh, look at you," Shirl said softly to Cat, who'd stalked out of the crate when Jane opened it, looking royally pissed off. "What do we know about this beauty?"

"Not much. He's a stray, but I don't think anyone lets him inside their house or has gotten him checked out."

"Aw." Shirl bravely scooped Cat up from the floor and set him on the examination table. "Don't you have a sweet cat mommy?"

"I'm not," Jane said. "He just lives in the alley behind the house I'm staying in, and I wanted to make sure he's taken care of."

"So a good cat mommy with a big heart." Shirl continued to love up on Cat, who'd lost his defensive stance and seemed to be enjoying the attention.

"This precious boy needs a real name," Shirl said. "That's the first step in making him yours."

"But he's not mine." Just saying it gave Jane's heart a squeeze. "I'm a nurse. I work twelve-hours shifts that always turn into more, so I'd be a terrible cat mom. Plus, I'm here only until the end of ski season, and then I'll be gone."

This seemed to startle Shirl. "Where to?"

"I think it's Haiti next."

Shirl paused. "Putting yourself on the front lines to take care of other people. I don't know if there's a more respectable job than that. Your mom must be so proud."

Jane's mom was something all right, but proud probably wasn't it. But then again, if she'd had a mom like Shirl, Jane probably wouldn't be running all over the world. Instead, she'd want a relationship with her family. She'd want to put down roots and live close.

You're living close to your grandpa . . .

At the thought of him, she was hit by the usual colliding mix of emotions. Some she knew—regret, resentment. More regret . . . The other emotions she couldn't name. She reminded herself that she didn't have a relationship with him because his health had been frail and she hadn't wanted to cause any more problems. How many times had her aunt Viv told her that? Too many to count. Jane wouldn't be the one to bring him any more stress, like reminding him of happier times, when his wife had still been alive.

And what about the fact that he hadn't fought to keep her? He'd let other relatives take her, pass her around like last week's leftovers, only a day from going bad.

Oh, wait. Seemed she could name the other emotions after all. Shame. Embarrassment. Fear of further rejection . . . "I'm not close to my family."

"Oh, I'm so sorry." Shirl clearly felt bad for asking in the first place, which didn't stop her from asking another question. "Well then, certainly the man in your life is proud."

"Um—"

"Oh, dear," Shirl said suddenly while still checking out Cat. "Interesting."

Jane's heart leapt into her throat. "What's wrong with him?"

"Well, that's just it. He's not a he, he's a she." Shirl beamed. "Isn't that something?"

Jane nearly collapsed in relief and put a hand to her heart. "Are you sure?"

"Yes." Shirl took in the look on Jane's face and her own creased in regret as she reached for the hand Jane had clasped to her chest. "I'm sorry. I didn't mean to scare you. It's just that it's clear she's already had a litter. You might want to get her spayed before she has another."

Jane scooped Cat up and hugged her close. "You're a mama?"

Cat gently bumped her face to Jane's and her heart nearly exploded. "You have babies?" And she probably didn't even know where they were, how they were doing, if they were okay. If they had homes . . . Jane's throat tightened so that it hurt to even speak.

Shirl leaned across the examination table and patted her hand. "You don't need to worry. Our vet here is one of the very best."

Jane hugged the cat tighter. "Thank you. Yes, I'll think about getting her spayed, as soon as possible."

Shirl smiled. "You're a good person, Jane. If you're worried about her, we've got personalized collars and tags out front. You can put your phone number on the tag. In fact, you can put multiple numbers on the tag. A lot of people put down their significant other's number too, so if their pet ever gets lost, you can both be contacted. Would you like that? Would your significant other want to be put on the name tag?"

A tag that would claim Cat as her own. That seemed like both a horrible idea and the best idea on the planet. "I'll think about that too," she said softly.

LEVI SPENT THE day in the back office at Cutler Sporting Goods. He purposely waited until everyone was busy to let himself into the stock room. He wanted to do an inventory check against what was in the system, because so far, as near as Levi could tell, Cal had dipped his fingers into just about every corner of the family business.

Levi needed to get the authorities involved so they could nail Cal's ass, but he didn't want to freak out his parents and Tess until he'd finished his audit. He wanted to have all the details before breaking all their hearts. And he was close.

But after last night's date, his mission at the store today was more than just the inventory check. He wanted to ask Tess what the hell she'd been thinking befriending his pretend girlfriend.

But his sister came to him, poking her head into the back storage room. "What are you doing poking around back here?" she asked.

He leaned against a wall of shelving. "Seems to me you're the one poking around in other people's business."

She blinked. Grimaced. And then came all the way into the room and leaned against the shelving unit opposite him. "You've got something to say?"

He resisted the urge to be the baby brother and come right out with it, because from experience he knew that would only make her defensive. No, the only way to get information out of Tess was to outwit, outlast, and outplay her. Ten years older than him, she'd been bossing him around since birth. On the other hand, she'd also been loving him since birth. He knew she'd been blindsided by her divorce and terribly hurt, all the while still managing to be there for his parents and her daughter. And him.

That's why she interfered, he reminded himself. Because she loved him, in her own messed-up way. Still, he just stared at her, knowing the value of silence when it came to gaining any intel from her. She hated silence and always rushed to fill it. And she would, in three, two, one—

"Fine," she said. "Clearly Jane told you about our coincidental meet-up."

Coincidental, his ass. "I don't know how you figured out where she would be scheduled that day and what time she would take her break, but that was no coincidence, Tess."

She shrugged. "So one of our regular customers happens to be an X-ray tech and knows her. It's not my fault you won't tell us anything about your girlfriend. Like the fact that she's *not* your girlfriend."

Never underestimate the depths of deception that an older bossy sister would sink to. That had been his first mistake. "I don't know what you're talking about."

Mistake number two, denial.

Tess smiled, knowing she had him. "She's clearly single, Levi."

"Or she isn't into gossiping about her love life."

"Is that the story you're going to go with?"

Damn. He could compound his errors by continuing the pretense, but his sister was better than any lie detector in the land. Besides, maybe she could help him find a way out of this farce that he never should've started to begin with. "Okay," he said. "So hypothetically, let's say I do have a *pretend* girlfriend."

Tess crossed her arms. "Uh-huh . . ."

"What if I wanted to make things real?"

"Let me guess," she said. "You're asking for a friend."

"Sure," he said. "Let's say that."

Tess looked at him for a beat. "Is your *friend* asking for advice to get into this woman's pants, or is he genuinely seeking advice on how to get to know this person—because I don't want to see her hurt, and you have a way of being effortlessly charming when you want to be and getting whatever you want."

"I'm asking for a friend, remember?"

"Is your friend an idiot?" she countered.

He sighed. "Forget it. Forget I asked."

The door opened and nearly hit his sister in the ass. Shirl Cutler came in, bouncing with joy. "Guess who I met today during my volunteer shift at the humane society!"

Levi turned and thunked his head against the steel shelving. "*Why?*"

"Don't worry. I didn't tell her who I was."

Mateo came in behind Levi's mom. "What did I miss?"

Levi sighed. "And you're here why?"

His mom gasped. "What kind of way is that to speak to your oldest, bestest friend?"

Behind her back, Mateo grinned at Levi.

Levi very discreetly gave him the middle finger.

"And I invited him here," his mom said. "Because we have all that leftover food from today's birthday lunch for Dusty. Mateo's just worked a bunch of days in a row and I bet he hasn't eaten a good home-cooked meal in forever. I'm packing him up leftovers."

Mateo was one of the best cooks Levi knew. The guy was actually a huge food snob. Even though Levi believed that Mateo had indeed worked a bunch of days in a row and was probably near dead from exhaustion, there was no way he hadn't eaten.

"Come help me, Tess." And with that, Levi's mom and sister were gone.

Mateo plopped into one of the two chairs in the corner and rubbed his hands over his face.

"Long few days?" Levi asked.

"You could say that."

Levi dropped into the other chair. "Want to tell me what's going on?"

"No."

"Okay, glad we could clear that up."

Mateo swore beneath his breath. "What do you know about your pretend girlfriend's best friend?"

"How do you know about Jane?"

"I have my ways. Tell me what you know about Charlotte."

Levi shrugged. "I met her last night. She seems really nice."

"Nice? That's it?"

"I know she's a doctor," Levi said. "At your hospital. Which means you know way more about her than I do."

Mateo leaned forward and put his elbows on his knees and his face into his hands.

Mateo was one of the most easygoing, giving guys Levi knew. It was a miracle, really, given his demanding profession and the needs his family put on him. When the Morenos had lost Amy, it'd left Mateo an only child of elderly parents. Elderly parents that he'd become solely responsible for. Between that and the demanding job, Mateo had no personal life outside his family. Levi had been a real dick for vanishing on him, leaving Mateo without emotional support. He wouldn't make that mistake again. "What's wrong?"

"She's smart as hell, sharp as hell, feisty and sassy and . . . hell." Mateo slid his fingers into his hair. "Gorgeous."

"Not hearing a problem."

"She's outta my league, man. But she's the One."

Levi stared at him. "Charlotte?"

"No, jackass, the Easter Bunny. Yeah, Charlotte."

"And this is a problem?"

"She doesn't like me."

Levi laughed.

"I'm serious."

"Come on. You've never had to work for a woman in your life."

"Until this one," Mateo said. "When I get home before her, I clear her snow. She yells at me to put it back. Sometimes I leave her snacks in her cubby at work because I don't think she remembers to eat. She thinks it's the asshole X-ray tech who always hits on her."

Levi burst out laughing.

"Not funny. Last week, I put air in her tires because I could tell they were low, and with icy roads . . ." He broke off and sighed. "I'm so screwed."

"Why not just tell her how you feel?"

"Really?" Mateo asked dryly. "Is that what you're doing with Jane? Being honest about your feelings?"

"Hey, we both know how *not* an expert I am on this shit. But what's so wrong with telling Charlotte how you really feel?"

"I'll mess it up."

Mateo had gone right from high school to college to medical school, then to residency and straight onward from there with his medical career. He was brilliant, but when it came to getting serious in a relationship, the guy had as little experience as, well, Levi. "You could just take it slow."

Mateo laughed mirthlessly. "Our current pace is a tortoise trying to wade through peanut butter. If we go any slower, we'll be going backwards."

"What's the hurry? Neither of you are going anywhere."

Mateo rolled his eyes. "Tell me you got better advice for me than that."

"Pretend girlfriend, remember?"

Mateo snorted, then shook his head. "We're both such dumb-asses."

"No doubt."

CHAPTER 14

Charlotte walked out of the hospital. It was the end of a shift, but the beginning of a day. At just past dawn, the sky was alight with an ocean of pinks, reds, and purples. She stood there for a beat, blinking at the bright winter light bouncing off the fresh snow blanketing the parking lot, face turned up to the emerging sun like a lizard.

Just concentrating on inhaling and exhaling.

When she could do so without that sharp stabbing pain of grief in her chest, she made her way to her car.

A young woman had died on her table last night while under her knife. As a horrible reality of her job, it happened. But it never, ever failed to take a little chunk out of her heart and soul.

Cranking on her heater, she turned the vents toward her as she drove home, but all the heat in the world couldn't warm her up.

Her patient—"*Talia*," she said out loud to her car. Talia, a twenty-two-year-old, had been a victim of domestic abuse. Feeling the prickle of tears behind her eyes, she blinked hard and pulled into her driveway. Which had been cleared.

Mateo, of course.

Dammit. Damn him. She was already trembling with the effort to hold back her own internal storm, the one that was playing havoc with her emotions, bringing them far too close to the surface.

Nothing good ever came of her emotions breaking free.

She stared at her house. He'd done the walkway too. How in the world was she supposed to deal with someone doing something nice for her right now? Answer: she couldn't. Especially from Mateo, for reasons she didn't quite understand.

Drawing a deep breath, she pulled her visor down to look into the mirror, needing to make sure there were no signs of her turmoil. She didn't need a knight in shining armor to save her day.

She would save her own damn day.

She got out of the car and lost a portion of her self-righteousness when she didn't have to wade through a foot of fresh snow as she made her way to his front door and knocked.

Nothing.

She tried again, rapping her fist harder onto the wood.

When the door finally opened, Mateo stood there wearing red knit boxers and . . . nothing else. No shirt. Bed head. Eyes heavy lidded. Bare feet.

He blinked blearily. "What's up?"

"Put it back."

"Put what back?"

"The snow," she said. "Put it all back."

He reached for her hand, pushed up her jacket sleeve, and looked at the time on her watch. When he saw it was five thirty

A.M., he groaned. "I didn't get out of the ER until an hour ago. I've had twelve minutes of sleep out of the past thirty-six hours. Are you crazy?"

"Yes. And you already know that. So you should also know that I'm completely capable of clearing my own snow, even after a terrible, horrible, no good, very bad day at work."

His eyes cleared and softened. "I know. I saw her in the ER. I had no choice but to send her to you in OR, but I hated it, because I knew what it would do to you."

To her utter horror, she felt her eyes filling, and though she worked hard to keep them to herself, a few tears broke free. Dammit. Needing space, she turned her back to him, hating he'd seen her at her worst—vulnerable.

"I'm going to touch you now," he warned in that same quiet, calm voice. Then she felt his hand on her arm as he slowly pulled her back around to face him.

She already knew he was perceptive. It was what made him such a great ER doctor, but it also made him dangerous to her heart, because though she hadn't said a word about her past to anyone except Jane, he'd clearly gotten the gist of it from her own actions.

"Charlotte," he said softly. "Come in, let me make you something to eat."

Great, and now he felt sorry for her. Which pissed her off. Tugging free, she started to storm off before remembering the ice. Having to slow down really fried her ass.

"Charlotte."

Nope, she was no longer speaking to him, but since he wasn't the most talkative person to begin with, she wasn't sure he appreciated the fact that she was punishing him. So she stopped and glared at him. "I don't want you to feel sorry for me."

"Good, because I don't." His voice was low. Serious. "You've had a shit night, and let's just say I know what that feels like."

"I'm not fit for company."

"Then we won't talk. We'll just eat. Then sleep." Slowly, giving her plenty of opportunity to back away, he reached for her hand. "But first, I'd like to hug you again. Okay?"

More okay than anything she could think of. Fact was, she hadn't stopped thinking about how safe she'd felt in his arms. Safe and secure and . . . *not* lonely. Because of her long hours, being alone was her norm, a by-product of her profession. And okay, yes, also because she'd chosen to be alone rather than let someone in to see what a hot mess she was on the inside. But she was tired of hiding.

"Charlotte?"

She nodded.

"I need the words."

"Yes, please," she whispered, and with a smile he stepped farther into the freezing cold morning in his bare feet and wrapped his arms around her.

She gasped as her hands came in contact with warm bare skin stretched taut over sinew. "Oh my God, you're almost naked!"

"That was an 'omigod, you're almost naked' in a good way, right?"

And that was how she found herself laughing and crying at the same time. Going up on tiptoes, she pressed her face into the crook of his neck, slipping her arms around him, holding on for dear life. "You're going to catch frostbite," she whispered against his throat.

He slid one hand up her spine, past the nape of her neck and into her hair, the other arm wrapped low on her hips as he held her close, and she wondered how something so simple as a hug could both give her such comfort and yet also rev her engines.

"Guess you'll just have to keep me warm," he murmured, his cheek pressed to her hair.

Closing her eyes, she breathed him in and held on for dear life. And he let her, cuddling her into him, her anchor in a world gone mad.

"You're shivering," she whispered.

"That's you." He pulled back but held on to her hand. "Come inside, Charlotte. I've got food. I even know how to cook it."

She stared up at him. "Just breakfast, right? Nothing more."

"I'd never ask you for more than you were willing to give."

She wasn't sure why such a simple statement felt so earth changing. No one had ever said such a thing to her.

He bent his head and looked into her eyes. "You in, or is it too much?"

That he would even ask her that meant everything. And he really had to be freezing, not to mention every bit as exhausted as she. But he was giving away none of that, just a calm, steady patience that was a balm to her soul.

That was when her stomach chose to rumble and grumble like a locomotive engine. Horrified, she pressed her hands to her belly while Mateo laughed and tugged her inside.

She'd been in his house a few times. Once for a holiday party, which had been the first time she'd seen him outside of his role as a doctor. It had fascinated her, watching him with friends and family, all of whom clearly adored him. A few months later, they'd had a disagreement at work and she'd stalked off, angry that he'd reported a coworker and gotten him fired, only to find out later that coworker had been harassing a female coworker. She'd gone to his house to apologize. On both visits she'd spent more time concentrating on the man, not the place he'd made his home.

This time, she was afraid to concentrate on the man. She felt too . . . exposed for that today, and when she was exposed, she didn't always make smart decisions.

So she looked around. The big living room had the same wall-to-wall windows hers did, framing the gorgeous mountains she loved. In her house, her furniture was feminine and a little flowery because, sue her, she loved a little flowery. Mateo's place was all warm woods and neutral colors, and big, sturdy furniture that was inviting in a whole new way. No flowery anything anywhere.

There were noises coming from the kitchen, making her realize she'd stopped in the living room and Mateo hadn't. She followed the sounds and found he'd pulled on sweatpants and a T-shirt, and she didn't know if she was relieved or disappointed.

Still barefoot, he stood in front of his stove, cracking eggs into a pan. His other hand was holding a spatula, which he used to point her to a barstool on the other side of his cooking station.

So she sat, watching him chop up some veggies and toss them

in with the eggs. Then he grabbed the handle of the pan and with a flick of his wrist, flipped the omelet.

Two minutes later he'd divided the eggs onto two plates, added toast, and served her with an easy efficiency that was sexy as hell.

"You've been doing that a long time," she said.

He shrugged. "My parents worked around the clock. So did my aunts, and being the oldest, I was the babysitter of a lot of kids. It was cook or go hungry."

She knew he had a big extended family, and that he took care of most of them. He was good at taking care of others, really good. "Who takes care of you?" she asked.

His gaze met hers, warm, curious, probably because normally, she did her best to keep some mental distance between them—it was the only way she knew how to resist him. "Sorry. I didn't mean to ask such a personal question."

He didn't say anything for a long moment, pouring them both juice, then sitting on the barstool next to her. Their thighs brushed, and when he reached for a napkin, so did their arms.

"I take care of me." He turned his head to hold her gaze. "The same way you take care of you. It's who we are, it's what we do."

She nodded. Then shook her head. "Does it ever get to you? Always being an island?"

Reaching out, he brushed the tips of his fingers along her jaw. "I guess I don't let myself think about it too much."

"That's usually my tactic too," she admitted. "But sometimes it gets old."

He watched her inhale the food he'd made for her, a small smile curving his mouth. "We could do something about that."

She nearly choked on a bite of toast. "Meaning?"

He just smiled.

Something low in her belly quivered. A good kind of quiver. One she hadn't allowed herself much of in a long time. "Um . . ."

"You telling me you haven't thought about it?"

She met his gaze. "To be clear, by *it*, you're suggesting we . . . sleep together."

"I'm suggesting I'm here to meet any need you have, any time."

If she thought about that for even another second, she was going to crawl into his lap and wrap herself around him. Instead, she stood up, took both their empty plates and went to the sink with them. She rinsed them and helped herself to his dishwasher, loading the dishes inside. When she turned, he was right there, close enough to touch, and she sucked in a breath. "That was the only need I'm capable of helping you with at the moment," she said, even as her body vehemently disagreed with her.

Mateo smiled, like no worries. Or maybe because he knew she was lying. "And you?" he asked. "Is there a need I can help *you* with?"

She had to bite her tongue rather than answer *yes, please!*

His amusement faded. "Want to talk about last night?"

"No." *Definitely not.*

He just looked at her for a long beat. "When you're ready, then."

She fussed with drying off his countertop. "Thanks for breakfast."

"Any time." He gently pulled her back around to face him. "But just so you know, I'm sure we could do much better than breakfast for you."

Her body, knowing it, shifted against his. "I . . . need to work up to that."

With a smile, he cupped her face and brushed a kiss across her forehead. "On your time, Charlotte. Always."

A FEW MINUTES later, Charlotte walked back to her house, carrying one of Mateo's mugs filled with his own special blend of coffee that might as well have been crack, it was that good.

The sun had risen. Gorgeous but not anywhere close to warm. Snow clung stubbornly to the pine trees and the icy air burned her lungs. She didn't care because it was still early, and Dr. Charlotte Marie Dixon was leaving a man's house and she was smiling.

She felt amazing. Absolutely nothing had happened beyond breakfast, but it'd been the most intimate she'd been with a man in years.

When she stepped into her kitchen, she found Jane sitting at the table staring at a small flat box on the coffee table as if it was a coiled rattlesnake. She looked up at Charlotte with obvious relief. "Hey. Where were you? You were off shift an hour ago and your car's here, but you vanished."

Charlotte laughed. "Sucks, doesn't it, the not knowing if someone's okay?"

Jane grimaced in acknowledgment that she was guilty of not checking in as often as she should. "You're the responsible one. You're teaching me, remember? Wait a minute." She narrowed her eyes. "Did you just come from Mateo's house? From Mateo's bed?" She eyed the mug in Charlotte's hands, leapt to her feet, and gasped. "Oh my God, you did!" She hopped up to sit crisscross on the counter. "Tell all. Don't leave a single thing out."

"He cleared the snow for us, so I went over there to, um, thank him, and he made me breakfast."

Jane stared at her. "Are you blushing?"

Charlotte clasped her hands to her cheeks. "No!"

"You are so!" She pointed at her. "He did more than make you breakfast."

"If I'm blushing, it's because he made me breakfast and didn't expect anything more." And she'd enjoyed herself so much more than she had in a very long time.

"Well, of course he didn't expect anything from you. He's Mateo," Jane said, reminding Charlotte that Jane trusted Mateo, when Jane didn't trust anyone.

Charlotte gave her a soft smile. "I'm starting to realize that."

"Tell me the truth. You didn't go over there to thank him for removing the snow."

"No." Charlotte laughed at herself. "I went over there to yell at him. I'd had a really bad night at work. I . . . lost someone. A young woman. Domestic violence."

Jane let out a soft gasp and slid off the counter. "Oh no. Honey, I'm so sorry." She pulled Charlotte in for one of those rare but magical hugs. "Are you okay?"

Charlotte held on tight. "Better now."

"So . . ." Jane's voice had a small smile in it. "You had a shit night, came home upset, found all your snow gone, and stormed over to yell at our sexy neighbor, and he defused you with his amazing food."

Charlotte dropped her head to Jane's shoulder. "Yes."

Jane pulled back, keeping her hands on Charlotte's arms, looking into her face. Jane didn't touch people casually, so whenever she did touch Charlotte, it meant something. This morning, it warmed a part of her heart she hadn't realized needed warming.

"I like it," Jane said. "I like him for you." She then turned back to the table to stare at the box some more.

"What's that?" Charlotte asked.

"You tell me."

"I have no idea."

Jane rolled her eyes. "You left it for me."

Charlotte gave a slow shake of her head. "Not me. Are you kidding? You break out into hives when I give you a present. You went through an entire packet of Benadryl last Christmas."

Jane frowned. "You're not playing me? This really isn't from you?" She opened the box, separated the gift paper inside, and pulled out a sugar plum fairy ornament, dangling it from her finger. "You're the only one who knows I once dressed up like a sugar plum fairy to go see *The Nutcracker* with my grandma."

"It's beautiful," Charlotte breathed, admiring the dainty glass ornament. "But no. I'm not playing you. Where was it?"

"At my cubby in the Sierra North clinic." She eyed Charlotte suspiciously, clearly still believing it had been her. "Who else knows my work schedule? No one."

"Okay," Charlotte said. "Let me stop you right there. When have you ever known me not to write a missive when sending a present?"

"True." Jane's shoulders slumped. "But if it wasn't you, then who the hell left it?"

"I don't know." Charlotte moved closer and put a hand on her shoulder. "I think the real question is, if it *had* been me who gave it to you, why would it upset you so much?"

Jane sank to a chair. "I don't know. Maybe because it feels like the past colliding with the here and now. The past hurts, and I don't like thinking about it."

Charlotte touched the pretty ornament. "This memory hurts you?"

Jane blew out a breath. "Okay, no. Not that one. It's actually one of my favorite memories."

"Then why don't you hold on to *that* feeling whenever you look at it? Trust me, you can't run away from your past forever."

Jane snorted. "One breakfast with Dr. Hottie Patottie and all of a sudden you're Dr. Phil."

"Ha-ha." Charlotte handed back the ornament. "Is it possible someone from your past left it for you? Like your grandpa?"

"I guess . . . but doubtful. He doesn't know I'm here." Jane turned the pretty ornament in the light. "It's so fragile. I don't know what to do with it. I'll end up breaking it if I take it with me when I go."

"Then leave it here, in your bedroom, for when you come back next season."

"I don't like taking up your space with my junk. Plus, you never know if you're going to need the room for another renter while I'm gone."

Charlotte's first instinct was to sigh with annoyance, but instead she took in the anxiety on Jane's face and ached for her. "There's always going to be a room for you here. For you *and* your stuff, Jane."

Jane stood up. "Don't say that, because you never know what's going to happen. Have you talked to Sandra? She wants to extend her stay."

"Yeah, I'm thinking of buying bunk beds for the downstairs bedroom. Zoe said she wouldn't mind sharing."

"You don't need to spend the money on a new bed," Jane said. "Seriously. The easier solution is for me to head out early."

Okay, Charlotte was done with this convo. Spinning on her heels, she opened her junk drawer, grabbed a Sharpie. Without another word, she headed down the hall.

She heard Jane mutter, "What the—" and smiled grimly to herself when she also heard footsteps following after her.

"What are you doing?" Jane asked.

Charlotte uncapped the Sharpie and wrote *JANE* in big letters across her bedroom door. "Does this make it clear?"

"That's permanent ink," Jane said.

"Yes, as permanent as your place is here."

Jane looked at her. "You do realize that paint could cover it up."

Charlotte pointed at her with the Sharpie. "Don't ruin this for me. We're having a moment."

"I'm not good at moments."

"No kidding. Now hush, or I'll make you hug me again. Maybe even cry too." She snagged an arm around Jane's neck and dragged her in close. "Never mind. I'll hug you." And she did just that, holding tight while Jane sighed dramatically. "Bad shit happens," Charlotte said. "To all of us. We'll deal."

"You deal better than me," Jane said.

"That's because when things get bad, I know I can fly home, where my mom has my name on my bedroom door. It makes everything so much easier knowing I have a room out there waiting for me, always. And I want the same for you."

"But what if you need the money?"

Charlotte's throat tightened at the genuine worry on Jane's face. "I won't. I don't rent out my rooms because I need the money. You know that. I need time with my best friend, the sister of my heart, whenever she can get into town."

Jane looked simultaneously touched and upset. "If I'm your best friend, you're in trouble."

Charlotte smiled. "I think I'm in good hands."

Jane sighed. "You are. You know how I feel about you."

"Well, I do my best to guess, since you're such a miser with words."

"I . . . we're . . ."

Charlotte raised a brow.

"You're my person, okay? Happy now?" Jane finally said, and Charlotte felt her eyes sting. She sniffed and Jane stared at her. "Oh my God, what are you doing?"

Charlotte's eyes filled.

"No. No crying in the hallway!" Jane blinked, her own eyes looking suspiciously misty. "I mean it. You know I have a sympathy cry thing, and you also know I hate to cry!"

Charlotte laughed through her tears. "Maybe I've just got something in my eye."

"Yeah, right." Then suddenly Jane straightened up like a light bulb had gone off over her head. "*Levi.*"

Charlotte blinked, confused. "Huh?"

"The present! I think it could be Levi. He's the one who got me back my locket. And he knows what a sugar plum fairy would mean to me." She shook her head. "I can't believe I didn't think of it before. *What was he thinking?*"

Charlotte watched Jane pace back and forth. "I don't know

about him, but I'm guessing you're thinking he knows you far better than you're comfortable with."

"It's like he can read me. What the hell is that?"

It was a man falling hard, not that she could say so without freaking Jane out even more. "And you're not comfortable with that, not even a little bit."

Jane gave her a "duh" look and Charlotte felt her mouth curve. "You know you have to thank him, right? And a gift with this level of sentiment requires an *in*-person thank-you. It's etiquette."

Jane leaned back against her bedroom door and thunked her head against the wood.

Charlotte knew better than to laugh, but as it was her greatest wish for Jane to find someone special enough to keep her here in Tahoe, she allowed herself a small smile.

CHAPTER 15

That night, Jane showered, pulled on her fave pj's, which were an old oversize tee and undies, and went into her favorite thinking position—curled up in her bed under a thick down comforter.

Nothing could get to her in here. Not destructive thoughts, not unhappy memories, not the stress of her job, nothing.

She intended to have a good think. Maybe over whether she was doing the right thing about not contacting her grandpa, letting him know she was around.

But that's not where her brain took her. Nope, instead it kept replaying snapshots in her head of how she'd felt the other night, making s'mores with Levi. Why had he left her a present when they were only *pretending* to be involved?

But maybe the better question was, why did she care?

When she opened her eyes again, it was morning. She'd slept the entire night through without waking up racked with anxiety.

What was that?

She had to laugh as she got out of bed. She hated anxiety, but now that it had gone missing for a night, she was anxious about losing the anxiety.

Which settled it.

She'd lost her mind.

She hustled through her morning routine. Then she and Charlotte hit up the diner for breakfast before their shifts. The cook came out and slapped a twenty into Charlotte's waiting palm before vanishing back into the kitchen.

"He lost a bet," Charlotte said. "Last week he sliced his hand open when I was here."

"Wait. You come here without me?"

"No, when you're busy, I stay at home, frozen in time until you come home."

Jane rolled her eyes and Charlotte smiled. "Jealous. Cute. Anyway, he sliced his hand wide open. I wanted to stitch him up, but he insisted on using Super Glue because he's got a needle phobia. I told him it was a terrible idea, but have you ever successfully talked a man out of a stupid idea? No, right? So he found some sort of construction glue and electric tape and told me to pick my poison. I told him that either would land him in the ER with an infection. We bet on it—his idea," she said, raising her hands like she was innocent. "Not mine. So he Super Glued his hand."

"And because you can't help yourself, you took the bet knowing you'd win, and it got infected and he landed in the ER," Jane guessed.

"Bingo. But don't worry, I'm putting the twenty into his tip jar when we leave."

Jane laughed. Charlotte couldn't resist a good bet that she knew she could win, but she also couldn't take advantage of anyone— she just wasn't built that way. "You work in the OR. So how did you find out?"

Charlotte's cheeks went red. Fascinating. Jane pointed at her. "You and Mateo have been talking."

"No! Well, not about patients. I . . . um, happened to be with Mateo in the staff room when he was paged, and I might have gone with him to the ER, since I was having a slow night."

"Mateo and Charlotte sitting in a tree," Jane sang. "K-I-S-S-I-N-G . . ."

Charlotte was head down on the table, ears flaming. "You're a child."

"Yep." Jane stood. "I've gotta go and so do you."

They walked out into the parking lot together. They'd gotten another foot of fresh powdery snow overnight.

"Stay safe," Charlotte said.

"Always. And right back at you."

It was a common refrain between them. Jane hit the road heading up to Starwood Peak urgent care and got caught behind a snowplow, which meant she made it to work with barely a minute to spare. She hit the job running and never slowed down.

Starwood was Jane's least favorite of the five, mostly because it tended to draw the hotdoggers, the reckless, the worst of the weekend warriors—which meant her day was filled with knee, shoulder, and leg injuries. Plus, there was an ever-higher ratio of what she privately called the splat syndrome—when people who weren't expert skiers or boarders attempted to ski the fresh powder off trail in the trees. Then went splat against those trees.

They could be horrifyingly serious injuries, which meant calling for the helicopter to get them airlifted to either Reno or Davis, depending on how many minutes they had to save them—a grim reality that *wasn't* in the glorious, exciting promo ads for Lake

Tahoe. The staff often reduced the tension by playing pranks on one another. Last week, Dr. Daniel Briggs, a known asshole to nurses far and wide, had decided he needed his own microwave because the nurses took up too much of their short lunch breaks heating up their food. And no underlings—nurses—were allowed to use his microwave.

For a few days, Jane and the others had debated on a way to prank him without getting caught. They came up with lots of plans, all discarded because Dr. Briggs had been known to get people fired for looking at him cross-eyed.

Charlotte had helped Jane come up with a brilliant plan. She'd changed his autocorrect settings in Outlook, so whenever he typed his title—something he did all day long, every time he entered patient info—his name autocorrected to *Dr. Daniel Briggs, his eloquence, master of duck herding, and debater of microwave etiquette.*

He'd not been able to point the finger at anyone, so Jane lived to prank another day. And better yet, Dr. Briggs wasn't on today. But the clinic was unusually cold, and not just because people kept coming in from outside, where the temp hovered around twenty-eight degrees. There was something wrong with the heating system, so she was working in her scrubs with her down vest on top.

In the vest pocket sat the sugar plum fairy ornament. Every time the small flat box pressed up against her ribs, a mixed bag of emotions hit her. Emotions she wasn't sure she could name even if she'd wanted to. She tried to go with angry, but somehow she was having trouble sticking with that.

On her break, she decided it was time to be a grown-up. So she sneaked into the supply closet—because nothing said grown-up more than that—and pulled out her phone to send a text.

JANE: Need to talk to you.

LEVI: Not that I'm easy, but when and where?

JANE: I get off at 6.

LEVI: Or you could wait for me to assist in the getting off . . .

JANE: Are you flirting with me?

LEVI: Depends on if you liked it.

LEVI: . . .

JANE: Okay, maybe I liked it a little. Leave me a text on where to find you. I'm going to go home and change first.

LEVI: Don't change on my account. I like you just the way you are.

Since she had no idea how to respond to him—well, okay, her body knew *exactly* how to respond to him—she did as she should have when she got to work: she turned off her phone and went back to her shift.

At six fifteen, she headed out to the parking lot and stopped short at the man leaning against her car, boots casually crossed, head down doing something on his phone. Long before he could have heard her coming, he looked up and unerringly landed that see-all gray gaze on her.

She faltered, then lifted her chin and strode directly toward him. *Remember, you're not happy he gave you a present. You're not at all charmed. This is pretend. Just pretend. Presents have no place in a pretend relationship. Especially presents that make you feel decidedly . . . un-pretend-like.*

And here was the thing. She'd spent most of her life living by certainties. The sun would rise, and no matter what part of the world she was in, she rose with it and went to her job. Then she'd go to bed and stare up at whatever ceiling happened to be over her head and tell herself that even though much of her life hadn't been ideal, she was doing her part to make people's lives better.

But then a certain blizzard had put her in a situation up close and far too personal with the man watching her approach. A man who had no place in her regimented, planned-out world. None. And as un-grown-up as it was, she felt a stirring of frustration with him for standing there looking like the best thing that had ever happened to her.

So she did what she did. She went on the defensive. She went toe-to-toe with him, pulled the box out of her pocket, and pressed it against his chest. "We agreed this isn't real, so why in the world would you do this?"

He opened the box and looked at the ornament, nothing showing on his face.

She stared into his eyes. Okay, not his eyes. She stared at his mouth. She didn't know why. "Your turn to talk," she said, crossing her arms over her chest.

"Well, thanks to my niece, I know this is a sugar plum fairy from *The Nutcracker*. Although I gotta say, you make a far cuter one."

"Why, Levi?"

"I don't know. Why did you tell me you didn't want to kiss me the other night, when all you've done since you got out here was look at my lips?"

Gah! She jerked her gaze off his lips, then rubbed her hands over her face. "I swear, I have no idea what that is."

He looked at her for a long beat, then set the box with the ornament on the hood. "This is why," he said and nudged her up against the vehicle. Moving slowly, clearly giving her time to resist, he reached out and removed her sunglasses. Then he closed the gap separating them and kissed her. Slow. Sweet. Almost as if he was asking a question.

Her heart drumming in her ears and throat, she pulled back and stared at him, her only thought being that this hadn't been nearly enough. Reaching out, she grabbed the front of his jacket and yanked him back into her. He went with the forward momentum, letting them bump into each other, chest to chest, thigh to thigh, and everything deliciously in between. "This is *just* a kiss," she informed him, her voice annoyingly soft and breathy.

This had him laughing softly against her as he nibbled her lower lip, then sucked it into his mouth. Someone gasped. Her. Dammit. With another of those sexy laughs, he kissed her. Really kissed her, nothing sweet or questioning about it this time. She moaned, closed a fist in his hair, and did the only thing she could: held on for the best kiss of her life.

Levi was slow to pull back, slower still to lift his head and reveal those sexy eyes.

"Okay." She nodded and licked her lips, because apparently she needed that one last taste of him. "So we got that out of the way, which means we're done with that now."

He looked pointedly at her arms, which were still wrapped tightly around him.

She yanked her hands from him and shoved her fingers in her hair, turning away from him while she tried to catch her breath and gather her thoughts. "You make me crazy."

"Ditto." He paused. "And I didn't give you that ornament."

She whirled back, took in the truth in his eyes, and felt her heart sink. She believed him.

That left only her grandpa. Which meant he knew she was in town.

Guilt flooded her because it was one thing to avoid the man when he didn't know she was here; it was another entirely if he was aware of her trips to Tahoe and knew she'd been avoiding him. And then there was the disappointment that he'd chosen to communicate via the gift instead of in person, or the guilt for avoiding him in the first place—she wasn't sure which.

"Jane? You okay?"

She dropped her head to his chest. His hard chest. Slowly shook her head.

"What can I do? Name it."

"Feed me."

"Done." He led her to his car and drove them toward town, parking at one end of the Lake Walk. All the shops, storefronts, and restaurants were lit with a myriad of lights, as were the old-fashioned lampposts, making the place seem like a movie set.

In less than five minutes, they were seated inside a pizzeria, near a huge brick fireplace that took up one entire wall. The heat felt wonderful, the scents teased her cranky belly, and as much as she didn't want to admit it, her dinner companion was a sight for sore eyes.

They ordered, and when they each had a beer in front of them,

Levi met her gaze. "I'm guessing you have an idea who the orna-ment is from."

She gave a stunned nod. "I think it's from my grandpa. He's the only other person who would know what such a gift would mean to me."

"Can you ask him?"

"I haven't talked to him in twenty years."

He didn't look judgy or horrified. He merely nodded. "I can understand why." Gently, he rubbed the pad of his thumb over the back of her hand, which was gripping her beer bottle with a white-knuckled grip. "What do you want to do?"

She wasn't sure. Did she want to make contact? Her first in-stinct was no, a decision made by hurt. But suddenly she wasn't sure. Wariness kept beating back her curiosity, but maybe it was time to let go of the past and make a present for herself. "I don't know," she said quietly. "If I just show up, I might upset him."

Levi continued to hold her hand, and she wondered if he knew that simple touch was the only thing keeping her grounded.

"If he's the one who got you the ornament, he already knows you're here," he pointed out. "You won't be a surprise. He gave you the ornament knowing you'd figure out who it came from. I'm betting he's expecting you."

She looked into his calm eyes. "But what if he's not? What if he's unhappy to see me. I can't . . ." She let her gaze break from his. "I don't want to be turned away."

Levi gently cupped her face, bringing it back around. "Either way, going to see him or not, you're in the driver's seat now. You can't make a wrong move."

She nodded, empowered by the reminder. "I'm just . . . wary. I don't know how to trust this. I have no idea what he expects. But you're right. This isn't about him, it's about me and what I want. And what I want is for bygones to be bygones, because family matters."

"I agree, family does matter. But it only works if it's a give-and-take."

"He did make the first move," she said. "Sort of."

He nodded, keeping a hold on her hand, gaze solemn. He was taking this seriously. He was taking her seriously. Just as Charlotte had, and Jane realized how much that meant. "When I lived with my grandparents . . . it was the best time of my entire childhood," she admitted.

"There's no harm in reaching out and seeing what's up."

How did he always make everything sound so simple, so easy, so right? She had no idea. All she knew was that when she was with him, she felt like she could do anything.

Their pizza came, and she practically fell onto it, inhaling the best-tasting loaded pie she'd ever had. "Oh my God," she said around a mouthful.

"Right?" Levi was working on his own big slice. "Only yesterday, I'd have said heaven on earth."

"What changed since yesterday?"

"I have a new favorite taste," he said, and laughed when she blushed.

She put her hands on her cheeks. "Are you always such a flirt?"

"No."

"So why me?"

He smiled at her. "Because when I'm with you, I feel like . . . me."

Everything inside her softened at that. Because the truth was, she felt the exact same way, which meant he was dangerous to her heart and soul. She decided to concentrate on eating rather than messy things like feelings. "I'm starving," she said, grabbing another piece. "Didn't get any breaks today."

"You work too hard."

She shrugged. "Not more than anyone else."

His look said he disagreed, but he let it go. He told her about his day, how he was balancing his own work with helping out his parents with the store's accounting, making her laugh with the antics of Jasper, the goldendoodle. How he'd put his nose where it didn't belong on the poor UPS guy and now they couldn't get their deliveries. And then there was the dog's choice of snacks— his humans' belongings, like his niece's socks.

"Maybe they're just lost," Jane said on a laugh.

"He horked up the evidence on the kitchen floor while we were eating breakfast, along with a pair of my mom's underwear—nude lace." He shuddered, looking so pained, she nearly snorted her beer out her nose. "No," she gasped.

"Oh yes. There was a lot of screaming. My ears are still ringing."

She laughed in sympathy and then eyed the last piece of pizza. Levi nudged it toward her.

"I couldn't," she said, trying to mean it. "You take it."

"It's got your name on it. I'm full."

She was halfway through the piece when she caught him smiling at her. Not laughing at her, just genuinely smiling. And yet . . . she realized that his smile was missing its usual wattage. "It was sweet of you to come to my work to see me," she said. "You didn't have to do that."

He grimaced a little at the *sweet*. "I wanted to make it easier for you to communicate to me whatever you needed to."

"I'm sorry I accused you of leaving me the ornament," she said on a wince. "Not my finest moment."

"I understand."

She met his gaze. "Are you sure? Because I feel like something's bothering you."

"I just heard myself tell you that story about Jasper, deflecting with humor, rather than having the courage to go deep, like you did." He blew out a breath. "I came to Tahoe because my mom hinted that she needed my help with something. I ended up on that gondola with you because an hour into the visit I needed an escape. You know what happened next, and it was a week before my dad told me the reason they'd needed me. The store's accountant was my sister's husband. When he left her, he took all their money and vanished. My dad was worried that he'd gotten creative with the store accounting as well."

"Oh my God. Did he?"

He pushed his plate away. "There was a month of time where no one was really on top of the books. I've been going through it all. And yeah, he helped himself to the kitty, getting very creative about it."

"Oh, no." Her heart sank for him. For his family. "Did you get the police involved?"

"Not yet. I'm not quite finished with the internal audit, but it's bad. And my family is going to be shattered when they find out that the store is now at risk. Telling them is going to suck."

"I'm so sorry," she said softly. "That's a heavy burden to carry alone."

"I don't feel alone at the moment."

She didn't question why it felt as natural as breathing to slide out of her side of the booth and into his to wrap her arms around his strong shoulders and hug him. He'd certainly consoled and supported her enough times. And when he buried his face in her hair and held on tight, taking comfort from her, something squeezed deep inside her chest in the very best of ways.

"How do you tell family that *family* screwed you over?" he asked.

Jane let out a small mirthless huff of laughter. "Being an expert on the being-screwed-over end of things, I'd say this—just rip off the Band-Aid rather than skate around the truth."

"I don't want to tell them until I have everything I need to nail my sister's asshole soon-to-be-ex."

"Are you always the family fixer?" she asked.

He shrugged. Which was a yes, and something deep in her gut twinged. Suddenly she felt like that once-homeless eight-year-old clutching her backpack with everything she possessed in the world, waiting for her guardians to realize what everyone always did eventually—that she was unfixable.

The waitress came by and offered them dessert. They ordered a brownie and ice cream to share.

"You still thinking of sticking around Tahoe?" she asked, digging into the brownie, dragging it through the ice cream.

He looked out at the lake. "I told myself I didn't miss it here. But lately, when I think of this place, I feel an ache. I keep brushing it off, but since I've been home, it's only gotten stronger. I think it's an ache to be back here."

She knew that ache, knew it well. She just didn't know where her home was.

"Jane."

She looked up.

"Your turn. How was your day?"

"Mostly filled with ski-related incidents. Oh, but I did meet another new friend. There's a new hospital volunteer, and he came out to each clinic to leave books for the waiting rooms. He's going to be starting a small library for each location. He wants to follow a theme each month, and he's starting with wilderness and exploration. He even had cute pop-up books for kids. Such a sweet, kind man."

"Wilderness and exploration," Levi repeated in an oddly strangled voice. "And I suppose also the history of the region."

"Yes! How did you know?"

"Lucky guess." He took a long pull of his beer and shook his head. "My mom's been demon-dialing me. They're getting antsy, wanting to know if you're coming to the anniversary dinner."

"Oh." She bit her lower lip. "I can't think of a good excuse not to."

He laughed.

"It's not funny! But I promised, so yes, I'm coming to dinner. I should bring something."

"Bring something?"

"Yes! Your *real* girlfriend wouldn't just show up empty-handed at her first dinner with your parents. She'd bring something that she thought would mean something to them, a sort of a please-like-me gift."

"Not necessary," he said.

"It is! Help me. Can I bring something for the meal? Wine? Dessert?"

"Well . . ." He thought about it. "My mom's a great cook, but not a great baker."

"Okay," Jane said, hoping her panic wasn't showing. She was a shit baker. "I'll bake . . . something. I'll get a recipe from Charlotte."

"It's only fair that I help," he said on a smile.

"Are you looking for pretend date number three?"

"Yes. Just name the day and time and I'll be there."

She'd never brought a guy home before. Not that she had a home, but she did have Charlotte and Cat, and their opinions mattered to her. She nodded, and he smiled. Then he leaned in and kissed her, his hand sliding up her throat, his fingertips sinking into her hair, his thumb gliding along her jaw. He tasted like hopes and dreams and brownies, and she was breathless when he pulled back.

"Was that pretend too?" he asked, voice low and husky.

She had to clear her throat to talk. "*Extremely* pretend."

The corner of his mouth twitched. "Whatever helps you sleep at night."

CHAPTER 16

Charlotte pulled up her driveway at four in the afternoon. It was the first time she'd seen daylight in . . . well, she couldn't remember how long. She got out of her car, noticing that Mateo had at least ten cars in his driveway, and two right on top of the snow on his front lawn. A few more cars lined the street, now that she thought about it, even though there was no parking on the street allowed between November and April for snow removal.

What was going on?

She followed the sounds of wild laughter and screeching past the driveway and around the side of Mateo's house. The snow was deeper here, and she sank into several inches as she moved, her boots making a crunching sound. Just as she rounded the corner of the house to the back, she realized all noise had stopped. In the odd and sudden silence, she cleared the corner. And then . . . whoosh!

A snowball hit her right in the face, breaking apart on impact, its momentum taking her down to her ass in the snow.

"Oh shit!"

"Oh my God!"

"Did we kill her?"

Charlotte sat up and wiped the quickly melting snow from her eyes and mouth, just as a tall shadow dropped to its knees at her side.

"Charlotte?"

She didn't answer right away as she was spitting out some snow, so Mateo hauled her upright, holding on to her hands, and he stared down into her face, his own creased in deep concern. "Charlotte, say something."

She looked past his broad shadows to find a whole bunch of what looked like Morenos of all ages scattered in the yard, clearly in the midst of a killer snowball fight. "Who threw it?"

Every single person pointed to Mateo.

She swiveled her head and looked at him.

He grimaced. "Look, you were tiptoeing in the back way. I thought you were my cousin Rafe. He sneaked in last time and took me down."

She arched a brow. Or at least she thought she arched a brow, but since they were frozen, she couldn't be sure.

"I'm so sorry," he said quietly, stepping closer, cupping her face to tilt it up to his. "Did I hurt you?"

"Hmm," she said noncommittally and bent under the guise of rubbing her ankle. "I think I sprained something. Do you have a first aid kit?"

"Of course." He turned toward the house.

"Mateo?"

He turned back just as she rose upright again, patting the snow she'd just scooped up into a snowball as she did. Which she threw at him.

And nailed him.

Also in the face.

His family erupted in wild cheers.

She grinned and took a bow.

This got her an ovation.

Mateo, who hadn't fallen to his ass, straightened—snow in his hair, dripping off his nose and sticking to the stubble on his jaw—and just looked at her.

"Mateo, can we keep her for our team?" someone called out.

"No fair," someone else yelled. "She's got a wicked right arm. We need her on our side!"

"Charlotte," Mateo said and swept an arm across his yard, "meet my wild and crazy cousins. Primos, meet Dr. Charlotte Dixon. And she's far too civilized to play with this lot."

"I'm not that civilized," Charlotte said. "And I want to play against you."

Cheers broke out on one side of the yard, groans on the other side.

Mateo met her gaze, his own lit with humor but also challenge. "You sure?"

"Oh yeah." She shrugged off her purse and computer bag. Mateo put them on his patio table and turned back to her. "You should know, there's no rules. First one to call 'tío' gets a cease-fire and a loss."

He looked a little worried for her. Cute. She turned to her team. "Let's do this."

It was mayhem. It was chaos. It was rough-and-tumble. Snowballs flew so hard and fast that it was a constant, unrelenting battle, and Charlotte loved every second of it.

A snowball took her beanie right off her head. When she looked up, Mateo stood there with a wicked mischievous unrepentant grin.

She mirrored his expression and quickly formed a snowball. Ducking his next hit, she came up and threw, and nailed him right between the eyes.

He wavered, but didn't go down, so she launched herself at him, and then they were in free fall. Mateo landed flat on his back, cushioning her as she followed him down.

"Say it," she said, laughingly holding him down, knowing that if he wanted to, he could easily have flung her off him. "Say it," she said again, their noses nearly touching.

His hands went to her hips, his mouth curved, but definitely not saying a word.

"Say it, say it, say it," her team of Morenos began to chant.

Charlotte wiggled a bit, realizing she was getting cold as the snow had slowly seeped into her clothing. Mateo's hands tightened on her hips to hold her still, and suddenly his eyes had gone from amused to hot.

She stared down at him, time suddenly stopping as she gulped.

"Tío," he said huskily.

She cocked a hand around her ear, smiling as she said, "Excuse me? I didn't catch that."

His eyes narrowed playfully. "Why, Dr. Dixon, I forgot how viciously competitive you were."

"Never have tried to hide it." She smiled and hoisted another handful of snow threateningly. "Say it, Moreno." Amongst the cheers, he rolled her to her back, came over on top of her, and dropped a kiss to the tip of her icy nose. "Our next round is a one-on-one," he said for her ears only, and then rose, hauling her to her feet as well.

After that comment, she felt her knees wobbling, so he held on to her for an extra second. "Yeah?" he asked.

She drew a deep breath. "Yeah."

LEVI WAS AT his dad's desk, ostensibly working while also playing that kiss with Jane on repeat. Good thing he could multitask. He was putting together a PowerPoint presentation to explain all the shocking accounting discrepancies to his family in an orderly fashion. *And* to hopefully mitigate their panic while he was at it. He'd also come up with a few possible solutions for the now-struggling store, not to mention a list of the evidence needed to put Cal away. The thought gave him a pang for Peyton, who deserved better from her dad, but they'd deal with how to tell her when the time came.

The problem was the mitigation of panic. Cal had managed to get his hands on a lot of the Cutler money, enough to put them under if the store didn't bring in a lot of money quickly.

And the high revenue season—the holidays—was behind them. Knowing that, Levi planned to present the info in a way that they could stomach.

Or so he hoped.

Making it worse, Cal had gone off the grid. With some time and the right resources, Levi felt confident they'd be able to find him and haul his ass back to Tahoe to face his crimes. But one thing at a time.

Jasper padded into the room and gave a soft *woo woo*. Translation: he was hungry.

"You're always hungry," Levi said.

Jasper nudged his arm.

"You had dinner. In fact you had your dinner and half of mine, because when I got up to get a drink, you got up on your hind legs like Scooby-Doo and helped yourself to my plate."

Jasper lay his head on Levi's thigh and gave him the "I'm starving to death as you speak" eyes.

"You know the vet told Mom you've got to lose some weight."

At this, the dog huffed out a huge sigh and plopped to the floor, propping his face on Levi's shoe so he would know if Levi moved so much as a single inch.

Tess appeared in the doorway wearing oversize plaid pj's and crazy hair. She helped herself to Levi's bed—aka the couch—and sighed more dramatically than Jasper.

Levi knew this trap. He'd grown up with this trap. So he just kept working on his laptop.

Jasper abandoned him to jump up on the couch, all ninety pounds of him crawling into Tess's lap.

Another very loud sigh came from Tess as she scratched Jasper's head.

Levi gave up and looked at her.

"I just spent the last ten minutes helping Peyton look for the cupcake she got from school."

"And?"

"And . . . I ate it two hours ago."

Levi laughed. "Isn't it past her bedtime?"

"She got up to go potty. Then she wanted another story. And then she needed water. We were in the kitchen getting a cup of water when she noticed the cupcake was missing."

Of course she would notice. Not much got by his niece. "I assume you lied your ass off."

"Yeah." She sighed again and hugged Jasper. "I'm a terrible person."

"You're not a terrible person. You're a single mom on the edge."

Tess burst into tears. "Oh my God, I'm a single mom! I don't want to be a single mom! How did this happen to me?"

With a grimace, he got up from the desk and sat next to Tess.

Jasper, an equal opportunity hugger, crawled from Tess's lap to Levi's.

"It's not your fault," Levi told Tess. "Your husband is a big bag of dicks."

She sniffed. "Yeah." She stared up at the ceiling. "Today Peyton got mad at me when I wouldn't let Jasper drive her home from day care, when her bath was 'too wet,' and when I wouldn't buy her shoes like her friend Skylar. And please do note that there is no Skylar."

He laughed. "Sounds about right."

Tess sighed. "Not that I'd change a single thing about my precious girl, but sometimes her bedtime is my favorite time of the day. No, scratch that. Her falling *asleep* is my favorite time of day."

"Hate to break it to you, but she probably never went to sleep tonight. She just pretends, and then she goes under the covers with a flashlight and reads."

Tess smiled. "I know. She thinks reading past her bedtime is an act of rebellion. It hasn't yet occurred to her that her flashlights never seem to run out of batteries."

He smiled. "You're a good mom, Tess."

She blinked in surprise, looking unbearably touched. "Yeah?"

"Yeah."

"Thanks," she whispered and cleared her throat. "And you're a good uncle. I know she wakes you up every morning. I know she gets into your things and makes you have tea parties, and you never complain. I can't tell you how much it means to me that you're such a good male role model, when her dad can't love her enough to do right by her."

"He's an idiot." He shrugged. "And she's an easy kid to love."

Tess nodded, then laughed. "Scary how easy it is, even if half the time I'm pretty sure she needs an exorcism."

"Maybe it's a female thing."

She chucked a pillow at his face and it landed with the accuracy only an older sister could execute.

THE NEXT MORNING, Levi asked everyone to meet in the kitchen at the table at eight A.M. sharp. He was there with copies of his presentation and an open laptop, ready to start the slide show. Jasper sat at his side, clearly hoping the show included breakfast.

Levi's mom and dad showed up two minutes past the hour.

Tess came strolling in fifteen minutes later. "Sorry I'm late," she said. "I didn't want to come."

Levi didn't blame her. He didn't want to do this either. "Can everyone see my laptop screen?"

"I wouldn't worry about that," Tess said. "I caught Mom and Dad ears to the wall, fully eavesdropping on you earlier. So chances are, they already know whatever it is you want to tell us."

His mom glared at her beloved daughter. "That's going to cost you my chocolate chip cookies."

"I already ate them," Tess said.

His mom looked at Levi. "I'm sorry. But you were on the phone and I was hoping it was with Jane."

Levi drew a deep breath. Everyone in the house knew that the study was directly overhead. They also knew that if you put your ear to the wall behind him, the one with the doorway to the living room, you could clearly hear every word said in the study. "I was on work calls. For Cutler Analytics."

"I know. It was very boring," his mom said, looking disappointed. "Though I did hear you swearing."

"I was swearing because your printer is ancient and prints a page a year. I'm buying you a new one."

"We don't need a new one," his dad said. "That printer works just fine. A new one will only break. They don't make things like they used to."

"Dad, you have to shake the ink cartridge after every page you print."

"So she's a bit touchy, that's all," his dad grumbled. "She still has a lot of ink left in that cartridge—don't replace it. Those fuckers are expensive. And I still don't see why we couldn't have done this in the study."

"Or in the living room on the comfy couches," his mom said.

"You don't allow liquor on the couches," Levi said, handing out glasses of orange juice. Then he grabbed the vodka from the freezer, pouring a healthy shot into the OJ glasses.

"It's eight A.M.," his mom said.

"Eight seventeen," Levi said. "Which means that somewhere, it's five seventeen. And a mimosa contains thirty-two percent of your suggested dose of vitamin C, so you're welcome." Then he pregamed by downing his.

His mom stared at him, looking worried. "It must be bad if my most well-behaved child is drinking so early."

"Excuse me," Tess said. "Most well-behaved child?"

"Honey, when you graduated and I went to have a little celebratory . . . 'mimosa,' my vodka was nothing but water."

"Fine," Tess allowed. "But Levi screwed up plenty too."

"He was an angel," his mom said.

Levi winced.

"Oh my God," Tess said, tossing up her hands. "He's no angel. You just never caught him at anything."

True story. "*Focus*," he said. He handed out the folders with the evidence of Cal's creative accounting, along with Levi's plan on how to steer the damaged ship without going under. "I've also sent each of you the digital file."

"What is this?" his mom asked, flipping through the pages.

"It's an accounting of where the store stands financially. I've run all the monthly and year-end reports, so what you're looking at are the balance sheets for the different departments, all of which have their own bottom line, debt-to-income ratios, accounts receivable and payables, assets, and inventory orders."

"Why does it look so much worse than last year?" his dad asked.

"Because it *is* worse than last year." Levi paused. "Orders were placed for store inventory, *large* orders. The money left your account to pay for those orders, but we never received the inventory."

"Well, that doesn't make any sense," Tess said. "Cal was in charge of all of that . . ." She gasped softly. "Oh my God."

His dad ran a hand down his face. "Fuck."

"Hank!" his mother gasped.

His dad slugged his OJ down.

Jasper farted. At least Levi was pretty sure it was Jasper.

Tess looked like she wanted to throw up. Instead, she also drank. Swallowed. Pounded her chest. Then pointed at Levi. "Are you telling me that the lying son of a bitch I'm still married to was stealing from Mom and Dad to fund his new life with his girlfriend on some gorgeous island near Bali that he could never find the time to take me to?"

He nodded grimly. "It looks like he was creating invoices for fictitious accounts to funnel the money to himself."

"Fictitious accounts?" his mom asked.

"Yeah, there are a bunch. One of them is called Buffy Slater."

His mom drank her glass down.

"*What?*" his sister shrieked and leapt to her feet. "Buffy Slater is the babysitter's name! We need to sue. We need to call the police! We need to kick his ass!"

"Yes," Levi said, pouring her another drink, nudging it toward her. "All of that, and not necessarily in that order."

Peyton stuck her head in the kitchen. She was in Wonder Woman pj's, hair looking like an explosion in a mattress factory, her face pink as if she'd been sleeping on it. "Hi! I wanna have a drink too!"

His sister drew in a steadying breath. "Not now, baby."

"Okay. Then can I have candy for breakfast?"

Levi went to the pantry and came out with a single-serving-size packet of natural fruit gummy bears and a to-go box of apple juice.

Peyton beamed her thanks. "Will you come to my tea party? I'm all set up in my room."

He crouched in front of her, opened the gummy bears for her, and then ruffled her hair. "Give me a few minutes."

"My mommy says that, but a few minutes never happens."

"Have I ever not come to you when I said I would?"

She thought about that. Then shook her head.

"So I'll see you in a few minutes," he said.

"Okay, but don't forget to dress up as a girl superhero! Only girl superheroes can come into my room."

He grimaced, but his sister pointed at the screen. "How long?" she whispered. "How long has this been going on?"

Shit. Levi really didn't want to tell her this. He gave Peyton a kiss on the forehead and gently nudged her out of the kitchen. Then he rose to his full height and looked at his sister. "Two years."

His mom grabbed the vodka bottle and refilled everyone's glass. Minus the juice.

His dad jabbed a finger at the laptop. "You didn't need this whole virtual presentation, or whatever you want to call it, to tell us our business is going under. You could've just called me into the office and had a meeting. Man-to-man."

Levi's mom whipped around to stare at him. "Why? So you could hide the fact that our company's going under? And then what would happen, Hank? You'd shoulder all that responsibility on your own and keep it from us?"

"This is all my fault," Tess moaned, dropping her forehead to the table and giving it a few hits. "Everyone needs to stop arguing. I'm the one who's going to fix this mess."

"Nonsense." His dad's fist hit the table and all the glasses did a little jump. Everyone grabbed theirs to keep them from spilling, and then, looking at one another, shrugged and drank again.

"*I'm* the one who gave that SOB a job," his dad said. "Instead, I should've kicked his ass."

Peyton poked her head in. "Uncle Levi? You're taking too long!"

Levi went back to the pantry, grabbed a box of cereal, and handed it to her.

She squealed with delight and vanished again.

"Are you kidding me?" Tess asked him.

"Hey, it was crunchy granola, not Frosted Flakes."

His mom pointed a spoon at her husband. "I need to know what you meant by your previous comment. Are you saying it's *my* fault, since I was the one who told you to give Cal a chance?"

"I'm just saying I should have gone with my instincts. If I had, we wouldn't be in this mess."

Tess drew a shaky breath. "I'm the one who should never have given him a chance. If you'll excuse me, I'm going to go back to bed and stay there until my life's on a better track."

"I want to go back to bed too," Levi's mom said.

Levi stood up. "No one's going back to bed. We need to talk, so everyone just take a deep breath and—"

"And what," his dad growled. "Stare at the stupid PowerPoint some more?"

"Hank!" This from his mom.

"Yes, I want you to look at the PowerPoint," Levi said as calmly as he could. He clicked over to the next slide. "Here you'll see I've created a five-step plan for how to get the store out of debt."

Dad stood up. "No offense, son, but I'm not going to find the answers on how to get my store back on its feet by watching a slide show from a tech guy."

"Dad, you *know* he's more than a tech guy," Tess said with censure in her voice. "He consults with businesses on how to manage their data, and—"

Their dad shook his head. "This isn't about data either."

"Hank, stop taking this out on Levi," his mom snapped at her husband. "He's just trying to help."

His dad was quiet a moment. Ran a hand down his face. "You're right." He looked Levi in the eyes with sincere remorse. "We appreciate what you've done. I just need a minute." He took another shot and walked out.

Levi let out a rough breath. *This isn't about you*, he reminded himself. His dad was battling his own ego. Cal had stolen money out from beneath the guy's nose, and that wasn't going to sit well.

His mom patted him on the arm. "I know it doesn't seem like it, but he loves you very much. We're grateful for your help, but I better go check on him. When he gets worked up like this, it's bad for his blood pressure."

When they were alone, Levi turned to his sister. "Dad has blood pressure problems?"

"Dad's got a lot of problems." She got up and patted him like his mom had done. She left too, and a moment later he heard the shower go on in her bathroom.

Levi looked at his PowerPoint, which for the record still had ten pages left to go on the plan that would've shown them how he could help fix some of the most immediate problems.

Square peg, round hole.

He eyed the vodka. Tempting. But there was a cure far better than alcohol, and her name was Jane. He wanted nothing more than to go drown himself in her pretty green eyes and the smile that made him forget all the bad shit. But at the moment, he had another woman waiting, one he couldn't disappoint.

Peyton beamed her welcome when he appeared in her doorway, and Levi felt a slight warming in the region of his cold heart. "I don't have a superhero costume. May I still come in?"

"Yes! And here, I'll help you." She pulled off her sash and wrapped it around his head like a bandanna. "Sit!" she commanded.

So he sat at her tiny little table in a chair that barely fit half his ass. But he made it work and drank her pretend tea and ate her pretend cookies, and they plotted how Superwoman might save the world if she was real.

JUST AFTER NIGHTFALL, Levi was on a Zoom call with clients when his cell phone buzzed an incoming text from Jane.

> **JANE:** I'm stuck and could use some help.

He immediately got out of his meeting and called her. "Jane."
"Yep."
She sounded not at all like herself. "Where are you?" he asked.
Silence.
"Jane?"
"I'll text you the address."
Yeah, definitely not herself, and maybe even tearful. His gut clenched. "Are you safe?"
But she'd disconnected.
He recognized the street name she'd given him, so he headed

out. The night seemed to glow thanks to the reflection of moon-light bouncing off the snow. Just outside of Sunrise Cove, he turned and headed up a hill from the lake. Here the streets were narrow thanks to thick snow berms on either side, some single file only because they'd barely been snowplowed. He shifted into four-wheel drive and kept going.

A handful of turns and five minutes later, he saw Jane's car. Dark. No lights. He parked behind her and got out, realizing she was sitting behind the wheel. He slid into her front passenger seat. "Why wasn't this locked?"

She let out a mirthless laugh and tipped her head back, staring up at the roof of her car. "There's not a lot of people who would ask me that."

"Then I'll make sure to keep asking." He reached out and let his fingertips brush the nape of her neck, wanting to comfort, but also not wanting to push her before she was ready. "Are you okay?"

Instead of answering, she closed her eyes. "I'm short on brave tonight. You got any to spare?"

"You can have any of me you want." *Or all of me . . .* "You said you were stuck."

"I think my battery's dead."

"That's easy enough." He looked around. "Where are we?"

"Up that steep driveway is my grandpa's cabin."

And with that, he finally understood. She was going to go talk to her grandpa for the first time in twenty years. "You've got this, Jane."

That got him a ragged but real laugh. "How do you always know the right thing to say?"

Now *he* laughed, thinking of his family and how they might

disagree. But Jane, a woman who didn't have a lot of reasons to trust anyone, trusted him. It had a warm glow filling his chest. "I never know the right thing to say."

She turned her head, met his gaze, and gave him a small smile. "You just get lucky?"

Her smile turned his heart upside down. "Once in a blue moon."

CHAPTER 17

Jane drew a deep breath at the way Levi was looking at her. Like she meant something to him, like she was important, at least enough to drive out in a storm for her. She'd texted him instinctively, not even thinking about it, which was a statement all on its own about how much she trusted him. And he'd shown up, no questions asked. "Thank you," she said softly.

"Happy to help."

She nodded. "Happy," she repeated softly and then shook her head. "I think I've had a problem letting myself be happy."

"Cherophobia."

She looked at him. "What?"

"It's the fear of being happy."

She laughed and felt some of the tension drain from her. "Thanks for that too, for always knowing what to say to brighten my day."

He smiled. "But it's night."

"You know what I mean."

His smile faded. "I do. And you should know . . . you do the same for me." He pulled off his ski cap and unzipped his jacket, even though the interior of her car was cold. She'd turned it off half an hour ago to save gas.

Then he put the ski cap on her head, wrapped her up in his jacket, and zipped it up to her chin, letting his fingers brush her jaw. "Better?"

Okay, so he had a question, but only one, and with that single word, uttered in his low, calm voice that said together they could handle anything, she knew that somehow it was going to be okay. "Yes." And not just because she was now enveloped in his body heat, but also because his scent was teasing her. Something woodsy and very male. "I need to go talk to my grandpa about the ornament."

He nodded, clearly not wanting to influence her on this, trusting her to be a grown-up. Which meant that she needed to actually be a grown-up.

They both looked up the driveway to the small old cabin at the top. A light flickered in the kitchen, her favorite kitchen in the whole wide world. Some of the best memories of her life had taken place there. The place had always seemed warm, and there'd been copious amounts of hot chocolate made with love, complete with marshmallows. "I've been avoiding this a long time," she murmured.

"I know. Just a reminder, you didn't do anything wrong."

"But—"

Very gently, he set a finger to her lips. "You didn't, Jane. No one in their right mind would blame an eight-year-old who was at the mercy of her relatives after her parents walked away from her."

She closed her eyes, then felt Levi's hand slip into hers. Even without his jacket and hat, he was warm and solid. Her only anchor at the moment.

"Will he be alone?" he asked.

"I don't know. Near as I can tell, my aunt Viv sold her house here in Sunrise Cove a bunch of years back. Word is her husband got a job on the East Coast and they all moved there."

Levi raised his right, scarred brow.

"Yeah," she said on a laugh. "I've got some excellent stalking skills."

"Good riddance. Come here, Jane."

She leaned in closer, but apparently that wasn't close enough because he hauled her up and over the console, effortlessly dropping her into his lap.

"What—"

He wrapped his deliciously warm arms around her and cuddled her into him.

"*Mmm*," she heard herself purr and pressed her face to his throat.

He dipped his head so he could meet her gaze, but she didn't know how to take the way he looked at her. Like he cared. Like he wanted to hurt someone for what she'd been through. Like he wanted to touch her. She'd honestly expected him to recoil from her history, from how screwed up she was. Instead, he'd done the opposite.

"What do you want to do?" he asked, his calloused thumb making slow sweeps over the knuckles of her hand.

Still with her face in the crook between his throat and shoulder, she just breathed him in for a moment. "I *want* to run away," she admitted. "Just like I always do. But I *need* to go talk to him."

"I'll go with you if you want."

The offer surprised and warmed her from tip to toe, and she squeezed him before lifting her head. "Just knowing you would helps. But I think I've got to do this alone. I'm sorry I called you out here before I did this."

"Don't be sorry. I'll wait. As long as you need."

She let out a breath, not taking that promise lightly. She wasn't sure how or when they'd become friends for real or when he'd become so important to her, but she felt grateful for him. "Thanks," she whispered, inadequate but all she could think of in the moment. She reached for the door handle, then hesitated, her heart pounding in her ears.

"Quick like a Band-Aid," he said quietly.

She snorted. "Do you and your family ever stop speaking to each other?"

He laughed, drawing her eyes. He was genuinely amused. "All the time. They mean well, but I'm very different from them, and different is sometimes hard to accept."

She pressed her forehead to his. "I like different."

"For which I'm grateful. You've got this, Jane."

She eyed the little cabin. "You sure?"

"Hey, you survived a near-fatal fall from a gondola. You regularly put yourself in war zones to save people's lives. You agreed to go to dinner with my crazy family. Trust me, you can handle this. Either way, I'll be waiting right here."

With a wobbly smile, she nodded, drew a deep breath, got out of the car, and walked up to the front door and knocked.

She wasn't sure what she planned to say, and the door opened far too soon, because suddenly her grandpa was standing there, squinting at her through bifocals perched on the end of his nose. He gasped, put a hand to his chest, and whispered, "Sugar Plum?"

She hadn't been sure what she would feel when face-to-face with him, and she still wasn't beyond the slight nausea of all the butterflies taking flight in her belly. "Hi, Grandpa."

His smile was trembling and there was a suspicious shininess to his eyes now as he reached for her hand. "You're actually here."

"Is that okay?"

At her question, a shadow passed over his face, but his voice, trembling before, was strong now. "Yes. More than anything. I'm sorry if you doubted it for even a second."

"There were more than a few seconds," she said, not willing to let herself be moved by his obvious emotions at seeing her.

"I deserve that," he said quietly. "Can . . . can I hug you, Jane?"

The eight-year-old in her spoke before the grown-up in her could, whispering yes.

He pulled her into his arms and pressed his cheek to hers. "Thank you," he said, holding on tight. "You're so much braver than I've ever been."

Leaving that statement alone for now, she pulled back. "You smell the same."

"It's mothballs."

She choked out a laugh as his gaze searched hers. "Did you get it?"

She pulled the ornament from her pocket.

"You carry it with you." He looked unbearably touched by that. "Come in, come in, before you catch your death!"

She followed him past the well-lived-in front room she remembered so vividly. She'd bounced on that very couch, huddled up to the woodstove for heat after playing in the snow. "It's the same," she whispered.

He shrugged. "I like the same." He brought her into the kitchen. "Let me make us something warm to drink. Sit."

She sat at the same scarred wood table where she'd memorized her multiplication tables and learned how to write in cursive. She could see the small burn she'd created when she knocked over one of her grandma's candles. And the Sharpie mark she'd accidentally left doing a school assignment.

Her grandpa brought her hot cocoa with marshmallows and whipped cream. "My favorite."

"I know." He hesitated. "I bought it the day I saw you watching me in the diner. I was stunned to see you, and . . ." His eyes went misty. "At first I was certain you were my imagination playing tricks on me. But then I saw you were wearing your grandma's necklace." He gave her a small smile. "And I knew. I knew it was you, even after all these years."

"I saw you too."

"Ah. I wasn't sure. You took off pretty quickly, and I knew after what I'd done, that I had to give you the time you deserved to decide if you wanted to see me."

Her throat felt tight. It'd been two years since she'd found him in Sunrise Cove, and she'd hesitated to make contact. For her own reasons, of course, and she knew those reasons were valid. But he'd seen her what, a week ago, and hadn't hesitated. Food for thought. "What you did?"

He looked away as if ashamed. "I let you go, Jane." He met her eyes again, and indeed, it was shame swimming in his rheumy blues. "I've never forgiven myself for that." He studied her for a beat. "I have a lot to make up for, but I want you to know that I've been dreaming of a second chance with you. I started with the ornament. It was a blatant bribe, but also a way to approach you without your feeling forced into something you weren't ready for."

She searched for the right words, but were there any? "I'm glad you made contact," she said carefully. "I always figured that if you'd wanted to see me after all that had happened, you'd get in touch."

"After all that happened?"

"You know, when you and Viv fought over me and it destroyed your relationship."

He looked stricken. "How do you know that?"

"She told me about it back then, how keeping me would have been too hard on you."

He sighed. Scrubbed a hand over his face. "She shouldn't have told you that. The truth is, Viv and I *always* fought. That wasn't your fault, Jane."

"It felt like it."

He drew a shaky breath. "I'm sorry for that. So sorry. Please believe me, none of it was your fault." He paused. "Do you remember what I used to tell you?"

"That Santa Claus was real? Which, by the way . . ."

That got her a small smile. "I meant when I once told you that family is blood. I was wrong. Family, real family, has nothing to do with blood. Family is who you pick. And I've not done a bang-up job of it with you. Your aunt Viv, and for that matter, also your mom . . . they are who they are. I'm angry that I allowed them to sabotage our relationship, that Viv made you feel like not only were you a burden, but that you weren't wanted. But mostly I'm angry with myself that I didn't come to you years ago. I don't even have an excuse other than shame. You have no reason to believe me, but I want you to know you are my family, Jane. The family that I'm choosing. Maybe it's too little too late, but you should know that I'm ashamed I waited so long to try and connect with you. Ashamed, and so very, very sorry. But I choose you. If you'll have me."

Jane lost the battle with her tears, as did her grandpa. They moved toward each other and held on tight for a long moment while she grappled with her emotions.

"Are you okay?" he asked quietly. "And the answer doesn't have to be yes."

"That's good, because I'm not sure how I am." She sniffed and gave a slow shake of her head. "I'm sorry."

"Don't be. I can accept your not being sure. It's better than a flat-out no." He looked out the window. "Do you want to talk about that handsome young fellow waiting out in the cold?"

Nope. Definitely not. She shook her head.

"Sugar Plum." He removed his fogged-up glasses to wipe them on his sweater. "It's twenty-two degrees outside."

And she was wearing his jacket and hat . . . "I can't stay."

He nodded his acceptance of that. "Maybe next time then, you'll let him come in."

Was there going to be a next time? She hadn't been sure, but now she was feeling maybe having a next time might be good. "Maybe."

He smiled, still looking emotional. And tired. And damn, older than she wanted him to be.

"When?" he asked. "I want to write it down because if my memory gets any worse, I could plan my own surprise party."

"Maybe we could have dinner one night after work."

"You just tell me when and where and I'll be there," he said.

She nodded and then put her contact info into his phone, which made him beam so happily it gave her a hard pang. "I'm going to go before *Family Feud* comes on, which you used to always watch after your stretching routine. You still do that, right?"

"Yes. It's a doctor requirement now, ever since . . ." He broke off. "Er . . ."

"Since your heart attack?"

Her grandpa winced guiltily. "You know about that?"

"Yes. Your cronies are all on Facebook. They posted pics visiting you in the hospital."

Her grandpa looked pained. "I told them the interweb is a terrible place, and I want no part of it. I need to call Facebook and have them delete all the pictures and burn the negatives."

"Yeah, that's not how it actually works—"

"*All* the negatives!"

Because his eyes were twinkling, she smiled. But she still wasn't ready to let him off the hook. "I assume you're eating well? Getting some walking in when it's not icy?"

"I'm fine," he said, waving all that off. "It's my damn TV that isn't. My friend Doug's grandson is selling TVs now, and he convinced me to upgrade my system. But the buttons are too small on the remote and I can't figure out how to do anything. I'm stuck on some sappy movie channel. I mean, what are the chances of that? I couldn't get stuck on, say, ESPN?"

Jane walked into the living room and looked his system over.

"It's voice activated. We could set it up so you can just talk to your remote."

"Talk to my remote?" He shook his head like she'd just said he could visit Mars.

"Almost as crazy as the Santa Claus story," she said dryly.

He had the good grace to laugh. "I just wanted you to believe in something good."

Her heart squeezed hard enough to hurt, but she concentrated on setting up his system and . . . failed. "Okay, I'm going to have to call in tech support," she finally admitted.

"It's a little late . . ."

"Oh, don't you worry, this tech support's open 24/7." She pulled out her phone and called Levi.

He answered with "You okay?"

Her heart swelled against her rib cage. "I am. I'm actually calling for tech support. You available?"

"Always."

She disconnected. "He'll be right here."

The doorbell rang and her grandpa's brows went up, but he headed to the door. "Are you her fellow?" he asked Levi.

Levi looked past him to Jane, and she felt him taking visual inventory. His gaze slowed on her face and she knew he could see the trace of tears.

"Right now I'm tech support," he said to her grandpa.

"And later?"

"Whatever she needs me to be."

Jane felt her heart warm for Levi in a whole new way as her grandpa let Levi in.

CHAPTER 18

Levi kept his gaze on Jane, wanting a sign from her that she was okay. She gave him a small smile, looking emotional but more relaxed than she'd been in the car.

"Grandpa," she said, "this is Levi Cutler. Levi, this is my grandpa, Lloyd Parks."

Her grandpa was the same height as Jane, and round and solid as a tree trunk. He wore round spectacles, but was looking over the top of them at Levi. He had a wild mane of white hair that seemed to defy gravity—except for the bald spot at the top—and a beard that ensured he could pass for Santa if he wanted. "Nice to meet you, Mr. Parks," he said and shook the man's hand.

"Call me Lloyd," her grandpa said. "In fact, if you can fix my TV, you can call me whatever you want."

"I'll do my best." Levi put a hand on Jane's shoulder, running it lightly down her arm to squeeze her fingers.

She smiled and squeezed back. She was okay, at least for now. Good enough for him.

She brought him over to the TV and handed him the remote.

"Hope this is in your realm of expertise." Then she turned to her grandpa. "Did you have dinner?"

"Yes, and the hot cocoa was excellent."

"Grandpa, when someone has a heart attack, that someone should change his entire way of living, including how he eats."

Her grandpa smiled. "You've got your grandma's bossiness."

She pointed at him. "Don't try to distract me with sentiment, because trust me, my heart's hard as stone. Did you really not eat yet?"

"I had some cookies."

"*Grandpa.*"

"I need them."

"You *don't* need them."

"Kuchi zamishi," Levi said.

Lloyd laughed in delight and pointed at him. "Exactly! See, he gets it!"

Jane looked at Levi, clearly waiting for the translation.

"Kuchi zamishi is a Japanese saying. It's the act of eating because your mouth is lonely," Levi said.

"Hence the cookies," Lloyd explained to Jane.

She narrowed her eyes. "You're saying you eat bad because you're lonely?"

"Maybe?"

"I'd remind you of whose fault that is," she said. "But I don't think you need the reminder. You're going to start taking better care of yourself."

"I—"

"You will," she said. "So that when I come back, you can tell me about it."

Lloyd's voice softened. "I will." He dropped himself into the recliner that had clearly seen a lot of years and looked at Levi with a wry smile. "My sweet, gentle, mild-mannered granddaughter."

"She's a lot of things," Levi agreed. "All of them incredibly great, but . . ." He smiled at Jane. "I'm not sure mild-mannered is one of them."

She rolled her eyes.

"I know," Lloyd said proudly. "She's amazing, isn't she?"

Jane went into the kitchen. A moment later they heard her mutter, "Oh my God. You're using real butter, cream cheese, and whipped cream? *Seriously?*"

Lloyd cackled, clearly enjoying himself.

As for Levi, he was enjoying watching Jane handle her grandpa. Not giving away her heart, holding her thoughts close to the vest, but being far more open than he'd imagined she'd be. In spite of her wariness, she was being sweet. Caring. Real. It was clear her grandpa loved it. And her, at least in his own way.

And crazy as it seemed, Levi was pretty sure he was heading that way himself. Shaking his head, he turned to his task. The TV.

"So . . ." Lloyd said, watching him work. "You and Jane seem close."

"Hmm," he said noncommittally. He held out the remote. "Okay, I think we've got it. Let me show you how to use this. I'll also write down the password for you."

"You think I'm old enough to forget things?"

Levi slid him a look. "I don't think age has anything to do with . . . *forgetting* things." Or people . . .

Lloyd held his gaze, then nodded grimly. "Yeah. But I intend to work on that."

"Good."

The old man sighed. "I'm glad you don't want to kick my ass. I'd like to kick my own ass for letting so much time pass."

"Not my place," Levi said, but didn't offer any empty platitudes about it being okay. Because it wasn't. Not in his book.

Lloyd gave a gruff nod. "Not letting me off the hook. I get that. I deserve that. She got passed around more than an offering basket in church, and I blame myself for that too. I let my grief overwhelm me, and then I let my embarrassment over how I'd handled things keep me from finding her. I don't deserve her, but I intend to try and make up for whatever I can for as long as she'll let me."

As frustrating as Levi's own family could be, he knew they'd never pretend he didn't exist or treat him like he wasn't welcome. "I hope that's true."

"It is. She deserved more from us, and I'm hoping it's not too late."

"If you two are finished gossiping, dinner's on the table."

The two men turned and found Jane standing there, arms crossed.

Lloyd looked like a kid caught with his hand in the candy jar. "We were just—"

"I know." Jane met his gaze. "I found frozen chicken bowls in your freezer. They're a little freezer burned, but there's veggies in them, so let's eat."

The old man got a little misty-eyed. "You made dinner."

"Well, 'made' is a bit strong. More like pushed a few buttons. Last one to the table has to clean up."

Her grandpa rushed to follow her into the kitchen. Never having minded the mindless task of dishes—it let his brain settle—Levi followed more slowly, watching Jane. Something about her was different tonight. She was still the kickass, smart-as-hell woman he was starting to get to know on a level he hadn't expected. But there was something new. She seemed . . . just a little more open.

And right then and there, he vowed to see that look on her face as often as possible. He wanted to be with her as often as possible. And where the hell that had come from and how it had sneaked up on him, he had no idea. He didn't want to be just another person in a long line of people who'd hurt her, but truth was truth.

She was leaving at the end of the season. And he . . . well, that'd been his original plan, but his goal was shifting, changing. But even when—yes, when, not if—he changed his home base back to Tahoe, he knew she wouldn't do the same. She already had a contract for her next job.

They had an expiration date, him and Jane.

And playing pretend wasn't going to change that or keep them from getting hurt. Nothing was. Unless he somehow changed her mind about him being a keeper.

CHAPTER 19

An hour later, Jane watched Levi out of her peripheral vision as he drove her home. He'd tried giving her battery a jump, but no go. He'd told her he'd get it charged in the morning. She'd told him not to worry about it, she had roadside service and would get a ride out there before work to get it handled.

And she would. She didn't need to waste any more of his rare free time helping her. Besides, if he kept being so nice to her, she'd forget. Right now it was pretend, and pretend was awesome because pretend wasn't real. Pretend was better than real any day of the week.

Levi was in a driving zone, watching the road, his hand on the gear stick, shifting into lower gears as needed. There were no streetlights out here, because the original town planners wanted the Tahoe night sky to shine bright.

And that it did.

It was no longer snowing, which always meant the temperature dropped even more. The roads had iced up, making her more than a little relieved to not be the one driving. The sky was a black velvet blanket upon which countless millions of stars glittered like diamonds. Having been all over the world, she could honestly say she'd never seen a sky so gorgeous as the one above Lake Tahoe.

Tonight . . . tonight had been a lot for her, though it'd gone better than she could have imagined. She honestly hadn't been sure she could actually knock on her grandpa's door and face him. But then Levi had shown up and soothed a place deep inside her where she kept her vulnerability and fear hidden from the rest of the world. With one easy smile, he'd made her feel like she could do anything.

And she'd faced her past.

"Thanks for tonight," she said quietly.

Without taking his eyes off the road, he reached for her hand, bringing it up to his mouth to brush a kiss to her palm. "After that night on the gondola and all we went through, I'd probably do anything for you, Jane."

As far as confessions went, that seemed like a doozy, at least according to the way her heart kicked it into gear. And he didn't seem to have any regrets about saying it either. She took in his profile by the ambient light of the dashboard. He had a few days' scruff on him that she loved. It went with his wavy hair that never quite behaved, and she loved that too. He was unapologetically himself, not to mention strong and steady, and . . . hot as hell.

"See something you like?" he teased and nipped at the palm he still had hold of.

Her insides quivered. Some outside parts quivered too. "Yes."

Clearly surprised at her response, he met her gaze briefly, then turned back to the road. "Good, because I can hardly take my eyes off you."

The words were more of a promise than an admission, and

something deep inside her shifted and clicked into place. For years she'd let herself be tossed around in the wind like a wild tumbleweed. And yet suddenly she felt anchored for the first time in . . . maybe forever. "Levi?"

He glanced over again.

"I'm not ready to go home," she said softly.

This got her another, slightly longer look. "Where should we go?"

We. She closed her eyes a beat. That's what she got from Levi. Unconditional support. Total acceptance. "Anywhere quiet."

"Trust me?" he asked.

He'd asked her that very same thing not too long ago, and she'd said no. But at some point over the past few weeks, her answer had changed. "I do."

He turned on the next road and suddenly they were going up a hill. And up.

And up.

Fifteen minutes later, they'd left all signs of Sunrise Cove behind and were on what was surely normally a dirt road but was currently covered with snow. Levi's four-wheel drive easily handled the road, and though she could see nothing past the midnight-black night and the dark outline of trees, he clearly knew exactly where he was going.

Finally he took a hairpin curve and stopped the truck.

She took in the view and gasped.

Above, a half-moon hung in the sky, streaked with fingerlike clouds, all of it surrounded by shimmering, twinkling stars, more than she'd ever seen in her life. With no city lights to mask anything, they had a clear view for as far as the eye could see. Far below lay the dark outline of Lake Tahoe, which she'd never seen from this angle, hundreds of feet up. "It's like we're on top of the world," she whispered.

"We are. We're up on the Tahoe Rim Trail. At 9,500 feet."

"Wow." She stared out at the night, enthralled and awed. "I don't even have words."

"Same."

She turned to find him with a forearm braced on the wheel, his other hand on her headrest, watching her. Thoughts hidden. She sensed a careful restraint, a rare hesitation.

She felt neither of those things. Around him, she'd never been able to control her emotions. Now was no exception, but he'd never seemed to have that problem, always steady, calm, in full control.

What would it take to make him lose that control? And why did she want to see it so badly . . . right now?

As if he could read her mind, he let out a rough laugh, the sound scraping at all her good parts. He'd come through for her tonight, giving her what she'd asked for, no questions. No pressure. No sense of impatience.

She'd asked for somewhere quiet. In the moment, she'd meant for somewhere to just be and think. She hadn't been ready to go home and call it a night, but her wants had changed. She wanted to climb over the console, straddle him, and have her merry way with him.

"I smell something burning," he murmured.

She let out a quiet laugh because yeah, she was *definitely* thinking too hard. "It's just that what I want seems . . . a little forward."

His eyes darkened. "You have my full attention."

With a nervous laugh, she pulled out her phone. "So . . . I found another questionnaire."

He groaned. "Not where I thought you were going with this." His hand, the one on the headrest of her seat, slipped to the nape of her neck, making thinking difficult. "Thought maybe we were past the quick tricks of the getting-to-know-you stage."

"It's called Ten Questions You Need to Ask Your Partner Before Having Sex."

He stared at her for a beat, then let out a smile that melted her bones. "Hit me."

Nodding, suddenly nervous, she looked down at the first question. *Are you attracted to your potential sexual partner?* Since that was a given, she skimmed past it. "Um . . . where's your favorite place to be kissed?"

This won her a slow, mischievous grin. "In bed or out of bed?"

She laughed, and just like that, her nerves vanished. She had no idea how he always did that, lightened her world every single time, but he was good at it. "Either," she whispered.

He pointed to his lips, and she shook her head with another laugh. "Yeah, I'm betting that's actually your *second* favorite place to be kissed, but sure, let's start there." Heart pounding, she unbuckled her seat belt, came up on her knees, and leaned over him. She put one hand on the back of his seat, the other on his chest, and started with a light closed-mouth kiss to one corner of his mouth, her plan to move slowly, wanting to drive him nuts, wanting to see him lose that famed control.

"Jane—"

"Hmm?" She bypassed his mouth for the second kiss because his jaw called to her, and then his sexy throat.

He shivered and his hands tightened on her. "If you want the same thing I do, we're in the wrong place."

"I like this place."

"So do I. A lot. But we're outside. In public."

"We're in a truck, and there's no one else out here, probably for miles. And besides, I'm just kissing you."

"Yeah, but—" He broke off with a sharply indrawn breath when she sank her teeth into his lower lip and gave a little tug.

His scent was delicious, and she heard herself moan in protest as he caught her wandering hands, which had opened his jacket and were working to get beneath his Henley. "Jane . . . I didn't bring you up here for this."

"I know. Also, I lied about the just kissing."

"Jane—"

She lifted her head. "You're not going to turn down your pretend girlfriend, are you?"

"Like I could turn you down for anything."

That made her smile. "Then there's just one more thing to discuss . . ."

"I've got a condom in my glove box. At least, I used to. It's been a while . . ."

Her heart warmed that he would think to tell her either of those things. "I was going to remind you not to fall for me."

His rough laugh made her grin, and then he caught her mouth in a kiss that was soft and sweet, but made her think of things hot and bare and sweaty—

"My turn to ask," he said huskily, lifting his head. "Where do *you* like to be kissed?"

"Um . . . everywhere?"

His eyes went molten lava as he hauled her over the console and into his lap so she could straddle him. With her knees tight at his sides, he slid his hands up her back and into her hair, pulling her down for a kiss that quickly ignited.

She couldn't get close enough, and seeing pleasure cross his face, hearing it seep into his voice, assured her he felt the same. His knowing hands went about discovering every sweet spot, shifting clothing aside as needed. Somehow they managed to free the essentials, and sweet baby Jesus, his essentials . . . He came up with the promised condom and she nearly collapsed in gratitude that one of them was capable of rational thought. She took it from him and fumbled with it a bit. He tried to take over, but she wanted to do it, and smiled while he quivered and swore and begged her to get on with it. The second she had them protected, he lifted her and then lowered her down until she'd taken all of him.

Time stopped, completely stopped while they both took in the shocking, heart-stopping pleasure of being one. She'd started this, wanting to see him lose control, but *she* was the one doing just that. They moved in unison, together, until she was lost, rocking against him, fingers digging for purchase as waves of release hit her like a tidal wave.

She had no idea how long it took her to come back to herself, but when she opened her eyes, Levi's face was still buried in her neck. He took several long, deep breaths before lifting his head. With the same hands that had just taken her to heaven and back, he adjusted their position so that she could slouch against him and set her head on his shoulder.

More time passed as he slowly swept his hands up and down her back. At one point, he started to say something and then stopped.

"What?" she whispered.

"I actually don't have words."

"Is that a good or bad thing?"

He nudged her face from the crook of his shoulder. Cupping it in his big hands, he kissed her, putting a whole bunch of what he was thinking into the kiss, so that by the time he pulled back, she could only smile dazedly. "A good thing, then."

"More like amazing." He looked around. The windows were completely fogged. The temperature had dropped too, and now that they weren't actively creating enough heat to start an explosion, the chill was becoming pronounced. Reaching behind his seat, he produced a duffel bag. "Emergency kit," he said as he pulled out a blanket and wrapped them up in it.

"You know what would be good? If you also had a cookies 'n' cream cupcake in there."

With a low chuckle, he wrapped his arms around her, nuzzling at her neck. "Sorry, no. But I've got some PowerBars and water."

She wriggled in closer, loving the feel of his hard body beneath hers. And he was hard. Everywhere. "How about another condom?" she whispered.

This got her a sexy, heated smile that she took as a *hell, yes.* This time when they came together, it was slower, deeper, and just as shockingly good. And with it was the unspoken agreement that this, whatever *this* was, would continue to their mutual pleasure for as long as it worked.

Or for as long as they were both in Tahoe.

Because as she reminded everyone as often as she could, she was going to be gone soon. There would be no future. She'd made him promise her that. And hell if it wasn't both a huge relief and her greatest regret.

THE NEXT MORNING, Jane jerked awake at the rude sound of her alarm. She'd set it early to get a ride from Mateo out to her car. Fumbling for her phone, she hurriedly slapped snooze, not ready to rise and shine.

She and Levi had stayed up on the Tahoe Rim Trail until two thirty in the morning. Which had been three short hours ago.

Basking in the wonderfulness of that, she staggered into the shower. Ten minutes later, she was back in her room, hunting for clothes, when Levi called.

"Just wanted to make sure you're okay."

The sound of his low, sleep-roughened voice had her smiling like an idiot. "I think you know that I am."

He gave a soft laugh.

Silence.

Memories.

Longing.

"So . . ." she managed. "Are we going to be uncomfortable around each other now?"

"Does it feel uncomfortable?"

She let out the breath she hadn't even realized she'd been holding as relief flooded her. She loved his candidness and felt grateful for it. "I'm glad nothing's changed," she said softly.

"Not even if we made this real."

Her heart stopped at the thought of doing just that, and because it did, she forced herself to joke away the odd ache his words had brought. "Oh, sure," she teased, "you say that now, but before I knew it, it'd be all healthy food and anal sex."

She heard a choking sound.

Then a rustling and a good amount of swearing.

"Levi?"

"Just snorted coffee up my nose."

She laughed.

He was quiet a moment and she assumed he was mopping himself up. Then he asked quietly, "Any regrets?"

"No," she said, and meant it.

"Good. Your car's out front. I charged your battery. You should be good to go."

"Wait— You did? But . . . you must have gotten up hours ago."

"Did it after I drove you home. Mateo gave me a ride out there."

That he and Mateo had skipped out on sleep to do such a thing for her boggled her mind. But maybe it shouldn't. Levi had already proven he'd do just about anything for her. "Thank you."

"Anytime. Later, Jane."

"Later," she whispered, wondering why it sounded like a promise. She went down to the kitchen and straight to the coffee maker, staring at it until it produced twelve ounces of blessed caffeine.

As she slurped it as fast as she could without burning the skin of the roof of her mouth off, Charlotte stepped into the room. She took one look at Jane and said, "Whoa."

"What?"

"You're wearing a smile. In the A.M. hours. What's that about?"

Jane had noticed the smile when she'd brushed her teeth, but she'd been unable to get rid of it, so she shrugged.

Charlotte studied her more closely and gasped. "Oh my God."

Jane did her best to ignore this, pouring herself a bowl of cereal. She made a big production of adding milk and searching for a spoon. When she looked up, Charlotte gave her a brow waggle.

Jane gave her a prim look. "I don't know what you're trying to say."

"Yeah, you do."

"Fine." Jane tossed up her hands. "Yes, Mom, he got to first base, okay? In fact, we had a couple of home runs and several victory laps. Are you satisfied?"

Charlotte's laugh was infectious, and Jane sighed and stopped fighting her ridiculous smile.

Coming close, Charlotte cupped Jane's face and looked into her eyes. "I'm happy for you."

"It was just one night."

"It could turn into more if you let it."

For a single second she allowed herself the luxury of wanting more. "You know I'm not built that way."

"Jane."

She grabbed her keys and turned back to her landlord, her roommate, her friend, and one of her favorite people on the planet. "I'm not."

"People change."

Jane pointed at her. "I will if you will."

"Hey," Charlotte said. Sighed. "And fair."

Jane stopped to refill her cup and then went still at the sight of a trophy on the counter. She had no idea what the original plaque said because it had been marked by what appeared to be a Sharpie, and now read:

Head in Charge of Everything and Ruler of the Annual Moreno Snowball Challenge

Jane looked at Charlotte.

Charlotte was suddenly fascinated with making her own cup of coffee.

"Charlotte."

"Jane."

"Did you partake in a . . ." She read the trophy again. "Snowball challenge?"

"I partook. I won." Charlotte grinned, looking way younger than her thirty-nine years. "I kicked ass. Including Mateo's."

Jane grinned. "That's my girl." She headed to the door.

"What if you're running from something that might turn out to be really good?" Charlotte asked her back.

The thing was, Jane hadn't survived on what-ifs.

"What if being with Levi would turn out to be one of the best things in your life? You're just going to ignore it?" Charlotte asked.

"Uh-huh. Pot, I'd like you to meet Kettle."

"*I'm* not running," Charlotte said. "*I'm* staying put."

"Physically, sure. But we both know that you're holding back emotionally with Mateo because you're afraid your past will keep you from leading a happy and full life. Problem is, that makes you a walking/talking self-fulfilling prophecy."

Charlotte sucked in a breath. "So you're saying I'm being a hypocrite."

Jane held up her hand with her first finger and thumb half an inch apart.

Charlotte sat back, looking surprised and then thoughtful. "Well, damn."

"What?"

"You're right."

Jane laughed. "Duh."

"But we're also both wrong. We're holding back with our hearts on two men who deserve the best of us, and I don't mean that our lives can't be full without a man in them. I mean that maybe love could *possibly* enrich or enhance our lives. But . . ." She bit her lip.

"Yeah. But." Jane drew a deep breath. "We need to find a way to move on from our pasts."

"I will if you will," Charlotte said, throwing Jane's words back at her.

Jane had to admit, it was tempting. On a rough laugh, she left for work.

But the smile stuck all day long.

CHAPTER 20

Levi awoke to someone poking him in the cheek. When he didn't open his eyes right away, little fingers pried one open for him.

Peyton's face was two inches from his, with her faithful minion Jasper right behind her. "*Hi!*" she said at a high decibel. "You're awake! *Hi!*"

Yes, they did this every single morning. And yes, every single evening when he kissed her good night, he also begged her not to poke him awake the next morning. She always smiled sweetly and said, "I promise," but yet here they were.

"Tonight's Grandma and Grandpa's anniversary dinner!" Peyton grinned. "We finally get to meet Jane!"

"Yes," he said sleepily. He hadn't gotten much sleep the last couple of weeks. The night up on the Tahoe Rim Trail with Jane had started it, but he'd gladly forgo sleep every single night just to be with her.

And had. The thought made him smile. Just last night, he'd met her at her grandpa's house, where they'd had takeout dinner, and afterward had made bread with one of Jane's grandma's old recipes.

"Betty's recipe never fails," Lloyd had said proudly as they'd all stuffed themselves with one of the two incredible loaves they'd made.

"Good enough to take to your mom's tomorrow night for their anniversary dinner?" Jane had asked, nerves evident.

He'd leaned over the cutting board that had only crumbs on it and had kissed her right in front of her grandpa.

Jane had grinned at him. "I'll take that as a yes."

"Everyone's going to love it, and you," Levi had promised, and meant it.

"What's not to love about a big family dinner?" Lloyd said. "I don't remember much, but I know how much I miss those."

Jane had paused. Looked at Levi, who had nodded, then drew a breath. "You can go with me, if you'd like."

Lloyd smiled. "Really?" he'd asked softly, hopefully, also disbelievingly.

"Really," Jane had whispered back.

Now Levi looked into Peyton's eyes. "Did you bring Apple Jacks?"

She gave a slow shake of her head, ponytails bouncing. "Momma said no more food outside of the kitchen cuz of Jasper."

At her side, Jasper panted a happy, ever-hopeful smile, completely unrepentant.

"I'm going to be an astronaut," Peyton said apropos of nothing. "I'm going to be the first human to land on Jupiter."

"Sounds good," Levi said. "But you can't actually land on Jupiter. It's made of gas and has no solid surface. Same with Saturn and Neptune."

She nodded sagely. "Grandma says I'm going to be as smart as you. Which means I'll find a way to land on Jupiter."

"If anyone can do it, you can," he said.

She beamed at him with her two missing front teeth. "You're smiling this morning."

He was.

"Just like yesterday morning."

True story.

"And the morning before that. Why are you smiling in the mornings now?"

"Are you six, or thirty?"

"I'm six, silly," Peyton said, giggling, and began climbing the couch to get to him.

"*Peyton!*" Tess yelled from down the hallway. "Are you bothering Uncle Levi again?"

"Nope!"

There came a snort from the desk. His dad.

"I really love my community bedroom," Levi said, just as it occurred to him that after tonight's dinner, he was pretty much free to leave. He was healed from his concussion. He'd found the source of the money leak, and they had a lawyer involved now. It was only a matter of time before Cal had to face what he'd done.

But he knew he wasn't going back to San Francisco. At least not permanently. There was land for sale not too far from where he'd taken Jane up on the Tahoe Rim Trail.

It was a great investment, but that's not why he wanted it. He wanted to build a house that he could someday raise his kids in. And maybe one of them would come back as an adult and bitch about sleeping on the pullout couch bed . . .

Not that he was ready to share that yet. Hell, he'd barely come to terms with the idea himself.

"Do you know what your mother is doing?" his dad asked.

"Not my turn to watch her."

"Smartass. She's rearranging furniture for tonight's anniversary dinner. She's so excited, she's already dressed for it, and is it because she and I are celebrating the big four-oh? No. It's because we'll finally get to meet Jane."

Welp, that did it. Levi's smile couldn't hold up to that. He rose to his feet. "Don't you mean you'll get to meet her for the *second* time? Yeah," he said at the flicker of guilt behind his dad's eyes. "I know you went to the hospital to meet her. Just like Mom coaxed her into the humane society with a fake email."

"Not fake," his mom said, coming into the room. "It was a real email. She got her adorable rescue cat treated at a discount."

"How did you even know she had a pet?"

"I didn't. I got lucky."

Levi shook his head at her. "You met her under false pretenses."

Tess appeared in the doorway, and Levi spared a hard look for her as well. "None of you told her the truth about who you are." Shaking his head, he went to walk past his sister, but stopped and looked her in the eyes. "What do you think is going to happen when she shows up later and finds all her new friends here? How is she supposed to feel about you guys and the deception you pulled off? Or *me*, for that matter, since I didn't blow the whistle on any of you."

His mom's expression was pure guilt, but she lifted her chin. "Maybe she's going to think you're so well loved that we just wanted to make sure she was good enough for you. Because it's true, honey. I've waited a long time for you to find someone after

Amy. And once you did, I had to know that she was going to be good for you."

His dad just nodded. In fact, they all nodded in unison like a pack of bobbleheads of the Three Stooges.

Levi just shook his head. "I'm going to shower. You all might want to work on what you're going to say to her when she arrives. I have my own groveling to do." Because he'd made his own mistakes with Jane, and at some point he was going to pay the price for those mistakes. A price that would undoubtedly be high.

As in losing her.

An hour later he was in the back booth at the Stovetop Diner, at what he'd come to think of as his temporary "office"—much to his mom's dismay, as she'd hoped he'd make a place for himself in the store's office. And he went there too, but the diner suited his purposes better.

He liked the organized chaos going on all around him, and yet not involving him. He liked the owner of the diner, who happened to be one of Mateo's cousins. He liked the way everyone left him alone to his own devices. Mostly, that is. Because just then Mateo slid onto the seat across from him.

At least he was bearing gifts in the way of two plates loaded with bacon, eggs, and pancakes. He slid one to Levi and then waited for him to take his first bite before saying, "Heard you put a bid in for that property up in Hidden Falls."

Levi choked on that bite.

Mateo smiled. "You're finally doing what I've been trying to get you to do for years. You're coming back."

Levi managed to suck air into his taxed lungs and eyed his

oldest, very smug-looking friend. "Want to tell me how you know about the bid I put on those fifteen acres less than an hour ago?"

"Ah, man, you know how it is. Everyone knows everyone. Hell, it's Sunrise Cove. You can leave your car unlocked, but there's no such thing as privacy."

Levi just looked at him. "Leave your car unlocked and you'll get a bear."

Mateo smiled. "God, that was fun. What were we? Seventeen? And you left a bag of chips in your dad's new car, not a week after he'd bought it, and a bear climbed in and ate the chips *and* his steering wheel."

And his console. "He nearly killed me." Levi scrubbed a hand down his face. "Good times. And how do you know about the land? And don't tell me a bear told you."

"Okay, fine. The real estate agent you're using for the purchase is my cousin's sister-in-law's mom. And yeah, yeah, I know, I've got a lot of cousins."

Jesus. Why did he want to move back here again? *Because even though they drive you crazy, you miss your family.* "Just tell me my mom and dad don't already know."

"They don't know. *Yet.*"

Levi groaned.

"You're surprised? Come on, you know them better than anyone. Your mom's name should be Sherlock Holmes. Face it, they're going to hear about this."

"If my mom finds out before I tell her, she'll tell everyone I'm going to build a house with a white picket fence and fill it with a wife named Jane and two point five kids."

Mateo laughed, but when he caught sight of Levi's face, his smile faded. "Come on, no one will believe that."

Right. Because other than his half-assed commitment to Amy, he'd never really made any commitment to anyone. He looked away, out the window. It was snowing again. It'd be a great powder day tomorrow. He hadn't skied since the gondola accident. Maybe it was time to get back on the horse. Maybe he'd see if Jane wanted to go with him . . .

"I've known you a long time," Mateo said. "I know when something's wrong."

"Nothing's wrong."

Mateo shook his head. "Calling bullshit, man. Is it Jane? She falling for you?"

"You know she's just doing me a favor." Which, for the record, he hated. He never should have started this ridiculous farce. Instead, he should've found a way to do this for real.

Mateo studied him for a beat. "It's you. *You're* falling for *her*."

Levi closed his eyes.

"You're serious about her."

"Yeah," he admitted. "I'm serious about her. Which means I'm screwed."

Mateo shrugged. "You could just tell her."

"She's leaving soon. Already has another contract lined up in Haiti, had it before she even stepped foot into Sunrise Cove. She'll be there at least three months."

"So? Do your feelings have an expiration date just shy of three months or something?"

Levi sighed. "It's not that easy."

"Have you tried?"

"Haven't wanted to scare her off."

Mateo looked at him for a beat. "You know what I think?"

"No, and don't tell me."

"I think you're complicating this on purpose so it doesn't happen. I think you're scared."

Levi sighed and pushed his plate away.

"And now you don't want to let another woman down. Or worse, hurt her."

"Don't."

"You won't hurt her, Levi."

He met Mateo's gaze. "How do you know?"

The guy took his time answering, crunching on a piece of bacon. Levi's, by the way. "When we were kids," he finally said, "you worked hard at making the people around you happy. Your family. Amy. You wanted your people happy, often to the sacrifice of your own happiness. But in the years since, on your own in San Francisco, you seemed to figure some things out. You've settled into who you are. You're good in your own skin now, and know what you want, what makes you happy. There's nothing wrong with that, man."

Levi took that in. Realized Mateo was right. He did know what he wanted. "I'm still not convinced it's that easy."

"Why not?" Mateo shrugged. "All that's left for you to do is to make your move."

"*Now* who's the old soul? Why don't you follow your own advice? Make your move on Charlotte."

"Because I'm like you—I'm in love, and every bit as terrified as you to admit it."

CHAPTER 21

Levi thought about Mateo's parting words for the rest of the day. He worked, then went for a long run, showered, and a few minutes before Jane was due to arrive, headed downstairs, feeling . . . nervous.

Wondering what the hell that was about, he walked into the living room and went to the big picture window to look out.

Jane's car wasn't there.

He turned to face the room and found his entire family standing there staring at him.

His mom clasped her hands together. "Levi."

"Mom."

"I've got everything prepped for dinner and the house cleaned. Does it look okay?"

"The house is always clean, Mom. It looks great. And I thought you were going to order food in so you didn't have to cook on your own anniversary."

"I wanted homemade food for Jane. Did it smell good when you came downstairs?"

"Yes, but it always smells good." He could tell by the look on her face that he'd given the wrong answer. "Though it smells *extra* good right now. You didn't need to—"

His mom sucked in a breath. "Oh dear God," she said. "She broke up with you, didn't she. She's not coming."

"What?" He shook his head. "No, I just mean that she wouldn't want you to go to any trouble for her."

"Well, of course I'm going to some trouble. I want her to love us."

"She will, Mom."

She narrowed her eyes. "You sure she didn't dump you?"

The doorbell rang and everyone jumped. Jasper lost his ever-loving mind, barking at a piercing pitch, warning the entire planet that there was a possible intruder.

Levi got out in front of the whole pack and faced them, hands up. "Sit," he said. "All of you."

Everyone but Jasper sat.

"Okay, now try to look normal."

"Honestly, Levi," his mom said, "we know how to behave."

"Do you?"

"It's his *girlfriend*," Tess said, putting an odd emphasis on the word *girlfriend* that made Levi grimace on the inside. "He's got the right to want everything to go perfectly. Isn't that right, Levi?"

He pointed at her, then the rest of them. "All of you, zip it." He gently touched his finger to Peyton's nose. "Except you. Never you."

She beamed her toothless grin at him.

To everyone else he said, "Not a single one of you is going to say another word. Not until I explain to her what you guys did. Because there's no way I'm letting her walk in here without first telling her about the con you all pulled."

Tess gave him a long look. "Do you really want to tell stories about con artists?"

Levi glared at her, but she'd been his big sister all his life and wasn't cowed in the least. In fact, she smirked.

Shaking his head, he opened the door to Jane and her grandpa. Jasper squeezed between Levi and the door and immediately put his nose to Lloyd's crotch.

"Whoa," Lloyd said. "The frank and beans haven't been nosed like that in a long while."

"Sorry." Levi pulled the dog away. "Jasper, sit."

Jasper sat, panting happily, smiling from ear to ear.

"Jasper, huh?" Lloyd patted him on the head. "What a big boy you are. Nice name too."

"He also goes by 'dammit,' 'don't you dare,' 'no!' and 'stop!'" Levi looked at Jane, trying to figure out how to do this. Like a Band-Aid, Jane would say.

Her smile was a little short of its usual wattage. In fact, it was her polite smile, the one she used with people she hadn't let into her life. The one Levi hadn't seen in a while, and he stepped over the threshold, pulling the door shut behind him. "You okay?"

"Nervous." She sat on the top porch step like her legs were wobbly.

"Me too," Lloyd said at a decibel that suggested he might have forgotten to turn on his hearing aids. "But not for the same reason as Jane. I'm nervous because I had bologna and cheese for lunch, and bologna gives me the toots."

"Don't worry, Jasper will have you beat," Levi said and crouched before Jane. "Don't be nervous. You don't have to be nervous. Trust me, they're going to be nicer to you than they are to me."

She lifted her head and nodded, studying him a moment. "You seem off too. What is it?"

How did she do it? How did she always know what was going on with him beneath the surface? No one had ever been able to read him in the same way he could pick up on her emotions. If he thought too hard about that, the meaning of that ability, it made him feel vulnerable like nothing else ever had.

"Whatever it is, tell me quick before I have a heart attack," she said.

"Heart attack?" Lloyd put a hand to his own heart and shook his head. "No, I'm fine. I'm great."

"Grandpa, are your hearing aids on?"

"Uh . . ." He blinked sheepishly as he turned them on. "Sorry."

Jane's eyes were still on Levi, anxiety swimming in her pretty eyes. She thought she was the problem. As if.

"What did I miss?" Lloyd asked. "I hope the meal isn't canceled. I was looking forward to dessert."

"Not canceled," Levi said. "But we could head out to Cake Walk if you want. I hear they've gotten some new flavors—"

"Levi." Jane took a deep breath and nodded. "You've changed your mind. I get it, believe me. We'll just—"

"No." Levi grabbed her hand before she could get away. "I haven't changed my mind. On *anything*," he clarified, looking her right in the eyes. "But—"

She closed her eyes. "There's a but."

He really hated that he had to do this. "There're a few things you need to know before we go inside."

"Maybe I should go inside to give you two a moment," Lloyd said, shifting his weight from foot to foot. "Besides, I drank a lot of water today, so I'll just . . ." He gestured to the front door and then opened it and vanished inside.

"Ohmigod," Jane said. "Should I go after him?"

"No." If anyone could handle Levi's family for a minute, it was Lloyd. He sat next to Jane, then turned her to face him. Their knees bumped and he took comfort from the touch, accidental as it was. He knew that in a minute she was going to be mad at him, very mad, possibly mad enough to walk away. And he wouldn't be able to blame her. "I'm not sure where to start."

"Then I'll start," she said. "You regret asking me to do this. You regret that night up at the Tahoe Rim Trail. And every night since then—"

"No. *No*," he repeated softly, reaching for her hand. Well, okay, yes, he regretted asking her to be a part of this farce, but only because he wanted it to be real. "I don't regret anything, most especially the times I've spent with you, including what happened up at the Tahoe Rim Trail in my truck. I smile every time I get into it now, like Pavlov's dog." *Not to mention, get a hard-on . . .* "That night will go down in history as one of my favorite nights ever. The other is last night."

She snorted, because long after they'd made her grandma's bread with her grandpa, after he'd taken her home and had gone to bed himself, they'd started texting, playing phone truth or dare. He'd learned that the little scar on her chin was from jumping off her grandparents' patio roof to see if she could fly. And that she'd skipped her last year of high school and graduated early. He'd also learned that she'd never brought a guy home before.

And then she'd dared him to come over—where they'd continued the truth or dare in person. In her bed . . .

"Zero regrets," he repeated, holding her gaze, willing her to believe him.

She drew a deep breath. "Then what is it? It's something, I can feel it."

"Remember that night on the gondola?"

"The one I still have nightmares about?" She gave a wry smile. "No, not at all."

Okay, she was trying to be funny, but he had a feeling it was also true about the nightmares, and he hated that. They'd circle back to that. "When I called my mom that night and told her I had someone in my life—"

"Because you thought we were going to die, and you were trying to say goodbye and realized how much she loved you and that all she'd ever wanted was for you to have love in your life . . . Yeah, I get it, Levi. I mean, I don't exactly have personal experience with a family like yours, but I've seen the Hallmark movies. And honestly? It's sweet, the lengths you'd go to for your family."

"Yeah." He scrubbed a hand over his face. "Let me tell you the rest of it and you'll probably revoke that understanding. See, after that night, they started hounding me about meeting you."

"Hence why I'm here," she said. "Wearing real jeans and not yoga pants that have never seen a yoga class."

He smiled. "I love the jeans. The jeans make me want to play truth or dare again."

"Hey, how was I supposed to know that daring *you* to remove a piece of clothing would turn on me and that you'd remove a piece of *my* clothing?"

"You were commando," he said reverently. "I'm never going to stop reliving that."

"*Focus*," she said on a laugh. "Your family was hounding you about meeting me and . . ."

"And I kept stalling, so . . ."

"Oh my God," she said. "You're the slowest storyteller on the planet!"

"*And* four weeks was too long for them. They didn't have that sort of time."

She covered her mouth with her hand. "Is someone sick? You should've told me. I'd have come sooner!"

"Not sick," he said. "At least not physically."

She shook her head. "I don't understand."

"Because you're normal." He sighed. "They got impatient. My mom is Shirley, the nosy woman you met at the humane society. My sister is Tess, the nosy woman who forced you into being friends with her. And my dad is Hank, the guy creating the libraries for the hospital and clinics."

Jane's mouth fell open and she just stared at him.

His heart kept skipping beats. "If you want to get up and walk away right now, I'll understand," he forced himself to say.

She blinked. Closed her mouth. Opened it again.

Nothing came out.

"Jane?" He slid closer, a hand on her leg. "Say something."

She was still for another very long beat. Then she slowly shook her head. "They did all that for me?"

"You mean stalked you? Yes, they did. They inserted themselves into your life under false pretenses, and I'm sorry."

He had no idea what she would do next, but he was stunned to see her suddenly smile and whisper, "Wow."

"Jane," he said, completely undone. "You should be running for the hills, not looking like you just won the lottery."

"Are you kidding? I was so freaked out about meeting your family, about somehow messing it up for you, because the only thing I know about close families like yours is what I've seen on TV or in the movies." She laughed. "But I'm not the one who messed it up!"

He softened and cupped her face. "You're not upset?"

"Well, I have nothing to compare this to because no one's ever searched for me or ever gone through that much trouble to find me before. But your mom and dad and sister did."

Just like that, his amusement was gone and he felt like a total asshole. Here he was, embarrassed by his nosy family, when he was talking to a woman whose own family had completely deserted her, tossed her out like yesterday's trash. Wrapping his arms around her, he brushed a kiss to her temple. "You're amazing, you know that?"

"I do, you told me that last night when I was—"

He kissed her. While laughing. Another first for him. When they broke from the kiss, he asked, "Are you really ready for this?"

"Yes. Because God knows what my grandpa is in there telling them." She smiled and squeezed his hand. "Let's do this."

When they walked inside, everyone was lined up looking sheepish, but to Levi's surprise, Jane smiled even bigger and walked right over to his mom, handing over the basket holding the loaf of bread she'd made. "Shirl, it's nice to see you again."

"Oh, honey." His mom yanked Jane in for a hug. "I'm sorry I

didn't tell you who I was. I just needed to know that my son had found someone worthy, and then once I started talking to you, I realized that in spite of himself he'd managed to find someone even *better* than I could have ever imagined."

"Thanks for the vote of confidence, Mom," Levi said dryly.

His mom ignored him and kept hugging Jane, who met Levi's gaze over his mom's shoulder.

Smiling.

Tess moved toward Jane next, sincere regret and remorse in her voice. "I'm sorry," she said softly. "I should've told you who I was from the very start. But you turned out to be so sweet, and so funny that I wanted to be your friend for real. I got carried away. I've regretted it every single day since, I just didn't know how to tell you."

"I get it. You were looking out for your brother." She hugged Tess. "Thank you."

His sister pulled back, looking grateful. "For what?"

"For being my first new friend in a long time."

"Hey," Levi said. "Standing right here."

Jane smiled at him, looking beautiful and *happy*.

"Okay, my *second* new friend," she corrected.

Levi smiled back as his dad came forward next, sheepish. "I should've told you as well. But I didn't because Shirley made me do it."

Levi's mom grimaced at being thrown under the bus, but didn't deny a thing. "We're just thrilled you're finally here," she said. "And that you brought your charming grandpa."

Lloyd was sitting on one of the recliners with Peyton. They were reading a book together, heads bent to the pages. He lifted his head and waved at Jane. "No one's ever asked me what my third favorite reptile is before."

"It's the T. rex!" Peyton said joyfully, her ponytails practically vibrating with excitement.

Jane moved over there to meet her, and after Levi did the introduction, Peyton immediately pointed at Jane's locket. "Pretty!"

Jane opened it, and from the moment Peyton caught sight of eight-year-old Jane dressed as a fairy princess, their bond was forged in unbreakable ties. Levi's heart stopped skipping beats and warmed.

"I was a fairy princess for Halloween last year!" Peyton said—aka yelled. "And the year before that! But this year I'm going to be something real. I'm going to be a *unicorn*!"

"Honey," Tess said, "unicorns aren't real."

"But they are! They have to be! Uncle Levi told me they're the national animal of Scotland!"

Tess gave Levi a look.

"Hey, it's true," he said.

A timer went off in the kitchen and his mom clapped. "To the dining room, everyone! Food's ready."

There was the usual mob movement. The Cutler family didn't mess around with meals. They got right to it. They might be shit at communicating with one another, but breaking bread together? That was their thing.

Hank started to give a toast to Shirl about their anniversary, but Shirl shushed him. "Enough about us, Hank. I want to talk to Jane."

Jane took this all in good humor, even as everyone peppered her with questions. In fact, she gave as good as she got, asking them questions too. She asked his mom about some cat they'd been worried about at the humane society. She asked his dad about the library, wondering when he was coming back with more books. She asked Peyton about her glittery pink nail polish, and then she and Tess bonded over the latest season of something they were both marathoning that Levi had never heard of. He was amused, but also grateful and relieved, not to mention a little surprised. The Cutlers didn't usually mess around when it came to eating, but they were interacting. And even more surprising, behaving.

"My teacher says we're all going to be murdered by the sun," Peyton said out of the blue.

Everyone stared at her.

"It's going to be blowed up," she explained. "So I was thinking we should ask Santa to come early this year. I want a new bike, but I want time to ride it before we all die."

Everyone turned in unison to Levi for translation. "I think Peyton's teacher probably told her class that the sun's getting progressively brighter and hotter, which will eventually evaporate our oceans, making Earth one big desert similar to Mars. And everyone will die off."

"Yep." Peyton nodded. "That's what she said."

"But you've got plenty of time," Levi told her. "Just over two billion years, in fact. So probably Santa doesn't need to come early this year."

Peyton looked hugely disappointed, and everyone laughed. Jane gave her a sympathetic hug while his mom beamed on. Okay, Levi thought, this wasn't so bad. His dad hadn't even tried to pick a fight with him. Not yet anyway. And his mom hadn't once asked him when he was going to produce a grandbaby like his sister had.

"Pass the wine?" his mom asked him, then turned to Jane. "You're so good with kids. Do you plan to have any of your own?"

And there it was. "Mom."

"What, it's just a question," she said innocently.

Jane laughed at whatever look was on his face. Probably horror.

"Why are you laughing?" he asked her. "And seriously, why aren't you running for the hills?"

"Don't pay any attention to him," his mom said. "He's got some drama in him. Always did, to be honest. We host a ski race for charity every year, and for years we competed as a family in the race, encouraging other families to compete with us. The year he turned ten, he announced he was refusing to be on our team."

"Because you were going to race in your pj's," Levi said.

"And?"

"And Dad sleeps in the buff."

"He was going to race in nude-colored long underwear."

"Yeah," his dad said, "I'm not stupid. If I'd fallen while buck ass naked, I'd get freezer burn on my—"

"*Dad.*" Tess reached over to Peyton and covered her ears.

"Mama!" Peyton was bouncing in her seat, pointing to the peach cobbler in the center of the table. "Look, your favorite—bitches. Are we going to eat bitches?"

"*Peaches*, baby."

"We like bitches."

Tess looked pained. "*Peaches.* And yes."

"So does Jasper."

At hearing his name, Jasper leapt up from where he'd been napping at Levi's feet, smacking his head on the table in the process. Undeterred, he came out to blink hopefully at everyone, eyes bright, tongue lolling, tail wagging.

"Jasper would eat anything that wouldn't eat him first." Tess looked at Jane. "My mom's secret to peach cobbler is to double the butter required. It's like crack, so I'm torn between looking good in a bathing suit or eating half the cobbler single-handedly."

"You shouldn't have to choose," Jane said. "Always eat the bitches." She grinned at Levi, her eyes sparkling. Her entire being sparkled.

She was having fun, and it looked good on her.

Levi's mom passed Jane's breadbasket around for the second time, and just like that it was all gone.

"It's wonderful," his mom said. "It's not easy to bake at altitude." She smiled at Peyton, who was inhaling hers. "And I bet one day, your and Levi's kids will love baking with you."

"Can you die from an eye twitch?" Levi asked the room, pressing a finger to his eye. "You can, right?"

Levi's mom rolled her eyes, but looked at Jane. "I don't mean to put you on the spot with the baby talk."

"What *did* you mean?" Levi asked.

Jane put her hand on his thigh, like she was trying to comfort him, which gave his heart a pinch. Had anyone ever tried to protect him? He couldn't remember.

"I do see myself with kids," Jane said. "Someday."

Levi looked over at her in surprise.

She looked just as surprised at herself. "I mean . . . I'm pretty sure. I love other people's kids."

"You'd be an amazing mom," Levi told her quietly. "A kid would be lucky to have you."

She seemed unsure. "I don't have a lot of experience with family. Good experience anyway."

Jane's grandpa looked across the table at her, eyes soft. "And yet you're still one of the two most amazing, warm, caring women I've ever met. Your grandma being the other, of course."

Levi's mom smiled. "Whoever manages to win you over as the mother of their children should count their blessings." She slid a look toward Levi.

He shook his head at her. He'd tell her to behave, but she wasn't programmed to behave.

"I'm not sure what kind of a mother I'd be," Jane said. "But I'd love to someday get a chance to be a part of a close-knit family like this one. Your son is the best man I've ever known. You all must be so proud of him."

"We are *very* proud," his mom said. "He's so smart. He always knows how to get rid of the gophers in the grass."

He had to laugh. What else could he do?

"I've missed this," Lloyd said. "My wife and I, we had it all, for a long time. I've been blessed, but I miss the family meals."

"How long were you married?" Levi's mom asked.

"Since the ice age." He smiled. "We kept things fresh by writing love notes. I saved them all. My favorite was one she'd left for me after a fight. It said: *I considered smothering you with a pillow last night but didn't.*"

Everyone laughed, but no one harder than Levi's dad.

Levi's mom gave him a long, hard look.

He winked at her.

Then she smiled.

"Peyton, slow down on that bread or you'll choke," Tess said. "Remember last week when you tried to shove a whole piece in?"

"What happened?" Jane asked.

"I threw up," Peyton announced. "All over. My throwed-up ate Grandma's new pillow."

"Stomach acid is strong enough to dissolve stainless steel," Levi said.

"Seriously?" Tess asked him. "Gross."

"Levi, we don't talk about stomach acid at the table," his mom said.

Levi reached for his wineglass and drained it. He should have started with that.

Jane smiled at him.

Yep, she was having a great time.

"Mommy says she has to walk around the block for every piece of bread she eats," Peyton said. "She said she could've walked to Hawaii by now."

"I'm not walking my bread off," his dad said. "I'm old. Old people don't have to walk if they don't want to."

"Amen," Lloyd said.

"I walk 10,000 steps a day," Levi's mom said proudly.

"When I'm working, I get well over 20,000," Jane said. "Yesterday I got 24,000."

"Wow." Tess shook her head. "All I get from work is the occasional dick pic."

Levi's mom choked. "*What?*"

"Oh yes," Tess said. "And it's disgusting. I mean, a real man gets out there and disappoints women in person."

"You know you could just turn off your AirDrop, right?" Levi asked.

Tess shrugged. "Sure, but it's probably going to be a while until I see one in person, so . . ."

"What's a dix pic?" Peyton wanted to know.

"Changing the subject now," his mom said, looking horrified. She turned to Jane. "You work so hard. I can't imagine all you go through on a daily basis. I always wanted to be a nurse, but I chickened out. I'd hoped one of my kids would be a nurse, but Tess loves working at the store, and Levi . . ." She looked at him like he was a puzzle she was missing a few pieces on. "He just wanted to play on the computer. How many steps did you get yesterday?"

Levi shook his head. "I don't know, Mom."

"You should look. I don't think it's healthy for you to sit at a computer all day."

"I ran five miles this morning."

"I'm just saying."

"You're just saying what?" he asked.

His dad pointed at him with his fork. "Don't sass your mom. She just means you spend a lot of time making big, fancy presentations when you could be doing something else."

"Do you mean the PowerPoint that I created to show you what Cal had done? Because—" He was about to put a whole lot more "sass" out there, but then felt Jane's hand on his leg again.

"I think it was really sweet of you to make that presentation," she said, smiling at him before turning to everyone else. "He was really worried about how to tell you all. I think it's impressive that he was also able to lay out the proof in case of prosecution, and also to figure out a fix for you."

Everyone looked at Levi as if seeing him for the first time.

"We really are so incredibly happy he brought the woman he loves home to meet us," his mom said.

Levi choked on his last bite of bread and nearly died, but his know-it-all sister pounded him on the back and revived him.

Jane kissed him on the cheek, probably in thanks for not leaving her with his crazy family. "Oh, and Shirl," she said, "you could totally be a nurse if you wanted. It's never too late."

His mom nudged her husband. "You hear that, Hank? I think I should. I'm going to go back to school to be a nurse!"

His dad looked at her. "Since when?"

"Since now. I put my life on hold to raise the kids, and now they're raised. One of them is even in a good relationship."

"Thanks, Mom," Tess said dryly.

Levi's dad was staring at his mom. "If you get to go back to school, then I get to go buy that Camaro I've always wanted."

"How is that the same as going back to school to better myself?"

"I bet my car is cheaper than your school."

"Are the car and nursing school free?" Levi asked. "Because as you both now know, you're currently broke."

"But you're fixing it all," his mom said. "See? I read your whole PowerPoint *and* listened in at the meeting with the lawyer."

Levi looked at his steak knife and wondered if he could hit his own carotid artery in one try.

"And anyway," his mom went on, "we're at rock bottom, right? Things can't get worse than this, so why not dream big."

"I found a Camaro I want," his dad said, bent over his phone.

"Wait a minute," Levi said. "You can find a car to buy online in less than two minutes, but not your own email?"

"I have to poop!" Peyton yelled.

"I'm pregnant," Tess said. "Pass the peas?"

And then she burst into tears.

"Tess?" her mom asked, looking horrified.

"I peed on a stick this morning and it turned b-b-blue," Tess wailed. "And no amount of walking around the block is going to be able to hide it soon enough. So you can stop hounding Levi now, I've got your grandbaby number two." She blew her nose noisily into her napkin and looked at Levi. "You're welcome."

Things deteriorated pretty quickly after that. Levi had nearly had to restrain his father from leaving the house and going after Cal to "tear him apart with his bare hands," only to be reminded by his mom that no one knew where Cal actually was. He did calm down after Levi promised that yes, they had enough evidence to put the guy away.

His mom was surprisingly serene about the whole thing. Of course, Tess's surprise pregnancy worked for her, giving her two grandbabies growing up right here in her house. Plus, she had Jane on backup, who'd said she'd like to be a mom someday . . .

After dessert, he walked Jane and her grandpa out to her car. Lloyd shook Levi's hand and thanked him for the best home meal he'd had since his wife had passed twenty years earlier. Then he got into the passenger seat of Jane's car and shut the door, giving Levi and Jane some privacy.

"That was fun," Jane said.

"You have a very odd sense of fun."

This made her laugh. "They're great, Levi. And they love you so much."

"So . . . you're not scarred for life?"

"Are you kidding?" She laughed again. "That was awesome."

Her eyes were shining bright with good humor. Her soft, kiss-able lips were curved, and she was looking at him as if he was the sun and the moon, and also her heart and soul. Unable to resist, he pulled her into him, cupped her face. "I want to kiss you."

"Please do."

He did just that, sweet enough not to insult her grandpa, deep enough to pleasure them both before he pulled reluctantly back. "Jane, about tonight."

She smiled. "I think we pulled it off, don't you?"

He froze because that wasn't what he'd wanted to talk about. He wanted to ask if it'd been real for her, but he managed a smile. "Yes," he said, his voice soft. "We definitely pulled it off."

CHAPTER 22

Charlotte didn't do idle well. She liked to keep busy so her mind couldn't get the better of her. It was one of the many reasons she loved being a doctor. Personal time, aka too much thinking time, was rare.

But today she'd actually had the day off and, for once, no errands to run, her laundry could wait, and she was caught up on her shows. She'd hung out with Jane until she'd left to have dinner at Levi's, and then, bored with herself, she'd made a Thanksgiving dinner. In the middle of winter. She'd done it because she hadn't gone home to Atlanta for Thanksgiving, and sometimes a girl just needed a big, carb-loaded comfort meal.

There was no one home to share it with. Zoe and Mariella were at work. And Jane was out, probably somewhere with Levi. There was no one else she'd want to spend time with.

No, that was a lie. Mateo had called her yesterday. She'd been in the shower, but she hadn't called him back. She didn't know why.

That was another lie, of course.

His message had stated—in his low, sexy voice—that he was going to his mom's for dinner and the Head in Charge of Everything was invited.

She was a big chicken.

She looked at the gorgeous meal in front of her and . . . packed it up. Because what she really needed was a brownie. Soft and warm and delicious. The problem was, baking had always eluded her. So she pointed at her oven. "We're going to do this, and it's going to be good."

Two hours later, she was covered in flour and on her fourth batch of brownies. The first batch had sunk. The second and third batches had burned on the bottom. "This is it," she told the dough. "I'm outta flour after this. You're my last shot." She put it into the oven and sat on the floor, watching them through the small oven window.

When the brownies began to rise, she pumped a fist. "*Yes!*"

Her phone buzzed. The scheduled OR doc was going home sick and she was up. She looked into the oven at the brownies. "So close . . ." With a sigh, she turned off the oven and headed to the hospital.

Hours later, she was in a corner of the hospital cafeteria in between patients, taking a rare break. They'd been beyond busy. Four cars had piled up on the summit because the roads had become ice sheets and people were always in a hurry. Two deaths. And then there'd been a crash of a different sort when a duo of skiers had thought it smart to sneak up High Alpine and ski down the ungroomed, blocked-off back side—by moonlight. Only problem, there was no moonlight tonight. They'd hit each other at over twenty miles an hour.

Neither had survived.

All needless deaths, and yet having had her hands on each of them, she felt the weight of their passing as if it'd been her fault. She didn't know why sometimes the chaos and trauma she saw hit her harder than others, but tonight was one of those times. Looking around the cafeteria at the groups of people talking and comforting each other, she reached for her phone. Craving the comfort only her mom could supply, she called home.

"Hey, baby," her mom answered softly, sleepily. "Are you okay?"

Horrified, she looked at the time. It was ten P.M. Which was one A.M. for her parents. "Oh my God, I forgot how late it was for you. Go back to sleep."

"No, I'm so glad it's you." Her mom's voice was more alert now, and there was a soft rustling, as if she was sitting up in bed. "I was hoping to hear from you this week. Are you okay? Is anything wrong? When are you coming home?"

"Mom." Charlotte couldn't have stopped the emotion in her voice if she'd tried. "I'm so sorry I woke you."

"Enough about that. Tell me what's wrong."

"Nothing really." She cleared her throat, but the emotion couldn't be budged. "I just wanted to hear your voice."

"Ah, honey. Tough night?"

"Yeah." She closed her eyes and let her mom's voice wash over her. She missed her. Missed the big old kitchen, where her mom had never had a problem baking. The whole house was always scented with something delicious.

"What happened, Lottie?"

"Oh, you know how it goes at work," she managed.

"I do." Her mom had been a nurse before she'd retired a few

years ago. A small-town private nurse, but she'd seen her share of horror. "Remember what I told you to do when it gets to be too much?"

Charlotte found a laugh. "Drink?"

"Find a partner. And jump their bones."

"*Mom.*"

"Look, I don't pretend to understand why you don't want someone in your life. I mean, okay, after what you went through, I actually do understand, but it's been years and lots of therapists, and—"

"I'm fine, I promise."

"But—"

"Not now, okay?" She rubbed at the tension headache forming between her eyebrows, the one that would've been erased by a thick, gooey homemade brownie. "Not here."

"Okay, baby. I hear you. How long of a break do you have?"

"Maybe twenty minutes."

"You're going to eat, yes? You *need* to eat. Preferably protein, not just a quick grilled cheese."

"I cooked," Charlotte said. "I went all out and made turkey and stuffing." She opened her glass food container and had to admit, she'd done a damn good job. "I brought my leftovers."

"You use my recipes?"

"Of course." She left off the failed attempts at baking brownies. "I miss you, Mom."

"Oh, honey. We miss you too. I sure wish you could've made it home for the holidays."

"Me too." Charlotte looked out at the sea of exhausted hospital employees around her. "But there are just so many staff members with young kids this year who wanted to be home with their families."

"So you volunteered." Her mom's voice was thick with emotion. "Now we only see you when we can come to you. Which is fine, I understand, I just . . ." She sniffed. "We miss you so much."

Charlotte was staring at the floor, trying not to lose it, when two sneakers came into view, topped by long legs covered in green scrubs. She knew those beat-up sneaks. She knew those long legs. "Mom," she said softly, closing her eyes, ignoring the man in front of her, "please don't cry."

"I'm not. I've just got something in my eye."

Yeah. Her too. "I've gotta go, okay? I love you. Tell Daddy I love him, too." She disconnected and pretended she didn't feel the weight of Mateo's gaze as he studied her. When she thought she had herself together, she lifted her face to his.

There was no doubt that he took in the ravages the night had brought because his eyes softened. "My mom doesn't understand why I can't always get the holidays off either," he said.

She looked at him for a long beat, quite positive that her reason for not going home was a whole lot different from his.

He looked at her right back. No smile, exhaustion in every line of his scrub-covered body. She knew his night had been just as rough as hers. With a sigh, she gestured to the empty chair across the table from her.

He sat, but in the chair right next to her, then eyed her food. "I'll swap you half my dinner for half of yours."

She eyed the huge piece of cherry pie he set in front of him. "That looks more like dessert than dinner."

"It's a dessert sort of night."

True that. "Homemade or store-bought?" she asked.

"Homemade, straight from my mom's oven from a big family dinner last night. Which you were invited to, only you didn't call me back."

"I'm sorry."

He chuckled, whether because he didn't believe her or because he appreciated the lie. "It's okay, family can be a lot."

"I like them," she said.

He lifted his head and held her gaze. "But?"

"But . . ." She squirmed. "I need to work up to that."

He nodded. Easy acceptance. That's what she got from him, always.

He divided the piece of pie in half and then put his half on the lid of the container and slid the rest to her. He'd given her the bigger half, and right then and there she knew. He was the One.

If she'd been ready for the One, that is.

Taking the deal, she pushed her food toward him.

With a fork, he scooped up a bite of turkey, dragged it through the dollop of gravy, then scooped some cranberry sauce on top.

She stared at him in horror.

"What?" he asked.

"You mixed everything up!"

"And . . . we don't do that?"

"Absolutely not," she said. "The foods shall never touch."

He slid her a look. "You do know what happens when we eat them, right?"

Okay, so he was definitely not the One. Huge relief.

He ate the bite and closed his eyes in bliss as he chewed. When she started to speak, he held up a finger, indicating he needed silence, so she shut her mouth, watching as his entire body relaxed and tension drained with each passing second.

"Oh. My. God," he finally said, opening his eyes. "First you kick ass in the OR, and then take the championship in the infamous Moreno snowball challenge, and now this? I'm going to need you to marry me."

She laughed. "You're an idiot."

"Yeah, no doubt. But damn, woman. You're an angel in the kitchen. This is amazing. You're amazing."

She tried and failed to keep the words from warming her from the inside out. "Do you have a lot of family dinners?"

"Yes. There are a lot of birthdays. I get out of most of them thanks to work, which they pretend to understand. But they don't, not really."

Oh, how she got that, and she relaxed a bit too. Aided by the cherry pie, which really was fantastic.

"So." He fixed himself another bite, very carefully not mixing any of the foods together this time. "You never go home?"

And . . . so much for relaxing. She shook her head.

"You're not close to your family?"

She took another bite of pie and gave him a vague shrug, but he simply waited her out with that endless patience of his.

"We're close," she finally admitted and met his warm, curious eyes. "But it's not that easy to get to Atlanta."

"No? They don't make planes that fly there several times a day?"

She snorted. "You know what I mean."

He nodded and didn't say anything, and damn if she didn't fill the silence for him like a rookie. "I don't like to go back there," she admitted.

"Why?" Simple question, no judgment.

"Bad memories," she admitted. "And I guess sometimes it's hard to remember the good memories over those bad and very loud memories, you know?"

Looking at her with those warm, dark eyes, he gave her a slow nod. He knew.

Unbearably touched for reasons she couldn't begin to fathom, she got very busy separating out the piece of cranberry that had gotten lodged in the gravy, like it was her job.

"Charlotte."

Oh, look, there was some gravy touching her stuffing, so that took another minute—

He put his hand over hers and she stilled, lifting her gaze to his.

"You don't have to talk about something you don't want to."

She swallowed hard and nodded.

"But in my experience," he went on quietly, "when the memories get loud, it's because they *need* to be heard."

Her heart skipped a beat, and then another. She played with her fork with suddenly clammy palms as her stomach turned. Same symptoms that assaulted her every time she thought about that night. "Something happened to me. A long time ago. And sometimes . . . sometimes I let it affect me now."

"Time's a bitch, isn't it?" He got up, went to the front counter, bought two water bottles, and brought them back, sitting right next to her again. "Sometimes, long-ago memories can feel like just yesterday." He opened one of the water bottles and handed it to her. "Or right now."

She took a long drink. Stalling. Not sure whether she wanted to run out of the cafeteria or keep going. But when she made herself look into Mateo's eyes, she saw compassion and understanding. "I know you're supposed to talk about this stuff," she said slowly. "That I should let it out and trust that people will understand. But they don't. Not really."

"Try me."

She took another drink, then set the water down and began to play with the condensation on the bottle. "It's a long, clichéd story about a small-town girl going off to college in the big city, and as a freshman who went out to celebrate her birthday, let herself get taken advantage of." She shook her head. "She was young and naive and stupid. So stupid."

"There's nothing wrong with young and naive, and I have a hard time believing you were ever stupid."

Her laugh held no humor. "I let myself get charmed by a southern accent similar to mine. He played me like a fiddle, bought me a drink, told me how out of his league I was, and took me dancing."

She scraped at the water bottle label with her nail, shredding it. Horrified at the tell, she clasped her hands together, wondering why her mouth kept flapping. "I got drunk."

"Not a crime."

"No, but it made me foolish, and foolish should be a crime," she said. "Because instead of calling my parents when I started feeling weird, I stayed."

"Weird?"

She looked away. "Yeah. Not drunk weird. Drugged weird."

"Someone put something in your drink," he said grimly.

"Yes." For so long she'd kept this to herself, but in doing so, she'd given that night all the power. She knew it was time, past time, to let it all go, because if she didn't, it'd continue to keep her from living the life she secretly dreamed about.

Which meant Mateo was right. She *needed* to say it all out loud and take away its power to hurt her. "I woke up the next morning alone in a strange bed, in a strange place, no clothes, not knowing where I was or what had happened." The not remembering was probably a blessing, but sometimes in the dark of the night her brain liked to fill in the missing time, and she had to admit her imagination might be a whole lot worse than the truth.

Mateo sat quietly next to her, calm and steady, but there was a storm in his eyes. "How badly were you hurt?"

She shook her head. "Not badly."

"There are levels of hurt," he said carefully.

As she knew all too well. Charges hadn't been pressed because she'd never been able to ID anyone. "I'm fine. No long-lasting damages." She made the mistake of looking at him again, seeing a genuine concern for her and a carefully banked fury for what she'd gone through. And also . . . understanding. "Well, no lasting physical damages anyway," she admitted with an attempt at a smile.

He'd stopped eating and set his fork down. "And the *not*-physical damages?"

She shrugged. "I've had counseling. I don't hate men. I just . . ." She shook her head. "I don't like to talk about it. People get weird."

"Weird how?"

She bit her lower lip. "Okay, they don't. Because I never talk about this, not with anyone."

"Not even Jane?"

"She knows, but only because she saw my reaction when a

man . . ." She shuddered. "There was a situation in Colombia, at a medical clinic. It got held up, and I reacted badly." She drew a deep breath. "But other than Jane and a bunch of therapists, no one else knows."

"What about in your past relationships?"

She froze for a beat. "I get claustrophobic in relationships," she finally said. "So I don't do them."

"You're sure about that?"

She blinked. "What does that mean?"

"Look, there are all kinds of relationships, right? Like us," he said quietly. "Technically, what we have could be called a relationship. We're two neighbors who fight over who plows the snow." He smiled. "It also might be the best relationship I've ever been in."

She was . . . well, she didn't know exactly. Flustered? "But we've never—"

"There are all kinds of relationships," he repeated softly.

She stared at him some more. He just flashed another small smile and went back to eating.

Around her, the sounds of the busy cafeteria kicked in and she realized she'd been holding her breath, so she breathed. He'd heard her deepest, darkest secret and he wasn't scared off. Even more than that, he hadn't asked invasive questions or pulled back in horror. He wasn't treating her like a fragile piece of glass that could shatter at any moment.

Normal.

He was acting completely normal.

"Normal's good, right?" she accidentally said out loud.

He shrugged. "Personally, I think it's overrated." Very briefly, so it might have been a mistake, he let his thigh and biceps touch hers. It felt like the very best hug. "Thanks for trusting me," he said very softly.

She turned her head and met his gaze.

He fed her a bite of her own delicious stuffing. "Charlotte?"

"Yeah?"

"What do you need from me right now?"

"Um . . ." She eyed her half of his pie.

"Think bigger," he said.

The truth was, she knew exactly what she needed. What she didn't know was how to ask for it. She looked at his mouth, imagined it on hers, on all of her, erasing all her nightmares . . .

"Anything, Charlotte. All you have to do is say it."

"Sometimes . . ." She had to lick her dry lips. "I think maybe I need a momentary diversion from my life."

"Such as?"

She bit her lower lip. How did you tell the man you'd spent months and months secretly aching for—while turning him down—that you wanted to do just as her mom had suggested: jump his bones? "Maybe a hug," she finally said.

He immediately stood up, and even though they were literally in the middle of the crowded cafeteria, he pulled her up as well, and right into his arms. And as they closed around her, not carefully, not gently, and *definitely* not like she was a piece of glass, she sighed out her tension and melted into him. Her past didn't fade away—she was the only one with the power to make that happen—but the memories became . . . muted. For now, at least.

Mateo ducked a little to look into her eyes, a question in his own. *Okay?* he was asking.

"Yes." More than. "I want . . ." She wanted them to be off duty. In his big, warm house. *In his bed* . . .

"Anything," he said.

She stared at his mouth.

A low groan rumbled up from his chest. "Especially that."

She nodded, then closed her eyes. "I'm sorry, I'm not trying to be a tease here, but . . . I really also like things the way they are."

"You mean with you yelling at me every time I do something nice for you?"

Her eyes flew open and found him smiling at her.

He tugged on a strand of hair that had gotten loose from her ponytail. "Never apologize to me for telling me what you want. And as for what else you might want, we could tackle those things one at a time. On your schedule."

"But what we have right now works for us."

He nodded. "Agreed. But more would work too."

She sucked in a breath. "Or ruin it."

"Oh ye of little faith."

"Not in you," she said. "In me. Let's face it, I've ruined every relationship I've attempted."

"Sounds like you haven't attempted very many. But in any case, it takes only one. The right one."

She opened her mouth with absolutely no idea what she planned on saying, but just then they were both texted at the exact same time.

They looked at their phones.

"I have to go," they said in sync and then laughed a little.

Charlotte gathered up her things, and he did the same. She gave him a smile and turned to walk off, but he caught her hand, waiting until she looked at him.

"Thanks for the best dinner in recent memory," he said.

"You hardly got to eat."

"It wasn't the food—which was off the charts, by the way." And with another playful tug on her hair, he went back to work. And so did she. But this time, she was smiling.

TWO HOURS LATER, Charlotte was relieved by another on-call doctor, and she drove home on autopilot. It was just after midnight and both driveways were cleared. That was no mystery, as Mateo's car was in his driveway.

He'd done it again. Tried to make her life easier. Better.

What he didn't know was that just his presence did that.

It takes only the right one . . .

It couldn't possibly be that simple, but the fact was she felt restless, lonely, on edge, and needing . . .

Gah.

She was pretty sure what she needed was in that house next to hers. And in the next moment, she was out of her car and knocking on his door before she could stop herself.

He answered in just sweat bottoms, slung low on his hips. No shirt. Bare feet. Bed-head hair. Sleepy eyes. "You okay?" he asked.

She felt dizzy just looking at him, but she managed a nod.

He shoved his fingers through his hair as if trying to wake himself up. "Let me guess. You've got a problem with the driveway."

She shook her head and found her voice. "Thanks."

He rubbed a hand over his jaw, the sound of the scruff there making her stomach twirl. "You're not going to ask me to put the snow back?"

She grimaced. "No."

He gave a slow smile. "Are you . . . hungry?"

"Yes." She took a deep breath. "But not for food."

He stilled.

She did not. She stepped across the threshold, kicked his door closed, turned, and pushed him up against it. "Mateo?" she whispered, setting her hands on his bare chest, only belatedly realizing those hands were probably frozen.

He sucked in a breath but didn't utter a complaint. "Yeah?"

"You said anything, anytime. Did you mean it?"

"Yes." One of his hands came up to touch her jaw as he lowered his head and brushed a kiss to her temple. Her eyes drifted closed as his mouth made its way to her ear. "Name it, Charlotte."

"You know what I want," she whispered.

He lifted his head. The look in his eyes as they met hers caused a rush of heat and desire. "Now?" His voice was low, giving her goose bumps over her entire body. The very best kind of goose bumps.

"Now," she said. "Here."

The words had barely left her mouth before he turned them, pressing *her* to the door now as his mouth came down on hers. Things got hazy then, in the very best of ways. Clothing became optional, pieces flying as fast as they were discarded.

"Charlotte."

She had her back to the door, her legs wrapped around him as he leaned into her, supporting them both, poised to give her the biggest diversion she'd had in a long time. She wriggled her hips impatiently. "Don't ask me if I'm sure," she gasped. "I am. I'm surer of this than anything. So not to be rude or anything, but do it, Mateo. Do me. Here. Now."

With a rough laugh, he gave her what she wanted, and then neither of them were laughing. There was no more talking either. Well, unless she counted the deliciously erotic dirty talk . . .

CHAPTER 23

Jane pulled up to her grandpa's cabin and smiled. "That was fun."

Hand on the car door handle, his face lit only by the ambient interior dashboard, her grandpa smiled back.

"Haven't been out past midnight in a long time. Levi's family was nice."

"Very," she agreed, realizing she was still smiling. They were nice. And funny. And irreverent. And . . . pretty great.

"Jane." Her grandpa waited until she looked at him. "You've changed everything for me, Jane. I hope you know that."

"What do you mean?"

"For coming to me and showing me what courage is, for reminding me that love had to be earned. For including me tonight like I'm family, like I'm important to you." He lifted his hands. "For everything, really." Reaching out, he put his hand over hers. "I love having you back in my life, Jane. I won't be careless with you, not ever again. I promise you that. I hope you'll agree to continue to see me."

"I'll be leaving soon, but we can stay in touch."

He gave a sad smile at the reminder she would be gone, and suddenly something seemed off about him, so she turned her hand over and squeezed his. "Grandpa? You feeling okay?"

"Never better."

She nodded, stared at their entwined hands, then into his eyes. "You're going in for regular checkups?"

"Yes."

"And all is okay?" she pressed.

"All is okay."

"Promise me," she said.

He looked her right in the eyes and smiled. "I promise. Good night, Jane. Love you. To the moon and back."

Her eyes filled. That had been her grandma's favorite saying. She'd whispered it to Jane every single night. "To the moon and back," she repeated.

He got out of her car. She watched him walk carefully up to his door and vanish inside. She stayed there until the lights came on, then pulled away and headed back to Charlotte's house.

She let herself in and then stopped short when she realized that she'd just walked right in without worrying about whether to knock or not, like she really did live here.

Like it was home.

It felt right. In fact, everything felt so right that it scared her. How she could be so fierce in her everyday life, but when it came to the personal, to the heart and soul of things, she always second-guessed anything good.

Shaking her head, she went into the kitchen and grabbed a can of cat food from the stash she'd been keeping in the pantry. She prepared a plate for Cat and opened the back door.

The big gray cat strolled in like she owned the place, sat back on her haunches, and gave Jane a haughty look. "Meow."

Cat-speak for "you're late."

"And you're not supposed to be in the house," Jane said and set down the plate on the kitchen floor anyway.

Cat sniffed at it, then settled herself in, eating daintily, tail twitching. She took her time finishing, and then without so much as a thank-you, she headed out into the night.

"You're welcome!" Jane called after her.

The house was quiet. Yawning, she tiptoed down the hall and then stopped short in shock.

Charlotte was painting Jane's bedroom door. "Meant to finish this and get in bed before you saw it," she said with a grimace.

Jane shook her head. "What are you doing?"

"Painting."

"It's two in the morning."

"And . . . ?" Charlotte asked.

Jane just looked at the big, curvy letters in blues and greens that spelled out her name. Well, they spelled out *J-A-N* because the *E* hadn't been filled in yet. There were mountains and trees sketched out around her name, also not yet painted.

"The paint's oil based," Charlotte said. "More permanent than Sharpie. Just to hammer home the point that this room is yours and only yours. Also, I had to watch YouTube videos on how to draw the mountains and trees, so if that's not love . . . Oh, and I printed up a billion-year rental agreement for you on your dresser. Sign it."

A billion-year rental agreement. Clearly, Charlotte had lost her noodles. "But—"

"No. No buts. We're doing this." She paused. "You're not going to freak out, are you?"

"I'm trying," Jane said slowly. "But I think I'm too tired for a freak-out." She grabbed a paintbrush and started filling in a tree.

Charlotte just stared at her.

"What?"

"You're *never* too tired to freak out when you think you're putting down roots by accident."

Jane just kept painting, concentrating very hard on the tree, making sure to fill it in just right.

Charlotte gave a low laugh. "You slept with Levi again. You must really like him. Like really, *really* like him. As in maybe even *love* him."

"I don't know." Jane bit her lower lip. "Okay, maybe. But we're not talking about it. Because if we did talk about it, I'd be putting it out there in the universe for karma to mess it all up somehow. That's how my life goes, you know. The good stuff isn't ever real. So yeah . . . not talking about it. Ever."

"Jane." Charlotte got to her feet. "You do realize you deserve to be loved just like any other girl."

Jane couldn't help it, she hugged Charlotte. "Yeah, and right back at you, babe." She stepped back and took a closer look at Charlotte and laughed. "You want to tell me why your shirt's on backwards?"

"Um . . . I dressed in the dark?"

"Uh-huh," Jane said, fascinated by Charlotte's sudden blush. "And the love bite on your throat?"

"Shit." Charlotte slapped a hand right to the spot. With her free hand she jabbed her paintbrush in Jane's direction. "You know what? I'm pulling a Jane. We're not talking about it. Ever. Because if we were to talk about it, that would be putting it out there into the universe for karma to mess it up somehow."

Jane stared at her for a long beat. "Fair. So . . . we're just going to paint?"

"Yes."

"Okay." Jane dipped her brush into the paint again. "Just tell me it was Mateo."

Charlotte grinned dopily. "It was Mateo."

Jane laughed, then stilled at the unmistakable meow right behind her. She turned and found Cat sitting there in the hallway, watching with her sharp gray eyes. "How did you get back inside?"

"I've got the basement window cracked open," Charlotte said.

Cat sauntered closer, all the way to Jane's door, which she gave a light, half-assed scratch to with her front paw.

"I think she's knocking," Charlotte said dryly.

Jane opened her bedroom door.

Cat stared at her for a long beat, then walked inside, head and tail high, as if she owned the place. Then she jumped up on Jane's bed and made herself at home.

On Jane's pillow.

Jane felt the last piece of her heart click into place and looked at Charlotte. "So . . . can we add a pet clause on that billion-year lease?"

CHAPTER 24

A few minutes later, Charlotte crawled into bed, satisfied from Jane's reaction to her newly painted bedroom door, but also still smiling a little dreamily about how she'd spent the earlier part of the evening.

In Mateo's bed.

And Mateo's shower . . .

Then his bed again.

Okay, yes, she'd then sneaked out of said bed and back to her place, but baby steps, right? Besides, he probably hadn't even realized that she'd left. She plumped up her pillow and told herself to go to sleep. She'd just finally drifted off when she was jerked awake by a knock at the front door. "*No,*" she said out loud.

When the knock came again, she blew out a breath and slipped out of bed. Because nothing good ever happened at three in the morning, she grabbed the fireplace poker on the way to the front door. She looked through the peephole and froze.

Mateo.

And he didn't look thrilled. Huh. Okay, so maybe he'd minded her sneaking out. But really, he should be thanking her. She was a restless sleeper and she liked to sleep diagonally across the bed and—

"I know you're in there, Charlotte," came his sleep-roughened voice. Which for the record, was almost as good as his sex-roughened voice. "I can hear you breathing."

That actually couldn't be true, because the minute he'd spoken, she'd stopped breathing.

"Charlotte."

With a grimace, she opened the door.

Mateo took in the sight of her. She was wearing one of his T-shirts, which she'd stolen. Nothing else. Well, except the fireplace poker. Not to mention her undoubtedly defensive attitude. "What are you doing here in the middle of the night?" she asked.

"Good question." He stood there in the freezing night wearing nothing but a pair of sweat bottoms, looking rumpled and roughly sexy—and good God, was that a bite mark on his neck?

She'd bitten him too?

"Normally," he said, "I prefer to share breakfast with the person I just slept with. But then again, you didn't sleep. Instead, you waited for me to fall asleep and then sneaked out. In the middle of the night. While it was snowing. Without a coat or your shoes. Without so much as a note." He gave a long once-over. "What kind of a southern woman doesn't leave a missive, Charlotte?"

Guilt swamped her and she sagged, dropping the poker. "I know, I'm sorry, it was awful of me, but I didn't know what to do."

Pushing off from the doorjamb, he took a step toward her, still not touching her with anything other than that piercing dark gaze. "You didn't know what to do," he repeated, sounding like he was trying to make sense of that.

She wanted to take a few steps back from him because she needed thinking room, which was hard with his larger-than-life presence filling up the entire foyer. But she didn't move away because she didn't want him to think she was afraid of him.

She wasn't.

She was afraid of her own heart, of what that heart wanted. "I didn't know what to do," she said again, softer now.

"Okay, then let me make a suggestion." He took another step until they were toe-to-toe. Lifting a hand, he traced a finger along her jaw. "After we make love, after we have pillow talk and cuddle, after you do that sexy-as-hell thing where you curl into me, murmur my name in that sensual little sated sigh, and close your eyes . . . you *don't* sneak out into the winter night wearing, near as I can tell, next to nothing. Instead, you talk or yell, laugh, cry . . . hell, climb on top of me and ride me like a bronco again, whatever you want. Sleep is also a good option."

"I didn't ride you like a bronco."

He gave her a heated look, which made her blush. He was right. She'd ridden him like a bronco and had practically yelled *giddyup* while she was at it. "Okay, one time."

"And after?"

Damn. Yeah. After, she'd curled into him and closed her eyes, trying to soak up his warm, hard body and the way it held hers, marveling at how he had a way of making her feel safe and secure. "But staying the night, that's what girlfriends do."

"Yeah. And?"

"I'm not your girlfriend."

"Really?" He shifted in closer now, so that they were sharing air. Like they had when they'd had their mouths fused to each other, sharing deep, sensual, erotic kisses . . . "Because only a few hours ago it felt a hell of a lot like you were my girlfriend. Like when you—"

On a choked laugh, she reached up and covered his mouth with her hand. "Don't." But it was too late. Memories washed over her, his worshiping every inch of her body, her turning the tables and doing the same to him, knowing she might never be able to get enough of him . . .

"Charlotte." His voice was terrifyingly gentle as he removed her hand from his mouth and held on to it. "Maybe we should talk."

"It's three thirty in the morning."

He just looked at her.

She squirmed. "Talking makes things real. And real things . . . well, they end, Mateo."

"I'm not going anywhere. Stop running."

"I'm not trying to." She tossed up her hands. "Look, in case you haven't noticed, I'm a handful."

"That's okay, I've got two hands."

She smiled, but her eyes also filled. "I told you from the very beginning," she managed around a rough throat. "I don't date. And I don't sleep in other people's beds either. I . . ." She broke off to breathe. "I *can't* sleep in other people's bed. And you know why."

His eyes softened as he reached for her, sudden understanding in every line of his body now.

"I'm sorry," she whispered. "I really am, but—"

"It's okay. It's okay, Charlotte," he murmured, slipping a hand in hers. "We could always try your bed."

She stared down at their entwined fingers, running the pad of her thumb over his calloused palm. She shivered, remembering some of the things his hands had done to her, all incredibly, amazingly perfect. "I don't sleep well if someone else is in my bed."

"Then lucky for you I don't mind sleeping on the floor. Did it for most of my premed college years actually. Couldn't afford my own room, so I couch-surfed. It was better than a park bench." He reached back out the door and picked up something he'd apparently left on the porch before knocking.

A rolled-up sleeping bag. "This thing has seen a lot," he said. "Your floor will be luxurious accommodations, trust me."

She stared at the sleeping bag and realized . . . he'd known her problem all along. Known and understood. And had come up with a work-around. As if maybe she truly, honestly did mean something to him.

"My floor is hardwood," she said inanely.

His eyes twinkled, but he didn't smile. "Doesn't bother me, as long as it doesn't bother you." With his free hand, he tipped her face up to his. "*Does* it bother you, Charlotte? That I want to sleep near you? That I want to be with you?"

Staring at him for a long beat, she slowly shook her head.

He smiled, stepped all the way inside, and closed the door at his back before taking her hand and just looking at her.

Letting her make the move, she realized. So she led him upstairs, her heart pounding in her chest and in her ears. Incredibly aware of him at her back, she brought him inside her room.

He shut the door, walked to her bed, and pulled back her covers, gesturing for her to get in. "You're cold," he murmured, "wearing only that stolen shirt."

"Borrowed."

"What's mine is yours. Besides, I love the way you look in it."

He pulled the covers up to her chin, planted a hand on either side of her head and leaned in to kiss her softly. "'Night."

Then he unrolled his sleeping bag and slid into it. On the floor.

She stared up at the ceiling, waiting for the familiar panic. Or at least unease.

Neither came.

She let out a breath and dropped a hand over the side of the bed.

Reaching up, he slipped his into hers. "Sweet dreams, Charlotte."

For a beat, she lay there, taking in the room. Quiet. Warm. Dark. She could hear Mateo's steady breathing from the floor.

Hers wasn't steady. In fact, she might not be breathing at all. Because it was decision time. Right here, right now. If she was going to face her fears, there was no better man to do that with than Mateo. She knew this because every time she was anywhere in his proximity, she felt a calm wash over her, as well as a sense of anticipation. The very best kind of anticipation. It was like her body recognized him as a soulmate.

Even as her brain pretended such a thing didn't exist.

She didn't want to be alone. She didn't want to give one horrific memory the power to steal away the hope of a happy future. She wanted to reach out and grab what was hers for the taking.

She was scared. Terrified, actually. But she was also a hundred percent positive she was doing the right thing. "Mateo?"

"Yeah?"

She slid out of her bed. "Move over?"

He scooted and made room for her, and she crawled into his sleeping bag.

CHAPTER 25

The next day Jane grabbed her lunch bag from the Homeward resort's staff fridge where she'd stashed it and headed outside. The temp was a brisk thirty-two degrees, but in the sun at high altitude, it would feel warm and glorious. And after five hours in the packed urgent care, she needed some warm and glorious.

But even working as hard as she did in Tahoe, she enjoyed the work. For one thing, she didn't see the death and gore up here as she did for the rest of the year.

But the biggie, the thing that kept her coming back, was the connections she'd made in spite of herself. She'd grown roots here. Her relationship with Charlotte. Mateo. Even Cat. Her grandpa . . . And she knew the list wasn't complete without Levi on it, no matter how temporary they were.

Temporary.

She'd always considered that word to be a part of her personality.

And now that she'd fulfilled her promise to be his pretend girl-friend for his parents' anniversary dinner— She froze halfway to a table. *She'd fulfilled her promise to be his pretend girlfriend.*

There was no need for Levi to see her anymore.

Little black dots danced in front of her eyes and she realized she wasn't breathing. Gulping in air, she put a hand to her aching chest. For the first time in her life, she'd begun to settle, feeling things that were the very opposite of temporary.

And it was over anyway by her own decree when she'd extracted that ridiculous promise from Levi in the very beginning.

The snow crunched beneath her feet as she began walking again, making her way through the maze of skiers to a small, empty table.

Was it over?

Would she see him again?

And what business did she have for wanting to so badly her heart was threatening to pound out of her chest?

When she opened her eyes again, she wasn't alone.

Shirl and Tess were seated opposite her, smiling.

"Heard you made an appointment for Cat to get spayed," Shirl said, looking pleased.

Jane had to clear her throat to speak. "We decided to keep each other. My friend Charlotte offered to keep feeding her after I'm gone, so she'll always have a home. What are you doing here?"

"We're not stalking you or anything," Shirl said.

Tess snorted. "We're *totally* stalking you." She looked recovered from her shocking pregnancy reveal last night. Serene and calm. "But we're the good kind of stalkers, because . . ." She opened a large lunch box. "We come bearing food."

"Thanks, but I brought my own." Jane pulled out a banana, a yogurt, and a package of peanut butter crackers, all pilfered from Charlotte's kitchen because she hadn't had a chance to get to the store. Oh, who was she kidding. She hated going to the store, she always waited until she was half starved to death, and by then Charlotte had stocked her up.

Shirl looked over Jane's lunch and shook her head. "That's just sad."

"I packed at five this morning," Jane said in her defense. "I wasn't feeling like much then."

"How about a meatloaf sandwich?" Shirl asked.

"It's her special recipe," Tess said. "It's crackalicious."

"It doesn't contain real crack," Shirl said. "I do have a few secret ingredients in there, but they're all perfectly legal, I promise you." She pushed a glass container at Jane. "Brought you one."

"How did you know I'd be able to eat with you?"

"Just hoping." Shirl smiled. "I wanted to tell you how good you are for Levi."

Jane's smile faltered as she realized the depths of the deception she and Levi had laid out and how it was not only going to destroy herself—something she was trying to come to terms with—but also hurt others. In trying to make his mom happy, they were now about to do the very opposite. "You know I'm leaving soon," she said carefully.

"Yes." Shirl reached for Jane's hand. "And you know about Amy?"

Jane nodded.

Shirl and Tess exchanged a knowing look.

"What?" Jane asked.

Shirl squeezed Jane's fingers gently. "Amy was his best friend for years and years. And then his girlfriend. And then his fiancée."

"I get that."

"But you might not get that he hasn't really let another woman in since. You're the first. That's how we knew before we'd even met you that you had to be special."

"Because I'm Levi's girlfriend," Jane said quietly, hating the facade she and Levi had created.

"No, because you're Jane Parks."

Jane froze, feeling that definitive statement clear through her heart like an arrow had pierced it. How ironic that all her life she'd shied away from commitments to keep her heart safe, only to fail utterly here. Because what she felt for Levi was shockingly real, and now she was going to hurt his family, who didn't deserve it.

"At least take a bite," Shirl said, nudging the meatloaf sandwich closer.

Not knowing what else to do, Jane took a bite of the sandwich and— "Oh my God."

Tess smiled. "Right?"

Shirl just sat back, looking pleased.

Jane practically moaned her way through the entire sandwich and just barely managed not to lick the container when she was done.

"Here." Levi's mom was going through her phone, tapping away, and then Jane's phone buzzed with a text. "The recipe."

"Are you kidding me?" Tess asked. "I've been asking you for that recipe for years."

"You don't need the meatloaf," Shirl said.

"Was that a fat joke? I'm pregnant, not fat."

"Honey." Shirl reached out and hugged Tess. "Of course that wasn't a fat joke, you're perfect. I just meant that you don't need the recipe because I'll always cook it for you. You've given me Peyton, and now another sweet grandbaby is coming . . ." She put her hand on Tess's still-flat belly. "And you indulge me by living at home and letting me be part of their daily village."

"It's because I can't afford to move out."

"Shh. Don't ruin my fantasy."

Tess laughed, but Jane actually felt her heart tug hard at these two women who'd somehow become a part of her life.

How was she going to let them go? How was she going to let Levi go? To distract herself, she looked at the recipe. "This might be above my pay grade."

"Levi loves this recipe," Shirl said.

"Are you suggesting that Jane cook it to snare Levi?" Tess asked in horror. "Mom, women don't have to cook for their men anymore. You know that, right? Love comes from the heart, not the stomach."

"Bull pucky," Shirl said. "Cook the meatloaf, Jane. Trust me on this."

"Mom, seriously. Stop. You're setting women back fifty years."

Shirl shrugged. "I'm still married to the man I married forty years ago. The proof's in the pudding. Or, in this case, the meatloaf."

Jane didn't want to be rude and disagree, but personally she thought if a man wanted her for her meatloaf, he was going to go through life greatly disappointed.

But if said man loved her for her and her alone . . . and if that man was Levi, she knew she'd do everything she could to make it work. How scary was that?

WHEN JANE GOT off work, she stopped at the store and bought the ingredients for the meatloaf. But *only* because it'd been a most *excellent* meatloaf.

She wandered into the kitchen and found Mateo, who had Charlotte up against the fridge. They were . . . well, kissing seemed too tame a word, but even from across the room Jane could see how much he loved her even as his hands slid up her back, pulling her even closer.

Jane cleared her throat. "Nice use of appliance."

Charlotte gasped and broke free.

Mateo grinned. "We got hungry."

Jane loved the look on Charlotte's face. Happiness. "Good thing I'm cooking then."

Charlotte blinked. "Did you say . . . cooking?" She smacked Mateo lightly on his arm. "I knew it. You kissed all my brain cells gone because I could swear she just said she was . . . cooking."

"Ha-ha," Jane said. "Watch and learn."

When she pulled the meatloaf out of the oven an hour later, the kitchen was crowded. Zoe and Mariella had joined them, brought in by the scent.

"Who are you and what have you done with my Jane?" Charlotte asked.

"Ha-ha. And it's just an experiment." Jane handed out forks and everyone dug in. Jane knew it had to be good when the only sound in the room was chewing.

"You've been holding out on me," Charlotte said, mouth full.

"On all of us," Zoe said, shoveling meatloaf into her mouth.

Mariella was eating and working on her laptop at the same time. "Is it *for fuck's sake* or *for fuck sakes*?" she asked the room. "It's a work email, so it has to sound professional."

Charlotte choked on her bite. "Honey, what have I told you about using the f-bomb for work?"

"To do it behind my boss's back, not to his face?"

Charlotte waved a hand like *Well, there's your answer.*

Mariella sighed. "And to think, I grew up for this shit." And then she hit the delete key a bunch of times.

"You know who should have some of this?" Mateo asked. "Levi."

"Seems only fair," Charlotte said, looking at Jane. "Seeing as his mama gave you the recipe."

Just yesterday, Jane would've agreed. But she'd been jerked out of her fantasy bubble after Shirl and Tess's visit, making her realize that one, she'd fallen for Levi for real and she still didn't know what to do with that, and two, continuing the charade and hurting the people Levi loved felt incredibly wrong. "I've got someone else in mind for the meatloaf," she said.

Charlotte smiled. "Your grandpa."

Jane touched the tip of her nose. Charlotte pulled her in for a warm hug.

"He looks good on you," Jane whispered.

"I rather think it's the other way around," Charlotte drawled.

Jane pulled back and looked into Charlotte's eyes. "You're okay?"

"Well, I'm still neurotic as hell, but okay? Yes."

Jane laughed, kissed Charlotte on the cheek, and headed out.

When she pulled into her grandpa's driveway, she stared at the truck parked in it.

Levi's truck.

Her heart skipped a beat in confusion, but also happiness.

She walked up the driveway and looked inside Levi's truck. Empty. And the hood was cold. She knocked on the front door, but when no one answered, she let herself in. "Hello?" she called out, walking through the living room before coming to a stop.

Levi was on a ladder, head into the attic access, so all she could see was a pair of long denim-clad legs and possibly the best ass in Tahoe. "What are you doing?"

There came a solid thunk, followed by an oath, and then Levi craned his neck to look down at her, rubbing the top of his head.

"You okay?"

He smiled. "I am now. And hey."

"Hey yourself," she said casually because it felt way too good to see him. "What are you doing here?"

"Your grandpa called me. He wanted to know who to hire to make this place a smart house. I told him I'd do it for him." He twisted and put his head back into the attic.

Fine with her. Great view. "You didn't have to do this." His jeans were faded and fit just right. His long-sleeved Henley rose up a bit when he stretched to reach something, exposing a strip of skin that made her mouth go a little dry.

"Don't stand too close," he called down. "It's dusty up here."

"Just appreciating the view."

He craned his neck and met her gaze, his own hot. "Say that again and I'll come down."

"And then?"

"And then you're coming too."

She laughed, but he began to climb down the ladder with intent and she almost swallowed her tongue.

He grinned at the look on her face. "Later," he promised huskily and kissed her. When he pulled back, he eyed the bag she held with great interest. "That smells delicious."

"Hungry?"

"Always." He kissed her again, a long, deep, drugging kiss that had her forgetting time and place. By the time she came out of the sexual haze he'd put her in, she realized he'd stopped kissing her and had taken ahold of the bag.

Grandpa came in the back door wearing a tool belt, and she walked over to him to greet him with a hug.

"Found my hammer," he said with pride, and Jane realized that Levi had clearly included him in the work, which meant that the job was probably taking him three times as long as it should.

Damn. He was truly the best pretend boyfriend she'd ever had. More than that, he was the best man who'd ever been in her life.

"Your man's had me working," her grandpa said, looking pleased with himself.

And here was yet another person who was going to be hurt now that her pretense was over. "Grandpa, you know he's not. That we're . . . not."

Her grandpa glanced over at Levi, who had moved away from them and was cleaning up, then gave Jane a rather impressive eye roll. "Yeah, yeah, I know. You got stuck on the gondola, thought you were going to die, promised his mom he was happy with a woman in his life so she wouldn't think her son had died lonely and alone. It's alllllll pretend."

"You don't believe it?" Jane asked.

"Sugar Plum, I'm not even sure *you* believe it."

"I have food," she said inanely.

Levi was back. "What takeout is it?"

"It's not. I actually cooked. It's your mom's meatloaf."

Levi's eyes widened. "She gave you the recipe?"

She nodded.

"She never gives anyone the recipe. Her own sister died without ever acquiring the recipe, and there were many, many attempts."

She gave him a smile that she hoped was her usual wattage. "She likes me." She took the bag back and carried it into the kitchen. She divided the leftover meatloaf into three portions and carried everything out to the living room, where they all sat squished on the couch and ate while watching *Jeopardy!*

Before Levi, she'd never eaten a family dinner like the one at his house, with fancy china at a decorated table that had looked like something off Pinterest. Here at her grandpa's, they were feet up on the coffee table, Grandpa yelling out all the answers to *Jeopardy!*

Even if her life had depended on it, Jane wouldn't have been able to say which dinner had been better. They'd both felt . . . right.

It's still not real . . .

Problem was, it *felt* real, more real than anything in her entire life.

After dinner, Levi followed her home. He parked and opened her door before she freed herself of her seat belt.

"This is usually where we argue about me walking you to your door," he said. "But just FYI, I'm still going to. Not because you're not capable of taking care of yourself, but because it's the right thing to do, and . . ." He smiled. "It gives me an extra few minutes with you, where I plan on stealing at least one kiss and hopefully copping a feel as well."

"You're going to get more than that." Yes, she was crazy to spend another night with him knowing she could no longer separate her feelings for him from the physical act of being with him, but she didn't care. She wanted him, even if it was for the last time.

They walked hand in hand to the door. On the porch, he looked around. "Where's Cat?"

"It's a surprise. Do you have a minute?"

He cupped her face and smiled. "For you, I've got *all* the minutes."

Her heart squeezed, which she tried to ignore. She unlocked the front door with her own key—smiling when Levi looked surprised at the fact she didn't knock first. Still holding his hand, she tugged him into the living room and turned to the couch. "Levi, meet Zoe and Mariella, two of my roommates."

Zoe and Mariella sat up straight. Zoe dusted some chip crumbs off her shirt and Mariella pointed at Jane. "Hey, you *do* know our names," she teased.

Jane felt her face heat up and heard Levi's soft laugh, but then there was a loud, demanding meow and they all looked down at the large gray cat unfurling herself from where she'd been lying in front of the woodstove. Chirping in happiness, she ran over to Jane.

"You invited her in?" Levi asked, crouching down to smile at Cat, who bumped her head against Levi's thigh, demanding to be petted.

Levi obliged and Jane found herself rubbing her aching chest as she stared down at two of her favorite living creatures. She no longer had any idea how she was supposed to do this and then leave at the end of the season. But she did know it was going to hurt like hell.

"Saw your name painted on your door," Zoe said. "Congrats."

"For what?"

Zoe smiled. "For coming in out of the storm along with Cat."

Damn. She felt her face heat up again, but not from embarrassment this time. It was an overload of something she almost didn't recognize—contentment. Which meant, of course, she was doomed. She didn't have a lot of experience with contentment, but she knew one thing for absolute certain.

It never lasted.

"Show me your door," Levi said softly in her ear.

Which was how she found herself taking his hand and leading him up the stairs.

Levi smiled at the prominently painted *JANE* and the landscape. "Nice. You going to invite me in too? Like you did Cat?"

"It's a little messy."

"I like a little messy," he said and kissed her softly. Letting her know he liked her just as she was.

A powerful realization. A little flummoxed, she pushed the door open and walked in. Levi followed, nudged the door closed with his foot, then turned her in his arms to face him. He let his smile fade as he looked into her eyes. "You're an enigma, Jane, and I love that about you. You have all these secret compartments and hidden locked boxes, and there's no instructions or manual. It's been a thrill of a ride, the not knowing what's around the next corner, but you know what's an even bigger thrill?"

Speechless, she shook her head.

Cupping her face, he slid his fingers into her hair, the pads of his thumbs brushing her jaw lightly. "Being on the inside."

Her breath stuttered in her chest. "You think you're on the inside?" she asked lightly, going for a teasing tone.

"I do." He paused. "I hope."

She dropped her head to his chest to muffle her startled laugh. Because when he was right, he was right. "You are," she said. "In, I mean. But we no longer have to pretend anything for anyone, so . . ." She shook her head. "What are we really doing here?"

"I don't know about you, but for me this is real." He brushed his mouth to her temple. "Has been for a while now."

She lifted her head again, suddenly having trouble drawing air into her lungs. "But you promised. You promised not to fall for me."

His gaze met hers, his own warm and loving. "Some promises are meant to be broken."

This had her breaking out into a cold sweat of sheer nerves. "How can you be so sure?"

He shrugged. "I've been sure on my end of things since that night you stood over me bleeding on the floor of that gondola, stripping out of your clothes."

She choked out a laugh past the emotions clogging her throat. "I didn't strip out of all my clothes!"

He smiled, but then let it fade. "You're a tough nut to crack, Jane. I've only been able to *hope* that I was slowly worming my way into your heart as well. But now . . ."

"Now what?" she whispered.

"Sometimes I catch you looking at me like I'm a cookies 'n' cream cupcake," he whispered back.

Was he right? No. Because he was better than a cupcake. "Maybe I'm really just thinking about a cookies 'n' cream cupcake."

He smiled. "You're a cute liar."

Maybe, but she wasn't capable of baring her heart and soul. She didn't know how. "I'll show you cute," she said, needing to change the direction of this conversation.

His eyes said he knew she was holding back, but he didn't call her on it. Instead he smiled and said, "Please do."

So she did.

All night long.

She'd been trying to prove a point to herself, but hell if she could remember said point. And it didn't matter because what had started out funny and teasing ended up being the most meaningful night of her life.

CHAPTER 26

The next morning, Jane jerked awake at the sound of her alarm. A long arm reached over her and hit snooze.

She turned and faced the naked man in her bed. The naked man with sexy scruff on his jaw and a glint of intent in his eyes as he pulled her into him and kissed her.

"Wait!"

Levi pulled back a fraction and lifted a brow.

"Um, hi."

His mouth quirked. "Hi."

She squirmed a bit, and not just because she didn't know how to do morning-afters, but because she was naked too, which was a whole lot of nakedness pressed up against more nakedness. He felt warm and sexy and . . . *hello*, ready to start the day.

"Ignore that," he said. "What did you want to tell me?"

"I don't remember."

He laughed softly and lowered his head again.

It was two snoozes and an orgasm later before she gasped and leapt out of bed. "Oh my God, I'm going to be late."

"I thought your shift didn't start until eight." He squinted at the clock. "It's not even the butt crack of dawn."

She was hopping into the clothes he'd so helpfully got her out of the night before. "I'm meeting my grandpa for breakfast. I'll grab a shower at work—"

He caught her at her bedroom door. He'd had time to pull on only his jeans, but hadn't fastened them. Gently he pressed her back against the wood, cupped her face, and gave her a drugging kiss so full of longing and desire and affection, she forgot she was in a hurry.

"Good morning," he whispered against her mouth.

She stared at him and then narrowed her gaze. "Do you hear that?"

He cocked his head. "Hear what?"

She slid out from between him and the door and went hands on hips, staring around her room. Her gaze landed on the blanket that had slid to the very bottom of her bed, balled up. There was a suspicious lump under that blanket.

And it was . . . purring.

"Cat?"

The lump stopped moving.

"I know it's you," Jane said. "I can hear you purring."

The purring stopped.

"Oh my God." She pulled the blanket back from the bed and Cat blinked her gray eyes up at Jane lazily. Innocently. "Don't even try," she said. "We've agreed that mi casa es su casa, but my bed is *my* bed."

Cat just stared at her.

"I mean it. You're nocturnal. The other night you batted my

hair in the middle of the night. You stole my pillow. You knocked things off my shelves . . ."

Cat's expression was boredom personified.

"We agreed you'd sleep on the floor," Jane said. "A point that we negotiated at two A.M. and was finally agreed on by both parties."

Cat began to wash her face.

Levi smiled. "Marches to her own beat, huh?"

She choked out a laugh. "That describes both of my current bedmates."

"And are you comparing me to your cat?"

"Well, she does remind me of you," she pointed out. "Confident. Pushing. And then there are those gray eyes . . ."

Levi scratched the cat's back, then along the side of her face and under her chin, and the thing actually rolled her eyes in ecstasy. The man smiled. "There are some similarities. But I'd say she's more like you than me."

Jane crossed her arms. "Oh, do tell."

"She lets me pet her on her terms, allowing a little friendship and affection—not too much, of course—and then goes back to her life."

Jane narrowed her eyes.

Levi smiled.

The cat looked back and forth between them until, with a last flick of her tail and a sniff, she jumped down and padded out the door.

"Humph," Jane said, and Levi laughed and kissed her again. "Later, babe."

She nodded, but struck dumb by his kiss, she didn't move. And why did that keep happening? Shouldn't she be used to their chemistry by now?

He grinned. "Cute. But you need to get going, remember?"

"Huh?"

"Your grandpa. Breakfast."

When he was this close to her, the only thing she thought about was getting hot and bothered with him. As if he could hear her thoughts, his hand brushed up her side, skimming the outer swell of her breast before palming her neck so his thumb could play with her lower lip. A rush of desire shot southward and she went hot all over. Damn. She pointed at him. "You do that on purpose."

"Feel free to get back at me any time."

She was still smiling ten minutes later when she pulled into the Stovetop Diner parking lot. Even after all the time she'd spent with Levi, she still wanted more. A lot more.

Because it is real . . .

Since that thought gave her heart palpitations, she looked around. She'd beaten her grandpa here, which was unusual, since she knew for a fact he was usually halfway through a meal by now.

He showed up five minutes later, moving a little slower than she'd seen so far. She stood up, kissed him on his cheek, and then watched him slide into the booth as if he hurt everywhere. "What's wrong?"

"I'm old." He flashed a grin.

She didn't return it because his mirth didn't go all the way to his eyes. "Grandpa—"

The waitress came by with a smile and a coffeepot.

"Bless you," her grandpa said, and the woman, three decades younger than him, gave him a wink.

"Hey, sexy. Your usual?" she asked.

"Yes, thank you, doll."

The waitress turned and headed back to the bakery display.

"What's your usual?" Jane asked him.

"Two Danish pastries."

"What? No. *Are you kidding me?* Look, I'm sure you're on a specific diet, right? One that I know damn well can't possibly allow for two Danish pastries."

He waved this off. "I'm like an old phone battery, Sugar Plum. Even when I charge myself overnight for twelve hours, by nine A.M, I'm already drained to forty percent. I need the sugar boost."

Jane gestured for the waitress. "Could we get two of your healthy start breakfasts? Hold the pastries?"

The waitress looked at Grandpa, popping her gum. "I like this one," she told him.

"Yeah, me too," Grandpa said. "But she's a little bossy."

"You could use some of that in your life." This time the waitress winked at Jane.

Soon as she was gone, Jane turned on her grandpa. "Do you *really* always eat Danishes for breakfast?"

"Unless you're here, yeah."

She was baffled. "But you had another heart attack."

"Yes. *Had.* And I'm not planning on having another unless you're going to keep yelling at me."

She sighed. "We've talked about this. You can't eat whatever you want anymore—that ship sailed. You have to give up the crap food."

He reached over and covered her hand in his. "You know I'm going to bite it and go to the farm someday no matter what I eat, right?"

"Yes, but not any time soon, right?"

He shrugged and dropped the eye contact. "No one knows. That's why it's called life."

She hesitated. "Something's off," she said quietly. "Something's wrong. What is it?"

"Nothing."

"Grandpa. You swear?"

He lifted a hand. "I solemnly swear. I'm fine, relax. And better yet, let me relax, okay? I've lived a long life, I deserve some joy."

She stared at him. For whatever reason, she couldn't get a bead on him this morning. She felt certain he was holding something back, but short of pushing him, which she knew would yield her nothing, she didn't know what else to do. "Can you find joy in something other than Danishes?"

At that, he looked into her eyes again. "I can," he said with quiet, warm conviction. "I have."

She felt the threat of tears in the back of her throat and gave him a smile. "Love you."

"Love you, too, Sugar Plum. To the moon and back."

An hour later she was at work, running her butt off as usual. Halfway through her shift, she got a rare lull in patients. She eyed the screen in front of her, where she sat typing her reports. Then she looked around.

No one was paying her any attention.

She sucked in a breath, cracked her knuckles, and did something she was not allowed to do. She typed in her grandpa's name, accessed his patient records—in Tahoe, all the doctors were contractors to the hospital, so all the records were stored in one system—and began to read.

CHAPTER 27

Charlotte's workday was its usual crazy, so by the time she made it to the break room, desperate for caffeine and a bite of something, she was beyond famished. She crossed the room, heading to the staff fridge before she remembered she hadn't packed herself anything.

Damn. She was channeling Jane now.

"Whatever is in your bag, it smells amazing when you open the fridge," Sandra said to her.

Charlotte turned in surprise. "What?"

"Your lunch. There's a big brown bag in there with your name on it. Smells like Mexican food, and I'm jealous as hell."

Charlotte opened the fridge and gaped. Because there was indeed a big brown bag in there with her name on it, and it smelled delicious. "I didn't pack myself anything."

"Well then, can we pretend it says *Sandra* on it?" the nurse asked with a laugh.

Hell, no. Because she was pretty sure she recognized that handwriting, and the person who'd written it could cook, maybe even better than she could. So she took the bag out of the fridge and to the counter, and opened it up.

There was a glass container filled with what looked like two enchiladas, a side of tortilla chips, and pico de gallo.

Her mouth watered as she pulled out the folded note.

C
Enjoy.
love, M

She stood there frozen in place.

Love, M . . . ?

In her pocket, her phone buzzed, indicating an incoming text, and she pulled it out.

MATEO: Check the fridge before the vultures get to it.

CHARLOTTE: You didn't have to!

MATEO: Actually, I didn't. If you'll remember, I ended up in your bed last night when I got home at midnight. My mom left me a fridge full of food. And I know you didn't have time to cook in your kitchen, since we were cooking in your bedroom until dawn, and I didn't want you to be hungry.

Charlotte laughed out loud, then bit her lower lip when Sandra glanced over at her. She shook her head at the nurse. "Nothing," she said.

"Nothing my ass," Sandra said on a grin. "I wouldn't mind having someone put that look on my face. The one that says you've been kept up all night in the very best of ways. Tell me it's Dr. Hottie Patottie."

"There are some things a woman should keep to herself," Charlotte said with a smile.

Sandra grinned back. "Well, whatever you're keeping to yourself, it agrees with you."

Charlotte headed to the ER and pulled Mateo into a corner.

"The note," she said.

"Good, you got it. I wasn't sure the food would be safe."

"The note," she said again, hearing a touch of hysteria in her voice.

Mateo just looked at her.

"'Love, M'?"

His dark eyes never wavered from hers. "Yes."

"You . . . love me?"

His hands came up to her face. "Yes," he said simply.

She drew in a shuddery breath.

"I don't expect—"

"I love you too. But—"

He winced at the *but*.

"But," she said softly, "I'm not the girl who dreamed about a wedding and kids. I'm . . ." She shook her head. "I'm still not sure I see those things for myself."

"A piece of paper linking us . . . kids . . ." He smiled into her eyes. "I can do without those things. What I can't do without is you, Charlotte."

Heart. Melted.

He started to kiss her, but someone was calling his name urgently from down the hall and he straightened. "We're swamped. I gotta go. But I can't until I know we're okay."

She smiled. "We're more than okay."

He smiled back and vanished.

Still smiling, she left the building and walked over to the urgent care next door to share her lunch with Jane.

She found her sitting behind the counter staring off into space, looking pale.

And maybe like she'd been crying.

"What is it?" Charlotte asked.

Jane just shook her head.

"Jane—"

"What is that amazing scent?"

Charlotte looked around. There was no one waiting to be seen. "Let's take lunch."

They went into the back, heated the container, then sat at the small staff table and shared the food.

"Mateo cooked this?" Jane asked after shoving in a few big bites. "You're going to have to marry him, you do realize that, right?"

"It's his mom's cooking."

"But he shared it with you."

"Yes," Charlotte said, unable to keep the small smile off her face.

Jane took in her expression and nodded with satisfaction, though the good humor didn't make it all the way to her eyes. "He's the One."

Charlotte set her fork down. "You ready to talk?"

"No."

"But you will anyway?"

Jane pushed the food back. "My grandpa has cancer."

Charlotte felt the breath stutter in her throat. "Oh, Jane. I'm—"

"—Sorry?" Jane shook her head. "I am too." She looked away. "I'm . . ." She stood up and paced the room. "I'm feeling a lot of things."

"You're angry," Charlotte said softly.

"Damn right I am."

"It's one of the first emotions to hit with a cancer diagnosis."

Jane stopped pacing, "I'm not one of your patient's family members."

Charlotte nodded. "Of course not. I'm sorry."

Jane closed her eyes for a beat, then sighed. "No. I'm sorry. I shouldn't have snapped at you. He didn't tell me about it. I wasn't important enough to him. I had to find out on my own."

Charlotte's first thought was pain and fury for Jane, who'd started to trust her grandpa after a life filled with hard-earned mistrust of her family. If the man had been standing here, Charlotte could have killed him with her bare hands. Her second thought gave her an icy shiver. "Jane. Tell me you didn't defy HIPAA—"

Jane's face closed off and Charlotte's heart took another hard kick. "Jane . . ." She broke off when her phone beeped. Work. She was needed in the OR stat.

"Go," Jane said. "I'm fine."

No, she wasn't, but Charlotte had no choice. "I'll call you soon as I can."

Jane turned away and nodded, and Charlotte had to walk away. One of the hardest things she'd ever done.

JANE MOVED ROBOTICALLY through the rest of her shift. The second it was over, she went straight to her car and started driving.

Charlotte had been right. She needed to talk this out with her grandpa. Without jumping to conclusions. It made perfect sense. It was the logical thing to do.

But here was the thing. She didn't feel logical. Which undoubtedly was the reason that when she parked, she found herself at Levi's house.

Probably because her heart knew what her brain had accepted: that in that moment, she needed Levi. She could feel the vibration of panic and anxiety just beneath her skin. She was scared and angry, and on the verge of losing it as she got out of her car.

Levi opened the door before she got to it. "You're off early—" he started, but then his smile faded as he came down the steps to meet her. "What's wrong?"

She bit down hard on her lip, but the tears came anyway, silently spilling down her cheeks.

"Are you hurt? Where?" He reached for her, reeling her in, eyes sharp as they ran over every inch of her.

"Not hurt," she managed. "Just . . . I got some hard news, but I can't say it yet." Not without completely losing it. "I need a minute."

His eyes were filled with a deep concern, and there was a grim set to his mouth as he gathered her into his arms and held her close, resting his cheek against the top of her head. "Whatever it is, Jane, I'm right here. We'll deal with it."

She had no idea how or why, but he never failed to strip her defenses away—a double-edged sword because oh, how she *hated* being vulnerable or seeming weak. But she fisted her hands in his shirt and held on tight.

They stood like that right in the middle of the front yard for a long moment, her a complete hot mess soaking up the comfort and peace she always found in his arms, him a solid, steady rock. And then suddenly she felt a gentle patting on her back from hands that weren't Levi's—which she knew because he had one hand cupping the back of her head, the other low on her spine.

And then yet a third person's arms hugged her from behind.

"Jane?" It was Shirl. "Baby, what's the matter?"

"Whatever it is, we got you," Tess said.

"I've got an extra taco. Do you want it?" This was from Peyton, and Jane lifted her head to find that the entire Cutler family had come out of the woodwork to check on her.

The front door was still wide open, and from inside the house came the most delicious scent of Mexican food. She'd interrupted their dinner. She looked up and saw Hank waiting on the porch, clearly not wanting to crowd her. Peyton had a makeshift bib of a paper towel tucked into the neck of her sweater and a taco in one hand. Jasper was at her side, very gently and stealthily licking the taco shell.

"I'm sorry." Jane swiped at her eyes. "I didn't mean to interrupt a family dinner."

"Honey, don't you give it a second thought," Shirl said. "Come inside, I've got food. And hot tea."

"Yes," Tess said. "And I've got something to lace the tea with."

"For me too, Mommy?" Peyton asked.

"No, but you can have a lollipop."

Levi looked at his mom and sister. There was a silent exchange, and then everyone nodded and went back inside except Levi. "We don't have to go," he said. "We can go somewhere else, anywhere you want, name it."

She sniffed. "The food smells good."

He smiled. "Here it is then. Talk, or food first?"

She'd never be able to eat until she got this out. "Talk."

He offered her a hand, and together they walked inside. He pulled her through the crowd of his well-meaning family and up the stairs.

Despite the mountains of paperwork on the desk, Levi's clothes over the back of the couch, and Peyton's toys strewn everywhere, the room felt warm and cozy. She sniffed again, trying to get ahold of herself. "You really are a slob like Tess said."

"Ha-ha." He reached out and swiped everything from the couch with a single swoop of a hand. "Have a seat."

When she did, he came up with a box of tissues from somewhere and sat next to her, pulling her into his side. "Tell me what's going on."

Right. Now she had to say it out loud. "At breakfast this morning, there was something off about my grandpa, but I couldn't place it. Last night I'd asked him about his health and he told me he was fine. Promised me, even." She gulped in some air. "But he's not. He's got cancer." Just saying the words out loud had the horror bubbling up all over again. Her eyes filled. "I just found him again and he's going to die."

"Oh, Jane." He hugged her tight, his jaw resting on the top of her head as he rocked her a little bit, and for a moment, she sank into him and let his strength seep into her.

"What kind of cancer?" he asked. "So many are curable, now more than ever."

"Yes, if the patient elects to seek treatment." A little bitter about that, she climbed off of his lap and began to pace the room, not easy with everything on the floor. But Charlotte was right, she was angry, very angry, and that was okay because behind that was a grief she wasn't ready to face. "It's lung cancer. Apparently he was successfully treated two years ago, but it's back and . . ." She swallowed hard. "He is refusing treatment this time. He's just going to let himself die, without telling me. How could he not tell me? How could he look me in the eyes and promise me that everything was okay when he knew, dammit, he *knew* that nothing was okay and it wouldn't ever be okay again."

Levi rose to his feet and stepped into her path.

She lifted her face to his. "*How?*" she demanded.

He ran his hands up her arms. "It's complicated. You more than anyone knows that. You're only just back in his life. It's possible he just hasn't worked up the nerve to tell you yet. Cancer isn't exactly an easy thing to talk about, especially with someone you love."

"No." She twisted away, turned her back on him and his empathy. "It's *exactly* the thing you talk about to someone you love. In fact, it's the first thing he should've told me. Like: 'Hi, I'm so glad you're back. You should know, though, that I've got cancer, but I love you enough to tell you the truth.'"

"Jane—"

"Stop." Deep in her head somewhere past denial and anger, she knew she was being unreasonable—irrational, even. She knew there was never an easy way or a convenient time to talk about something like this, but she had thought when it came to her and her grandpa, their relationship was real this time. Clearly she'd gotten it wrong. Hell, maybe she was still nothing but an inconvenience. He certainly couldn't possibly really love her "to the moon and back" if he'd kept such a huge, unforgivable secret.

"This might have nothing to do with you or your relationship with him," Levi said quietly. "This might just be about him, and, Jane, you may have to accept that."

"He still should've told me right away." She hugged herself, staring out the window. "He knows I'm going to be gone again soon."

"Is it possible that he didn't want to spend the last of his time with you talking about death and being sick, or defending his choice of treatment? That he just wanted to soak up every moment he could with you before you go?"

There was a tightness to his voice, but she shook her head. "He chose *no* treatment. None. Zero. Zilch."

"Again, his choice."

Fueled by panic and anxiety and fury, she whirled on him. "Are you actually trying to defend his decision to me? There are treatments available, Levi. There is no defense for what he's doing."

"I assume you've talked to him about this. Calmly. Rationally. No judgment."

She tossed up her hands. "Of course I haven't. I came straight here." She felt her eyes fill. "I'm just so mad at him," she whispered. "*So* mad."

He nodded and came slowly toward her, making his way through the roadblocks without any trouble. "It's understandable," he said. "But it's possible he made his choice *before* you were back in his life."

She stared at him as his words hit her like a one-two punch to the solar plexus. "So it's my fault for not reaching out to him sooner?"

"No, of course not. But I do think he might've made a different choice now—something you won't know unless you talk to him."

She pressed the heels of her hands to her temples. "You don't get it. His decision was made months and months ago, and cancer doesn't waste time. There's no going back and fixing this in the here and now."

"You don't know that."

"Oh, Mr. Fix-It, but I *do* know it. I accessed his records, Levi. All of them."

He was toe-to-toe with her now, but not touching her, looking suddenly both incredulous and angry, and she'd like to know what he could possibly have to be angry about. *She* was the angry one, as was her right.

"Let me make sure I understand," he said carefully. "You said he seemed off. Then he told you he had cancer, and you pressed for more information and he showed you his medical records. Yes?"

She looked away. "He *did* seem off. And I didn't press him for answers because he wouldn't have given them to me."

"So you, what, accessed them without permission, meaning you risked your entire nursing career, not to mention your license, to avoid a difficult conversation with your grandpa?"

Shit. Well, when he put it like that . . . But her fuse had been lit, which meant rational thought and logic were backed up behind the huge ball of emotion in her throat. "Family matters more than any job," she said. "Or at least it should. And you're one to talk about avoiding a difficult conversation. You made up a pretend girlfriend!"

"Guilty. And for the record, I stopped pretending a long time ago. As I told you, this"—he paused to gesture between them—"is real for me, Jane. *Very* real."

She sucked in a breath. She was never going to get used to that.

Levi gave her a small, tight smile. "But clearly you haven't gotten there yet."

"I haven't *let* myself go there," she corrected. Paused. "I do know you're important to me, Levi. Very important."

"As important as your job? As important as your love of going far and wide without any tether longer than the length of your next contract?"

"Work doesn't factor into this."

"The hell it doesn't. Work gives you an excuse to leave."

For a heart-stopping moment, she was eight years old again, too much trouble to keep, to fight for, to want. She'd fixed that, though, by always leaving first. "That's not fair."

"No? You're the one who, in the same sentence about your grandpa's cancer, also talked about leaving Tahoe. How convenient for you to have a built-in escape route. But things change, Jane, and you could change with them. Because no one's asking you to leave this time. You don't have to take another contract. You could stay here and enjoy the time you have left with your grandpa."

She stared at him, trying to fight the rising panic she couldn't explain. Maybe because he made it all sound so simple when it was anything but. Wasn't it? "I've never lied to you. You've always known I was going to leave."

He looked . . . disappointed. Hurt. "You're running away again, this time from people who really care about you, because you're too afraid of getting hurt to even try and build a real relationship."

Is that what she was doing? Finding reasons to take off before she could be asked to leave? Holy shit. Abruptly, she sat down on the couch, ashamed and furious with herself. She didn't know how to respond.

Levi sat on the coffee table facing her.

Still not touching her . . .

The silence stretched where she didn't say anything, could hardly even think over the blood pounding in her ears and the panic squeezing her throat. Panic, because this was it. She was going to lose her grandpa and Levi in one fell swoop because of the ever-present desperate need to run from anything that made her feel too much.

"Jane, what do you want me to do here?"

"I want you to do whatever you want," she said dully.

He nodded and stood. "All right." He was clearly waiting for her to do something. Walk out, she realized, so she stood too, and without another word, did just that, without looking back. That was the trick, she reminded herself. Never look back.

But for the first time, she wanted to.

CHAPTER 28

Levi heard the front door shut and felt it reverberate in his gut. *Well, you screwed that up pretty good, didn't you.*

He ran his hands through his hair and then asked himself why he wasn't going after the best thing to ever happen to him. To hell with that, and he strode down the stairs and to the front door.

Jane's car was gone.

Okay, so onto the gut-wrenching portion of the evening, apparently. He turned in a slow circle in the living room, wondering how in the world he was such an idiot when it came to women. And why had he ever made that stupid promise to not fall for her? He stopped when he realized the double doors leading to the kitchen were closed.

They were never closed.

He pushed them open and his entire family leapt away from the doors, trying to look busy. His mom was suddenly doing dishes, his dad reading his newspaper—upside down, which wasn't a dead giveaway at all—and his sister was searching through a drawer looking for . . . he had no idea. He doubted she knew either. Only his niece was left standing suspiciously close to the wall next to the kitchen door.

The eavesdropping wall.

She gave him a guileless smile. "Hi! We had our ears to the wall listening to you and Jane upstairs. Grandma was using a glass cuz she said it carries sound better."

Levi cut his eyes to his mom, who had the good grace to grimace. "Kids," she said. "They say the darnedest things."

"Why is Jane mad at you?" Peyton asked him. "Did you do something bad? Cuz you gotta 'pologize when you do something bad."

Ignoring the three guilty-looking adults in the room, Levi crouched before Peyton. "First, never change, okay?" He tugged her ponytail. "You're perfect. And second, sometimes adults disagree, and that's okay." He rose to his feet and shook his head at the rest of his family. "You couldn't give me ten minutes of privacy?"

His dad snorted. "Son, you blew that whole thing up in under five."

Tess nodded her agreement. "I don't even think one of your PowerPoints could have saved you."

"I've got this," he said with a certainty he didn't feel.

Tess looked at her parents. "Please note that, in fact, he does not 'got this.'"

Levi shook his head and turned to his mom. "And you? The leader of the pack, the nosy instigator, you don't have a smartass comment for me too?"

"*Ask* is a bad word," Peyton said.

"Peyton's right," his mom said, nose in the air. "And anyway, the answer is no. I don't have any comment for you because I'm not talking to you. You felt the need to make up a girlfriend. And then lied to me about it."

Levi tossed up his hands and walked out of the kitchen, no particular destination in mind as he was already in hell. And oh, goody, Mateo was walking in the front door. The guy took one look at Levi and his smile faded. "What happened?"

"He just destroyed his relationship with Jane," his mom said over Levi's shoulder, having followed him from the kitchen.

"Not quite true," Tess said, coming in behind his mom. "*Jane* dumped *him*."

"Actually, what Jane said was that he could do whatever he wanted," his mom said.

Mateo shook his head. "Ah, man, when a woman says that, you do *not* do whatever you want. You stand still. You don't blink, you don't even breathe, you just play dead."

"Awesome," Levi said. "That was super helpful, thanks."

His mom looked at Mateo. "Can you tell your best friend he's an idiot?"

"I think he already knows," Mateo said.

Levi sighed and turned to his mom. "I thought you weren't speaking to me."

"I'm not!" She sighed. "Okay, yes, I am. I'm sorry you messed it up, Levi. So sorry. Are you okay?"

Levi pressed his hand to his aching heart and shook his head. "I'll let you know if I ever get sensation back in my soul. Not that I *should* let you know—my personal life shouldn't be up for debate."

"Aw, sweetheart." She cupped his face. "Who taught you that your personal life has to be separate from your family?"

"Who do you think?"

Sadness filled her eyes. "I'm sorry," she said softly. "You were just always so private that we tended to do whatever we had to in order to find out what was up with you. I can see now, with perfect twenty-twenty hindsight, that wasn't always healthy for you. But in our defense, we just love you so much."

"I love you too, Mom, but you guys couldn't even give me two minutes to process what just happened before you were breathing down my neck about where I went wrong. You think I don't already know?"

Looking stricken, she sucked in a breath. "You're right, we should've given you time. We just didn't want you to take so long that you missed out on something that made you so happy." She drew a deep breath. "That night you called me from the gondola. It wasn't to tell me you had a girlfriend. It was to say goodbye, wasn't it?"

The regret was yet another bitter pill.

"But you couldn't do it," she said. "You loved me so much that your last thoughts were of how to make me happy." She pressed her hand to her chest. "Your heart's in the right place. You meant well. I'm sorry that I ever made you feel like you had to be something you weren't. I'm sorry you felt judged by us. I know we over-react to everything, but, Levi, you uprooted your life and moved away, and we miss you so much. So yes, when you come home, we go a little overboard. But it's not because we want you to be someone you're not. It's not because we don't love you. It's because we can't help ourselves." And then she did it, she killed him dead when her eyes filled with tears.

"Mom," he whispered, reaching for her. "Don't cry."

"I can't help it. I want to go after Jane for you and fix this myself."

"Okay, but you won't, right?"

She both cried and huffed out a laugh against his chest, and he realized that while maybe his family didn't always understand him, he'd never taken the time to understand them either. He never imagined that his moving away would bother them so much. At the time, he'd been desperate to find his own space, so much so that he'd unintentionally cut the people who loved him right out of his life.

And wasn't that what he just accused Jane of doing?

Shit.

Legs weak, he dropped onto the couch and realized everyone was giving him a moment, offering silent support. "I really am an idiot."

His mom started to open her mouth, but Tess gave her a subtle shake of her head and his mom pinched her mouth together.

Progress, he supposed. Too bad he couldn't appreciate it with the taste of failure swamping him. Why had he pushed Jane so hard? Why push a truth she hadn't wanted to hear, making her face her past and inadvertently playing off her worst fear—being walked away from. She'd done the walking, but still. He'd definitely pushed her into it.

He hated that, and at the moment, hated himself too. He needed to prove to her that it was real between them. "I made mistakes."

"Well, who hasn't?" his mom asked. "You're a fixer, always have been. It hurts you when you can't fix something. Like what Cal took from us. Or when Amy died—"

"Mom—"

"No, baby, listen. There are always going to be things in life that can't be undone, no matter how badly you want it. But there are also plenty of things you *can* fix. Like you and Jane. I know you can fix this."

Mateo nodded.

Tess nodded.

Hell, even his dad nodded.

Peyton opened her hand and offered him a melted chocolate kiss.

What the hell. He popped it into his mouth. "How?" he said. "How do I fix this?"

"Whoa." Tess looked amazed. "He's asking for advice. Quick, someone write the date down."

His mom ignored this. "The fix isn't easy," she warned him. "You're going to have to listen to your heart, which already has the answer."

Great. Because Levi had no idea how to listen to his heart—which was pounding at the moment, so hard and fast that it hurt. "I might actually be having a heart attack."

"Or . . . ?" Tess prompted.

"Or . . ." He swallowed hard. "Or I love her."

"For such a smart guy," his dad said, clapping a hand onto his shoulder in a rare display of affection, "it sure takes you a while to catch on."

His mom was smiling. "Proud of you, baby."

Levi moved to the door. "I've gotta go."

"You're going to go ask her to be your girlfriend for real, right?" his mom asked his back.

"I suggest groveling," Tess said.

"Ditto," Mateo said.

"Good luck, son," his dad said. "You're going to need it."

CHAPTER 29

Jane pulled off the road for two reasons. One, because her defroster was on the blink and swiping her sleeve across the inside of the windshield to see the road better wasn't working. Two, she was crying. Which might be why she couldn't see the road.

Life officially sucked golf balls.

But hey, she'd been here before and had survived. All she had to do was keep one foot in front of the other and push through. So she swiped at her face and eyed her reflection in the rearview mirror. "Since when do you let anyone get close enough to hurt you? Because that's just plain dumb. You know better."

She did.

But she'd somehow come to believe that she'd been on a new trajectory, where the people she was slowly letting into her life could be trusted.

Turned out the joke was on her, because both the men she loved had just gutted her.

By the time she parked in front of her grandpa's house, the tears were gone, but she had some things to say. She stormed up the walk and lifted her hand to knock, but the door opened before she could, taking some of the wind from her sails.

Her grandpa took one look at her and sighed. "You always were a nosy little thing."

Fine. They were going straight to the thick of it then. Suited her perfectly. *"How could you not tell me?"*

"Easy."

She gasped, actually gasped, and through the pain in her heart, stared at him.

Suddenly looking far older than his years, he seemed to cave in on himself. "Look, I knew if I told you, it'd be all you'd want to talk about. And I didn't want to talk about it. Still don't."

"But—"

"Jane, do you know when I made my decision about treatment? A year ago, far before you came back into my life. And back then, all I could think of was getting to see your grandma again." He looked at her with regret shining in his eyes. "I had messed things up with you and couldn't even imagine a scenario in which you'd ever want to see me again. I honestly thought I was done here."

She sat down before her knees could give out, right there on the top step of his porch. "I feel like I just found you," she said through a thick throat. "I don't think I can bear the thought of losing you again."

He sat on the step next to her and took her hand. "I'll still be with you. Just like I always have been."

Her eyes filled. "But there are treatments that can make it so you can stay with me longer."

He was already shaking his head. "What time I have left, I want to spend laughing with you, enjoying life with you, not you coming to visit me in a sterile hospital bed. Jane, I'd rather have three incredible months with you than three long, painful, terrifying years." He looked her right in the eyes, letting her see everything he was feeling, which was enough to bowl her over. "Can you try and understand that?"

She had to force herself to really hear his words. To process what he was saying. She had to ask herself . . . if he *hadn't* been her grandpa, if he'd been one of her patients, how would she feel?

If she was being brutally honest, she'd agree with him.

And something else. Levi had said no one was pushing her away this time, she'd done that all on her own. And he was right, painfully so. There would always be another job. There wouldn't be another grandpa, not for her. "I'll be here," she said fiercely, clinging to her grandpa's hand. "I'll be here with you no matter what."

The tension drained from his shoulders and he leaned in and kissed her cheek. "Thank you," he said with such meaning, her heart squeezed.

And in that moment, she realized that Levi hadn't been trying to be cruel or to underplay the seriousness of her grandpa's situation *or* her reaction to it. He'd simply been attempting to help her understand what her grandpa wanted, from the point of view of a man who himself had never been fully understood by his own family.

This is real for me . . .

He'd put his heart on the line for her. He'd bared heart and soul to her, and she'd turned away from all he'd offered, basically doing to him what people had done to her for her whole life. She'd walked. She sucked in a breath, feeling a new wave of grief. "I messed up," she murmured. "Big-time."

"Not with me you didn't," her grandpa said genuinely.

She held on to his hand. "Thank you for that. But you're not the only one I hurt today by thinking only of myself."

"Levi?"

"Yes." She swallowed hard. "He told me that what he and I have is real."

He nodded. "I could see that in his eyes."

"I walked away," she whispered.

Her grandpa nodded again.

"You're . . . not surprised."

He let out a rough laugh. "After all you've been through, *no one* would be surprised to know you don't trust love. But, Jane, people *are* going to love you just for being you. You don't have to run from it or be scared by it. I know you've had very good reasons to do and feel both of those things in the past. But you aren't your past." He cupped her face. "It's okay to let people in, let them love you. It's a beautiful thing. You don't have to live in the shadows of your past anymore. Once you realize that, you'll be able to stop shoving it deep, where it festers inside you."

She wanted to stop. She did. But could she? Was it that simple?

"That boy loves you. Go to him like you came to me. He'll listen. Then you'll listen. Just like we did here, you and me."

She gave him a watery smile. "Funny, that was his advice to me to begin with." She covered her face. "I handled it badly. I'm not sure he can forgive me. I'm not sure I would if I were him, but he wanted something real with me, and now I know I want that too, more than I could have ever imagined."

Her grandpa stood up and offered her a hand, and then a hug that she really needed. "You've got a lot of people here who care about you. You're not alone. This time, *every* time, it's your choice to stay or go."

She hugged him tight, but he pulled back and gave her a *shoo* gesture. "Go. Go do what you need to."

She turned and started down the path, only to stop short, nearly tripping over her own feet.

Levi's truck was parked at the end of the driveway. She could see his tall silhouette in the fading daylight, Levi leaning against his truck, presumably waiting for her.

It was snowing lightly, individual flakes floating in the air, silently making their way down in slow motion, sparkling on the ground, the trees, in Levi's hair, dusting his shoulders.

He looked like the rest of her life.

He'd asked her where he stood in the lineup of her jobs and her love of going far and wide. She hadn't answered. She'd been too scared.

She'd lied to herself about that.

But she knew exactly where he stood in the lineup. She would choose him, any day, *always*. Swiping the tears off her cheeks, she moved closer, her boots crunching on the snow. "Hi."

"Hi." He looked at her with a self-deprecating smile while a light gust of wind playfully ruffled his snow-glistened hair. "I thought maybe you might need an Uber or tech support."

Though his tone had been light, his eyes were anything but. "Maybe I just need you," she said.

He studied her. "I'd like to think that was true, but you don't often let yourself need anything or anyone."

"I know. I was an island, and I was good at it." She shook her head. "But coming back here this time, bonding with Charlotte, my grandpa. *You . . .*" She held his gaze this time. "Being alone doesn't hold the same appeal anymore."

"Good," he said. "Because you're not alone. I'm standing right here."

Her own miracle. "You came for me."

"I'll always come for you. But you should know that I lied about the Uber and tech support. I'm here because I forgot to tell you something pretty important."

"What?"

He straightened up from his truck but still didn't touch her. "I love you, Jane."

Her entire body softened. In fact, she nearly melted into a puddle right there on the icy ground. Stepping into him, she slid her hands up his chest and around his neck. Drawing in a breath, he hauled her in closer so there was no space between them. Then he kissed her, revealing everything he felt, not hiding a thing, telling her with his mouth, his touch, the way his body held hers that she really was the love of his life.

Just as he was hers. "I left something out too." She drew in a deep breath, because here went everything. "You said it was real for you. I need you to know it's real for me."

His eyes searched hers, dark, serious. Intense. "From when?"

"From the moment you showed up at my work with my grandma's locket. I wasn't sure I'd ever be a good partner for someone. The way I grew up, the way I led my life . . . Before I met you, I never even considered it an option for me. To be honest, I wasn't even sure I had it in me to fall in love. I'm still not sure how it happened."

He made a low sound that said it hurt him to know she truly had believed herself incapable of love, and she shook her head. "But a part of me knew from that first night on the mountain that you would change everything." She cupped his face. "I love you too, Levi."

He let out a breath like he'd been holding it for just that. Looking touched, marveled, and relieved all at the same time, he gave a low laugh.

"You didn't know?" she asked.

"Hoped. Suspected. But no, I wasn't sure."

"I really was going to Haiti," she whispered.

"I know."

"I'm not now."

He rubbed his jaw against hers and nodded. "But even if you had, it wouldn't have changed anything for me."

"Me either." She burrowed into him. "Thank you for loving me, Tarzan."

"You're easy to love." He kissed her again. His lips were cold, and she realized he wasn't even wearing a jacket. "You're freezing!"

"Left in a hurry. Jane, there's one more thing."

Her heart stopped at the seriousness in his voice. "Okay . . ."

"I bought a piece of land near the Tahoe Rim Trail."

She blinked. "Where we—"

He smiled. "Yeah. I think of you every time I drive up there. I'm going to build a house. I'd like it to be our house. Our home."

A home. That belonged to her and that she belonged to. A permanent place . . . with him. Her heart swelled so that she wasn't sure how it could possibly still be fitting inside her rib cage. "I've never had a house."

"I know."

"A home either," she said. "Though Charlotte's place is getting pretty close."

He smiled. "So you'll have two now, though I hope you're going to sleep in ours." He tipped her face up to his. "I'm not telling you this to put any pressure on you or to tie you down in any way. I'm just letting you know. I want you to be mine, Jane. But more than that, I want to be yours, on your terms, however that looks. If it means seeing you during ski season when you're here working, or if it means flying to visit you wherever you happen to be, I don't care. I just want to know that we're each other's person."

She stared up at him. "You'd really have come to visit me wherever I was working?"

"Even if it was Mars."

For some reason, this got her in the feels more than anything else he'd said, and she shook her head. "You deserve more than having to follow me around. And plus, I like the idea of a home base, taking shorter and fewer contracts. And I think I'd like to transfer from the urgent care clinics to the actual hospital. It's better shifts and more stability."

He was already shaking his head. "Don't do that for me, Jane. I don't want to change anything about you."

"I'm doing it for me," she said. "Because I need more of us than a visit here and there. You *are* my person, Levi. And I'm yours." She took his hand. "You could stay with me until your place is ready. Unless you'd like to keep sleeping on your parents' couch?"

He grinned. "So I'll be a kept man. I like it. Don't worry, I'll put out as often as you like."

She laughed. "How long can I keep you?"

He cupped her face. "How does forever sound?"

Her heart turned over in her chest, exposing its underbelly. "It's a date."

EPILOGUE

Five years later

Jane staggered down the stairs, plopped into a dining room chair, and did *gimme* hands toward Levi's coffee mug.

He slid it to her.

She sipped, grateful it was still steaming hot. It also had more cream than coffee, which meant . . . "You made this for me."

There was a smile playing at the corners of his mouth. "Sleep well?"

She smiled, scooping up Cat, who'd been winding around her ankles. "When you finally let me go to sleep."

Levi flashed a grin. "I don't remember hearing any protests."

"Not a single one."

In response to this, he hooked a foot around the leg of her chair and pulled her closer.

Miffed, Cat jumped off, and Levi scooped Jane into his lap, pulling her in for a heart-stopping kiss that had her melting into him.

"*Ew.*"

They broke apart and looked over at Nicole, their four-year-old daughter, who with the exception of Jane's own green eyes was the spitting image of her daddy. Their daughter was still in pj's, wearing—if Jane wasn't mistaken—syrup. A quick glance around the kitchen told the tale. Waffles had been made. Messily.

"Why do you and Daddy kiss so much?" Nicole wanted to know.

"Because we love each other."

"Is he your boyfriend?"

"Sort of," Jane said. "But we're married, so that also makes him my husband."

"Did you like kissing him before you were married too?"

She glanced at Levi, who was watching the twenty questions quiz with amusement. "I've always liked kissing your daddy."

"My friend Shelley at school says her mommy thinks my daddy's hot."

Levi choked on the unfortunate sip of coffee he'd just swallowed.

Jane laughed. "I'd have to agree with her."

Nicole crawled up into Jane's lap, and as she was still sitting in Levi's lap, it was a very tight fit. "Do you have to go to work today, Mommy? Can we go sledding down the hill?"

The house that they'd built had a slope in the backyard—perfect for sledding. Jane kissed the tip of Nicole's cute little nose. "I'm not working today." She was now employed at the Sunrise Cove hospital and loving it. She'd taken the week off because Mateo had finally talked Charlotte into saying "I do," and as her best friend's matron of honor, Jane had a lot to take care of.

But today was all about Nicole. "Sledding sounds perfect. Why don't you go get ready?"

"Yay!" Nicole leapt down and ran out of the kitchen. They could hear the pitter-patter of her feet moving through the house and presumably into her bedroom. There was the sound of drawers opening and closing as she searched for the sledding gear she'd picked out herself from Cutler Sporting Goods. Cal had been arrested and had done some time, but unfortunately had never paid back a penny. Still, after floundering for a bit, the store was beginning to thrive again on its own merit.

Jane leaned back against Levi's chest and sighed in pleasure as he dragged his mouth down the side of her neck. "*Mmm . . .*" she murmured. "You going to work for a little while?"

"No. Thought I'd go sledding with my two favorite girls."

She twisted around to face him and smiled. "I love you."

"I love you more." He leaned into her and was halfway through giving her another heart-stopping kiss when those little feet came running into the kitchen again.

"Daddy! Leave her alone, we're going sledding!"

Levi gently nudged Jane off his lap and stood to face the sweetest little tyrant they'd ever met. "Can I go too?"

Nicole giggled. "Of course, Daddy. Can Peyton come over and sled with us? And Taylor? I promised my cousins. Oh, and Aunt Tess too! And Grandma and Grandpa! And Auntie Charlotte and Uncle Mateo!"

"*Everyone* can come."

"Really?" Nicole asked, bouncing up and down.

"*Really.*"

Nicole ran to him, flinging herself into the air. Levi caught her and then snagged Nicole's mommy in close too. "Caught you both."

"Careful," Jane warned. "The syrup's sticky."

"Perfect. Now we can stick together." He pressed his forehead to Jane's. "For always."

Sounded like the perfect plan.

Reading Group Guide

1. If you thought you only had a few minutes to live, what would you do during that time?

2. Did you think Levi's deception was justified?

3. Under what circumstances would it be acceptable to lie to your family, or is it never acceptable?

4. Would you have agreed to help Levi if you were in Jane's position? Why or why not?

5. Do you have any regrets about your past relationships? How do they impact your current relationships?

6. What is your definition of a family?

7. If you could choose your own family, would it look the same? Different?

8. What do you think about Jane's decision to make amends with her grandfather? Why was this important for her?

9. What do you think the characters' lives are like in the years after the novel ends?

An Excerpt from
The Friendship Pact

**Keep reading for an
exclusive excerpt from the next
Sunrise Cove story by Jill Shalvis,
The Friendship Pact
On Sale Summer 2022**

Comfort food. That was the only thing
on Tae's mind as she loaded up her arms
in the convenience store. Comfort food
and . . . Riggs Copeland. Big, strong,
protective, annoyingly sexy Riggs
Copeland.

She didn't think much could surprise
her, but Jake's brother being back in
town most definitely had done just that.
He'd grown up too, and right into those
long, lanky limbs, looking better than
any man who'd seen her naked should.
Soon as she paid for her loot, she was
going to sneak out the back door and
hitch a ride home if she had to. Anything
to avoid the discussion she knew he'd
want to have.

*But, hey, look at that, two-for-one
donut packs. Score.* As she took her
bonus pack and moved to the ice
cream freezer, she felt the weight of

the cashier's gaze. "Ms. Riley," she said politely as she walked past.

"I *knew* it was you."

Tae ignored the woman's sharp, assessing, and judging tone. Truth was, she deserved it. She'd been a rotten teenager. Desperate too. She could think of a handful of times she'd lifted food from this very store, then gone home and quickly put the food into grocery store bags so her mom would think she'd purchased it.

Her mom had worked multiple jobs at all times, pretty much either working or asleep at any given hour of the day, and even then there hadn't been enough money. Tae picking up babysitting jobs had helped, but not nearly enough, so they'd often couch surfed with friends or lived with whomever her mom had been seeing at the time.

Fun memories, reliving the shame of the things she'd done.

Not.

She eyed her ice cream options. Thankfully, there were many. Double fudge chocolate. Mint. Cherry and nuts. But what was *nuts* had been Mr. Schwartz being so sure that her dad was alive.

He'd obviously backed off because of her shock and disbelief, and not because he'd been mistaken or unsure. She'd been a newborn when he'd gone ▶

into the marines, but her mom had kept him alive with stories. They'd wanted to marry, but April hadn't been of age and it'd been prohibited without parental consent. So they'd vowed to get married when Andy came back.

Only he'd died less than a year later.

Clearly Mr. Schwartz was wrong. But if not, it meant one of two things. Either her dad had lied to her mom. Or . . . her mom had lied to Tae.

But her mom would never, ever do that. She didn't even have the ability to lie, she literally got hives whenever she tried.

Ms. Riley's spine was ramrod straight, bringing her to her full five feet in height—at least three inches of which was hair. For as long as Tae could remember, the woman's black-as-night hair had been piled up on top of her head, resembling a beehive. It was shot through with gray streaks now, no doubt thanks in part to Tae herself. "You can't fool me with that expensive designer dress, you know."

"It's a rental!"

Ms. Riley didn't smile. "I've got my eyes on you. Tonight, you're going to pay for every single thing you take out of here, if I have to search you myself."

Tae pulled her debit card from her bra and waved it, trying to ignore the heat of shame she could feel creeping up her face because, let's face it, Ms. Riley had the right to doubt her. "No searching necessary."

"Hmph."

Tae went back to the very important decision of choosing the right ice cream for her impending breakdown, doing her best to shrug off Ms. Riley's piercing gaze that she could still feel stabbing her right between the shoulder blades. And rightfully so. But she'd long ago dropped money into the tip jar to cover the things she'd once taken. Yet it was still hard to maintain the high ground with water dripping from her hair down her arms and chest, her teeth rattling, and her body covered in goosebumps.

Between the gala not being as big as she'd hoped, then running into her tall, dark, and sexy past, and now Ms. Riley, she felt like the scared, insecure teenage girl she'd once been.

There was no cookies-and-cream ice cream in the freezer. Which meant it was official. The evening had gone to hell in a handbasket. Maybe tomorrow she'd get out of bed with an adjusted attitude. She'd go back to her come-what-may facade. But for that to happen, she needed ice cream. Copious amounts of it. She had cookies, chips, and a candy bar. All that she needed now was to settle on a different flavor of ice cream. Double fudge or Neapolitan? ▸

An Excerpt from *The Friendship Pact*
(*continued*)

She loved Neapolitan, but sometimes a girl just needed her chocolate—

"Take one of each, let's go."

Riggs. Of all the places in all the land, why had they collided tonight with her confidence at an all-time low? She could feel him behind her, the heat of his big body both a bad and good memory. Okay, *great* memory. But she waved him off like a pesky fly without looking at him. "Some things can't be rushed."

Two long arms reached around her and took everything out of her hands, dumping them all in the bin of candy bars at her hip.

She tried to push him away, but he caught her arm and held tight. She stared up at him. His brown hair was military short. His eyes studied her calmly. He looked exactly like the teenager he'd once been, and yet also like he'd lived two lifetimes since she'd seen him last. "You can yell at me in the car for being a pushy asshole," he said. "We're out. Now." Still holding on to her, he turned toward the door and then stilled, before turning them back to the ice cream. "Okay, don't look, but the kid behind you—"

She craned her neck.

"Jesus, Tae, I said *don't* look. The guy behind us might have a gun."

"You mean the kid? He can't be a day over fourteen."

"A gun doesn't give a shit about the age of the person holding it. Now here's what's going to happen. You're going to take my hand and we're going to walk out of here, easy-peasy." He started to tug her along, but she dug in her heels, pulling free.

"And leave Ms. Riley alone to fend for herself?" she hissed.

He took her hand again. "No, we'll take her too. But if she refuses, there's a loaded shotgun under the counter, and trust me, she knows how to use it."

True story. "You know she won't budge from this store. I think she's glued her ass to that seat. But I think you're wrong about the kid."

Riggs stared at her like no one had ever dared question him before. "And if he's planning on using that gun to rob the place?"

"Maybe he's just a kid trying to buy candy. Don't be so quick to judge."

"I'm not the judgy one here."

She wasn't even going to try and attempt to decipher that comment. Or the look in those eyes of his, which were a startling, almost hypnotic green.

She took another look around. There were no other customers in the store. Riggs was looking at Tae, or at least pretending to while actually eyeballing the mirror over the end of the aisle, which was giving him a bird's-eye view ▶

of the checkout counter. They both watched the kid reach into his coat, but faster than a blink of an eye, Ms. Riley had her shotgun out and pointed at the kid's nose.

"Go ahead, make my day, punk," she said, not missing Clint Eastwood's tone by all that much.

Here was the thing. Tae knew that the gun was all for show, that Ms. Riley, annoying as hell and mean as a snake, was not a murderer. She wasn't going to shoot at the kid.

But obviously, the kid didn't know that. He tried to make a run for it, making Riggs swear and head him off, with Tae right on his heels.

A shotgun blast sounded and ceiling-tile dust rained down on all of them. "There's more where that came from!" Ms. Riley yelled, moving the gun so that it was always aimed at one of the three of them.

Tae couldn't hear past the ringing in her ear from the close proximity to the shotgun blast. She'd instinctively jumped in front of the kid—while at the very same second, Riggs had slid his big body in front of hers.

"What kind of idiot jumps in front of a gun?" he growled at her.

"What kind of an idiot jumps in front of a woman who's jumped in front of a gun?" she growled right back.

Riggs looked incredulous. "I was trained by Uncle Sam."

"Yeah, and I got my education from the school of hard knocks. I've got this under control!" She looked at Ms. Riley. Not easy, since she had to peek around the stone wall that was Riggs, which meant the diminutive Ms. Riley now had her gun, Dirty Harry, pointed directly at his chest. "Okay, whoa," Tae said as calmly as she could with her blood thundering in her ears. "Let's all just calm down here and—"

"*No.*" Ms. Riley had her gun up to her cheek, one eye closed, the other clearly holding the three of them in her sights. "Hands up. All of you."

The kid was frozen in place, visibly shaking as he raised his hands.

Ms. Riley narrowed her eyes at Tae. "I *knew* you were trouble. You're with this little punk-ass thief, aren't you."

Tae had faced a lot of questionable circumstances in her life, several that she probably shouldn't have lived through. She'd long ago decided she was like a cat and had nine lives. She sure as hell hoped she had at least one left. "Ms. Riley, please lower your gun."

"Dirty Harry stays until you all empty out your pockets on the counter right now. The big guy first."

Tae could feel the tension in Riggs's body, but he didn't move. ▶

An Excerpt from *The Friendship Pact*
(continued)

"I don't care who I shoot!" Ms. Riley said. "*Now!*"

Tae started to take a step toward the counter, but Riggs gave her a hard look and she stilled. Then he slowly reached into his pockets and set the contents on the counter. Wallet. Keys. Phone.

"Turn around," Ms. Riley told him. "Slowly. Are you armed? You seem the sort to be armed."

"I'm not armed." Riggs raised his hands and turned in a slow circle.

Ms. Riley nodded her satisfaction and looked at Tae. "You next."

"Look at me. I had to shoehorn myself into this ridiculous dress. Do I look like I'm hiding anything?"

"Bullshit. I know you. You're carrying *something*."

Tae reached into her bra, pulling out the debit card she'd already revealed, along with two twenties and a small lip gloss.

The kid looked agog.

Riggs was showing nothing.

Ms. Riley gestured with the gun for the rest. "I know there's more."

"Fine." It wasn't often that Tae felt thankful for her D's, but she was in that moment as she reached back in for a small can of mace and then under her dress for the pocketknife she had sheathed to a thigh.

"You still carry that thing?" Riggs asked.

"Of course."

The very corners of his mouth quirked slightly. "What else is in there?"

"Wouldn't you like to know." Tae looked at Ms. Riley. "We good?"

"*Everything*, Tae Holmes."

Tae sighed and pulled out a just-in-case tampon. "There. Happy?"

"Not until the kid empties his pockets."

The kid shook his head.

Tae eyed him. She'd been right. He looked to be *barely* fourteen, and he was definitely still a flight risk. "Listen," she told him. "She's not kidding, okay? Whatever you've got in there is way less dangerous than Ms. Riley with a gun, trust me."

He shifted on his feet and yep, it was in the whites of his wide eyes. He was going to bolt. "No!" she cried. "*Don't—*"

The little idiot darted for the door.

Ms. Riley swung her gun his way.

Riggs dove for Ms. Riley—and the gun.

And suddenly life became a slow-motion movie montage. Riggs literally flying through the air *toward* the locked and loaded gun. The kid running faster than the speed of light. Ms. Riley taking aim . . .

On Tae's left was a bank of coolers ▶

An Excerpt from *The Friendship Pact*
(continued)

holding last-minute items like eggs, milk, soda. On her right was a display of beer, the cans stacked like a castle turret against the endcap. She snatched a can and flung it, beaning the kid right between the shoulder blades. He went down just as Ms. Riley's gun went off with an earsplitting BOOM.

Immediately on its heels came a shattering sound, and more ceiling tile rained down on them, and glass from the lights. Everyone but Ms. Riley hit the floor. Tae felt a piece of something, either part of the ceiling or a shard of glass, smack her in the face. Raising her head, her eyes locked on Riggs as he got to his feet. No big hole in him anywhere, thankfully. She crawled through the ceiling debris, insulation, and broken glass on the floor to the kid, who hadn't moved. "*Hey, are you okay?*"

Riggs tried to nudge her aside, voice gruff. "Careful, we still don't know if he's armed."

Tae patted the kid's back, going for that bulge Riggs had seen, and lifted up his jacket to find a sweatshirt rolled around his waist. She glared at Riggs. "Some weapon." Then she pulled two granola bars and a small carton of milk from the kid's various pockets and sent Ms. Riley a scathing look. "Shame on you."

"Stealing is stealing," the woman said, not looking sorry in the least.

"I swear I'll never do it again," the kid whispered.

Tae stood, feeling an ache around one eye and the sting of glass cutting into her skin from several different places. Since she'd had worse, she ignored all of it and pulled the kid upright. Glass and bits of ceiling tile rained off them both to join the mess on the floor. Miraculously, the kid didn't appear to be hurt. "You *really* picked the wrong place to steal from."

He looked panicked, and tried to scramble free, but Riggs had him by the back of his jacket. "I was seventy cents short," the kid burst out with. "My little sister's been crying all day and there's nothing in the apartment."

Tae felt a clamp on her heart. She pushed one of her two twenties toward Ms. Riley. "Here. For what he's got. Keep the change." The other twenty she handed to the kid. "What's your name?"

"Ty."

"Okay, Ty. Go across the street to McGregor's market. Make sure you pay this time."

The kid nodded like a bobblehead as he took a step backward, keeping a wary eye on Ms. Riley.

When the woman lowered her gun, ▶

An Excerpt from *The Friendship Pact*
(continued)

the kid turned and hightailed it out of the store.

Tae felt a trickle of blood down her arm and looked down at her now very dirty dress. And dammit, the slit had ripped up to nearly indecent heights. "I *knew* I should've bought the insurance!" She narrowed her eyes at Ms. Riley. "You're going to pay for this dress!"

"The hell I will! And you're going to pay for this whole mess." She gestured to the broken glass. "I should've called the cops on the lot of you!"

"You've got two ceiling tiles out, some insulation, and a few light bulbs." Riggs pulled money from his wallet. Two hundred-dollar bills from what Tae could see. "This should cover it," Riggs said to Ms. Riley. "We good?"

Ms. Riley snatched the two hundred bucks and shoved them into her pocket.

Riggs nodded and then turned his sharp and—*whoa*, seriously pissed-off eyes—on Tae. "You're bleeding," he said.

She took his left hand and turned it over, looking at his cut palm. "So are you."

"It's nothing," he said grimly. "You shouldn't have—"

"What? Not stood up for the kid who was stealing for his starving sister? Not given him money to get more food? Not let him go so he could feed her? Which?"

"All of it." He moved close, eyes on her like he might be approaching a wild lioness. Then, closer still, until they were toe-to-toe. Moving very slowly, he lifted a hand, tipped up her head, and eyed her face, turning it right and then left, studying her carefully.

She jerked her chin free. "I'm fine. And if I hadn't helped him, then who would have?" She turned to Ms. Riley. "You got a broom?"

Ten minutes later, she and Riggs had cleaned up the mess. Ms. Riley sat on her stool watching Netflix on her phone, ignoring them both.

Riggs looked at her face again.

"Still fine," she said.

"Is there someone I should call for you?" he asked. "Let them know you're okay?"

"Nope."

"*Someone's* got to be worried about you."

"Nope."

"No one?"

She slid him a look. "Are you fishing to see if I'm in a relationship?"

"Are you?"

"No." She'd had boyfriends, but no one to write home about, and nothing lately. Her first serious relationship had been five years ago, but they'd split when he'd fallen in love and she hadn't been there yet. Her last involvement ▶

An Excerpt from *The Friendship Pact*
(*continued*)

had been a year ago, and they'd split because, according to him, she was closed off and "grumpy." True, and she'd made an attempt to change that. But even then, when he'd come back a month later to try and make up, she'd told him she hadn't missed him when he was gone.

Except . . . she had.

Okay, so not *him* exactly, but she'd missed having someone in her life, someone to have fun with, be physical with, someone to talk to.

Was that her problem? Was she lonely? Good God, that made her sound so pathetic, but she suspected it was true. But for so long, she'd been motivated by circumstance, money—or lack thereof—and she'd told herself over and over again that nothing mattered but the security and safety money could bring her. Certainly not love.

At her continued silence, Riggs grabbed two pints of ice cream, taking the time to hold them up to her for approval. The double fudge chocolate and Neapolitan.

She nodded, and then he slapped more money on the counter. Without looking at Ms. Riley, he grabbed a plastic-wrapped spoon and came back to Tae.

"You're going to pollute your body with dairy and fat?" she asked in disbelief, knowing he ate clean. Or at least he used to.

"After tonight? Yes." He gently pressed one of the containers against her aching eye. With his free hand, he offered her the other carton and spoon.

She nearly melted. *Nearly.* Instead, she narrowed her eyes. "This doesn't make us friends."

"Agreed." ∾

$\mathcal{D}$iscover Wildstone in the delightfully addictive

Wildstone series

Available now

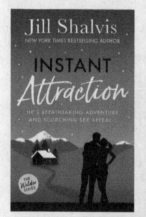

Meet the friends of Heartbreaker Bay as they discover that falling in love can be as glorious and tempestuous as the beautiful San Francisco waters.

Meet Prue, Willa, Ella, Colbie, Kylie, Molly, Sadie and Ivy in